DARK IMMOLATION

Also by Christopher Husberg and coming soon from Titan Books

Duskfall
Blood Requiem (June 2018)

DARK IMMOLATION

THE CHAOS QUEEN QUINTET

CHRISTOPHER HUSBERG

TITAN BOOKS

Dark Immolation
Print edition ISBN: 9781783299171
E-book edition ISBN: 9781783299188

Published by Titan Books
A division of Titan Publishing Group Ltd
144 Southwark Street, London SE1 0UP

First edition: June 2017
10 9 8 7 6 5 4 3 2 1

Names, places and incidents are either products of the author's imagination or used fictitiously. Any resemblance to actual persons, living or dead (except for satirical purposes), is entirely coincidental.

A CIP catalogue record for this title is available from the British Library.

Printed in the USA.

FOR RACHEL (AGAIN),
BECAUSE WE ARE WOVEN TOGETHER,
YOU AND I,
AND THIS IS AS MUCH YOURS
AS IT IS MINE.

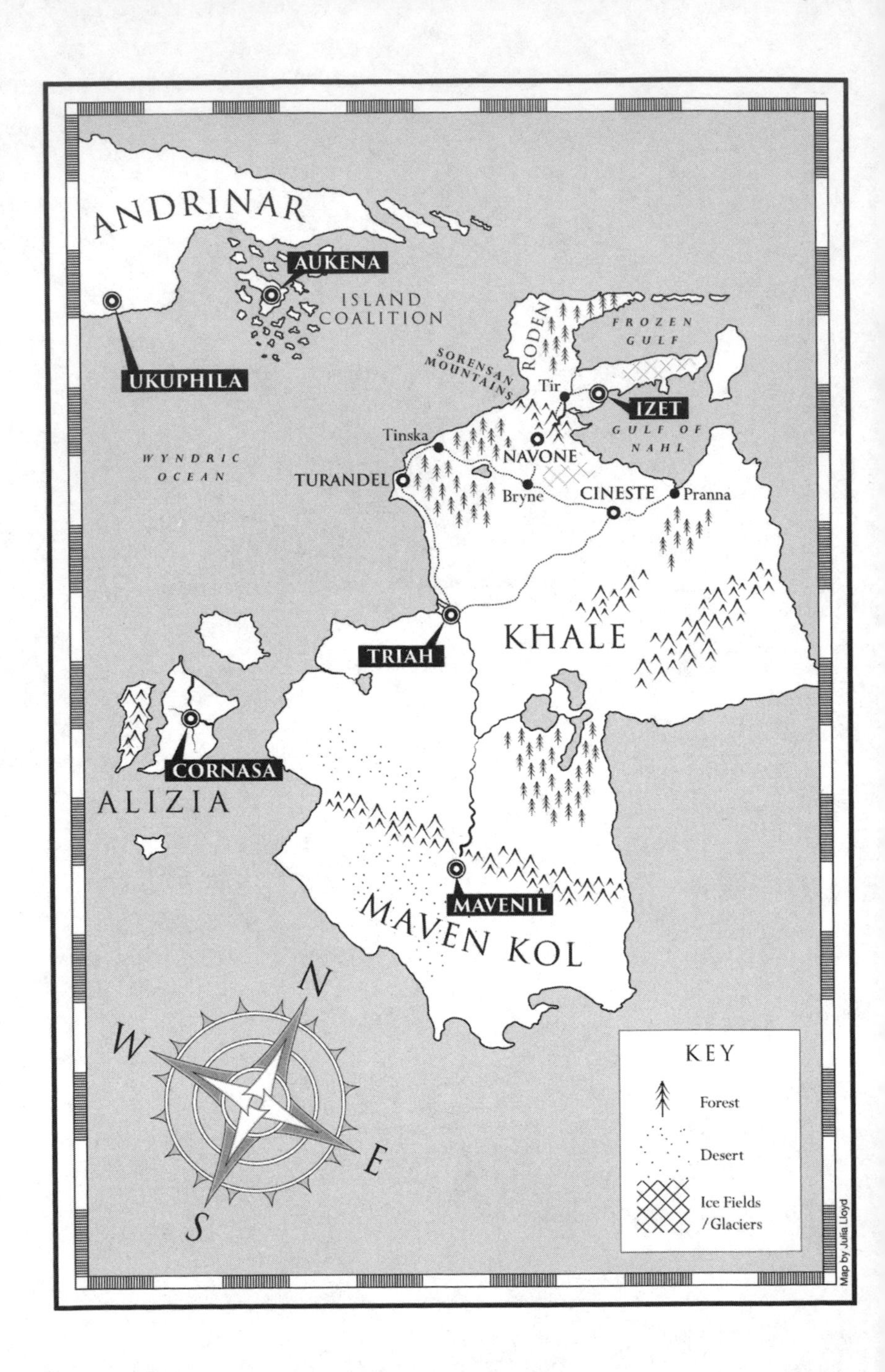
ANDRINAR
AUKENA
ISLAND
COALITION
UKUPHILA
RODEN
FROZEN
GULF
SORENSAN
MOUNTAINS
Tir
IZET
GULF OF
NAHL
Tinska
NAVONE
WYNDRIC
OCEAN
TURANDEL
Bryne
CINESTE
Pranna
KHALE
TRIAH
CORNASA
ALIZIA
MAVENIL
MAVEN KOL
N
W
E
S
KEY
Forest
Desert
Ice Fields
/ Glaciers
Map by Julia Lloyd

PART I

THOSE LEFT BEHIND

1

172nd Year of the People's Age, dungeons of the imperial palace in Izet, Roden

A WOMAN SLEEPS. A woman sleeps, and she dreams.

Her dreams twist together, littered with holes, and even as she dreams the woman wonders who she is. The woman is a woman, she supposes. She's tiellan, too, and this seems important, but the woman has difficulty defining herself in this moment. If the woman is tiellan she is also a daughter, a daughter who loves to hunt and fish, who loves to be among the trees and out on the water. If the woman is tiellan, and a daughter, then she is a wife, as well. The woman's husband must be dead. The woman loved her husband, but when she thinks of his face the image is blurred. If the woman is tiellan, a daughter, a huntress, a fisherwoman, a wife, if she is all these things then she is at least one thing more.

The woman is a weapon.

But her mind shies away from this thought. The woman knows she must not think of this. The woman knows that this only brings her pain, and sorrow, and sadness.

So, instead, the woman lets her mind wander. Her mind expands, and she begins to soar through the thoughts of those around her. That guard, walking past her door, for instance. The woman's mind watches him, follows him, sees what he sees and knows what he knows until she becomes him.

* * *

Outside the sky is gray and the air is cold, and inside the air is not much warmer. Enri Crawn walks briskly through the dungeons, making one final round before he returns home to his wife.

Enri shivers as he passes one of the cells, though Enri can't tell whether the shiver comes from the cold or the girl in the cell. The damn tiellan girl. The girl who seems to have turned an entire empire on its head. Rumors say the girl is an assassin from Khale, that she was sent to kill the emperor. And now, the emperor lies dead. Whether the tiny girl in the cell—just a tiellan, for Canta's sake—could have killed the most powerful man in Roden, though, does not seem likely. Almost makes him want to ask questions. But Enri has never been one for asking questions.

Enri never much cared for the emperor. Enri Crawn will live and die a gaoler, and the emperor will never be the wiser. Enri is dully surprised by the emptiness he feels inside himself when he thinks of his emperor, dead. And the Tokal-Ceno, too. He remembers what he overheard in Wazel's bar the other night, that a man like the emperor leaves an emptiness when he passes, a great space that demands to be filled. Such philosophical thoughts flee his mind as he exits the dreary stone dungeon and walks to his home.

The air is not much warmer inside than it is out. His wife Lisala is in the kitchen, and so is Keiten Gliss. Enri frowns. Bloody Keiten Gliss. Gliss is one of the cooks for House Amok, and having connections to such a house—especially in times like these—is important. But Enri Crawn can't help but wonder why the man spends so much time with his wife. Enri is of half a mind to get to the bottom of the situation… but no. *Not this time*, he tells himself. This time, he's just going to eat his dinner, kick up his feet, and smoke a pipe. After all, Enri Crawn never asks questions.

"I'd best be going," Keiten finally says.

Lisala smiles. "Thank you for stopping by," she says. "We always appreciate your company." With a thud, Enri's booted feet kick up onto the tiny table in front of his chair, and he fishes in his coat pocket for his pipe and weed.

Keiten Gliss walks out into the dreary evening, already feeling the sadness of leaving Lisala. Keiten pities the poor fool Enri, of course, but Enri is not a bad man. He is not a good man either, but then again neither is Keiten. Enri simply married the wrong woman. And, with any luck, Keiten's plan to change that will finish marinating very soon.

It begins to rain, and Keiten curses. Winter snows are one thing—bloody cold, to be sure, but beautiful in their own way and sticking to everything. Rain, on the other hand, he despises. Rain does not make the world beautiful, only wet and slippery and annoying as all Oblivion. And, of course, today Keiten has not worn his coat. It is that time of season, just between winter and spring, where the weather can't seem to make up its mind. Keiten pulls his jacket more tightly around him as the rain falls heavier, soaking through the fabric and through his skin.

He rushes along the wet streets, annoyed at the rain and disappointed at leaving Lisala, until he finally reaches his destination: Castle Amok. With a sigh of relief, Keiten slips through the gate and into the courtyard, nodding at the guard, and rushes up to his quarters where he can make a warm fire.

Sergeant Desmon Durii, gate guard of Castle Amok, frowns at the idiot cook as he runs past, but nods in return nonetheless. Politeness never hurt a man, Desmon's gramm used to say. Other tools hurt a man, of course, and Desmon knows a great deal about those. But not politeness.

Rain patters on Desmon's armor. He looks back out into the city from his post at the gate and wonders what will happen to House Amok, to Izet, and to Roden as a whole. The emperor is dead, and Desmon does not know how to react to such news. Even less so to the death of the Tokal-Ceno, leader of a religion that had not existed in Roden for centuries, but had re-emerged in the last decade. Desmon's sympathy would lie much more with the emperor than the Tokal, if his own lord had not been so involved in the Ceno re-emergence.

Lord Daval Amok has treated Desmon well, and thus while Lord Amok grieves, Desmon grieves, too. But tensions rise as houses swirl around the vacant throne; Emperor Grysole left no children or heirs. His rumored betrothal to Andia of House Luce is a topic of constant conversation. House Luce, of course, has made the plans for this betrothal public in an attempt to place Andia on the throne, but without any proof their claim is still weak. House Amok, while it doesn't have the largest army, or the greatest wealth of the noble families of Roden, is still a high house and thus its members are eligible for the throne. Whether Desmon's master wants that burden or not, Desmon is not sure. Desmon has always considered Daval Amok a timid man.

Desmon worries about what will happen in the coming weeks. There will be more assassinations as the noble houses vie for the throne. Which is why Desmon Durii must be on guard. His lord is under threat, and it is Desmon's job, and the job of his fellow soldiers, to protect Daval Amok.

"Excuse me, Sergeant Durii," someone behind him says.

Desmon turns to see a young boy, barely fourteen, fidgeting behind him. Desmon straightens, absently brushing imaginary dust from his armor and instead flicking rainwater everywhere.

"What is it, boy?"

"Your replacement is late," the boy says. "Weslin wanted me to tell you so."

Desmon sighs. "Very well." It's not the first time Weslin's been late, Canta knows. Desmon will have words to exchange with Weslin, to be sure. He could bring Captain Urstadt into it, but Desmon prefers to keep his own men in line. "Thanks for letting me know, boy. On your way now."

I'm not a boy, Fil Parce thinks, as he runs back towards the keep of Castle Amok to escape the rain. If Mistress Hamma thinks he's spent even one more moment outside than he needs to, she'll make him scrub garderobes for a week. Fil sees two maids exiting the narrow servants' door on the side of the keep. Fil picks up his pace and slips through the door, barely making it inside. Fil smiles at the cries of surprise from the maids outside. Fil doesn't care; they don't understand his game.

Fil, his work done for the day, trots through the servants' hallway. Desmon is only a house guard. If Desmon were as good as everyone said, he'd be in the emperor's personal army, or even a Reaper. Instead, Desmon is here, at Castle Amok, guarding a gate that no one cares about.

Fil reaches the door that leads into the great hall of the keep, covered in tapestries, paintings, and glistening suits of armor. No, a good man is a good warrior, but he also makes something of his life. Desmon's life doesn't seem to be going anywhere.

Fil's life, on the other hand, will be different. He has been training with the sword, which will surely help. Or rather with a stick that he figures is about the size of a sword. Weslin has been helping him. Fil does not like Weslin. While he has some good things to say about sword fighting, he says strange things to Fil, things that make Fil uncomfortable. Fil thinks about telling Desmon. Perhaps Desmon will want to help Fil learn to fight, too. But Weslin has told Fil not to mention anything about their training to Desmon.

The door he waits by opens slightly, and Master Frenn walks through, head held high. Master Frenn looks down disapprovingly at Fil, but before the old man can say anything, Fil slips through the door before it closes. Fil smiles. Twice in a row. A lucky day!

Fil walks through the great hall. He does not care much for the tapestries, or the paintings, but he loves the suits of armor. He imagines himself wearing one someday, fighting great battles. For good measure, Fil takes the fencer's stance that Weslin has been teaching him, and holds his arm out as if he were holding a sword. But, before he can take one lunge, Fil hears a soft laugh behind him.

"Fighting ghosts again, Fil?"

Fil turns to see Cova Amok, Lord Daval's youngest daughter, smiling at him from the end of the hall. Fil immediately blushes, because he thinks that Cova Amok is certainly the most beautiful person he has ever seen, and now she has caught him play-acting, *again*, and thinks of him as a boy just as Desmon does. Cova is only five years his senior, but she acts like she is his mother.

"I was just practicing," Fil says, looking down at the ground.

"Practicing is for practice yards, not noble halls," Cova says. The light-blue silk dress she wears falls perfectly over her hips and onwards to the floor. Fil is careful not to look at Cova's dress, or the shape beneath it, for too long. Mistress Hamma has warned him that to do so is a serious offense against those of noble birth. Fil has to take one look, though. He doesn't think Cova is the most beautiful thing in the world for nothing. He sees her face, fair and framed by hair the color of spun gold. Fil smiles.

Cova Amok grins back at Fil, expecting him to say something, but he does not. Cova feels a stab of regret—perhaps her comment was too harsh. She does not care whether the lad "practices" in the great hall or not. But now he stares at her, eyes wide, that silly grin on his face. Cova sighs.

"I'd love to stay and talk," she says, "but the hour grows late."

Fil nods almost imperceptibly, eyes still wide. Cova shakes her head, and crosses the great hall. She is fond of the boy, even if he is absent-minded. Even if he stares. Cova has never appreciated the stares of men, and makes no exception for Fil. But he is only a child, and can hardly know better. Men are different. Men lie, men change. Even Cova's father, who she has loved and respected her whole life, has changed. Cova can't quite put her finger on how, but something is off. The way he speaks. The look in his eyes when he smiles at her. He is still her father, but he is not the same. Cova knows her father was close with the Tokal-Ceno and the emperor, and such deaths would change any nobleman. Canta knows, they have an effect on Cova.

Perhaps I *have changed*, Cova thinks. *Perhaps I'm the one who is different*. Cova is a grown woman, now—the youngest of four, but no longer a child. The world's worries have become her worries; the looming war threatens her family and the future of their house. Cova reaches out a hand, brushing against a tapestry. Her mother, if she were still alive, would tell her not to touch. Cova had never gotten along with her mother when she was alive, but she misses her now.

Cova walks up the steps at the end of the great hall, up the floors of the keep, to her family's chambers. She walks past the rooms that once belonged to her brothers. They are all married now, living on estates outside Izet or moved to other cities. Cova is all but alone now. Cova sees the door to her father's chamber is wide open, and inside he stands tall and still. He turns, perhaps at the sound of her footsteps.

"Cova," he says, and smiles, but again Cova is disturbed at how hollow his eyes look.

"Hello, Father," Cova says, returning the smile and curtsying politely.

"Come in," Cova's father says. "Come in and sit with me, like you did when you were a little girl. I could have Rolof ascend and read us some of Tolokin's *Tales*; you always loved them as a child."

Cova does not respond for a moment, taken aback by her father's sudden nostalgia. They have not spoken of such things in years. A part of Cova wants to do as her father says, to feel that connection with him once more. But another part of Cova compels her to remain outside the door.

"I'm sorry, Father," she says, "perhaps another night. I'm very tired, and I need to sleep." Cova can't say why, but she does not trust her father in this moment. She does not know what he will do or say to her, alone in his chamber.

"Of course, daughter," Lord Amok says. "Another time, indeed. Sleep well, my dear."

Lord Daval Amok smiles as his daughter departs. He loves his daughter, wants only the best for her. Just as he loves his family and Roden itself. Just as he loves the Sfaera, and will do anything to make it the best it can be. Lord Daval Amok walks silently through his chamber towards the large looking-glass above his mantel. He is old, but the pain that once plagued his joints and the fatigue that once beset him after a simple flight of stairs are no longer present.

Lord Daval Amok stops before the looking-glass and gazes into it, seeing his own reflection. But, looking back at him is not the old man he has grown so used to seeing, skin wrinkled, gray hair receding, eyes dark and hooded. No, what stares back at him is something very different. A darkness. A skull, bare and black as if charred and polished, wreathed in dark flame.

Winter woke with a start, cowering in the corner of her cell, although she knew immediately that she had not been sleeping. Her mind seemed looser, lately, prone to wander and latch on to the closest consciousness. Winter had almost grown accustomed to it; the sensation was not unpleasant, and anything that could get her away from this wretched cell, from reality, from the memories of what had happened Before, was welcome.

This time was different, however. This time was not welcome. The man whose mind she had entered at the last was not a mind she had ever entered before. And what she saw as the man looked into the mirror...

A darkness. A black skull wreathed in dark fire.

The image flashed in Winter's mind when she closed her eyes. It reminded her of what happened Before, of the terrible things she had seen, and with those sights the feelings, and with those feelings knowledge.

Winter clenched her fists, clenched her jaw. Took deep, slow breaths. But the tightness in her chest, the constricting force around her heart, did not leave her.

Murderer, a voice whispered in her mind.

Winter shook her head, rocking back and forth on the floor of her cell. She was alone. Her friends were gone. Her power was gone. She was alone, and only death awaited her.

2

Keep of Castle Amok, Izet, Roden

"My Lord, it is time." Urstadt's voice was soft but clear from the hallway.

"Just give me a moment," Daval said, excitement flowing through him. Surely Urstadt would be even more excited than he; this was her plan coming to fruition, after all.

Daval dressed. The large dark-green robe with the oversized hood commanded a different type of respect than his decorated clothing, clothing that befitted his position in a high, noble house. As Lord Amok, Daval had great power and respect. But as the new Tokal-Ceno, Daval had something more.

"My Lord," Urstadt greeted him as he exited his chamber.

Daval nodded to her, smiling. As always, Urstadt wore her half-armor: steel cuirass and faulds, each plated with a thin layer of rose gold, and matching gauntlets and greaves. She wore a suit of micromail—a recent invention of the imperial smithies, both lighter and stronger than traditional chain—beneath the plate. In one arm she carried her helmet, a barbute of the same rose-gilded steel, etched to make the face of the helm look like a skull, accented by black gems near the eyes. The contrast was odd; Urstadt looked somewhat feminine in her armor, but the skull contrasted sharply against the rose gold. Of course, when Urstadt had been promoted to Daval's guard captain, he had granted her whichever armor she desired. In fact, since the suit had been finished, Daval couldn't think of a moment he had seen his guard captain out of armor. She slept in the bloody set for all he knew.

At Urstadt's waist was a short sword, scabbard and hilt also of rose gold, but her preferred weapon she carried in one hand. Her glaive—a poled weapon with a curved blade on one end—was an inelegant, ugly thing, taller than she was with a dented, dark steel blade and scarred, blackbark handle. Some laughed at and derided Urstadt's rose-gold armor; but her glaive, and her skill with it, was not something to jest about.

"Tell me everything," Daval said, as they walked down the hall. "How goes our little example?"

"Well enough," Urstadt said. "House Farady took the bait."

Daval nodded. He knew they would. The potential power they might accrue by undermining Daval's fish trade would have been irresistible. House Amok, of course, was one of the high houses for many reasons, but first and foremost for commerce. Fish and other fruits of the sea had been their specialty for hundreds of years, but as time passed the Amok lords had sought other sources of income, from the marble quarries near the western coast to the logging beastmen on the Cracked Horn, the northeast peninsula of Roden. But, by striking the Amok fishing industry, a tiny house like Farady could shake the very foundation of House Amok.

But a shaken foundation was not a broken one, which was why he and Urstadt had orchestrated the whole thing.

Urstadt led Daval to the cells below the keep. Unlike those in the imperial palace, Castle Amok's dungeons were very modest: a few cells below ground, near the wine cellars. Not particularly high-security.

They didn't need to be. They were generally only for

holding other nobles, soon to be released on negotiated terms. A certain level of comfort was expected. Daval was not surprised to see Darst Farady lounging on a cot with a smirk on his face in one of the cells. Two other men sat in the cells on either side of Darst, but he was obviously the leader.

"The great Lord Amok himself." Darst grinned as he saw Daval approach. "I'm honored by your accommodations."

Daval bowed to Darst, watching the young man through the iron bars. Darst did not move from his lounging position on the cot, one leg up, the other dangling over the edge, one arm curled behind his head in a makeshift pillow.

"I trust you're being treated fairly?" Daval asked. Despite Darst being only a stripling and of a house significantly less powerful than Amok, Daval wouldn't skimp on formalities. He must not give any impression of skirting the law.

The young man—perhaps no older than Daval's daughter—shrugged. "Fairly enough, I suppose. When will I get out of here?"

Daval took a deep breath. "I can't be sure, my Lord. You were caught attempting to set fire to my property."

Darst laughed. "You surely can't blame me. Given the rumors about your warehouse, you had to expect trouble of some kind."

Daval sighed. "We did, of course. Which is why you were caught."

"I don't think you have any witnesses who actually saw us attempt this alleged arson," Darst said. "So, considering the fact that no damage was done, I'd think being held a day or two in your cells would be sufficient punishment, wouldn't you?"

In times of peace, this was often the way light disputes were settled between houses. The offending party was held in the injured house's dungeons for an agreed-upon amount of time, and then released without further prosecution. If the offense was severe, a formal trial might be held, but such instances were rare. House representatives settled most disputes through informal negotiations.

This was not peacetime, however. Daval could not be so lenient. And, of course, their plan dictated he act otherwise.

"No damage was done?" Daval asked. "You expect me to believe that?"

Darst snorted. "Of course I do. Go check your warehouse yourself, old man. It's still standing."

Urstadt slammed her glaive against the cell bars with a resounding *clang*. Daval flinched at the sound, and Darst nearly leapt out of the cot.

"You will refer to Lord Amok with the proper respect," Urstadt said, her voice as hard as the iron she'd just struck.

"Canta rising," Darst muttered, sitting up on the cot. "No need to get so touchy about it."

"You should take my captain's advice, my Lord," Daval said quietly. "She is an intelligent woman."

"Just tell us our sentence. Two days? Three? I'll stay four if you insist, if that'll end this discussion sooner rather than later." Darst shifted on the cot, and Daval resisted the urge to smile. The boy was uncomfortable now. Good.

Daval sighed. "I'm afraid things aren't that simple, my Lord. The fire you started spread, and was unquenchable by the time help arrived. We had to watch it burn."

Darst's brow furrowed as he looked up at Daval. "That can't be possible. Your men caught us before we even started the fire."

Daval shrugged, raising his hands. "You say that, but how can I believe you? You've already admitted intent to commit arson."

"I... it wasn't us," Darst said. "We were only meant to scare you, anyway. Never were going to start a real fire. We were to lurk around your property a bit, get caught. That was all."

Daval pursed his lips, stepping closer to the bars. He peered in at Darst. "Do not lie to me, my Lord. Lies don't become men of power. Truth is our greatest ally."

"I… I'm not lying. We did not start any fire, Lord Amok. I swear it."

Daval felt the fear within this young man as if it were his own. It was beautiful.

"Despite your avowals otherwise, we *do* have witnesses," Urstadt said. "Three people can assert they saw you, each of you, starting the fire that decimated the Amok warehouse."

"But…"

"You're lying."

Daval frowned. That last assertion had not come from Darst, but from one of his companions. Daval was of half a mind to ignore the idiot, but this one's defiance irked him. Daval felt the fear radiating from Darst like the sun's rays on a summer day; this other one, the one who had just spoken, emitted no such fear.

Daval walked a few paces to the left to confront his accuser. "You say I'm lying?" Daval asked.

"It is a great offense to accuse a High Lord of dishonesty," Urstadt stated. "The penalties are severe."

"I don't give a shit about penalties," the young man said. This one was different than Darst, and was closer to thirty than twenty. His face, pale and unshaved, was not the face of a Rodenese nobleman.

"Perhaps you should," Daval replied. "It seems they may be more severe for you than they would be for your friends." If Daval's suspicions were correct, then this man was not a noble, and was not protected by noble tradition. High Lords had executed men for less impertinence.

"Keep quiet," Darst hissed from the other cell. "Let me do the talking."

The pale, scruffy-looking man glared at Daval, but said nothing more.

"We did not burn down your warehouse," Darst said, his voice strained. "But… but say we did. What sort of sentencing agreement would we negotiate, then?"

Daval nodded slowly. He wanted the boy to think he was actually considering his response. "I couldn't say for certain," Daval said. "An offense this weighty has not been levied against my house in many years. Perhaps… perhaps six months' incarceration."

The way Darst's eyes widened in panic brought a shiver of excitement through Daval's body.

"*Six months?*" The pale commoner spoke again. "You can't keep us here for *six bloody months*!"

"*Shut up*, Svol," Darst said. "He can, and he will."

"Of course, six months is what we would negotiate if arson were the only charge against you three," Daval said. It was time to close in for the kill. "Unfortunately, there is more."

Darst looked at Daval in disbelief. Incredible how the boy had transformed since Daval had first entered the room. His languid rebellion had turned into tense panic. It was lovely to observe.

"What else is there?" Darst asked, his face now almost as pale as Svol's.

Daval nodded to Urstadt. Urstadt stepped forward, so her face was practically touching the cell bars. "Darst Farady, you and your companions are charged with malicious arson in the form of burning down one of House Amok's most productive warehouses."

"We already know that one," the third prisoner said. "What's the other?"

Interesting, Daval thought. He peered into the cell of the man who had just spoken.

"And," Urstadt continued, "you and your companions are charged with the murder of five people, workers under the protection of House Amok, who perished in the fire."

To the left, Svol gasped. Darst stepped back, his face almost as white as the washed walls of the cell. Ignoring them, Daval met eyes with the third man, and wondered. There was fear here, yes. And defiance, too. But there was something else.

"The penalty for your crimes is death," Urstadt said. "You will be executed the morning after next, at dawn. Notice of your crimes and your sentences will be sent to your respective families."

Svol's gasps intensified; Daval heard a broken sob echo from Darst's cell. This third man, however, only looked at Daval.

"Have you something to say, my Lord?" Daval asked.

"I do," the man said. He stepped forward, so he and Daval were face to face, apart from the bars between them.

"I can testify against them," the man said in a whisper, and nodded his head towards his cellmates. "I saw them light the fire. They knew there were people in the warehouse, and still they lit it. I saw it all."

Daval raised an eyebrow. He glanced at Urstadt, who gave a tiny shake of her head. This man was not one of hers, then. This was unexpected.

"And what of you?" Daval asked, turning back to the man. "You were with them, and yet you did nothing to stop such crimes? Why should we not prosecute you, as well?"

"I accompanied them, yes," the man said, lowering his head. "To my everlasting shame. But I wish to make amends for my wrongs. If you spare my life, I will testify against them, and I will owe you a great debt. I will do whatever you ask of me."

Daval narrowed his eyes. Cowards came in all shapes and sizes, he supposed. This man, this third man, was the one lying. Urstadt had spread the rumors of the abandoned warehouse, and had sent someone to start the fire. She had planted the bodies of murdered Amok workers. If one thing was certain, Darst and his companions did *not* start the fire. Nor were they responsible for the deaths.

And yet this man was willing to lie, and say they were, to save himself. He was also offering Daval a lifetime of favors.

"Whatever I ask of you?"

"*Anything.*"

"What is your name?"

"Urian, my Lord."

Daval looked at Urian for a moment. Then he nodded. "I will consider your offer."

The man nodded, and stepped back to sit calmly on his cot.

"Come, Urstadt," Daval said. "We must inform their families."

"You will not get away with this!"

Daval turned. Darst had found his balls after all.

"My family will not allow it! They will come for us."

"Yes." Daval smiled as he walked out the door with Urstadt. "I'm counting on it."

3

Outskirts of Tinska, on the western coast of Khale

"WAKEY, WAKEY, NOMAD."

Knot sighed. "I'm not sleeping. I'm literally walking right beside you."

"You're being boring. Plus, we're almost there. Look."

Knot felt like he'd been walking, eyes fixed on the ground, for ages. Snow had fallen from the skies, and he'd walked. Sun beat down on his shoulders, and he'd walked. The damned vampire next to him had tried to joke with, pester, and annoy him in every way imaginable, and still he'd walked. He, Astrid, Cinzia, and Jane had been walking for months, now.

"I can see the town as well as you." Tinska was not a large place. Knot had heard of the town before, but had no memory of being there. He'd thought that a town unfamiliar to him would be a welcome change, but his anxiety only grew as he approached.

"Don't act so happy about it," Astrid said. The hood of her large gray cloak was drawn up around her face, despite the sun. *Or because of the sun.* Knot'd seen what direct contact with the sun did to the vampire. Wasn't pleasant.

"I'm happy about it," Knot muttered. "Just smilin' on the inside."

Astrid snorted, but said nothing more. Knot yearned to banter with her they way they had before Roden, but things had changed. Knot had changed, that much was true.

Astrid's cloak hid her small, waifish frame. Knot'd once had difficulty figuring where the monster ended and the girl began. But in the time they'd spent together, he'd decided they were both in there. The girl and the monster coexisted, somehow. Knot was okay with that. Astrid wasn't the only one who shared space with a monster.

"Where is your family staying, again?" Astrid asked.

"They'll be at our uncle's estate," Cinzia said. "Outside the town."

"Is your uncle as rich as your parents?"

Knot glared at Astrid. Her passive-aggressiveness when it came to the Cantic priestess was starting to wear on him.

The two sisters, Cinzia and Jane, shared a glance, but said nothing.

Astrid chuckled. "*Richer?*" she asked, incredulously. "Will I get my own wing of the mansion, then? Or just my own floor?"

Astrid cried out as a pebble struck her hood. Knot turned in surprise to see Jane tossing another small pebble repeatedly into the air with one hand. She was smiling. "Our family is wealthy," Jane said. "Get over it."

Knot chuckled. And, as Astrid turned away in a huff, he caught a smile beneath her hood as well. While Astrid repeatedly clashed with Cinzia, she seemed to have no problem getting along with Jane.

Cinzia's face wasn't easy to read. She was frustratingly adept at hiding her emotions. She'd tied her auburn hair behind her head, making her wide hazel eyes and high cheekbones more prominent. But beneath the austere exterior, Knot could hazard a guess as to what Cinzia might be feeling. They'd both lost people in Roden. It'd taken weeks before Cinzia and Jane had revealed what had happened to Kovac, Cinzia's Goddessguard.

Knot would've thought such a tale was crazy, if he hadn't seen far worse with his own eyes. Either way, Kovac was dead. And Knot could tell it weighed on Cinzia, just as another death weighed on him.

"I hope they are well," Jane whispered, looking down at the town below. The younger of the two sisters, Jane looked very much like Cinzia, although with blond hair and blue eyes where Cinzia's were auburn and hazel.

"The Denomination will not have sent another Crucible," Cinzia said. "Not yet. They will regroup, try to figure out how to approach us next. They will calculate their next move very carefully."

"With any luck, they still haven't figured out where we are," Jane said.

Cinzia shook her head. "They know exactly where we are. Or, at least, where our family went after Navone. They are tracking us."

Knot nodded. What Cinzia said lined up with his own fragmented memories of the Cantic Denomination. The Denomination was calculating, meticulous, and hoarded information from every corner of the Sfaera.

"You said the Denomination won't have sent another Crucible *yet*," Knot said. "But they will eventually?"

Cinzia shrugged. "I can't say. They will not let an insult of this magnitude go unanswered. But they may try… different approaches, before they resort to sending another Crucible."

"What other approaches are there?" Jane asked.

Knot felt Cinzia's gaze on him. They all knew who he'd been, before he lost his memories. They all knew who he'd worked for, what he'd done.

"Oh," Jane said quietly.

Knot pursed his lips. Part of the reason he'd come with

these two was to protect them. Or so he told himself. But, as he'd spent more time with Cinzia and Jane, as they told him what had happened to Kovac, and of what they'd translated from the Nine Scriptures, Knot felt like he might have found something like a purpose again. He'd seen darkness in the imperial palace. He'd seen the face of fear, and seen what daemons wanted to bring into the world. Sacrifices had been made to protect the Sfaera. Knot couldn't let those sacrifices be in vain.

Sticking with Jane and Cinzia seemed to be the best way to honor Winter's memory. They at least had a direction. Knot didn't.

The four of them made their way down into Tinska, and the smell of the sea reminded Knot of Pranna. Pranna was as close to a hometown as he'd known. It was a village, a tiny place compared to Tinska, but they shared the smell of the sea and the ocean wind, the dock jutting out into the harbor. Those smells reminded Knot of other things, too. Things that were not his own, and yet were in his head, anyway. They reminded him of an attempt to sail the entire circumference of the Sfaera, where he'd almost died off the coast of Andrinar. They reminded him of pirating in the warm waters near Alizia, taking gold, ships, and lives as he pleased. They reminded him of the great city of Triah, located at the mouth of the world, and the dark purposes he'd once served there.

To say his memories were becoming more clear since he'd learned who, and what, he was in Izet wouldn't be right. They were muddier than ever. But there were more ingredients, now, more bits and pieces thrown into the mix. The feeling of having been at a certain place before, having said a certain thing, returned more frequently. Knot didn't like it. Once already the memories had taken him too far, had buried who he was. Jane had been there to help him, but he didn't want that to happen again.

He had to remember what was real. The memories of

others, while they may have happened, were not real to *him*. Not in the way that Pranna was. Not in the way that Winter had looked at him on her father's fishing boat.

As they walked through Tinska, however, the nostalgia passed. Where Pranna was hardly more than a dirt road surrounded by a cluster of houses and shops, Tinska was home to thousands of people. Pranna was surrounded by windswept plains and tundra, with occasional pockets of red pine forests. Tinska, on the other hand, was surrounded by green trees and sat on a shelf of sorts above the water, with sandy beaches below, dark after a recent rain.

"Where's your uncle's place?" Astrid asked.

"The Harmoth estate is just over that hill," Jane said, nodding at the rising land ahead of them.

"Canta rising," he heard Cinzia whisper when they reached the top of the hill.

A massive manor house rose before them, sited on a large grassy ledge above the rocky beach. Tents, lean-tos, wagons, and small campfires dotted the large fields surrounding the house. A few large trees rose above the tents here and there, and horses, oxen, and other beasts of burden milled about amongst dozens of people who had made the estate their home.

"What in Oblivion…" Astrid did not seem to have the words to finish.

A young woman of sixteen or seventeen ran up to them, a great smile on her face. She walked immediately up to Jane. "You're her, aren't you?" the girl asked.

Knot looked at Jane, who seemed taken aback. "I… I don't know…"

"You're Jane," the girl said, more confident now. "You're Jane. You're the Prophetess."

Knot raised an eyebrow.

"I… I suppose I am," Jane said, hesitantly.

The girl laughed in delight. "Blessed be Canta's name. You're finally here." She turned and ran down the hill towards the crowds of people. "She's here," the girl shouted. "The Prophetess has arrived!"

4

Harmoth estate, Tinska, western Khale

CINZIA FROWNED. THIS COULD not be good. "Prophetess?" she asked, glaring at her sister.

Jane shrugged. "I never asked for such a title."

Heads began to turn at the young woman's shouting. Many were staring up the hill at Cinzia, Jane, Knot, and Astrid.

"I doubt you're hating it, either," Cinzia muttered.

Astrid nudged her. "Nice," she said, winking up at Cinzia.

Cinzia rolled her eyes. "Come on," she said. "We'd best find our family."

"Go on ahead," Knot said. "Me and Astrid will take our time."

"Are you sure?" Cinzia said.

Knot nodded. "You haven't seen your family in months. Take some time with them."

Cinzia glanced at Astrid, who was looking out at the crowd, her hood shrouding her face. Cinzia did not think her family was aware of what Astrid really was. By the time Astrid had been revealed in Navone's city center, the place was already in chaos. If her family was aware of Astrid, there might be problems, but they would have to be told sooner or later anyway.

"Very well," Cinzia said. "But we will find you two soon afterwards."

Knot nodded. "We'll be close."

Cinzia was comforted by his words. Kovac's death had left

a void in her heart. She had loved him like an older brother. Knot, despite his darkness, made her feel safe in the same way Kovac had.

As Cinzia and Jane approached the milling people, hands reached towards them, eyes bright with anticipation. They seemed to be waiting for Cinzia and Jane with a kind of charged patience. *They are not waiting for both of us,* Cinzia reminded herself. *They are here for Jane, not me.* She heard cries of "Prophetess!" and "Jane the Chosen!"

"They won't let us pass, sister," Cinzia whispered. "You're going to have to address them."

Jane raised an arm, and almost immediately the crowd quieted. Cinzia felt a chill run up her spine. This kind of power was dangerous.

"My name is Jane Oden," Jane said, loudly but without shouting. "This is my sister, Cinzia. Some of you may know, she is a priestess in the Cantic Denomination."

Murmurs rippled through the gathering. Most of them had not known this, apparently. Cinzia was immediately on guard. She looked around for Astrid and Knot, but she could no longer see them.

"You say I have been chosen. You say I am a prophetess."

Here we go, Cinzia thought. This was it, her sister's moment of glory.

"You're wrong," Jane said. Cinzia looked at her sister in surprise.

"I'm only a servant," Jane continued, "and that is all. I had a question, and I chose to bring it to Canta. The Goddess, by her grace, responded. And now something has begun that will change the Sfaera. In these times, as we prepare for the darkest days the world has ever seen, Canta has chosen to reveal herself. But I am only her servant. I am not a leader; I am not a revolutionary. I'm only a woman who wishes to do the will of her goddess." Jane turned to Cinzia. "My sister, Cinzia, has served Canta faithfully her whole life. She has studied Canta's word at the great seminary in Triah, and taught Canta's children of Her nature and doctrine. And now she travels with me, still serving Canta's will."

Jane hesitated for a moment before continuing. "You're all here, each and every one of you, for a purpose. Some of you will be teachers. Some of you will build Canta's kingdom on the Sfaera. Some of you will raise children, teaching them the way of the Goddess. And, among you, there are those who, like me, will be able to communicate directly with Canta Herself. You each have a purpose, my brothers and sisters. You are *all* Canta's servants."

Cinzia could *feel* the energy radiating from the crowd. *No, not from them*, Cinzia realized. The energy came from *Jane*.

Jane paused again, as if to let that feeling of crackling energy sink into her audience. "My sister and I have traveled a great distance," she said. "We have seen great darkness. We have seen what threatens our world. So now we need to be reunited with our family but soon we will return. Canta has great things planned for her children."

Though the energy had faded, the residual effect was still there. Jane's audience stared at her in perfect silence. Even the children seemed captivated.

"May Canta be with each of you," Jane said. Then, she walked forward. Cinzia hesitated a moment before falling in behind her sister. The small crowd parted easily in front of them, staring at Jane as she passed, faces eager, but somehow changed.

Cinzia was surprised to see tiellans among the predominately human crowd. Their shorter, slighter frames and pointed ears made them stand out. Tiellans had never been excluded from Cantic ceremonies and doctrine within the Denomination exactly, but their services were separate, and slightly different, to cater to tiellan tradition. Or so Cinzia had been told.

Cinzia knew why tiellans would be drawn to an alternative to the Denomination. The Denomination had not treated them well. The Denomination claimed to accept them, but in reality only heaped more persecution upon them.

Cinzia sighed. She saw one tiellan girl, a few years younger than herself, and was immediately reminded of two tiellans lost in Roden. Winter, Knot's wife, and Lian, their friend.

Cinzia and Jane made their way across the grounds of the Harmoth estate—named after her mother's family—the mass of people parting a few paces in front of them the whole way. The effect was eerie. Jane seemed to have a bubble of force around her that repelled the crowd as she walked. Cinzia glanced back, and, sure enough, the people fell into place a few paces behind them. Finally they reached the large double-doors of the manor house. Jane turned and waved to the crowd, a large smile on her face. "We know many of you have traveled great distances to see us," she said, her voice carrying across the throng. "Canta knows, we are grateful. We will be among you soon."

"I don't appreciate your constant use of the word 'we,' sister," Cinzia said as she closed the doors behind them. "I have no intention of walking among them any time soon."

"I'm sorry you feel that way, Cinzia," Jane said with her maddeningly calm demeanor.

Cinzia's jaw clenched. How could Jane be so serene when she felt such rage? "Why are they even here? How did they hear about us? How did they find our family?"

"I don't know," Jane said.

"If people like this can find us—simple people, tiellans, villagers—then who *else* will arrive at our doorstep?"

"Canta will direct us," Jane said. "As long as we are doing what she asks, we needn't worry."

Cinzia shook her head in disbelief. Could Jane really not see cause to worry? And yet she wondered why she was reacting so strongly. Since she had arrived in Navone last year to confront her sister, she had felt as if she had no control over her life. This aggravated older resentments, and since Kovac's death in Roden, those emotions had been amplified.

"There must be almost one hundred people out there," Cinzia seethed, "and we don't know what drew them here. The Denomination is surely taking steps to eliminate you—and your movement—and you can rest assured they will not be peaceful. And I lost my Goddessguard—" Cinzia stopped, choked up. "I lost my Goddessguard to a force neither of us know or understand. The Sfaera is in danger, Jane. You can't tell me I have nothing to worry about."

"Hello, girls."

Cinzia whirled to see her father, Ehram, standing in the entryway. "Father!" she cried.

"Hello, Father," Jane said.

Ehram smiled. "I'm so glad you're here," he said. He opened his arms, and both Cinzia and Jane sank into his embrace. "I have missed you both," Ehram said.

"We've missed you, Father," Jane said.

Cinzia said nothing, not trusting herself, and just buried her face in the soft leather of her father's jacket.

"Where is your Goddessguard, Cinzia? Kovac, was that his

name? And where are the others that accompanied you?"

Cinzia's face fell at the mention of her Goddessguard. Of course it would be the first thing to come up. "Kovac was killed," she explained. "In Roden."

Her father's face whitened, but he nodded slowly. "I'm so sorry, my dear. I could tell that he was someone special to you."

Cinzia did not know what else to say. That night in Izet carried so many different feelings for her. Just before Kovac's death, Cinzia had been alone on a rooftop, watching the snow fall around her. She had felt love. She had felt *meaning*. She had felt Canta's presence, felt that she, Cinzia, *mattered* to the Goddess.

And then, moments later, something terrible had possessed Kovac, and Cinzia had been forced to kill him with her own hands.

"But you're both safe? Healthy?"

Jane nodded. "Yes. We have traveled a long way. And outside..."

Ehram nodded vigorously. "Of course, of course. You'll be wondering about that." He beckoned them to follow as he moved down the corridor. "Come, come," he said. "The others will be anxious to see you. Especially your mother, bless her soul. She has had trouble sleeping. Not that that's your fault, but she worries—you know how she is."

"Well now we are home, Father," Jane said. "And we have work to do."

Her father laughed. "Of course, of course. Come, then. Let's get something warm in your bellies."

He led them into the dining hall, where Cinzia saw that her family sat around a large table, chatting loudly. They were all there, Cinzia saw with surprise—including Uncle Ronn, although with more gray in his hair and a bit thinner than she remembered him.

Ehram stepped forward as if to announce Cinzia and Jane, but Cinzia put a hand on his shoulder. He looked back at her, an eyebrow raised.

Cinzia shook her head. "Give us a moment," she whispered. "I want to watch them."

Her uncle Ronn sat at the head of the table, looking around in dismay. Cinzia smiled. The chaos of dealing with six Oden children was surely wearing down the man's formality.

Cinzia's mother, Pascia, bustled about the table, her blond hair in a loose bun. She was herding the two youngest children—Sammel and Ader, boys of twelve and eleven—to their chairs, where two steaming bowls of oatmeal waited for them. Directly across the table from Sammel and Ader sat Wina, Lana and Soffrena, the triplets, each fifteen. Lana was dumping spoonful after spoonful of what Cinzia could only imagine was sugar into her oatmeal.

"Lana!" Pascia said sharply, one hand on Ader's shoulder keeping him in his chair, the other reaching out to swat Lana's hand. "Not so much sugar, darling. Your blood will turn solid."

"I can't bear another morning of oatmeal, Mother," Lana said, pouting. "I *need* the sugar. I won't be able to eat it otherwise."

"We only have so much of it, Lana." Cinzia's other sibling, Eward, reached over Lana's shoulder to grab the small jar. "Save some for the rest of us." Eward, tall and powerfully built, was much closer to Cinzia and Jane in age. He was coming up on his twentieth summer, now, four years Cinzia's junior and just two years younger than Jane.

At that moment Eward looked up and locked eyes with Cinzia. Cinzia saw the grin spread across his face immediately. She put a finger to her lips and Eward nodded.

"Give me that!" Lana shouted. "Mother! Eward took the sugar!"

"Good thing he did," Pascia said, still struggling with Ader. The boy did not seem to want to sit in his seat.

"I don't see how you eat so much of it," said Soffrena. Wina sat eating quietly. While the triplets looked identical, with red-brown hair, hazcl eyes, and freckle-studded faces, their demeanors could not be any more different. Wina was shy and quiet—much like Sammel, Soffrena had always been even-tempered, while Lana had hardly had a serious moment in her entire life.

"I suppose you wouldn't. You're far too boring," Lana said.

"The fact that you think sugar consumption is an indication of vigor tells us all we need to know about you."

Cinzia glanced at Jane. They both smiled. While they were much more similar in demeanor to one another than Lana and Soffrena, they had experienced many similar exchanges. *We practically just had one,* Cinzia reminded herself. Although their arguments did not much seem like arguments anymore. Not with Jane refusing to shout back at her.

Lana turned back to her oatmeal, arms folded, pouting once more. Then she glanced towards the entrance of the dining hall. Her pout transformed into a grin.

"*They're home!*" Lana ran towards Cinzia and Jane, wrapping her arms around both at once.

After they had all said their hellos, after tearful hugs and the excited chatter of the younger children, things calmed down. Even Uncle Ronn seemed happy to see them, giving each of them warm, if somewhat stiff, embraces. Cinzia and her family moved back to the dining-room table, where they all sat down.

At that moment, Gorman, Uncle Ronn's head servant

appeared at the door to the kitchen. He looked over the shoulders of the younger children disdainfully.

"I see your breakfast has gotten cold," he said. "I suppose I'll have Shal make more."

"No," Pascia said, quickly. "The children will eat their oatmeal, cold or not. Isn't that right, children?" Soffrena, Lana, Wina, Sammel, and Ader nodded unenthusiastically.

Gorman did not seem happy either, but he nodded nonetheless, and began to clear dirty dishes. Then he noticed Cinzia, Jane, and Ehram at the table. He bowed. "Miss Cinzia. Miss Jane. I'm happy to see you both arrived safely."

"He hasn't changed much," Jane whispered, as Gorman walked back into the kitchen.

Cinzia nodded. "Although he never would have stooped to carrying dishes before. Something is different."

"Please, girls," Pascia said. "We want to hear all about your adventures."

Cinzia paled. Just mentioning Kovac to her father had been too much.

"Perhaps we can tell you of our… adventures another time," Jane said smoothly.

"Sooner rather than later, I hope," said Ronn. "I have heard much about you two."

"We have told Ronn everything," Pascia explained.

"I'm not a believer," Ronn said, his graying mustache drooping over his frown. "But what your parents have told me… intrigues me, to say the least."

Cinzia was surprised at her relief. It might be good to have someone who was a bit more skeptical around.

"But at least tell us of the translation," Eward said, his eyes wide. "What have you learned? How much have you translated?"

Cinzia looked from Eward to Jane. She was not aware the rest of their family knew of Jane's intention to translate the Nine Scriptures—the Codex of Elwene—while traveling to Roden. Cinzia herself had not been aware of the plan until their journey began.

"The translation goes well," Jane said, ignoring Cinzia's look. "There are ten major portions to the Codex. The first nine, of course, are named for the original disciple who penned each section. We have translated the books of Elessa, Baetrissa, Arcana, Sirana, Danica, Lucia, and Ocrestia. We are about to begin translating the book of Cinzia."

Ader and Sammel grinned at Cinzia at the mention of her namesake. Cinzia, like most firstborn daughters, was named after one of the original Nine Disciples that served Canta while she walked the Sfaera.

"And what have you learned?" Ehram asked. "What do the Nine Scriptures teach you?"

For the first time, Jane hesitated. She and Cinzia looked at each other. *They are not ready,* Cinzia thought. The Codex had taught them many things, about the creation of the Sfaera, the origins of Canta and the other gods and goddesses. But it had also contained warnings, of things happening now and of things to come. A tremor slithered up Cinzia's spine.

Jane apparently thought so as well. "We will reveal what has been taught to us in time," she said. "But I think we have more pressing matters. The dozens of people camping outside, for one."

"Bloody squatters is all they are, if you ask me," Uncle Ronn muttered.

"They're your followers, Jane!" Ader could not hide his excitement.

"They are calling themselves after us, our family name," Lana said, obviously proud of the fact. "They call themselves Odenites."

Jane smiled but Cinzia thought she saw a shadow of uncertainty in her eyes. *Good,* Cinzia thought. *Let her be uncomfortable. She knows this is going too far.*

"Is that who they are?" Jane asked.

Ehram and Pascia exchanged a glance. Ehram nodded. "More or less," he said. "We know the dangers of such things. We know that we only just escaped the Crucible's hand in Navone. But…"

"We couldn't turn them away," Pascia said. "And there were only a few of them, at first. People who sought refuge, people whom the Denomination—" she glanced at Cinzia when she said the word—"has harmed, or neglected."

"We wanted to invite them into the house," Soffrena said, "but Uncle Ronn doesn't think it's a good idea."

Ronn grunted. "This is my house. I will run it how I see fit."

Pascia smiled, although Cinzia could tell her mother disagreed with Ronn. "We have had that conversation many times over the past few weeks, and we know where you stand, Ronn. We will respect your authority here."

"But they are already too numerous to live in the house," Eward said, "and they just keep coming. New arrivals almost every day, now."

"How are they living?" Cinzia asked. "Are we providing for them?"

"Not exactly," Ehram said. "They take water from the pond and the stream that feeds it. Some of them catch fish from the sea, and a few have begun to find clams on the beach, and there is fruit in the orchard and other forage. The wealthier ones go into Tinska to buy food and supplies. While he does not want them in the house itself, Ronn has nevertheless been gracious enough to allow them access to the resources of his estate."

"I don't know how much longer that grace can last," Ronn said. "We have had a good few years recently, but my resources will only go so far. And the local fishermen will not be happy about the encroachment upon their business."

Cinzia felt a rush of affection for her uncle. Ronn had always had a compassionate soul beneath his stern exterior. But his compassion, in this case, was not exactly necessary.

"We gave the servants the option to leave, if they desired," Pascia said. "A few left, but most stayed. A good thing, too—we need their help more than ever."

"Father says the people are a blessing in disguise," Soffrena said. She was looking at Jane. "Is that what they are? A blessing?"

All eyes turned to Jane, including Cinzia's. Jane was silent.

If she does not say it, Cinzia thought, *I will.*

"They're a problem," Cinzia said, her voice harder than she meant it to be. "They will only bring trouble. The Cantic Denomination won't ignore such things. They will bring their fist down on us, and it will not be like Navone. They will not be nearly so... accommodating."

Ehram made as if to speak, but Cinzia continued over him. "And even if the Denomination *does not* come, how much longer can we accommodate such a gathering?"

"You're both correct," Jane said. Cinzia rolled her eyes. "Cinzia, the people outside *are* a problem. They will only bring trouble, if we seek to manage them ourselves. But Soffrena, too, is right." Jane smiled at Soffrena, who smiled tentatively in return. "Canta often sends us problems to bless us. To help us learn. This is one of those times."

"We should send them away," Cinzia insisted.

Jane was shaking her head when Gorman cleared his throat at the entrance to the dining hall.

"I apologize," he said stiffly. "I do not mean to interrupt, but someone wants to see Cinzia and Jane. Someone very insistent—"

Astrid sprinted into the room. "You need to come with me," she said. "There's a problem."

"I knew it," Cinzia said. "The people are already causing problems—"

"It isn't them," Astrid said. "It's Knot."

5

"ANOTHER EPISODE?" JANE ASKED, as they made their way through the mass of people.

"Yes." *That's a good thing, right?* Astrid thought. *It's happened before, and he got over it. He'll get over it again.*

"You left him out here? With *them*?" Cinzia asked.

Astrid shot the woman a glarc. "What was I supposed to do? He wouldn't come with me. He didn't recognize me."

"What do you mean? He didn't recognize his own daughter?"

Astrid glared at the young man who'd spoken. She looked at Jane. "Who's he? Why's he coming with us?"

"He's our—"

"I'm their brother," the young man said. "I just want to help."

Astrid rolled her eyes. Cinzia sighed, and placed a hand on her brother's shoulder. "Eward," she said, "we appreciate your eagerness to help, but…"

Their voices faded as Astrid and Jane walked quickly to where the people had gathered. Astrid frowned. Apparently Cinzia and Jane's brother—Eward—thought Astrid was Knot's daughter. She had never liked that particular cover; it felt fake.

It is *fake, idiot. How else did you expect it to feel?*

The rest of the Oden family, thankfully, had remained inside. Astrid didn't want their first impression of Knot to be… this.

With Jane's help they made their way through the gathering to find Knot in the middle of it.

"For Canta's sake," he was saying, "will one of you tell me what is going on? How did I get here? Who *are* all of you?"

Astrid ran up to him. The small crowd had given Knot a wide berth; a young woman with bright orange hair was trying to reason with him. Knot did not seem to be responding well. His eyes were wide and rolling.

"I'm back," Astrid said.

Knot looked down at her, and she hated the disdain in his eyes. "You," he said. "The child. You said you would bring help. Well? Where is the help?"

"I'm the help." Jane stepped forward. The crowd took a collective step back.

The red-headed woman who had been trying to calm Knot turned to face Jane. "Your Grace," she said, bowing. "This man is troubled. He does not seem to understand how he got here. We have informed him he is in Tinska, but he claims he has never been here before. He claims to be from Alizia."

Knot, or whoever he was, huffed. "Not just Alizia," he said, raising his chin. "The great city of Cornasa, on the island of Alna. I am High Prince Dorian Gatama, and I demand an explanation of what has been done to me. If I have been kidnapped, you must inform me immediately. I can have the ransom paid quickly and we can all be on our way." He looked at Jane. "You," he said, "you say you can help me. So help me."

Jane approached Knot, slowly. She thanked the woman, who stepped back into the crowd. Then Jane looked at Knot.

"You have not been kidnapped, High Prince Gatama, I assure you. You are in Tinska, in northern Khale, at the Harmoth estate. I am Jane Oden, daughter of Ehram and Pascia Oden.

You're perfectly safe. If you will please come with me, we will get you the help you need."

Knot, or Prince Gatama, or whoever the hell he was, shook his head. "No. I'll not leave this spot until someone has told me how I got here."

Cinzia stepped forward. "Your Grace," she said, bowing, "I am Cinzia Oden, Jane's elder sister. I can vouch for her words, and for your safety. But first, I'm afraid there is another issue at hand." Cinzia began speaking quietly enough that only Jane and Knot could hear. And Astrid, of course, but Astrid could hear a whisper from a dozen paces further away.

"You have a blood blight, Your Grace," Cinzia whispered.

Knot's face immediately paled. "A blood blight," he whispered, almost choking on the words. "How… how long?"

"You contracted it months ago, on Alna, and were sent north to find treatment in Triah. Then you went missing. The blood blight must have already gotten to your brain, Your Grace. You were missing for months, and have only now been found."

Knot's knees almost buckled. "Are you… are you sure?"

Cinzia nodded, and Astrid gave her credit for her solemnity, and the ruse itself. Alizians, especially Alizian nobles, were notoriously afraid of the blood blight.

"We will return you to the proper care, but in the meantime my sister is a physician, a healer. Allow her to help you."

Knot nodded, vigorously. "Yes, of course. Please, do anything you can."

Cinzia looked back at Jane, who stepped forward. "Please, Your Grace. If you would kneel."

Knot hesitated. *Jane, don't be a fool,* Astrid thought. *You never ask an Alizian noble to kneel.* But Knot's—or Prince Gatama's—terror took precedence, and he knelt. Jane walked behind him and placed her hands on his head. She looked up to the sky, and began moving her lips, although Astrid heard no words.

The people around them had fallen eerily silent. A chill shook Astrid, the same feeling she'd experienced the other time Jane had done this to Knot. Jane was healing him, she claimed. With Canta's power. Astrid wasn't sure it was that simple, but it made Knot come back, and that was all she cared about.

There was perfect silence for a moment, as Jane's lips moved. Then she stopped.

Knot stood, looking around him. His eyes found Astrid. "Happened again?" he asked.

Astrid nodded, trying to keep from showing emotion. She wanted to grin, and she wanted to cry, and she wasn't sure which she would do first. "You're back now, nomad."

The people gathered around them were already whispering. "Did you see that?" "She healed him!" "She brought Canta's power down from the skies!" "She cast the daemon out of him!"

That last one stuck. "Great," Astrid said to herself.

"What're they talkin' about?" Knot asked. Astrid was relieved to hear the usual gruffness in his voice. "Was I really that bad?"

Astrid shrugged. "Pretty bad, but not in the daemonic way. You were an Alizian noble."

Knot glanced at Jane, who was now moving among the people, trying to calm them down, to explain what had happened.

What had *actually* happened was inexplicable, at least not without context. The fact that Knot had a bunch of other souls inside of him, souls that seemed intent on getting out recently, wouldn't go over well. Perhaps daemonic possession *was* the best explanation, for now.

"She healed me?" Knot asked, still looking at Jane.

Astrid nodded. "Why can she bring you back?"

"Don't know. But I wouldn't mind finding out."

"Finding out what?" Cinzia asked. She, too, did not seem particularly comfortable with her sister's relationship with the people now flocking around her.

"What your sister does to Knot, to make him come back," Astrid said. "Don't suppose you know anything about it?"

Cinzia shook her head. "I don't understand anything going on with Jane. This is all so…"

"Absurd?" Astrid offered. People travelling across Khale just to see a woman who stood up to the Denomination. What was the point? The Denomination would never stand for it, not in the long term.

"That was clever what you did back there, anyway," Astrid said when Cinzia didn't respond. "A blood blight was quick thinking. You got him to calm down when I didn't think there was anything that could."

Cinzia shrugged. "It was nothing. I'm going back inside. You're both welcome to come with me."

"Wouldn't mind getting away from this lot," Knot said.

"Me too," Astrid agreed. Her ears still picked up whispers of "casting out daemons." As ridiculous as the idea was, the phrase made Astrid wonder. Jane, of all people, had never treated Astrid with the blunt mix of terror and disdain that everyone else showed when they discovered what she really was. Even Knot, when he'd first realized she was a vampire, had hated and feared her. But Jane had never treated her that way.

Maybe Jane truly did have power when she placed her hands on Knot's head. Maybe what she claimed when it came to the Goddess was true.

Maybe Jane could cast out daemons.

6

Dungeons of the imperial palace, Izet

"Eat your food, girl."

The gaoler glared at Winter through the bars in her cell door. Winter stared back at him dully. The gaoler had slid a tray with Winter's "food" on it through the hatch at the bottom of the door an hour or so ago. The mush had long gotten cold.

"Boss said you got to eat," the gaoler growled. His Rodenese accent was thick, his words clipped and halting. "Orders is orders, and you must follow them much as me."

Winter said nothing. She did not move. The man slammed his fist against the door, making a sound that echoed throughout the dungeon. Winter might've jumped, if she'd cared enough to be frightened.

"Just look at your bloody meal," the gaoler said, almost whining. "Something there we ain't given you before. Boss thinks you'll enjoy it."

Winter frowned. This wasn't the first time she'd not eaten her food, but it was the first time they'd heckled her about it. She didn't care much what it was the gaoler thought was so interesting, except that it might break up the monotony of her captivity. It'd been months, and they hadn't killed her yet. Hadn't spoken to her, either, except for the occasional word or two from a guard. Winter was beginning to wonder whether she'd been forgotten—and whether that was the point; she'd been framed for the murder of the emperor and the Tokal-Ceno, the two highest-ranking men in Roden. She had assumed her punishment would be death, perhaps preceded by torture. But maybe being forgotten *was* the torture. Maybe this would be her routine for the rest of her life.

Which was why the mere implication of something different made Winter stand and walk towards the door to inspect the food.

"Aye, missy. Do as you're bloody well told."

Winter ignored the man. Hubb was his name, and he was simultaneously the cruelest and the stupidest of the gaolers. Enri Crawn was the kindest, although his kindness was closer to indifference, if you could call it as much.

Enri Crawn likes to kick up his feet and smoke a pipe, Winter thought. *Enri Crawn isn't one to ask questions.*

She stopped.

There, on the scarred wooden tray on which sat the bowl of cold mush and the cup of stale water, was a crystalline substance, roughly the size of Winter's thumb, pale and opaque.

Winter started sweating. The whole world fell away, and only the crystal remained. *Faltira*, or what many termed frost, was a powerful narcotic with highly addictive properties. It was also the only means by which a small percentage of the human population could access the cognitive arts. Psimancy. Winter, as a tiellan, shouldn't have been able to use frost for that purpose. But she could.

The last time she had used it had been months ago: in the throne hall of the imperial palace, when she'd smashed the place to rubble, and a number of huge, otherworldly monsters along with it. When she had watched her friends die.

Winter was immediately suspicious. Why would they give

her *faltira*? Who would dare to risk it? With one dose Winter could probably kill half the people in the bloody palace. They had to know this, whoever her captors were. And yet there, before her, was a frost crystal.

Perhaps it was scratch, a placebo that offered none of the effects of true *faltira*.

There was only one way to find out. Winter picked up the crystal, felt the familiar lightness of it. She hesitated. The last time she had taken *faltira*, when she had annihilated the Outsiders in the throne hall, she had done it for a specific reason. She had done it to help her friends. It had felt like a revelation, like something that would change her life. And, perhaps, if her friends had survived, it would have. Perhaps if Knot were still here, if she still had people who cared about her, Winter would be different. She might fight the compulsion to take the crystal.

But Winter knew the truth. She was alone. Her revelation seemed petty, inconsequential. There was nothing left, now. There was Winter.

And, now, there was *faltira*. Winter raised the crystal to her lips, and swallowed.

Her suspicions that the crystal might be scratch dispelled almost immediately. The power began to course through her within moments, the fire roaring, the ice cooling her skin. Winter smiled. Then, she reached out with a *tendron*. This would be her prison no longer. She would punish those who had put her here, who had killed those she—

Nothing happened.

She reached again, with multiple *tendra* this time, the sinewy invisible limbs snaking out from her mind to the door, the bars before her, the lock, and the guard outside. Nothing. They must have given her scratch, after all. Some drug that made Winter feel the high, but gave her no access to the power. The Void was as far from her as it had always been, without *faltira*.

This has happened before, Winter thought, and she remembered the Ceno monks who had attacked her on the River Arden. She had taken frost then, but it hadn't worked. Something had blocked her.

Winter rushed to the bars on the door of her cell. The gaoler jumped back in surprise, but Winter only snarled at him. She was looking for someone else. She scanned the dank corridor outside of her cell as much as the limited space would allow. It was dark, lit only sporadically by dull torches. Winter couldn't see anyone.

"I know you're there," she called out. "You're blocking me."

No response came from the darkness. Hubb looked at her like she had lost her mind. Perhaps she had.

Winter reached a *tendron* into the shadows, but still nothing happened. "You can't block me forever," Winter said. "You can't hold me here." She knew the moment she said the words that they were untrue; she had no idea how long these people could block her powers, and as long as they could, they could keep her here until the day she died.

Still no response came from the darkness.

"You'd best calm down, girl," Hubb said. "No use getting upset."

Winter, the frost still burning in her veins, did not look at Hubb. She turned away from her cell door and collapsed to the ground. She let the effects of *faltira* take her away, away from her cell, away from her solitude, away from her pain, and she began to drift.

The woman does not dream because she no longer sleeps. She lies on a filthy pile of straw in one corner of the cell, legs angled awkwardly beneath her, arms outstretched. She is uncomfortable but the feeling is vague and distant. Sensation no longer matters. The voices in the woman's head, whispering and whispering, seem to no longer matter, either.

Murderer, they whisper.

Harbinger. Something new. Something she has not heard before. Something she does not understand.

Revenge, another part whispers. That part of her that still thinks she has control. That still thinks what she does matters. *Punish those who hurt us. Avenge the fallen.*

But another part of the woman wonders why revenge is necessary. Those she loves are dead. A permanent condition, and once it takes hold that person ceases to exist and enters the inescapable pull of Oblivion.

The woman is not dead. She knows that well enough. And, quite clearly, she does not wish to be dead. She does not fear much, anymore, but that is one thing she does: ceasing to exist. *True* oblivion. Nothingness.

But, beyond that fear, the woman feels nothing. The dungeon does not frighten her; loneliness does not frighten her, although there is a faint tug at her mind asking what the difference truly is between loneliness while living and loneliness in death. She responds to herself with the assertion that in living, at least she is alone with herself, while in death, she is alone without herself.

The woman feels sadness for those lost, but even that is only a dull ache, where it was once a tortured hollowing of her insides.

She lies back and lets her mind drift, lets it jump. She wonders whether she could just leave her body behind, and live in the minds of others. Perhaps she could be free, both of her dungeon cell and the prison of her body.

Then, her mind fixes upon the person closest to her.

* * *

Hubb worries about his brother, Darb. Darb has fallen in with rough company, rougher than either of them is used to. They have always enjoyed the occasional smoke of tark leaf, or even a hit of devil's dust when they can afford it. Darb has been spending more and more of his time, and silver, on such things. Darb has even told Hubb that he's tried hero. Hubb has not asked Darb how he's been able to afford hero; the drug is the most expensive thing, measure for measure, that Hubb can imagine buying. Now Darb owes hard men hard money, and Hubb has no way of helping him. Between his wages as a gaoler and his time spent bouncing at the Trundleback, he barely has enough to support either of them—

The woman jumps from Hubb's mind, unable to listen to his thoughts anymore. She jumps into the person nearest Hubb, and keeps jumping again and again.

—Huri can't believe he's still in this bloody dungeon when his parents should have bailed him out long—

—Grante wishes he could tell stories like his father—

—wonders whether her mother noticed her throwing up this morning—

—can't wait to get home to play with his newborn son—

—watches the people around her, hating them—

—thinks the Lords' Council shouldn't—

—waits for her husband—

—sees how sorry—

—doesn't realize—

—loves—

—herself—

—no longer—

And suddenly the woman's mind travels far away. It is a

sensation the likes of which she has never experienced; it is a sense of traveling a great distance and looking at things from a distant perspective, or perhaps the opposite, traveling far inward, moving in so close on things that they become completely different. She finds herself in what looks very much like the night sky. She thinks she is floating, but she can't be sure. Millions upon millions of tiny lights, looking for all the world like stars but of infinitely different colors, surround her on all sides. She sees varying shades of white and gold, countless others of red, blue, green, purple, orange, and other colors she can't fathom.

She looks down at herself, sees her hands and her feet, her body, but she is no longer clothed in the rough, reeking burlap that she has worn since the first day of her imprisonment. Instead, she wears the dark leather clothing Kali the assassin gave her, tight-fitting and sleek, in a memory outside of time.

The woman takes a step forward and her foot lands on an unseen surface; she can still see millions and millions of the tiny star-lights below her. Ripples of light echo away from her foot, like multicolored ripples from a stone tossed into still water. She takes another step, light waving away from where she treads.

In between the stars is the blackest of blacks, a true nothingness that reminds her of what it is she fears, the only thing she fears. *Hello?* she shouts, but her mouth does not open, nor does air move through her lungs. *Is anyone here? Can anyone hear me?* She wonders, for a brief moment, if this is death, if they have killed her, after all.

As soon as the thought enters her mind, she knows that is not this. While she is alone in this space, she does not feel alone. The lights around her radiate meaning. No, the death she fears couldn't be this forgiving. The death she fears could never be this connected.

But, through the connectivity she feels, she does notice something dark on the horizon. A shape, moving towards her. The shape looks to be a giant, looks far, far bigger than the woman herself, and she feels fear. She takes a few steps back, color and light rippling with each footstep, but the shade continues to advance.

What are you? the woman asks, her voice timid within her own head, but the shade does not respond, if it hears her at all. It only presses forward, growing bigger, larger, blocking out a multitude of the small star-lights. The shadow grows, and the lights dim and fade. Fear grips the woman's heart, wraps its sharp claws around her, and she closes her eyes, wanting to be anywhere but facing this shade.

And, just like that, the woman returns to herself. She feels the familiar pull of her own body. She opens her eyes, and she is in the dungeon, the orange glow of torchlight leaking through the bars of her cell door. She is once more alone.

7

Council chamber of the imperial palace, Izet

DAVAL SLIPPED QUIETLY INTO the council chamber and sat toward the back of the room, observing. The Ruling Council—the group chosen both to help the emperor rule, and to rule in his absence—had already begun their meeting.

The ornate throne at the head of the long table drew Daval's eyes immediately. The throne, made of gold and glass, was reserved for the emperor. It was, of course, empty.

Not for much longer, if Daval could help it.

His eyes met those of Kirkan Mandiat, the emperor's First Counselor, seated at the right hand of the throne. Mandiat nodded to Daval. "The Council acknowledges the presence of Lord Daval Amok."

Each member of the Ruling Council turned in their chairs to regard him, and Daval bowed in greeting.

"I assume he's here for our discussion about House Farady." Hirman Luce, Second Counselor to the emperor, did not like Daval. Daval did not care for the man either, but he was a strong contender in the succession. Luce sat at the left hand of the throne, opposite Mandiat.

"I'm only here to observe," Daval said, bowing once more. It was a lord's right, of course, to observe the workings of the Ruling Council. Daval wouldn't have much say in the Council's decisions unless he filed a formal petition, but he could learn and prepare for however the Council's decisions might affect his house.

Of course, he was also there for the Council's discussion on House Farady. Many already suspected his involvement in the house's demise, which was advantageous, but it wouldn't do to acknowledge such a thing publicly.

"Can we continue?" Jemma Rowady, the Cantic high priestess of Roden, sat next to Mandiat, frowning at Daval.

Not surprising. The Cantic Denomination had been the only religion of Roden for decades. Now the Ceno order and the worship of the Scorned Gods had revived, and Daval was at the head of it. It was a shame that Daval, as Tokal-Ceno, did not have a position on the Ruling Council. Emperor Grysole had been about to grant that right to the previous Tokal, before his demise. It did not matter much now. Daval would control the Ruling Council soon enough.

Mandiat nodded. "Of course," he said. "Our next item of business is the dome of the throne hall, and the repairs to be made to the imperial palace. Leader Dagnatar, have you found a lead architect?"

Arstan Dagnatar, Roden's merchant leader, was a tall, thin man, young for his office. He had sharp eyes behind the rounded spectacles he wore, and was quite handsome.

"We have, Councilor. A woman, by the name of Forst. She is a—" Dagnatar stopped, glaring at the snickering man across the table from him. Borce Kuglen, the Watch Commander of Izet, was a large man with a graying beard, a growing bald spot on the top of his head, and a face that, for whatever reason, was perpetually flushed. "Did I say something funny?" Dagnatar asked, frowning at Borce.

Kuglen grunted. "You said a woman was going to redesign

the Great Dome of the throne hall. And, yes, I find that funny."

"What's so funny about it?" High Priestess Rowady interjected.

As the Council descended into an argument about the pros and cons of a female architect, two figures approached Daval. A man and a woman in dark-green robes, cowls pulled back. Both knelt before Daval.

"Rise," Daval muttered. "What is your report?"

"We administered the drug as you ordered, Tokal," the man said. His name was Torun, and he was one of Daval's most trusted servants in the Ceno order.

"The block was effective?"

Raya, Daval's second-in-command, nodded. "I made sure of it myself."

"And you felt no threats to that block?"

Raya's lips pursed. "No, Tokal," she said after a moment of hesitation. "No… threats."

"Good," Daval said. "We don't know the extent of the woman's powers. She is not like the other psimancers we have dealt with, that much I know. As long as we keep giving her the drug, we'll need to post Ceno guards with the blocking ability near her at all times."

"It will be done, Tokal."

"Is there anything else?" Daval asked.

"No, Tokal," Torun said.

Raya was silent. Daval watched her thoughtfully. "You've something to say, Raya?" he asked.

The woman frowned. "Why are we toying with the tiellan, Tokal?"

Daval took a deep breath. Of course Raya would be the one to ask such a question. That was why the woman was his second.

"You're wondering why we don't kill her?" Daval whispered. "You're wondering why we don't eliminate someone who could be such a threat to our cause?"

"With respect, Tokal, she has *already* threatened our cause. She killed your predecessor, and..." Raya looked around the room again. "And she nearly thwarted the Rising. She is a danger to us all."

Daval nodded. What Raya said was true; the tiellan girl was a danger. His own first instinct had been to kill her. But there was a power greater than Daval that ran things, now. A power that understood what he could not. Azael's—the Fear Lord's—instructions rang clear in his mind. *She is the key to everything. Convince her. And if she can't be convinced, she must be coerced.* Now that they had given her frost, it would soon be time for the next phase of Daval's plan.

"She is a danger," Daval agreed, "but she is something else, too. She could be our greatest weapon in the Rising, Raya. She could be the weapon that turns the tide in our favor." He needed the tiellan. He needed her as much as he needed to become emperor.

Raya's lips pursed. "That seems a great risk."

"Risks must be taken on the path to victory," Daval said. "It is a fact of war."

Raya nodded, but Daval could tell she was not convinced. No matter. It was good that she thought this way; Daval needed the check on himself, on his plans. "Thank you for your reports," he said. "You are dismissed."

Daval turned his attention back to the Council. They had finished their argument over the woman architect, apparently, and had now moved on to the subject Daval had been waiting for. Daval felt Luce's eyes turn to him, and the high priestess's as well, as Mandiat brought up House Farady. Daval ignored the stares. Let them suspect what they might.

"Tragedy has struck House Farady," Mandiat said. "And I regret to say that it must be dissolved."

A few of the Council members gasped. Daval felt immensely satisfied. Urstadt's plan had worked.

"After an ill-advised affront to House Amok," Mandiat said, glancing at Daval, "in which five Amok workers were killed, House Amok responded within their rights by imprisoning the suspected perpetrators, putting them on trial, and sentencing them to death. These actions were overseen by a judicator, and given warrant. In response to these judgments, House Farady took another imprudent route of action, and attempted to break out House Amok's prisoners. This attempt resulted in the deaths of all Farady members involved."

Mandiat cleared his throat. Everyone in the room was staring at Daval. Daval made no indication that he noted or cared about the attention. He kept his face expressionless.

"That same night," Mandiat continued, "evidence suggests an attack was made on House Farady as well. All members of the house were killed."

"Oh, Goddess," the high priestess whispered softly.

This moment was the payoff—proof that Daval's plan was working. It was why he, with Urstadt's help, had orchestrated the affair. Word would spread and all of Roden would know that House Amok was not to be trifled with. That the head of House Amok was an ideal candidate for the imperial throne.

"You don't know who attacked House Farady?" Luce asked.

"No sufficient evidence was left behind," Kuglen said.

"And by that you mean no witnesses?" Luce asked.

"No witnesses," Kuglen replied.

"But surely you don't mean *all* of House Farady," the high priestess said. "There were children. Infants..."

It had not been an easy decision to make. Daval took no joy in ordering the deaths of children. But when the fate of Roden was at stake, Daval was willing to make sacrifices.

Mandiat cleared his throat once more, and slowly the Council turned its attention back to him. "We face now the business of dissolving House Farady's assets," Mandiat said, "and distributing them. In House Farady's Last Bequest..."

Daval stopped listening. He did not care where the Farady land and possessions fell. He had accomplished what he had wanted to accomplish. And, in the doorway, he saw an imposing frame in armor, helm held under one arm, a wicked-looking glaive held in the other.

Daval beckoned for his guard captain to approach. Urstadt walked into the room—surprisingly quietly, given her armor.

"Report," Daval said, keeping his voice low. Many eyes in the room still lingered on him.

Urstadt leaned in close. "House Luce has been communicating with House Mandiat," she said. "Rumors speak of another betrothal."

Daval's eyes widened, and he glanced at Hirman Luce. *That crafty bastard.*

"Luce is eager," Daval said. The man had betrothed his daughter to Emperor Grysole months ago in a desperate grab at power. Luce wanted grandchildren on the throne. So Kirkan Mandiat, Grysole's First Counselor, was the obvious next choice. Of course, being First Counselor said nothing about succession, but between that title and Andia Luce's previous betrothal, it might be enough.

"Send for my daughter when we return home," Daval said.

"If betrothal is the word of the season, we might as well throw our card onto the table." Daval had always hated the game of betrothals, but he would play by his enemies' rules, for now. Soon enough, he would force them to play by his.

"Anything else?" Daval asked.

"Nothing of concern," Urstadt said.

Daval nodded. "Very well. Wait for me outside, Urstadt. The meeting will end soon."

Daval turned back to the Council, but his mind was elsewhere. If Luce was already arranging marriages, he might have a serious chance at the throne. Daval would have to move quickly.

8

Harmoth estate, Tinska, western Khale

KNOT AND ASTRID WERE taking an evening walk around the estate when they heard the commotion. Near the pond in the northeast corner of the grounds, a group of Jane's followers had gathered and were having a heated conversation.

Astrid growled. "Goddess, is it too much to ask that these people should have some autonomy? They can't stop themselves from forming into crowds at the slightest provocation."

Knot stopped, leaning on his blackbark staff. "We should go over there," he said. "Don't want whatever the argument is to get too heated."

"Not sure you'll have much credibility, nomad. The last time they saw you, you were a blabbering noble from Alizia. And these people don't seem stable to me."

"How do you mean?" Knot asked, heading towards the commotion.

"They're a mob," Astrid said. "Right now they're fawning over Jane, but one little shift in the wind and things could go sour."

"You're worried they might want to roast a vampire at the stake?" He looked back at Astrid with a smile, although he was only half joking.

"The thought's crossed my mind," she muttered.

"Sounds like you've dealt with crowds like this before."

"Always amazed at your speed of mind, nomad. You catch

on to all the subtleties. Shouldn't we get Jane for this?" she whispered. "Or Cinzia, at least?"

"No time. They're translating, anyway."

Knot could tell Astrid wasn't won over by that argument, but it was too late now.

"Who else would have taken it?" Knot heard someone say as he approached the arguing group in the center of the gathering. "No one around here needed an extra meal except you two." The speaker was a man, tall, and skinnier than a fishing line. The way his clothing hung loosely on his body didn't indicate wealth, but the way he looked down at the two tiellans before him bespoke pride.

"We ain't got nothin' to do with your horse," one of the tiellans said. He was short, as most tiellans were, just a few fingers taller than Knot's shoulder, perhaps, and dwarfed by the tall human looking down on him. His companion was female, with silvery blond hair and pale-gray eyes. Her *siara*, the traditional scarf that almost all tiellan women wore around their necks, was thick and reached up well past her chin. The man, too, wore the traditional *araif,* a wide-brimmed hat, jaunted at an angle on his head. Both tiellans were gaunt.

"Just like a tiellan to lie," the human said. His voice was full of anger, and Knot didn't like the tone of it.

"We ain't lying," the tiellan man said; Knot could see the fear in his eyes. Knot couldn't blame him for being scared; the majority of the crowd around them was human. The woman did a better job of hiding her fear, but Knot could still see it in her clenched jaw and darting eyes.

"Don't do anything hasty," Astrid whispered. "I can tell you're aching for something."

"I'm achin', all right," Knot said. He walked between the two arguing parties. "Mornin', folks," he grunted. "What's the issue?"

The people recognized him immediately. "The Healed One," they called him. Knot could sense the importance of the way they said it, like it was a title. Wasn't a title Knot cared for. But if it'd lend him authority to settle whatever in Oblivion was going on here, so be it.

The tall human who'd made the accusation looked at Knot with wide eyes. He seemed unsure of what to do. Eventually he settled on a sort of half bow. Knot would have laughed at the gesture if his temper hadn't been up.

"No need for that," Knot said. "Just tell me what's going on."

The man raised himself up, standing tall once more, and looked at Knot. "My name is Dannel, my Lord. And these two—"

"Dannel, is it?" Knot took a step towards the man. Dannel nodded and attempted to speak again, but Knot spoke over him. "A moment, Dannel. I'd rather hear these two, first."

"But, my Lord—"

"*A moment*, Dannel. And I ain't no lord." He turned to the tiellans. "Tell me what happened."

"I'm Cavil, and this is my wife Ocrestia, my Lord."

"Don't call me lord," Knot said, though he made an effort to sound a bit gentler this time.

Ocrestia stepped forward. "That man," she said, nodding at Dannel, "accused us of stealing his horse. We ain't seen no horse of his, nor would we know what to do with one if we did. Fool probably neglected to tie it up and is looking for someone to blame."

Knot raised an eyebrow. He liked Ocrestia already. But, judging by the murmurs around him, the crowd was not so taken with her. A tiellan woman referring to a human that way wouldn't go over well. But Ocrestia didn't seem to care, and Knot liked that.

Dannel did care. "How *dare* you accuse me of such a thing," he said, advancing. Ocrestia took a step back.

Knot grabbed Dannel by the collar of his coat and yanked him away. "What'd I tell you about silence?" Knot asked, glaring at the man.

"Who the hell are you, anyway?" Dannel asked. He'd apparently caught on to the fact that Knot was more than a little biased in this dispute. "What right do you have to tell me what I should do?"

"He is the Healed One."

The response came before Knot could mouth one of his own. He turned to see a young woman who looked vaguely familiar. She had flaming orange hair. *She was there when I woke up from the last episode,* Knot realized. Astrid had pointed her out, said she'd tried to reason with him.

"He is the Healed One," the woman said again. "He has been touched by the Prophetess's own hand, and thus touched by Canta herself. He is chosen, a special vessel for us to witness Canta's power. Let us hear his arbitration on this issue; we owe him that much."

"Arbitration?" Knot muttered. He'd only been interested in getting this tiellan couple out of trouble. Arbitration was entirely different. Then again, he hadn't really had a plan in the first place. Maybe this was the best option.

Knot looked around in what he figured was an authoritative manner. Strangely, just like fighting, just like knots on a fishing boat, the attitude came naturally to him.

"Know what you're doing, nomad?" Astrid whispered.

Knot ignored her. "This man claims you stole his horse," Knot said, pointing at Dannel.

"He says we ate the stupid thing," Ocrestia said. "Proves he's truly an idiot. Who in their right mind would eat a perfectly good horse?"

Knot looked to Dannel. If arbitration was the name of the game, he supposed he'd better hear from both parties. "This true? You think they ate your horse?"

Dannel didn't look nervous, and he didn't need to be. Most of the humans would likely go along with his accusation. "They were hanging around my camp the other day," he said.

"Your *camp*," Ocrestia said, stepping forward, "is right next to the pond. That's our only source of water, case you forgot."

Knot raised an eyebrow, looking at Dannel. Dannel shrugged. "Of course. Where else would I camp?"

"Anyone else camped near the pond?"

This time, Dannel at least had the dignity to break eye contact. "The other side of the pond is forested, too many trees to make camp. There was only enough room for my group and a few others."

Canta's breath, this community ain't going to last long, Knot thought.

"Did you tie your horse up last night?" The young woman with red hair asked the question. She was dressed simply, but in well-fitting clothes. Difficult to tell what kind of background she came from.

"Of course I tied my horse up last night, what kind of half-wit do you think I am?" Dannel replied.

"Can your wife confirm that?" she asked.

"My wife?" Dannel said.

The woman spoke to someone in the assembled group. "Karia, what have you done for your husband almost every night since you arrived?"

Another woman spoke from in the crowd. She must have been

short; Knot couldn't see her, anyway. Knot found the idea that someone so short was married to someone so tall oddly humorous.

"I've been tying up his horse," the woman said. "Almost every night."

"Not every night," Dannel muttered quickly. "I've done it a time or two."

"And did you do it last night, Karia?" the woman asked.

"No, I did not."

Knot nodded to himself. He looked at Dannel, whose face had paled.

"Why didn't you say anything this morning?" he asked, his voice strained. "You could have saved us all this trouble, woman!"

Karia's quiet voice responded. "You didn't ask me. You stormed off shouting about tiellan thieves before I had a chance to say anything."

Dannel's mouth was moving silently. Knot snorted, and then realized that everyone—except for Dannel—was looking at him.

"Right," Knot said. "Cavil, Ocrestia, you're both cleared of the, er, charges." Knot looked at Dannel, and smiled. "If you actually find your horse, you can start tying it up yourself for a change."

The crowd was already dispersing. Knot shrugged off Cavil and Ocrestia's thanks. The red-haired woman and Dannel's own wife had done most of the talking. The tiellans said their goodbyes, and moved off towards what Knot assumed was the tiellan district of the camp. *Might be useful to know where that was.* He wondered if it was something they could change. No need for the tiellans to be separated. He'd talk to Cinzia and Jane about it.

"Thank you for your arbitration, Healed One," the red-headed woman said.

"Didn't do much," Knot muttered. "Should thank yourself, you seemed to know the lay of it better than me."

"Don't call him Healed One," Astrid interjected.

The woman ignored Astrid. "Nevertheless, I'm grateful for your participation. It is good for the others to see you interact with them, to see what Canta has done for you, Healed One."

"I said don't call him that," Astrid said.

Knot placed a hand on her shoulder. "The girl's right. I'm Knot; this 'Healed One' business ain't my style."

The woman raised an eyebrow. "Titles are never about *who* you are, but rather what. Nevertheless, I will do as you say, of course."

"Don't care much for whos or whats. Just know what I do and don't like to be called."

"Curious," the woman said, cocking her head to the side.

"What d'you mean?"

"You speak like them."

Knot didn't have to ask what she meant. "You got a problem with the way I speak?"

"Not a problem," the woman said, "I am simply curious. And even more curious that you tolerate such company."

Knot frowned. "Just because I hang around the tiellans doesn't mean—"

"I wasn't referring to the tiellans," the woman said, staring at Astrid.

Knot's eyes narrowed. "How do you know—"

"Don't worry," the woman said. "Your secret is safe with me. The Prophetess seems to accept this… creature. I will, too. The Prophetess knows Canta's will."

"You've got a long way to go on figuring out what 'acceptance' means," Astrid said, glaring back at the woman. "If this is your idea of it, you can go—"

"Hey," Knot said, squeezing her shoulder. Astrid shrugged him off and walked away.

Knot frowned at the woman. "You made her angry."

"She'll get over it."

"Don't be so sure. If you're trying to get on my good side, it ain't working. Who in Oblivion are you?"

"My name is Elessa," the woman said, meeting Knot's eyes. "You'll forgive my bluntness. I don't mean to offend. I'm not used to being around so many people. Let alone so many different… types." She held out her hand. Knot raised an eyebrow. He took her hand, though. No sense in making enemies, and Elessa exuded an energy, a crackling that Knot could almost feel.

"You been here long?" Knot asked.

"Longer than most," Elessa said. "I arrived almost one year ago."

Knot frowned. "What business did you have here a year ago?" He mentally calculated the timeframe. "The Oden family wouldn't have arrived here until five months ago, at the earliest. Word of what had happened in Navone would've taken some time to travel, too. Are you from Tinska?"

"No," Elessa said slowly, "but how I came here is a story for another time. Please excuse me. I will see you soon, Healed One."

9

CINZIA RUBBED HER EYES. She was tired, but nowhere near the level of exhaustion that she should feel. Once again, she and Jane had translated through the night, and most of that day. She yearned for sleep, but was also grateful to avoid it. After nearly six months, she still saw Kovac when she closed her eyes. She saw him in her dreams, the way his eyes glowed green, iridescent smoke trailing upwards. His face, sideways on the wooden floor after Cinzia had shoved his own dagger through his eye.

"Are you well, Cinzia?"

Cinzia shivered. She took a deep breath and nodded at Jane. "Just tired." Even in the house, she could smell the ocean. It made her smile.

"I know the feeling," Jane said. They were in Cinzia's old bedroom, which seemed completely different than Cinzia remembered it from her trips here when she was a young girl. The great wooden chest, the collection of sashes and scarves she had kept here, the sheets and the curtains and everything she remembered were gone. Everything except for the set of dark oak figurines of different heroes from the Age of Marvels, crafted and carved by her father and given to her on one of her birthdays. That was still here, the figures set up on a small stand in one corner of the room.

Jane stood at the window, looking out at the grounds. She beckoned for Cinzia to join her. "Come here and watch with me. I think something is happening outside."

Cinzia stood and yawned. "What is it now?"

"I can't be sure," Jane said, "but I think it involves Knot."

"Goddess, not again," Cinzia muttered. Panic was beginning to rise in her chest. "We have to go out there and help him."

"No," Jane said. "I don't think this is another episode. I think he is helping them."

Cinzia joined her sister at the window. Near the pond, a small group had gathered. She could barely make out Knot at the center of it, along with another very tall man.

"I think the tall man was arguing with some others," Jane said. "It is difficult to tell from here. Knot seems to have intervened."

Cinzia frowned. But she assumed Astrid was with him; if there was a problem, the girl would come running.

"There was an argument?" Cinzia asked.

"It seemed so."

"They don't know how to govern themselves," Cinzia said. "None of them have ever lived like this, humans and tiellans so close, here for the same purpose."

"We need to do something about it," Jane said.

"What can we do?"

"Canta has spoken to me," Jane said.

Canta has spoken to you. Cinzia was no longer surprised by such words.

"I've received visions, commandments," Jane continued. "We're translating the Codex of Elwene. We now need to form all of that into something organized."

"A religion," Cinzia whispered. Then her betrayal of the Denomination would be complete.

"A religion, yes," Jane said.

The crowd near the pond dispersed. Sure enough, Cinzia saw Astrid standing by Knot's side. Relief coursed through her. Not an episode, then.

Cinzia turned from the window and sat down on her bed. "Why don't we just send them all home?" she asked.

"Cinzia..."

"Why don't we? What use are they to us, Jane?"

For the first time since Cinzia and Jane had been reunited after their seven-year separation, Cinzia sensed anger from her sister.

"Is *use* your only concern?" Jane asked. "What they can do for us?"

Cinzia hesitated. "That's not what I meant." But it was what she meant, was it not? The people surrounding her family's mansion were a burden, and Cinzia wanted them gone. But that was not the only reason.

"It is less that they are useless," Cinzia said, "and more that they are actively harming us. Our family. You, and your crusade."

Jane's eyes widened. "My crusade? What are you talking about?"

"They are not good for you, Jane. The last thing you need is a group of sycophants inflating your ego, and the last thing *this*"—Cinzia gestured to the Codex of Elwene, open on her bed—"needs is a bunch of unstable people threatening its very existence."

"Cinzia, these people *are* the crusade. We do all of this *for them*. They've traveled hundreds of miles; many gave up their homes to come here."

"So let them go back to their homes. To their lives! We don't need them."

"You keep saying that, but I don't think you understand.

I know you've felt sorrow. I can't imagine how devastating Kovac's loss was to you. But you seem to have forgotten the circumstances under which he was killed. He was *possessed*, Cinzia. By one of the Nine Daemons. The worst of them, if what we have been translating is correct. So we *do* need these people. We are fighting a war. You've not yet realized it, but you will."

Cinzia said nothing. Whatever Jane was, whatever power was controlling her or leading her, one thing was clear. What they were translating, this conflict with the Nine Daemons—the Rising itself, for Canta's sake—was all real.

"You need to choose your path," Jane said. "I know you're struggling. You've all but severed ties with the Denomination, and yet you still resist what we have seen—what we have done together. You told me what happened to you on the rooftop in Izet. I know you believe in this translation; why can you not believe in everything else?"

"I have not felt it yet." Cinzia had asked herself this question many times, and the answer always came back to the same thing. "Your visions, they make no sense to me. All I have is the fear of what may happen if we do nothing. Fear of the Nine Daemons; fear of the Rising. I have felt nothing besides that."

"And why must you feel it?"

Because I need to know before I trust, Cinzia wanted to say.

"Sometimes faith requires us to act before we know, sister," Jane said, as if in response to Cinzia's thoughts.

Do you not think I already know that? Cinzia had been a priestess. She had taught about faith and studied it for years. And yet, had she really been practicing it?

"I know this is difficult for you, but I can't make it easier for you to believe. All I can do is tell you the truth, and hope you come to believe one day, as I do."

Cinzia wished she believed in Jane. It would make everything easier. But it went against everything she had known.

And yet… there was what she had experienced on the roof of an inn, in Roden. Facing the expanse of her own despair and inadequacy, amplified by the presence of the Nine Daemons, she had come within a hair's breadth of ending her own life. But then the sweeping hollowness that threatened to devour her had disappeared, and suddenly she had felt peace. She saw that, while the Sfaera and everything in it was vast, she nevertheless had a place in it. The ease with which she forgot that revelation disturbed Cinzia. Overshadowed by Kovac's death, overshadowed by the Rising of the Nine Daemons and what they had learned from the Nine Scriptures later that night, but it was there. It was so easy to forget.

Cinzia knew she needed to do what she could with what was given her. Perhaps these strangers who had been drawn to their family's estate were a gift. Jane's question echoed in her mind. Why *did* she think she had to feel it?

"We need to work to stop the Nine Daemons," Cinzia said finally.

"That's first on the list of many things Canta has in store for us."

"Will I ever be privy to these plans?" Cinzia asked.

Jane took a deep breath, but before she could answer, the door behind them opened. Cinzia sensed a soft green glow, and for a moment was back in the inn in Roden, was seeing Kovac's eyes.

"You two need to do something about these damn followers of yours. Bloody Odenites. For Canta's bloody sake."

"We were just discussing that exact issue," Jane said.

Cinzia stood to face Astrid. Sure enough, Astrid's eyes

glowed a soft green in the twilight. Cinzia no longer shuddered at the sight, but the hairs on her arms stood on end. During the day, there were moments that Cinzia almost forgot what Astrid was, what she was capable of. At night, however, it was impossible to forget. The darkness made the girl's eyes bright green that reminded Cinzia, oddly, of the stars.

"Something's got to be done," Astrid said. "These people are already at each other's throats. They're finding ways to segregate, and the tiellans naturally fall underfoot. Is that how your goddess runs things?"

It was a good question. The Cantic Denomination claimed that tiellans were equal to humans in most ways, and it had done since the King Who Gave Up His Crown emancipated the tiellans. But, while it claimed to treat tiellans and humans equally, the ideal was poorly executed. Cinzia wondered what Jane's version of Canta would say.

"I'm not sure Canta runs things," Jane said.

That was not the response Cinzia had expected.

"Um… okay?" Astrid did not seem impressed either.

"She allows us to govern ourselves, for the most part," Jane said. "We are not puppets on strings."

"Look, if I'd wanted a history lesson, I would have—"

"You're right," Jane said. "All of Canta's children are loved in her eyes."

"So you're for equality, then?" Cinzia asked. *This* interested her. She had long thought that tiellans were treated harshly, but had only dabbled in the idea of equality academically. In Triah, she had rarely had occasion to associate with many tiellans. They mostly kept to their own parts of the city, far from Cinzia's jurisdiction.

"I don't know if it is necessary to take a political stance,"

Jane said. "But yes, equality is the ideal. As we saw with Winter and Lian, there is nothing humans can do that tiellans can't. No intellectual or physical feat that is impossible for one but not the other."

"Blah, blah," Astrid said. "What are you going to *do* about it?"

"We are going to reform Canta's religion," Jane said.

"You're going to what?" Astrid asked.

"We are going to reform." Jane paused. She cocked her head, for all the world as if she were listening to someone who neither Cinzia nor Astrid could hear. "No," Jane said after a moment. "We are going to *revive* Canta herself, through Her religion that once existed when She walked the Sfaera, but has since died."

"And here I thought you two would do something sensible," Astrid muttered. "Instead you're going to start a religion exactly like the one that caused all your problems."

"It will not be like the Denomination," Jane said patiently.

"If you say so," Astrid said, "but a stone's a stone, and a religion's a religion."

"Is that a saying?" Cinzia asked. She had certainly never heard it before.

"Might be."

"A religion is a religion, and yes, we may have similarities to the Denomination. They did, after all, begin with the truth. But ours will also be very different. In all the ways that matter." Then, Jane did something Cinzia did not expect. She stepped toward Astrid, knelt down before her, and placed her hands on the vampire's shoulders. "Did you not listen to what I said earlier? All of Canta's children are loved in her eyes. *All* of them, Astrid."

Astrid seemed quite speechless. Cinzia did not know what

to think. What sort of love did a creature like Astrid deserve? And if Canta loved such a thing, that meant she might have to as well. Such a thought did not sit comfortably.

Jane stood. "We have much research to do. Cinzia and I need to continue translating; there *must* be some useful information in the Nine Scriptures. As for you… can you read, Astrid?"

Astrid scoffed. "I've been around for a few hundred years. I can read just fine."

Jane smiled. "Our family's library is relatively intact. You might want to start there."

"Library?" Astrid asked, a light sparking in her eyes that made her normal green glow seem dull in comparison. "I… I suppose I might help, if you need it."

The girl looked no older than nine, but she had seen things that Cinzia had only read about. She was on the Sfaera when some of the most incredible events of the past centuries had taken place, Cinzia realized. The Emancipation, the King Who Gave Up His Crown, the end of the Thousand Years War. Astrid may have even been *eyewitness* to some of them.

Canta rising, what a treasure trove of information this girl must be.

Cinzia did not know why the idea had not occurred to her before. The things she could *learn* from this girl…

"Of course you can help us," Cinzia said. "We'll need every bit of help we can get."

10

Castle Mandiat, Izet, Roden

Daval Amok walked into the keep of Castle Mandiat, Captain Urstadt close behind him. He shook water from his cloak, removing it and handing it to a young servant. He then straightened his Ceno robes and turned to face his welcoming committee.

A committee of one, in this case, not including the servant. There, waiting to greet Daval, was Kirkan Mandiat, fellow High Lord of Izet, and the First Counselor to the late Emperor Grysole. He was younger than Daval by at least twenty summers, and nearly as tall as Urstadt. Mandiat was broad, too, but it was broadness of muscle that had not degenerated into the fat that many men allowed with age. Mandiat wore his house colors proudly, violet stripes on a gold field, although he was not armored. A good sign. If Mandiat had worn his gilded armor, it would have all but destroyed any potential negotiations between the two of them. Unarmored, Mandiat must be willing to consider Daval's proposition.

"Lord Amok, my friend," Mandiat said, a broad smile splitting his face. Gray streaked the man's thick brown hair and beard, only making him look more handsome. "Or should I call you Tokal?" Mandiat bowed, ever so slightly. "You have many titles these days, Daval."

Daval bowed more deeply in return. Such humility was necessary. It was a lesson learned long ago.

"I suppose Tokal *is* the more appropriate title, now," Daval said with a sigh. "Not a name I would have ever chosen for myself, but one I'm stuck with, nonetheless." The statement was only partly true. When he was a young man, he would never have dreamed of choosing the title of Tokal for himself—the religion had been long dead then.

"And stuck with it you are," Mandiat said, smiling. "Although it seems a difficult position to hold for any extended amount of time." Mandiat's words doubled as both a threat and a dismissal. Whether he meant either or both, Daval was not sure.

"Things change, after all." Daval nodded to Urstadt behind him. "You remember Tirelle Urstadt, captain of my guard?"

"Of course," Mandiat said, nodding in Urstadt's direction. "Welcome to my home, Captain. We are honored to host a warrior of your prowess."

Urstadt bowed her head. "Thank you, my Lord."

Mandiat turned. "Come," he said. "Accompany me to the smoking room, we can converse more earnestly there." Mandiat turned, and Daval and Urstadt followed. "You may leave your captain," Mandiat said over one shoulder. "My servants will see to her needs."

As Mandiat spoke, two more servants, dressed in violet, emerged from a side corridor. Urstadt looked to him, and Daval nodded. Bringing Urstadt was a formality in this case. There was no need for her fighting abilities in the Mandiat smoking room. Better she attempt to pry bits of gossip from the servants.

Mandiat and Daval turned a corner to see Hama Mandiat, Kirkan's wife, walking towards them. Hama had not aged quite as well as her husband, but she was still beautiful. Daval could remember when Hama's frame had been less voluminous and more curvaceous, but five children and the weight of years had changed her. As such things did for all people. Daval did not mind; while he had admired Hama as a young, beautiful woman, he could now admire her as a formidable, older one.

"Ah, Hama," Mandiat said as the woman approached. They embraced. "You know Lord Daval Amok—er, the Tokal, as he likes to be called, now."

Hama bowed before Daval, showing significantly more respect than her husband had. While Kirkan was a well-intentioned, relatively intelligent man, everyone knew who the real mind behind House Mandiat was, and it was not the man who wore the circlet.

"I'm pleased to see you, Tokal," Hama said, a bright smile on her face. "I offer both congratulations and condolences. The latter on the recent attacks that have befallen your house, the former on your new appointment. It must be a cumbersome load to bear in addition to your many other responsibilities."

Daval breathed out slowly. "You're right, my Lady. But by the grace of the Gods I believe I will do what I must." No need to mention the attacks from House Farady. That business was over and done with as far as Daval was concerned, although it was good to see the results were still in effect.

"Of course," Hama said. "Such is the prayer in each of our hearts." She bowed once more to Daval, then turned to kiss her husband. She whispered something into Kirkan's ear. Kirkan nodded, and then Hama swayed past them.

"Very well," Mandiat said, nodding to Daval. "Shall we?"

The Rodenese smoking room was a tradition among nobles, although it was really nothing more than an excuse to socialize, and to discuss politics and business. Mandiat's smoking room was just as Daval remembered. It was both cozy and expansive—every lord in Izet could fit in the chamber with room still to spare. Oil paintings decorated the walls, sculpted busts rose from half-columns, and large stuffed sitting chairs were scattered about. Daval had been here many times, years ago, when the two men conspired to put Grysole on the throne.

In many ways, Daval longed for those simpler days, with so much less at stake. And yet what he had now was far too valuable to give up.

"I have traditional gradiant, very high quality from the western planes," Mandiat said, "or more local stuff, grown on the Burly Peninsula. Got something of a kick to it; it's what I prefer, personally." He leaned in close. "Of course, I've got stronger stuff, too. Devil's dust, hero. Even some frostfire, if you're interested, old friend."

Daval snorted. "I appreciate the offer, but I'll take the local gradiant. I haven't touched any of the stronger stuff since I was a lad."

Mandiat shrugged. "Suit yourself." He nodded to the servant who waited at the doorway. Mandiat smiled at Daval. "Since you were a lad, eh? I find that hard to believe. Hama says she saw one of your people seeking frostfire just the other day." Mandiat laughed. "Can't imagine that was for your staff."

Daval waited for Mandiat to seat himself, then sat down in a large chair opposite him. Daval smiled back at Mandiat, although inside he kicked himself. Of course such activities would have been noticed. He needed to be more careful when it came to providing *faltira* for the tiellan woman. Psimancers were rare in Roden; the Ceno order had enlisted the few that were known. "I like the feel of it, from time to time. You're still young, Kirkan. You'll understand when you get to be my age."

"Still young?" Mandiat barked. "I don't know who you think

you're talking to. If I didn't know any better I'd think I was catching up to you." He leaned in close, grin widening. "Of course, that doesn't mean I don't take a hit of frostfire myself every once in a while. *That* stuff can really kick, no?"

"Indeed," Daval said, glad he had deflected the issue. Mandiat obviously had no notion of how much *faltira* Daval had been buying. Good.

The servant entered the room carrying two trays, each piled high with gradiant, which he placed on a table between Daval and Mandiat. Daval reached into a pocket of his robe for his pipe. Soon, the room was full of the comforting smell of pipe smoke, swirls of it reaching towards the ceiling. This particular batch had a sweet, almost sugary casing, and Daval breathed it in deeply.

After a few moments, Daval coughed. "You're right about the local stuff," he said, eyes watering. "It does have a kick." Normally gradiant had a soft, slow burn of a taste that warmed one's entire throat. This batch from the Burly Peninsula had a harsher burn, but a sweeter taste.

"It does, doesn't it?" Mandiat said, leaning back in his chair and casting his eyes upwards. "Hope it isn't too strong for you?"

"Not at all," Daval said. "I rather enjoy it." He'd have to inquire about Mandiat's supplier.

The two men sat in silence for a few more moments. This was all part of the game; to start talking about business before lighting the pipes would be rude. It was a tradition Daval considered ridiculous, but necessary.

"Very well, Daval," Mandiat said, when the pleasant buzz of gradiant reached all the way to Daval's toes, "what is it you've come to discuss?"

Daval smiled. "Betrothals."

Mandiat nearly choked on the next draw from his pipe. Daval smiled.

"Betrothals?" Mandiat repeated. He sat up straight, staring at Daval through the haze. "What of them?" Mandiat was trying to look casual, but the way he crossed one leg over the other—such an unnatural position for Mandiat, something he only did when he was nervous—told Daval all he needed.

"You've been discussing a betrothal with Hirman Luce between his daughter and your eldest son Girgan. I've come to make you a better offer."

Mandiat slowly relaxed back into his chair. Daval smiled. The man was open to offers, at least. Mandiat took a long drag on his pipe. "I may or may not have been entertaining such discussions."

Daval leant closer. "I'll make it simple, Kirkan. My daughter is younger than Andia Luce, smarter, and I think you'll agree that she's far more beautiful."

"You think I care what my son's wife looks like?"

Daval grinned, raising his hands. "Of course you don't. But my daughter has another quality that Andia Luce lacks."

"What's that?"

"Ambition."

"Andia Luce was betrothed to an emperor," Mandiat said slowly.

Daval laughed. "And Cova is the daughter of the Tokal-Ceno. Tell me true, Kirkan, which matters more? A nullified betrothal to a dead emperor, or the living daughter of one of the most powerful men in Roden?"

Mandiat grunted. "Don't give me that power shit, Daval. You may be Tokal, but you're also a High Lord, same as me."

Daval wanted to point out how that made the match all the more appealing, but refrained. He should have realized that referring to himself as one of the most powerful men in Roden would put Mandiat on edge.

"But you make points worth considering," Mandiat said. "Such a match may have merit. But what do you gain? You've never been keen on betrothals, Daval. We all know this. Most of your other children married whomever in Oblivion they wanted to marry, sensible offers be damned. Why play the game now?"

"I play it because I must," Daval said. From Mandiat's view, Daval had everything he needed: he was the leader of the Ceno order, was a powerful High Lord. What more could he want? Mandiat clearly suspected Daval had something else up his sleeve. To his credit, Mandiat was right.

"Let us speak frankly," Mandiat said. "Why do you not just take the throne now, Daval? Why not become emperor tomorrow? You could do it. We all know you could."

Daval nodded. "If you prefer we speak frankly, then we shall. Yes, Kirkan. I could vie for the throne tomorrow, and likely have it by the end of the year, if I was fortunate. But such a thing would lead to war between the noble houses of Roden. Many people would die. The nobles would betray one another a dozen times over. Blood would flow freely, and I can't have that."

Mandiat laughed out loud. "Since when does Daval Amok care for betrayal? For avoiding bloodshed?"

Daval bowed his head. "Since I learned that there is much at stake. Far more than I ever realized."

"The throne, you mean?"

Daval shook his head. He needed to bring Mandiat in to the circle. "No, Kirkan. Far more."

Daval left a bewildered Kirkan Mandiat in the smoking room. Bewildered, but recruited to Daval's plans nonetheless. Mandiat had agreed to the betrothal between his son, Girgan Mandiat, and Cova. He had agreed to do whatever was necessary to see that Daval was put in power.

Daval respected Mandiat's commitment. It was one of the man's strengths.

Urstadt was waiting for him near the gatehouse, talking stiffly with a servant. Daval supposed this was as close as he had ever seen Urstadt to flirting; his guard captain was not one to make much of her personal life. That was partly why Daval chose her; it meant he had one of the most dedicated captains in the city.

Urstadt saw him coming, and quickly ended her conversation. Daval nodded curtly as he passed. He hoped she had not been in the middle of obtaining valuable information. While Urstadt's mind was keen when it came to politics, and brilliant when it came to battle, her social instincts were unrefined.

Urstadt stepped in behind Daval as they exited the gatehouse. "Any discoveries to report?" Daval asked, once they were sufficiently distant from Castle Mandiat.

"Nothing of consequence," Urstadt said, shaking her head. "Only gossip."

"Gossip can always be useful," Daval said. "What did you hear?"

Urstadt shrugged. "One of the cooks is sleeping with Girgan's cousin," she said.

Daval chuckled. "I suspect making small talk is more painful for you than any physical fight."

Urstadt's lack of response was answer enough.

"What else did you learn? Anything?"

"There are still rumors of a psimancer in House Luce," Urstadt said, "but no one could tell me who it might be."

"There have been rumors of psimancy at Castle Luce for almost a year, now. Nothing to show for it, though. Very well. That's all?"

"That is all, my Lord."

"And what did you tell them?" Daval asked. Part of hearing gossip was spreading it; Urstadt had learned not to listen without giving a bit of information herself.

"That you haven't been sleeping," she said. "Although they did not seem to find that very interesting."

Daval nodded. Without context, it was utterly dull. But it was true; he slept less and less lately, and it had more to do with his relationship with his new master than anything else. His transformation had come with many perks, some of which Daval was still discovering. It was like going through puberty again, but with much more interesting—and useful—results.

"Whether they latched on to it or not does not matter," Daval said. "They'll talk about it eventually. What else?"

"Rumors of what happened in the throne room when the emperor died. And that's all, my Lord."

Daval considered. Things were moving, but moving slowly. He needed to remember the Fear Lord's advice: moving cautiously was far better than plunging forward with abandon.

Back at Castle Amok, Daval went straight up to his daughter's chambers in the keep. He had business that couldn't wait. He found Cova in her room, reading a book.

"Hello, Father," she said, looking up as he approached.

"Good evening, my dear," Daval said. "All is well?"

"All is well."

"What is it you're reading?" Daval asked, looking around at his youngest daughter's room. The place was a mess, clothing strewn everywhere, bed unmade. They had servants who could take care of such things for her, but Cova insisted on keeping her room herself. Some job she did of it. Books lay open in the strangest places—on top of the dresser, beneath the bed, on the windowsill.

"*The Romances*," Cova said.

Daval cleared his throat. His daughter was clever, vastly more intelligent than any of his other children. Why she chose to read such drivel was beyond him.

"I have some news for you," Daval said. He lifted an abandoned book from a chair and placed it on Cova's desk, which was already covered in papers, books, and other odds and ends.

"News of the impending war?" Cova asked, her nose already back in her book.

"In a way," Daval said, taking a deep breath. His daughter wouldn't be happy with him. But she did not understand what was at stake. Daval sighed. Cova was his favorite. She was unique, intelligent, she thought about things in a very different way than anyone else he had ever known. Which was why what Daval was about to say was very difficult.

"I've found you a husband," Daval said.

Cova laughed. Just a short laugh, the brief chuckle made when someone was hardly listening. Then she looked up from her book.

"You've what?"

"I've found you a husband," Daval repeated.

"I..."

"You are officially betrothed to Girgan Mandiat. He is a good man, and will make a good husband."

"Father... are you serious?"

"Regrettably."

Cova tossed her book aside. "All my siblings have married

for love. You've not arranged a betrothal for any of them. Why do so for me?"

"Because we need it."

Cova stared at him, tight-lipped. Thick strands of blond hair had fallen across her reddening face. Hair like her mother's. *This is the moment*, Daval thought. *This is where I discover whether my daughter has truly grown up or not.*

Cova stared at him for a moment longer. Then, slowly, the anger drained from her face. She sat up straight.

"Why exactly do we need it?"

Daval smiled. She truly was unique. "We need to stand strong with House Mandiat," Daval said. "As two of the most powerful High Lords in Izet, the union of our children would garner the support we need. One marriage could give us the votes."

"Votes for what?"

"For the throne, of course."

Cova glared at him and shook her head. "You are the Tokal, now, as well as a High Lord. Why would you possibly want the throne?"

"Because it is what must be."

Cova rolled her eyes. "I don't like you since you've become Tokal, Father. You're all mysteries and crypticisms. You don't speak plainly any more."

Daval felt a stab of pain. Had his transformation changed him that much? Daval did not feel any different. Not in his mind, anyway. Physically, yes: the burdens of old age no longer weighed him down, and he had strength that men a third his age only dreamed of. His vision was better than it had ever been, he heard things that no human should be able to hear.

And yet he was the same man he always had been. Wasn't he?

"You're right, Cova. Things have changed. Even I have

changed in some ways, but the truth is the *world* is changing. An emperor lies dead, along with the previous Tokal. Roden is on the verge of collapse, and Khale is poised to attack. We need strong leadership."

That wasn't exactly Daval's motivation, of course, but it was close enough.

"And you are this person?" Cova asked. "You are the person with the strength Roden needs?"

"I may be," Daval said. "But if I am not, I know who is."

Cova stared at him for a moment, until he finally saw the dawn of understanding on her face.

"Me?"

Daval said nothing. It was always best to let Cova work things out on her own. Cova laughed nervously, the laugh she exuded when she was on the verge of discovering something.

"I'm your youngest child," Cova said, shaking her head. "I can't rule an empire."

Daval remained silent, watching his daughter, the daughter he loved more than anything in the world. His hand twitched at his side; he ignored it.

"If Girgan and I marry, he will rule. He's a graduate of the Citadel, after all. But none of that matters, Father. If you don't rule, it will be Sraven. And if not him, surely Valan. I'm the youngest of your children, the legitimacy lies..."

Daval smiled as he watched one begin to form on Cova's face. "The legitimacy lies with the strongest match, and a match is invalid for the throne unless arranged by the parents of the couple." While it was not uncommon for some noble couples to marry without formal arrangement and still keep their privileges—as all of Daval's other children had done—the law still dictated that any marriage involving the imperial throne be arranged.

Cova skipped over to Daval, wrapping him in a large embrace. "And that's what you've given me, isn't it, Father? A valid match, the strongest in our family. And Girgan is the eldest, so we will have full support from his family."

Daval breathed in his daughter's scent. It seemed a long time since she had embraced him like this.

Cova pulled away. "But this is different, isn't it?" she said. "What are you not telling me?"

Daval stepped back. It was so short. The hug, the embrace, the moment of trust, over so quickly. "Nothing that concerns you now, darling," he said. "You are betrothed to Girgan Mandiat. You and Girgan will ascend to the throne when I'm gone. You will rule this nation. For now, that's all you need know."

And, just like that, the joy was gone from his daughter's face. She had been so excited a moment before. The thought of her ruling, of his child on the throne, especially *this* child, made Daval's chest swell with pride. But of course she was too smart to take such a gift freely. Cova would want to find out what Daval wasn't telling her. And he couldn't allow her to do that.

"You really are not going to tell me," Cova said, eyeing Daval with a narrowed glance.

"I know you're going to want to find out on your own," Daval said. "Please don't attempt this, Cova. Take your father's advice. All will be revealed in time."

Cova shook her head. "That's nonsense, Father."

"You will reject the throne, then?"

Cova hesitated. No, she wouldn't be so emotional as to reject the throne. Not yet. "I don't know what I'll do," she said. "But I won't be your pawn. If you want me to be a part of your schemes, then you need to tell me what they are."

"And if I know how you'll respond?" Daval asked. "If I know

already what you will think of my schemes?"

Cova matched his gaze. "Then you know." She picked up her book and splayed herself out on her bed once more.

11

Harmoth estate

ASTRID CLOSED THE BOOK with a happy sigh. She'd been reading the early work of Cetro Ziravi, the renowned poet from the Age of Revival whose later writings challenged the Essera herself, including a grand epic that spanned the history of the Sfaera and beyond. Astrid didn't care much for them, though. His earlier writings were far more interesting, more human: poems about life, love, and death, what made people mortal and temporary. What made them good, and what made them monsters. Matters she knew she would never comprehend herself.

Astrid ran one finger—one claw, rather, razor sharp and half as long as her finger—along the spine of the book, felt the ridges there, the worn leather. Before her eyes, she watched her claw retract, merging once more with her finger. The sun was rising. Astrid had been reading all night. It was time for a walk.

Outside in the grounds, people were just beginning to stir. Astrid walked among them, her boots slick with dew. It felt good to move about; she had stayed up through the late hours of the night, reading about the Denomination and how it was formed. Cinzia insisted that if they were going to renew Canta's religion, they needed to do it right. And to do it right, they had to understand history.

Astrid had scoured through the main philosophers of the Age of Revival first, through Bronstin and Hustenheim.

Their writings had not been particularly helpful, though, so Astrid had turned to lesser-known thinkers. Nuria had been particularly interesting. While she said nothing about religion in particular, her treatise on mob mentality was fascinating. Astrid had shared what she'd learned with Cinzia and Jane, both of whom seemed appreciative, neither of whom seemed satisfied. Astrid suspected there would be more research to come.

She was excited at the prospect, but also uneasy—not because of the research itself, but because by doing it she was choosing to not do other things. Astrid was bound to forces beyond herself, and she had neglected those forces of late.

Her ears pricked. In the distance, near the pond, someone was speaking loudly. Curious, she moved closer. As she approached the pond, she saw the speaker was an old woman, her thin, gnarled arms protruding from the folds of a large brown cloak. She stood tall, though, unbent by her age, her short gray hair clumped in damp curls.

"There is a reason we are all here," the woman was saying. A half-dozen people from the camp had gathered around her. The woman's voice was low and smooth—Astrid thought she might make a good singer. "We did not come here by chance," the woman continued. "A higher power guides us! Dark times approach, and powers greater than ourselves direct us toward the end."

Astrid rolled her eyes and was about to move on when she was halted by the woman's next words.

"The Nine Daemons rise. They rise, and we will fall unless we heed the counsel of the Goddess."

Hold on a bloody minute. Astrid approached the crowd and tugged the hem of a young woman's skirt. "Who is that?" she asked, pointing at the speaker.

"I don't know her name," the woman said. She seemed

simultaneously annoyed at and enthralled by the old woman. "I'm not sure if anyone does, but they call her the Beldam. She arrived hardly more than a week ago."

The Beldam? Astrid wanted to laugh out loud.

"They come to destroy," the Beldam was saying, sweeping her scrawny arm towards her growing audience. "They come to destroy, and to lay waste to the Sfaera. They come to take all we have away from us. They *hunger*, and they will never stop."

"The Nine Daemons are nothin' but fables!" someone shouted out. "We came here to hear about Canta, not children's stories."

Astrid was glad at least someone was willing to ask what she was wondering herself.

"When we speak of the Nine Daemons, we speak of Canta," the Beldam said. "She and they are inseparably connected. Without our Goddess, we are powerless against them. And without them… our Goddess would have no power." She swept her eyes over the crowd. "I will tell you what I know of the Nine Daemons. But I admonish all of you—don't let what I'm about to tell you fall upon deaf ears. We are all here to serve a power greater than ourselves.

"Some say the Nine Daemons are the descendants of the Brother-Gods Emidor, and the Sister-Gods Adimor. Others say they are the lost children of the First Parents, Ellendre and Andara themselves. Others say the Nine Daemons were once men and women, long since corrupted and cursed, banished from our realm. They are shrouded in mystery, but the truth about them is all around us, if we choose to see it.

"We think what we experience—our emotions, our anger, and our sorrow—are because of our mortal lives. That wouldn't be wrong, but there are influences beyond ourselves, and the Nine Daemons are the most powerful of them all. Each of the

Nine Daemons manifests in one of our darkest, deepest pits of self-loathing. Each of the Nine Daemons feeds on the worst parts of ourselves.

"Mefiston is the eldest, and his vice is wrath. He was forged in the inferno of war and bloodlust, and his ire is like the Sfaera engulfed in flames. When we are angry, Mefiston is there, and he rejoices. Hade devours our sorrow in death and loss. He is ethereal and ever-present, and feeds on that which we can never truly escape. Luceraf, the fallen, manifests herself in our pride. Enmity, rebellion, arrogance, narcissism, she takes them all and they fuel her power. Iblin, the monstrosity, delights in greed and gluttony. Estille, both man and woman and the most beautiful of both, feeds on lust. Estille perverts the fire of our passion, rendering us powerless to resist. Nadir is unpredictable, and consumes the sanity of others. Bazlamit, her twin sister, enjoys deception and fraud. Samann is the youngest, and takes his strength from envy. And, of course, their master Azael, the Fear Lord, is more powerful than all of them combined. They come to destroy, and they come to consume. Their Rising has begun, and they, too, will soon walk the Sfaera."

Astrid stood rooted to the ground. The Beldam put to words what Astrid knew instinctively. *There are daemons even daemons fear.*

"But what are we supposed to do?" someone shouted from the crowd.

"Look around," the Beldam said. "You can see evidence of the Daemons everywhere. Some of us were made in Canta's image, strong, tall, and pure of form. Humans."

Oh no.

"Others descend from daemonic ancestry. And, if we are to truly begin the fight against the Nine Daemons, we must begin the fight against their children."

The crowd was murmuring, now. Some looked angry, others fearful. Astrid heard one word whispered more than any other.

Tiellan.

"Shit," Astrid said. Not quietly enough that some of the people around her didn't hear—she got more than one odd glance. Little girls weren't supposed to swear, after all.

She turned and walked quickly back to the house. Knot, Cinzia, and Jane needed to hear about this immediately.

12

Knot pulled the rope taut, stretching the tent-cover as far as it would go. Cavil, the tiellan man he had met during his "arbitration," pulled the opposite end, making sure it was tight across the tent below.

"Good," Knot said. "You'll want it tight as can be. A lot less likely for rain to get through, that way."

"Thank you for helpin' us," Cavil said earnestly. Pale-blond hair protruded in tufts from beneath his *araif*.

"Ain't something to make a big deal about," Knot muttered, securing the rope to the tree. When he'd stopped by to say hello to Cavil and Ocrestia—Ocrestia had gone into Tinska to buy provisions—Knot had noticed the conditions in which they were living. None of the tiellans had adequate shelter against the recent rain. Their primitive tents were hardly more than sheets strung up between trees. The tiellans were already in the process of moving their tents, anyway—relocating from a spot of land adjacent to Dannel's group, closest to the pond, to a new location under a large ash tree, some distance away.

For the past few hours Knot had shown Cavil and a few others how to construct a tent that provided more shelter, and the advantage of hanging up a second layer above the tent. Ader, Cinzia's youngest brother, had been helping, and Knot was pleased with the lad. Ader took a keen interest in Knot, although Knot suspected it had more to do with the sword Ader must've seen in his pack rather than anything Knot himself had to offer. He'd been teaching the lad to play warsquares, and he couldn't say it was time misspent. But it felt good to get outside and work with his hands. Knot's muscles itched, wanting to exert themselves.

"Where'd you learn all this about tents, anyway?" Cavil asked.

What he knew of wilderness survival, staying dry and warm in harsh conditions, came naturally to him, as did a host of other things. Knot could only assume the knowledge came from one of the sifts—one of the souls—within him, but there was no way he could explain that to Cavil.

"My father. A man needs to learn how to live on his own, my da always said. So what spurred your relocation, anyway? If you don't mind me askin'?" If that idiot Dannel was involved, Knot wasn't above talking some sense into him.

Cavil shook his head. "Some insane old woman has been preaching by the pond," he said. "She claims tiellans are descended from the Nine Daemons."

Knot scoffed. "That's ridiculous."

"Try telling the other humans that. They don't want us around anymore. Want to segregate the camp."

Knot was dumbfounded. "I'll talk to someone," he said after a moment. "Life shouldn't be this way round here."

Cavil shrugged. "Don't matter now. Not all the humans seem to have taken this woman's word for truth, mind you. Some of them are sympathetic to us. Most of 'em are indifferent, I'd say. But the ones against us are the most vocal."

"Ain't right," Knot said. He'd definitely talk to Jane and Cinzia about this old woman, whoever she was.

A flurry of motion caught Knot's attention on the road nearby. Atop the hill, Ocrestia was riding towards them. The tiellans had managed to secure one horse among all of them, and Ocrestia had taken it on her supply run into town.

But she wasn't alone. A group of five men rode with her.

"What is it?" Ader asked.

Cavil swore, and ran towards Ocrestia, picking up speed as he went.

"Cavil, wait!" Knot said, but the man did not look back. Knot frowned, and then looked to Ader. "Get help, boy. These men may not be friendly. *Go*." Giving the boy something to do was better than simply ordering him away. Knot grabbed his staff, and went after Cavil.

Two men rode along either side of Ocrestia, while three rode behind. It almost looked as if Ocrestia was being escorted back to the camp, but Knot knew enough to see the difference. She was hunched forward in her saddle, shying away from the men. They were heckling her.

Cavil had almost reached Ocrestia as Knot continued towards them, more cautiously. He could hear Cavil shouting, and some of the humans riding alongside Ocrestia laughed, pointing at the tiellan. Knot gripped his staff loosely, conscious of it and the dagger at his side as he approached. When he was within hearing distance, he stopped in the middle of the road, watching.

"This your husband, then?" One of the men riding beside Ocrestia pointed at Cavil with an axe.

"Looks more like her father," one of the others chortled. "Come spend a night with me, you'll see what a real man's like." The other men laughed.

"Are you all right?" Cavil asked his wife, ignoring the men. He took the reins of her horse.

Ocrestia, in tears but doing her best to hide it, nodded. "Yes," she said. "Just want to get home."

"And where is that, exactly?" one of the other men said.

"It surely can't be here," another man said. "Tiellans don't live in such fancy houses. Not unless they're serving in them."

"Runaways, then. Trying to escape the only life they deserve."

Knot nodded towards the camp as Ocrestia and Cavil reached him. "Go on. I'll be along shortly." They moved silently past him.

The men, all five of them, slowed. "And who is this?" one of them asked, the one with the axe. He was a tall man, certainly taller than Knot, with pale hair and even paler skin.

The other men circled Knot, their horses stamping their feet.

"A human," one of them responded, behind Knot now.

"What're you doing here with a bunch of elves?" the pale one asked, eyeing Knot. The man held his axe loosely—it was a wood axe certainly not meant for battle, but it could still do damage.

"Ain't no business of yours," Knot said, returning the man's gaze.

The pale man laughed. "Maybe not," he said. "But I don't care. Tell us what you're doing here. What's the commotion at the Harmoth estate?"

Knot gripped his staff, saying nothing.

The pale man frowned. "What's your name, friend? No need for there to be animosity between us. I'm sure we're very much alike, you and I."

"Name's Knot," Knot said. "And you and I ain't got nothin' in common."

The pale man frowned. "Name's not what?" he asked.

"No, Mik, I think he said his name's Knot," one of the other men said.

Mik snorted, looking down at Knot. "Your name is *Knot*?"

Knot laughed.

"What're you laughing at?" Mik asked, frowning. He held the axe out in front of him.

Knot's muscles tensed and relaxed. This was what his body'd been itching for. The other men were armed, but with weapons of occasion, not profession. Bludgeons, wood axes, a long dagger or two. A staff.

"I'm laughing at you," Knot said. "This Sfaera is full of idiots."

And, just like that, the pale man's face turned red, and with a grunt he swung his axe down at Knot.

Knot leaned his body to the side, neatly avoiding the strike, and thrust his staff upwards into Mik's chest. The familiar calmness of the fight overtook him.

Knot's blow knocked Mik to the road in a cloud of dust, and for a moment the others stared in silence. Knot sensed their surprise, knew the expression on their faces. They had not expected their de facto leader to end up in a pile of dirt on the road today.

Knot walked over to Mik. He reached down, pulling the sleeve back from the man's wrist. Sure enough, on the underside of Mik's wrist was a cross-and-crescent tattoo.

The sign of the Kamites—those who wanted a return to tiellan slavery.

Knot cursed. The other men were still staring, dumbfounded. Knot didn't hesitate. He slipped his hands to the edge of his staff and swung it around him with all his might. It connected with the nearest man's skull with a crack, and the man toppled from his horse. A twinge of shame ran through Knot. Knot didn't think he'd killed the man, but the blow, combined with the fall to the ground, might've been enough.

But the shame fled as quickly as it came. What these men had been doing to Ocrestia wasn't right. How many people had treated Winter that way? The tattoo on Mik's wrist was all the condemnation Knot needed.

The remaining three finally sprang into action. Knot rolled out of the way of a charging horse. The rider steered the steed around using only his legs, while he wielded a long pitchfork in both hands. One of the other men had dismounted, reaching down to help his leader. Rather than take his chances with the pitchfork-wielding horseman, Knot charged at Mik and the man who'd dismounted.

In his mind, Knot saw only Winter, and what these men would do to her, what they would say to her. With that thought, Knot felt his control slipping. He gave no quarter, no time for the men he approached to prepare. They were merchants, perhaps one of them a farmer. They weren't soldiers, but Knot didn't care.

Knot kneed the first man, doubling him over, and then threw him forcefully into the dirt. Knot then kicked the man in the face enough times for him to stop moving. Mik, stumbling to his feet, met Knot's boot and collapsed into the dust once more.

Hoofbeats behind him. Knot rolled as the man with the pitchfork rode past. The other man left on his horse was not moving; he sat in his saddle, staring, at Knot and at his three companions bleeding on the ground.

The pitchfork-wielding horseman spun his mount around once more, then he hesitated.

"Let's get out of here," the other thug said, moving his horse tentatively towards his companion. "This isn't worth it."

Knot wiped at his eyes, but the red in his vision was not

from blood. "Go," he growled. If they didn't leave now, he wasn't sure he could stop himself. As much as he wanted to defend the tiellans, if he killed any of these men and one of them lived to spread the word, things would only get worse.

The man with the pitchfork locked eyes with Knot for a moment longer, then slowly nodded. The two men bent to help their fallen comrades up. Knot watched as they remounted and rode back toward Tinska.

He felt a hand on his shoulder and spun around, grabbing the person by the wrist, twisting their arm behind them.

Ocrestia's cry brought Knot back.

He let go immediately, staring wide-eyed at Ocrestia doubled over before him. Cavil rushed to her, and Knot recognized the rage in Cavil's eyes. It was the same he'd felt himself, not moments ago.

"What in Canta's name is wrong with you?" Cavil asked, his eyes daggers as he held Ocrestia close to him. "She was about to thank you."

Ocrestia wouldn't look at him, her face buried in Cavil's shoulder. Knot didn't know what to say.

"You could've broken her arm," Cavil said. "After what those men had just done to her, this is your reaction?"

Ocrestia looked up at Knot. "It's all right, Cavil," she said. "He saved me." But she stayed in her husband's arms.

13

CINZIA SAT ON ONE of the large armchairs in the library, the Nine Scriptures open wide on her lap, in the segment of the L-shaped room that was furthest from the door. If someone walked in on them, they could hide the Codex before it was seen. Jane sat at the desk, a stack of papers before her, quill in hand.

Jane had her visions, yes, but Cinzia had this. The Nine Scriptures, open before her. Cinzia did not speak Old Khalic—she was not sure anyone did, in this age—but she could read the words of the Nine Scriptures nonetheless. Jane had called her a seer. Cinzia did not know anything about that. When she looked at them objectively and with a close eye, the words engraved on the metal pages were nonsense to her; but when she sat back and looked at the page as a whole, she could read what was written. The words sometimes blurred on the page, or at least they did in her vision, shifting back and forth between the original Old Khalic and what Cinzia read them as now, which was Rodenese. But all Cinzia had to do was close her eyes for a moment, take a deep breath, and open them again, and the words were legible before her.

There were some oddities; strange symbols dotted the pages of the book, symbols that were illegible despite Cinzia's ability to read everything else. Neither sister had been able to guess as to what they could be. So they had kept translating, hoping that at some point the meaning would be revealed.

The pages of the Nine Scriptures were an equal wonder. How they could be formed of a metal that could be minted so thinly, and yet be so durable, Cinzia did not know. And the dark metal shimmered every so often with a slight red color, catching the light in a strange way.

"Shall we go on?" Jane asked, rubbing her hands.

"Yes," Cinzia said. "Let's continue."

The book of Cinzia had begun with a brief liturgy to Canta's divinity, but then tackled headlong the very topic Cinzia and Jane had been talking about the previous night: the organization of Canta's religion. Was it coincidence that they stumbled upon this section when they did? That as soon as they had decided it was their duty to reform Canta's religion, they were led to a book that discussed that very subject?

The book had begun by delineating the structure of the Canta's religion. Canta, of course, was its eternal head, and She spoke directly to Her chosen servant on earth—deemed the Prophetess. Beneath the Prophetess were to be ordained nine disciples, just like the Nine Disciples that walked the earth with Canta Herself, who had written the Nine Scriptures.

That much already seemed far simpler than the structure of the Denomination. The Essera was the highest-ranking official; beneath her was a group of three—the Triunity, and the highest council of the Denomination—equal to one another in power and authority: the Oracle, the Holy Examiner, and the First Priestess. While the Essera oversaw each individual member of the Triunity, the Triunity combined was equal to the power and authority of the Essera herself. And, in turn, each member of the Triunity oversaw one of the three branches of the Denomination: the Mind of Revelation, the Arm of Inquisition, and the Sect of Priesthood.

Things did not get any less complicated beyond that. Answerable to the Triunity was the High Camarilla, the second-highest governing counsel of the Denomination, consisting of three diviners, three Holy Crucibles, and three high priestesses, again each representing their respective branch of the Denomination. The High Camarilla, when combined, was equal in power and authority to the Triunity.

From there, each branch forked in its respective responsibilities. The Sect of Priesthood was by far the largest of the three, and was responsible for running the logistics of the Denomination: performing ordinances for members, the upkeep of chapels, cathedrals, and Canta's Fane, and serving the various congregations. The Sect of Priesthood was governed by nine high priestesses—the number nine, it was easy to see, had been preserved in the Cantic Denomination—including the First Priestess and the three high priestesses on the High Camarilla, each of whom in turn oversaw up to nine matrons each. Each matron oversaw up to nine priestesses—Cinzia's own office within the Denomination—and each priestess oversaw up to nine disciples.

Strange that the "disciple" designation—the lowest rank in the Cantic Denomination of today's world—had actually been the highest rank during Canta's time.

The Mind of Revelation consisted of eighteen Diviners, including the Oracle and the three Diviners on the High Camarilla. Other than various disciples who helped the Diviners, there were no other dedicated servants in the Mind of Revelation. Their responsibility was to keep track of the records of the Denomination and to prepare it for the future.

There were twenty-seven Holy Crucibles in the Arm of Inquisition, and, like the Mind of Revelation, otherwise had no dedicated servants other than a few disciples to carry out the grunt work. The responsibility of the Arm of Inquisition was to keep Cantic doctrine pure by enforcing correct teachings within the Denomination, and eliminating incorrect teachings outside of it. Nayome, the Holy Crucible who had traveled to Navone to charge Jane and the rest of Cinzia's family with heresy, had been fulfilling her duty as part of the Arm of Inquisition. The Arm of Inquisition, with its white flame sigil behind the Trinacrya, was feared far and wide, and for good reason.

And the Denomination's bureaucracy did not stop there; there were Goddessguards and the Sons of Canta, there were appointments to the minor council in Parliament, and much more besides.

Suffice it to say, the organization of Canta's religion was nowhere near as complicated as the Denomination.

"'Disciples after Canta's Order of Priesthood,'" Cinzia dictated, the strange symbols swirling into words before her,

> have the right to officiate in their own stature, under the direction of the Prophetess, in administering to all followers of Canta. The Nine Disciples embody the basis of Canta's teachings and doctrine; they keep pure the doctrine, and thus keep pure all followers of Canta. Theirs is the responsibility that kings and rulers could never have, nor want, for they sacrifice all for the people they serve, and for the Goddess they represent.
>
> These Nine Disciples are called to be a light unto Canta's people, acting as servants of the Prophetess and thus servants of Canta Herself, in aiding, helping, teaching, healing, and defending the people.
>
> But behold, the people of Canta will grow, even

> so much that the Nine Disciples will no longer be able to sustain them. And thus others must be called: priestesses, prelates, seers, and sibyls. These are called and sustained to aid the Nine Disciples in their work, aiding the people of Canta.

"Cinzia? Are you all right?"

Cinzia looked up at Jane. "It is so different," she whispered.

"To the Denomination? It is, isn't it?" Jane stood and walked over to Cinzia. "Perhaps we should take a break. We have been translating all day. It is nearly suppertime."

"Yes. Perhaps we should."

"Come. Let's go see what everyone else is up to."

Cinzia allowed Jane to take her hand and help her to rise. The Codex slid from her lap into the seat of the chair.

"Do you know what this means?" Cinzia asked. "Priestesses, prelates, seers, and sibyls. We have a *lot* of work to do, Jane."

Jane smiled. "We do, don't we?"

"These are *so good*," Cinzia said, taking another of the sticky rolls from the large pan. The rolls were baked to perfection, flaky and golden and smothered in a layer of sweet icing that clung to Cinzia's fingers.

Gorman cleared his throat. He was clearly not very pleased with the way the food was being served. The two pans of sweet rolls were sitting on the table, unadorned. There were no plates or silverware to be seen. Gorman and a few other servants stood by. Cinzia had said they could go about some other business if they liked, but Gorman had insisted they stay, in case they were needed.

"Oh, calm yourself, Gorman," Cinzia said. "Just because we

did not want to bother with all the pomp and circumstance of a formal meal does not mean that you must cough over my shoulder every few moments."

"Of course, Miss Cinzia," Gorman said stiffly.

Cinzia rolled her eyes. She would see that man smile one day. What good was life without an occasional smile?

The rest of her family understood as much. Her parents were laughing, heads leaned in close to one another. Even Eward, who had been far too serious in Navone, was smiling with the rest of them, especially when Soffrena, Lana and Wina began telling jokes.

Other than Gorman—whose solemn exterior Cinzia had always supposed was a front—her uncle Ronn was the only one who did not seem taken into the levity, although even he could not resist licking icing from his fingers.

"Can we share some of these with the followers outside?" Ader asked.

His question had been directed at Pascia, but everyone in the room heard it. An awkward silence followed.

Pascia smiled down at her son. "I'm not sure we would have enough for everyone," she said. "It wouldn't do to share with only a few and then run out."

"Couldn't we just make more?" Ader asked.

Pascia glanced at Gorman. "Well… I'm not sure we have the ingredients to make that many, son."

Gorman sniffed but said nothing. Cinzia did not know if that meant they didn't have the resources, or if Gorman was just reluctant to share.

Jane stood and tousled Ader's hair. "Mother is right. It would be difficult to make sticky rolls for that many people." Jane looked up at their parents. "But this is something we need to discuss. Do we know anything about their welfare? Is there anything we can give them?"

Ehram and Pascia exchanged a glance, then Pascia spoke. "Eward and I have walked among them a few times, just to make sure no one was starving. A few have come asking for supplies, but other than that we don't know much."

Uncle Ronn cleared his throat. "We must remember that we don't have unlimited resources. We are already allowing them access to the pond and fish from the ocean. I don't see what else we could reasonably do for them."

Cinzia nodded. Her uncle's words were gently spoken, but she could tell he did not relish the idea of sharing his wealth with the pilgrims outside. Cinzia couldn't blame him. They knew nothing about these people.

"Of course, Uncle," Jane said. "But I do think it might be a good idea to carry out a census of some kind, just so we can be aware of what needs there really are." She glanced at Cinzia. "This is all the more reason to get organized as quickly as possible."

A chill echoed down Cinzia's spine. They had not discussed their plans to reform Canta's religion with their family. Perhaps now was as good a time as any.

"Get organized for what, Jane?" Ehram asked.

Before Jane could respond, the door to the dining hall burst open and Knot appeared, breathing heavily. He stopped immediately when he saw he had interrupted. "Er. Sorry, didn't realize—"

"It's not a problem, Knot," Jane said with a smile. "Join us. Help yourself to a sticky roll."

Knot shook his head. "Need to talk to you both," he said, looking at Cinzia and then at Jane. "Something's come up. You both need to hear about it."

Goddess, what is it now? First Knot's episode, and then the conflict between the tiellan couple and the human man about a horse. That morning Astrid had come to them ranting about how some woman—what was it she had called herself? The Beldam?—was preaching human superiority over tiellans. That had seemed bad enough. What could possibly be worse?

"Of course," Jane said. She looked around at her family. "Please excuse us."

"Everyone is safe?" Jane asked.

Cinzia paced back and forth in the hallway, while Knot and Jane stood facing one another. "We're safe, yes," he said. "Can't say as much for the men who attacked us."

"Oh, Goddess," Cinzia whispered, pacing more quickly.

"You mean you injured them?" Jane asked. "Or you… did you kill any of them, Knot?"

Knot cleared his throat. "No, but… I hurt a few of them. Badly enough they won't forget it."

"Canta's bloody bones," Cinzia muttered, rubbing her temples. Things were spiraling out of control. She felt Jane's shocked eyes on her, but did not care.

"One of them was a Kamite," Knot said.

Cinzia looked up. "One of them… how do you know?"

"A tattoo on his arm. Likely the others were too, but I can't be sure."

Cinzia and Jane looked at one another. "What would the Kamite order want with us?" Jane asked.

"You're accepting tiellans into your… into whatever it is that's going on here," Knot said. "That's enough to draw their attention."

Jane took a deep breath. "I didn't realize things would progress this quickly."

"Then let's slow it down," Cinzia said. "We can tell the followers to go home. Get our bearings. Figure out exactly what Canta wants from us first."

"They are here, it must be Canta's will. We must do what we can with what we have."

"We are risking too much, Jane. Our family can't possibly avoid the trouble these people will cause. The humans and the tiellans don't get along. That insane Beldam woman isn't helping. Who knows what discord she sows. And she's teaching about the *Nine Daemons*—"

"Wait," Knot said, "what's a Beldam?"

"—and now," Cinzia continued, ignoring him, "the *Kamite order*? Jane, see reason. These people are only bringing us trouble. We can't help them."

"You're right, sister."

Cinzia breathed a sigh of relief. *Thank you*.

"But Canta can," Jane continued. "We must do as we have been asked. We must reform her religion. Canta will take care of the loose ends."

Cinzia's eyes felt like they were about to pop out of her head. Then Jane placed her hand on Cinzia's, and immediately a wave of calm swept over her.

"Things will be all right, Cinzi," Jane said. "They were in Navone when I turned myself in to the Crucible. They will be now, too."

They were not all right in Izet, Cinzia wanted to say. *They were not when Kovac died. When I killed him.*

But Cinzia knew that was different. They had ventured into Roden because Cinzia had insisted upon it—because of a "vision" that had turned out to be from someone very different than Canta. They had been deceived.

As much as Cinzia hated to admit it, following her sister might be the best course of action. At least Jane had a respectable record. Jane had not yet gotten anyone killed. And if Cinzia wanted to trust, was this not as good a place to start as any?

"I understand your concerns," Jane said. "But I believe the best thing to do is move forward."

Cinzia threw up her hands. "Do what you want," she said, completely helpless. It seemed she had no choice but to trust.

Jane was silent for a moment, staring off into space. "I must meditate on this," she said finally. She walked away, up the spiral staircase to the upper floors of the house.

"What is she talking about?" Knot asked.

Cinzia blinked, still surprised at Jane's sudden exit. "What do you mean?"

"Reforming Canta's religion. What's she talking about?"

Cinzia sat down on a wooden bench and placed her head in her hands. "She thinks the solution to all of this is to reform Canta's religion, the same one the Goddess created when She walked the Sfaera."

"The Denomination's around," Knot said. "Haven't they already done that?"

Cinzia shook her head. "This is different. Jane thinks the Denomination has been led astray. She thinks the religion has changed too much since Canta's time. She says Canta wants her to restore it to its original form."

"What do you think?"

"I think the idea sounds ridiculous," Cinzia said, laughing. But the question did make her think. She looked up at Knot. "I can't say she is wrong about the Denomination. I don't know about being led astray, but... but they don't seem to embody Canta's doctrine. Not in the way I once thought they did. And

I don't think the way they treat the tiellans is right. Things shouldn't be so segregated. There are some good people in the Denomination. And yet, after all I learned as a priestess, I'm far less certain about the institution itself. If rumors are to be believed—and given everything I have seen in the last year, I might as well believe them—then there are some not-so-good people in the Denomination, as well." Cinzia laughed. "I'm sure the last thing you want is to hear me rant. I apologize."

"Sounds like you might agree with your sister, after all."

"But the followers—"

"Not about the followers. About the religion."

Knot might actually have a point there. "Yes, perhaps we agree on the religion, or at least on the fact that it needs reforming. I don't know if we agree on *how*."

"Then why wait?" Knot asked. "Your congregation's already here. The legwork's been done for you."

"You think this is a good idea?" Cinzia asked. "Wouldn't it be better to just send them away?"

Knot shrugged. "Doubt they'd leave, even if you told 'em to."

You remind me of Kovac, sometimes, Cinzia wanted to say. But it wouldn't be appropriate.

"Who's the Beldam?" Knot asked.

"Has Astrid not told you? She saw her this morning. An old woman who calls herself the Beldam was speaking to a small group of followers. She seemed to know a great deal about the Nine Daemons, and..." Cinzia hesitated. Knot, especially, wouldn't like what the Beldam preached. But she couldn't lie to him. "...Astrid seemed to think she was preaching that humans are superior to tiellans."

"Bloody Oblivion. That must've been who Cavil was talkin' about."

Cinzia blinked. "You've heard of her?"

"Whatever she's bloody preaching seems to have already taken hold on some. I had to help some tiellans move their tents this morning because a group of humans didn't want to camp next to them."

"Canta rising," Cinzia muttered. "We need to do something about that woman. I will talk to her myself. I will not let her cause such a schism among these people."

Be careful what you promise, Cinzia told herself. But she wanted to reassure Knot that things wouldn't get worse.

It was difficult to believe that Cinzia had once been suspicious of this man. She trusted him now more than she trusted most other people in her life, she realized.

Cinzia took a deep breath. "These people are more of a liability than anything. But organizing them might be the only way to deal with them, at the rate they're growing." Cinzia attempted a smile. "We have spent this whole conversation talking about me," she said. "Have you settled in to the Harmoth estate well?"

Knot frowned. "Well enough," he said. "I..." he paused for a moment. "When I found out who I was, what I was, in Roden, I thought I wouldn't have to worry about harming the people around me any longer. But twice someone who isn't me has taken over my body."

"It has not been that bad," Cinzia said, trying to comfort him. "We have resolved it both times."

"What happens if Jane ain't around, next time?" Knot asked. "What happens if it's one of the other, less peaceful sifts?"

"I don't know," Cinzia said. "But we will deal with it. And I'm sorry. I can't imagine what you must be going through."

Cinzia lowered her head, her hair falling around her eyes.

She stared at the cracks in the mortar once more, and laughed softly to herself. "Some ragtag group we make, right?"

When Knot did not respond, Cinzia looked up, only to find him gone.

"Goddess," Cinzia whispered. "How does he do that?"

14

Keep Mandiat, Izet

THE FIRST PERSON COVA Amok saw as she entered the anteroom of the Castle Mandiat ballroom was her father. This couldn't be helped, as her father would be the one to escort her onto the floor for her own engagement ball, but Cova cringed inwardly when she saw his scowl.

It lasted only for a fraction of a second, and his face had nearly returned to normal when he reached his daughter. In the past few weeks her father had become talented at hiding his emotions. This slight change had happened around the same time her father changed in other ways—ways that Cova struggled to define.

"Daughter," Daval said, smiling now, his anger only a hint around his eyes. "Welcome to the ball. I thought we agreed you would wear your cerulean gown?"

"We might've," Cova said, "but I changed my mind. This dress seemed far more appropriate, given who I'm going to meet this evening." Her cerulean gown, the one she and her father had indeed agreed that she would wear, was like those modeled by the other women in the ballroom: bright-colored, long-sleeved, tight-waisted, with the fabric billowing out in a wide arc.

Daval's eyes almost bugged out of his face at Cova's comment, but he again regained his composure. Cova frowned inwardly. The father she knew, the man she knew a few months ago, would never have been this calm. A few months ago, she would have given anything for her father to take his emotions down a notch, especially in public. Now Cova actually *wanted* him to fly off the handle.

"You think *this* is suitable?" Daval asked. His voice was strained, but he managed to mask the growl laced beneath.

Cova shrugged, looking at the gown she'd made. "I thought it was as appropriate as anything else," she said.

"*Appropriate?*" Daval repeated, through clenched teeth.

"Yes, Father," Cova said, smiling. "Appropriate." She spun in her gown, just to allow it to take full visual effect. It clung tightly around her breasts and waist, and rather than billowing out at the waist it hugged her hips, only fanning out at the top of her thighs. It was a style Cova had never seen before; she was quite proud of herself for thinking of it. Although it didn't leave much to the imagination.

The point from which the fabric flowed was not the only difference between her dress and the other ballgowns in the room. The fabric was a dark emerald color rather than a bright pastel, and while the other gowns had long sleeves that hugged the arm tightly to the wrist, Cova's dress had no sleeves at all. She wore long gloves that nearly reached her shoulder, but her shoulders themselves were bare.

And, as she slowed her spin, looking once again at her father, Cova noticed the servants in the anteroom staring at her, wide-eyed.

Cova's smile grew wider. It was the exact response for which she had hoped.

"I know this is a surprise to you, Father," Cova said, "and I'm sorry." She genuinely meant it; she had no desire to make her father's life more difficult. "But if you meant what you said in our last conversation, then I need to be my own woman. I must stand out, and I must begin now."

Her father's face softened ever so slightly, and he held out his arm for Cova to take. "I suppose you're already here," he grumbled. "There is no going back now."

Cova took Daval's arm, and together they walked forward. The anteroom was a small chamber with a curtained threshold that led to the grand entrance stage of the Mandiat ballroom. Daval nodded at one of the servants in the room, who in turn slipped out a side passage to inform the herald of Cova's arrival.

"No, there isn't," Cova said. "Plus, this will be fun. Don't you think?"

"Not at all. But I realized long ago that you and I are very different, daughter."

The herald's voice boomed through the ballroom beyond the curtain.

"Lords and ladies of Izet, it is my pleasure to announce our guest of honor, Miss Cova Amok, daughter of High Lord Daval Amok!"

A pair of servants opened the curtain, and Cova and her father stepped into the ballroom amidst thunderous applause. Cova smirked. Her announcement had been woefully short; she had no other titles, was not the firstborn, had no accomplishments worth attaching to her name—certainly not like the great empresses of Rodenese history. But she had time to forge her own list of titles.

Cova waved at the cheering crowd. She wonderd where Girgan was. He had spent the last seven years at the Citadel, and she had not known him before that. He would have been announced earlier, of course, given that his family was hosting the ball. At the end of the evening, the herald would make the official announcement of their engagement.

Daval pulled Cova into an embrace. "I'm proud of you, daughter."

Cova laughed. The cheers of the noble throng in the ballroom had died down, and a group of musicians had begun to play. "I don't know why. There's nothing to be proud of."

"There will be." Then her father released her and walked out into the crowd.

Cova stood for a moment, taking in Castle Mandiat's ballroom. Half a dozen chandeliers hung from the ceiling, each with lit candles and hanging crystals. Gilded columns lined the edges of the chamber, although whether their detailing was real gold Cova doubted. Mandiat was rich, but she did not think he was *that* rich. She preferred the paintings, tapestries, and sculptures that decorated the Amok ballroom. While the Mandiat ballroom was expensive, it had little soul.

Cova moved elegantly through the other nobles, smiling and greeting everyone. Wherever she moved in the room, stares followed, as she'd planned. There were whispers too, which was even better. Her father had put the idea in her head that she might be empress one day. She'd damn well better play the part.

"Ah, Miss Amok," someone said, and Cova turned with a broad smile. Her smile almost faltered when she saw who it was.

"Lord Luce," she said, curtsying. "Miss Luce." Hirman Luce stood before her, his daughter Andia at his side. House Luce had sought Girgan Mandiat's hand in marriage, too. They had lost their bid, and wouldn't be happy about it. Cova was not surprised to see them here—not showing up to congratulate the new couple would have been bad manners, and manifested a problematic ill-will during a tumultuous time.

"What a beautiful ball," Andia Luce said with a smile that seemed genuine enough.

"It is," Cova said. So unfortunate. Cova had always liked Andia, but this would likely ruin any chances the two of them had at being genuine friends.

"Mandiat could have done better," Hirman Luce muttered, his waxed mustache, as red as the hair that remained at the top of his head, quivering. He attempted a smile, but was obviously a far poorer actor than his daughter. The double meaning of the man's statement was not lost on Cova, but she let it go.

"Cova, your dress… your dress is so interesting," Andia said. "Where did you get it?"

Cova blushed. It was good to appear innocent. "I made it myself, actually. Do you like it?"

"It's difficult to say. It's so different," Andia said. Her own gown was of the style that most other women at the ball wore, with fabric billowing outward from the waist, covered shoulders, and long tight sleeves. It was light peach, which clashed in a very unfortunate way with her red-orange hair. If Andia and Cova ever did become friends, Cova would have to lecture Andia's stylist and tailor. Fools the both of them, apparently.

"You can be honest, Andia, I don't mind. It *is* different, and people are bound to not like it. That's fine with me."

"Well then… I suppose I don't like it. Not immediately, anyway. I shall inform you if it grows on me."

Cova laughed. This encounter contained far less animosity than she had feared. "Very well. It was good to see—"

"Did you sleep with him? Is that how you convinced them to pass our offer?"

"*Father*," Andia said sharply. "Don't make a fool of yourself."

Hirman Luce stepped toward Cova, now uncomfortably

close. While the delicate smell of sparkling wine was in the air, and almost everyone at the ball had a glass in hand, Luce's breath smelled of something much stronger. Cova took a step back instinctively, then immediately regretted the reaction. An empress does not step back.

"You did, didn't you?" Luce grumbled. "You slept with him, and now you'll get his hand because you're a bloody whore."

Luce took another step towards Cova, and this time Cova refused to back down.

"*Father*," Andia said, but she obviously had no control over the man.

"Please step back," Cova said, with as much calm as she could muster. Cova was already the center of attention. Hirman Luce would be a fool to try anything.

"You stole him from us," Luce said, jabbing his finger sharply into the bare skin below her neck.

The action didn't hurt, but it was insulting as all Oblivion. Cova's anger bubbled over. She pushed Luce away. The force of the push, along with Luce's already intoxicated state, made him stumble and fall flat on his back, his legs waving in the air. The image would have been comical had Cova not been so full of rage.

"You will keep your distance from me, my Lord. The next time you touch me, I shall have charges brought against you. Or I'll have my father's guard captain take that finger of yours."

Andia had already rushed to her father's side. Cova felt bad for the girl. Not only did her stylist have exceedingly poor taste, her father was a drunken idiot, and Cova had stolen her one shot at gaining more power for her house.

Cova met Andia's gaze for a brief moment, but Cova couldn't tell what the glance contained. Anger, and embarrassment, surely.

"Miss Cova," someone asked, "are you all right?"

"Fine," Cova muttered, still watching Andia as she helped her father stand. The two walked toward a distant corner of the ballroom. Cova blinked. She had not realized a group had gathered around them. She wondered when that had happened.

"I'm terribly sorry I couldn't get here sooner, I'd have liked to push that man off you myself."

"Excuse me?" Cova raised an eyebrow. The young man speaking to her was tall, even for a Rodenese man, with short dark hair and dark-blue eyes. His face clean-shaven, as was tradition among Rodenese nobles.

"I wish you wouldn't have had to do that," the man said. "Isn't right, a woman having to defend herself."

Cova refrained from rolling her eyes. This one was attractive, that much was sure. Didn't seem too bright, though. The young man tried to take her by the arm, but Cova shook him off.

"I'll defend myself when necessary," Cova said, scowling. "Now, if you'll excuse me…"

The man's eyes bulged, and he blushed. "Oh, Miss Cova, I'm terribly sorry. Of course you wouldn't recognize me. I only knew you because my parents pointed you out to me. I'm Girgan Mandiat. I am your betrothed."

Cova gulped. "Girgan… of course. It is good to finally meet you."

"Oh, we've met before." Girgan once again reached for her arm. "Now, if you'll just let me lead you away…"

"I'm sorry?" Once again, Cova shook her arm out of his grip. Betrothed or not, this one couldn't take a hint, could he? She hoped he wasn't this thick all of the time.

"I'm sorry, Miss Cova, I don't mean to offend. I'm just trying to take you somewhere more—"

"You said we'd met before," Cova interrupted. "To when were you referring?"

"Oh." The smile was back on his lips. "When we were young, we met. I was only eight years old; it was before my parents sent me to the Citadel. You were at a ball my parents were throwing with your father..."

Cova shook her head. "No, I would never have gone to a ball at that age. You were eight, I must have been seven."

"You misunderstand me," Girgan said. "You had arrived with your father, but only to drop off one of your older siblings. I can't remember who at the moment."

"If that's the case, then I didn't misunderstand you; I think you misspoke."

"Er... sorry?"

"You said I'd misunderstood you. If I'd misunderstood you, that means you would have stated something correct that I didn't understand. But I understood you completely; you merely misspoke, which was the source of our misunderstanding."

"Sure, I guess—"

"You're right, though," Cova said. "I would often come with my father to drop off my older brothers at balls."

Girgan's smile returned. "Yes, that's what I was talking about. I'm sorry for the misunderstanding."

"No need to apologize." Cova offered him her arm. "Come. Call me Cova and I'll call you Girgan. It will make things easier, will it not? Now, I think you were suggesting we should go somewhere more private? Or perhaps quieter?"

"Ah, yes," Girgan said. "That is what I meant to say."

"Which one?" Cova asked. She was aware she was talking too much. Her siblings always made fun of her for it. "Never mind," Cova said, smiling at his puzzled frown. "We've met now, and that's what's important. Take me where you will, my betrothed. I have to say you're handsomer than I'd feared, although I don't know why. Your parents seem attractive enough."

"My parents..."

"Of course, if we're judging by that standard, you must have thought I would be a hag," Cova said, laughing. "My father has never been on the attractive side of anything, and my mother... well, I can't really say much about her, can I? And I suppose, neither can you."

"No, I'm afraid I never knew your mother, Miss Cova."

"Cova, please. Call me Cova. If we're to be married, we had better get used to it, no?"

"Of course, Miss—" Girgan stopped himself with a laugh.

Cova laughed with him. That laugh, the spontaneity of it, was good enough for her.

"Of course, Cova," Girgan said. "You're right."

He looked down at her as he led her through the assembled people. "I like your dress," he said.

"Thank you," Cova said. "Do you mind if I ask you why?"

Cova felt Girgan's eyes taking her in. She couldn't tell whether she enjoyed the experience or not. "It accentuates your beautiful figure," he said, smiling at her. "You're beautiful, Cova. I hope you know that."

Cova had hoped he might say something about the stitching, or the way it was different than what everyone else was wearing. But he only liked it because it accentuated her figure. Perhaps that was the result of making a dress that fitted her hips so tightly, Cova mused. Some wouldn't be able to see past her body.

"There are my parents," Girgan said. "Come, let's tell them we've met."

"All right," Cova said absently, watching the couples who

danced to the music played by a small orchestra. "Can you dance, Girgan?"

"Can I… why yes, I can dance. I was instructed at the Citadel."

"I would like for you to dance with me," Cova said. "After we speak with your parents."

Girgan smiled. "Very well."

The meeting with Girgan's parents went well, but Cova had a difficult time thinking of anything during the conversation except dancing with Girgan. Growing up, Cova had been obsessed with dancing, and had persuaded her father into allowing her to begin lessons at a very early age. Rodenese formal ballroom dancing was different from the dances in the rest of the Sfaera; it was more technical, more focused on the beauty of two bodies moving together rather than a means of socialising. But even Rodenese balls had degenerated recently and, for every Rodenese waltz played by the orchestra—the waltz being considered the highest form of dance—there were three or four more "social" dances played, in which the dancers could still hold a conversation. Those who could dance—truly *dance*—the Rodenese waltz seemed fewer and further between. Cova had all but given up trying to find partners that could keep up with her. But whenever she was at a ball, when she heard the slow, dark tones of a Rodenese waltz, she felt the pull.

Cova gripped Girgan's arm. "Come, you promised me a dance. Don't deny me on the night of our celebration."

Girgan smiled at her. "Of course not." He looked to his parents. "If you'll excuse us, we have an appointment on the ballroom floor."

Hama Mandiat smiled. "Of course, son. This night belongs to both of you; enjoy yourselves."

As Girgan and Cova walked arm in arm towards the dance

floor, Cova felt a rush of sensation through her body. She rarely felt more alive than when gliding across the floor.

But, to her dismay, the orchestra began playing a fast-paced piece, not the waltz she wanted. The crowd on the dance floor began moving together, forming pairs of long lines along the floor, the men and women facing each other. Girgan led Cova to one of the lines before she could resist.

Cova recognized the song; it was called "Another Rabbit Chases the Gull," and the group dance was widely known. It was also the last thing Cova felt like doing at the moment, but she was already in line, facing Girgan.

"This isn't the type of dancing I had in mind," Cova said, as the two lines began moving. The men bowed to the women first, and then the women curtsied in turn. They then approached their appropriate partner, right hands held out in front of them, and circled one another.

"What was that?" Girgan asked. "I can't quite hear you, the music..."

"Never mind," Cova said. There was no use complaining about it now.

"So you've lived in Roden all your life?" Girgan asked. The music, still upbeat and fast, dictated that Cova and Girgan walk away, do a series of taps with their feet, and then come back to one another, hand in hand. The rest of their rows followed suit.

"All my life," Cova said, tapping her heels onto the ground. The move seemed incredibly undignified, but it admittedly didn't take much brainpower.

There was silence, and Cova could tell Girgan was trying to think of something to say. Cova sighed. Might as well help the boy out. If they were going to rule the empire together, she'd likely need to get used to it.

"You recently returned from the Citadel, then?" Cova asked. They were holding hands, walking down the line. This was what constituted dancing, now. Walking. Cova resisted the urge to laugh.

"I did!" Girgan said, almost shouting, although whether to be heard over the music or from excitement Cova was not sure. "Only a few weeks ago."

"I have heard many things about the Citadel," Cova said. "What did you think of your experience there?"

"Very good indeed," Girgan said. If possible, his smile was growing wider. "We are taught so much there, and by experts in every field. It was the best seven years of my life."

And you are how old? Cova wanted to ask. If it was the best seven years of his life, and he had only seen twelve summers when he entered, that wasn't saying much. "And now you're ready to rule?" she asked. The Citadel existed to train the leaders of the Sfaera. Noble and wealthy families from nations across the world sent their children to the school. The late Emperor Grysole was the most recent Rodenese graduate. The Citadel, based in Triah, the capital city of Khale, had understandably accepted fewer and fewer students from Roden, given the growing tension between the two nations. Girgan's acceptance and graduation said much about his character. Or at least about his intelligence.

Girgan did not seem to know how to take her comment, however. Perhaps his parents had similar aspirations for him as Cova's father did for her. Perhaps promises of the throne had reached his ears, too.

"Not that anyone ever is, really," Cova continued.

Girgan looked at her strangely. They had finished walking along the line, and were now turning in place. Cova began to wonder whether he would be a suitable partner for a waltz. As she understood it, all students of the Citadel were instructed in dance, but she had no idea to what level. His movements seemed awkward, and his limbs, slightly too long for his body, seemed disappointingly unsure.

Perhaps it was best they were dancing to this music, then. The desire to waltz, to Cova's dismay, was slowly leaving her.

"I'm sorry," Girgan said, after a few moments of silence.

"For what?" Cova asked.

"I… I don't know. I'm new to all of this. Engagement. Roden. Our customs. Even my own ballroom. If I seem awkward I apologize. I don't mean to be."

They approached one another once more, hands held before them. "Don't apologize," Cova said. "I hadn't even noticed."

"Good to hear. And… I really do have much to say about the Citadel, but I don't want to bore you."

"I'm not easily bored. But save it for another time if you wish. It seems we will have all the time in the world together, after all."

Girgan chuckled at that, and Cova realized that she wasn't completely disappointed by the idea. Then the music slowed, and Girgan and Cova slowly backed away from one another. Cova curtsied and Girgan bowed, signaling the end of the dance.

Cova smiled. "Thank you," she said. It had been relatively pleasant, after all. And now that her desire to waltz had all but left her, she could focus on Girgan, and they could perhaps find her father.

She was about to say as much when the orchestra began playing a Rodenese waltz. The music began with a single guitar, and Cova recognized the tune immediately. It was one of her favorites: "A Flower in Winter." A violin joined the guitar after a few moments, and more and more instruments added to the dark melody, slow and drawn-out.

Cova stopped in the middle of the floor. She could ask Girgan to dance. He *had* to know something of the waltz, coming from the Citadel. But... but he might also be miserable at it, too.

"Let's find my father," Cova said, resolved, although the music still called to her. "It's time we speak with him."

Girgan looked at her for a minute, not saying anything. Then his hand slid down her arm and gripped her hand, squeezing it.

"Can you waltz?" he asked.

The smile came quickly to Cova's lips. "I can. And you?"

"A bit," Girgan said with a smile. "Care to have a go? I quite likc this onc, anyway."

Cova's smile broadened. Soon she'd be grinning like an idiot. "Let's give it a try."

Girgan took a step back. As he looked at her, he frowned. "Uh... your dress... is it..."

Cova looked down at her dress, confused. Had she spilled something on it? Then she realized what he meant. Her dress, with the fabric line below her hips, was very different than the normal ballroom gowns. Girgan was likely concerned it would impede her movement.

Cova smiled at him. "I made the dress myself, specifically for dancing," she said. "I'll be fine." And it was true; she had tested it just to be sure. While the fabric hugged her hips, it allowed more than enough room to take the long steps necessary for the waltz.

"Very well," Girgan said. Then he raised his left hand; the signal to take up position. Cova moved towards him, clasping his raised hand in her right. He reached his other arm around her, placing his hand just below her shoulder blade, and she rested her left arm delicately on his.

His dance position isn't terrible, Cova thought.

Girgan pulled Cova gently towards him, and Cova knew immediately that this dance would be different. The Rodenese waltz relied on perfect unity between two bodies, the connection between partners. The obvious points were where the hands touched, and where the woman's arm rested on top of the man's, and the man's hand held the woman's back. These connection points were important; a certain tension had to exist between partners, both pushing away and pulling together at once.

What really separated the good dancers from the great, however, was the connection at the hip. Most dancers, whether because they had not been taught or because the idea of touching hips with someone of the opposite sex was uncomfortable, had very little connection other than through the arms and hands. But one needed to move together at the waist, the hips, and upper thighs, as one. Cova had never felt that connection with anyone else she had danced with.

Until now.

Girgan swayed, and Cova swayed with him. In the traditional Rodenese waltz, the male usually took the lead. Cova often found herself having to take that responsibility, but with Girgan she knew immediately she wouldn't have to. He swayed, she swayed, they swayed together, and then they *moved*.

Cova and Girgan swept across the dance floor, their bodies locked to one another. Cova felt the rush of the music, the movement. Girgan understood the subtleties of the rise and fall; he powered forward, then rose gently on his toes only to move low and forward once more. Cova followed him, ecstatic that she could finally allow her long legs to take strides they were meant to take. Even her dance instructor had shorter legs than she did, making it difficult for Cova to dance to her full potential. With Girgan she moved with wide strides, sailing across the floor, only to pause at a moment in the music that groaned with tension, and then move again, this time twirling and spinning around one another, always locked in their dance position, delicate tension buzzing between them.

The music ended too soon; Girgan slowed to a stop, stretching their bodies out in a final posture, Cova's back stretching, the muscles in her legs burning. A sheen of sweat masked her skin. What had just happened was a dream.

As the last strains of music echoed throughout the hall, and Cova and Girgan stretched out their final pose, the ballroom erupted in applause. Cova blinked; she had forgotten that anyone else was present.

Girgan spun Cova away, and she curtsied as he bowed. Then he took her hand once more, and they left the dance floor.

"That was… that was incredible," Cova managed, when she had caught her breath. The Rodenese waltz was danced to slow music, and while much of the movement was incredibly fast, the dancers' topline remained very still, giving the illusion of ease and serenity. In reality, the intricate footwork required great coordination and balance, not to mention endurance.

Girgan was once again smiling that ridiculous, silly grin of his. "*You* were incredible, Miss Cova. No lady of the Citadel could dance the way you did just now."

Cova found herself blushing, genuinely this time, at the compliment. She smiled back at him, hoping hers was a bit more serene. "There are no men in Roden who could have done what you just did, I assure you." She punched his arm lightly.

"And call me Cova. What did I tell you?"

Girgan laughed. "Of course. I'll not forget again."

"Best not."

They circulated once more, arm in arm, and this time Cova's dress seemed the last thing on people's minds. Or on their tongues, at any rate. *Everyone is enthralled by me,* Cova thought, not without excitement. *By us,* she corrected herself. It was perfect. If she was to rule one day, this was exactly the sentiment she needed from the nobility.

Her father told her as much when they found him. He smiled at her, a rare occurrence, and embraced her, whispering in her ear. "You've done well tonight, daughter. Better than I could have ever imagined. You will make a powerful empress."

Those words echoed in Cova's mind for days.

15

Harmoth estate

CINZIA STOOD NEAR THE pond on the estate grounds, listening to the Beldam preach. The Beldam's principal choice of topic was the Nine Daemons, and while Cinzia's curiosity was piqued—the woman seemed to know more about them than she did—what she said about the tiellans was not right. Not to mention the woman's rhetoric was troubling in and of itself. Why go on about the problem if you can't offer a solution? "Be afraid," was the Beldam's message. Fear was dangerous. Fear could override all of the progress Cinzia and Jane had made.

"The Sfaera is being reborn, whether we like it or not," the Beldam was saying. "The world changes, and we must change with it. We must leave behind the things of the old world. We must shed ourselves of those that would hold us back. There are some around us—even in this camp—who would stop us from progressing. Who want us to go back to the ancient ways. We must not let them."

The crowd that had gathered around the Beldam today was completely human. Cinzia had seen a few tiellans the last time she had come to hear the Beldam speak, but most had walked away before the Beldam had finished. Cinzia could understand why.

The Beldam was sowing discord. She was dividing the camp rather than uniting it.

After the speech, Cinzia waited until the crowd had

dispersed, then approached the Beldam.

"Ah, Priestess Cinzia," the Beldam said, her wrinkled face splitting into a smile. "I wondered when you might come see me."

Cinzia was surprised at how short the Beldam was—Cinzia herself was short for a human, but this woman barely reached her shoulder. "And what should I call you? I'm afraid I don't know your name."

The Beldam chuckled, the sound of her laugh like paper. "You're not the only one. I may have forgotten it myself. Around here, people just call me the Beldam."

"And that is how you… prefer to be called?" Why anyone would choose to be called such a name was beyond Cinzia's comprehension.

The Beldam shrugged. "I don't mind. Better I call myself such a thing than others call me worse behind my back."

"You're beginning to draw quite the following," Cinzia said, nodding at the departing Odenites, who were speaking excitedly to one another. It was an excitement Cinzia had always sought to create with her own sermons, but only achieved on occasion.

The Beldam's smile broadened. "What a miracle that is, isn't it? That someone like me can become an instrument in the Goddess's hands to reach so many."

Cinzia returned the smile, not without effort. Did this woman truly think she was doing the will of the Goddess? "We are all instruments in the hands of the Goddess, in one way or another. That's one of the many miracles of life, although precious few of us ever become cognizant of that fact."

"If I can help others realize that very thing, I can die happy."

Cinzia had hoped the Beldam might reveal more about why she thought she had the authority to preach to these people, but it was obviously not going to be that easy.

As the Beldam shuffled around gathering up her belongings—including a few books, the titles of which Cinzia was intensely curious to know—Cinzia thought of a different approach.

"And what brought you to our estate, Miss... er... Beldam?"

"Canta brought me here, just as She has brought everyone else. Just as She continues to bring people."

"But everyone has a story about where they came from and what prompted them to come here. I love hearing those stories, I think it... I think it gives me strength, reminds me of the importance of what we're doing. Would you tell me yours?" In fact, the tales Cinzia had heard she found disturbing: people hearing voices, experiencing strange feelings, not being able get Tinska out of their minds. Elessa, it seemed, had only been the beginning.

The Beldam hefted her satchel. "I suppose I could," she said. "If you would accompany me to my tent?"

Cinzia nodded. "Of course." She reached out her hand. "I can carry your bag, if you like."

The Beldam waved her off, already walking away. "Don't worry about me, my dear. I may be old, but I'm not weak. Not yet, anyway. I'm not sure you'll like my story as much as some of the others." She walked quickly for one of such age.

"I'm only curious," Cinzia said, hurrying after her.

The Beldam sighed. "Very well. I came, most recently, from Cineste. I was traveling to the west coast to meet an old friend of mine. But when I got to Tinska that friend was no longer there to greet me."

"She left?"

"She died," the Beldam said. "It happens when you get to be my age. And at least she's avoiding all of this." The Beldam spread out her hands wide.

"You mean the Rising?"

"That's not the only thing to despair of in our day, if you know what I mean."

"I'm not sure I do. Are the Nine Daemons not enough of a threat?"

"No, my dear, I'm afraid they are not."

"You're referring to the tiellans?"

The Beldam paused, glancing around. "I'm referring to all the things wrong with the Sfaera today. It's impossible to pinpoint any one thing."

"You're deflecting my question," Cinzia said. She could feel the frustration growing within her. "You don't think your rhetoric is against the tiellans?"

"I only speak truth."

"And you believe the truth is that tiellans are descended from the Nine Daemons?"

"Truth is truth, my dear."

Cinzia refrained from rolling her eyes. "Where do you get your information? And how do you know about the Rising?"

The Beldam's smile returned. "Ah yes. I'm afraid you're not the only woman to have left the Cantic Denomination's Ministry, Cinzia."

Cinzia's eyes widened. "You… you were with the Ministry? A priestess?"

"For a time, yes. And then a matron, and then a high priestess. And now I am what you see today."

"You were a *high priestess*? How long ago?"

"I was a high priestess before you were born, my dear."

"But you… left. Why?"

"Why did *you* leave? Why would anyone? Because the goings-on in the Denomination were no longer directed by our Goddess. I'm sure things have only gotten worse, now. I'm surprised the Ministry isn't hemorrhaging women by the day. I would pay my weight in gold if it meant I could've gotten out earlier than I did."

"And this is how you know so much about the Nine Daemons?" Cinzia asked. "Because you were in the Denomination?"

The Beldam stopped. They had arrived at a small lean-to tent at the edge of the grounds. "This is me," the Beldam said, tossing her satchel down.

"This is where you sleep?" Cinzia asked, trying to contain her surprise. She knew some of the Odenites did not live in ideal conditions, but it was something else entirely to see it up close.

The Beldam sat on a tree stump near the lean-to and looked up at Cinzia. "Dozens of people come to hear me speak. Not one of them cares where I lay my head. That's the nature of the world, isn't it?"

"I suppose so."

The Beldam reached down to massage one of her feet. Cinzia stood awkwardly, not sure what else to do. Eventually her curiosity got the better of her.

"How did you come to know so much about the Nine Daemons?" Cinzia asked. "Even in the Ministry, information was scarce."

"As a high priestess I had access to certain texts and other... things. Things we do not show the matrons or priestesses, let alone the general public. One of those things is a fragmented copy of the Nine Scriptures."

Cinzia blinked.

The Beldam chuckled. "They didn't tell you that at the seminary, did they?"

Cinzia shook her head slowly. "No," she said, "they did not." She wondered what the Beldam would say if she knew that Cinzia and Jane were translating the Nine Scriptures, that they actually had the *original version*. "Could you tell us what you know?" Cinzia asked. Whatever the Beldam was teaching about the Nine Daemons, Cinzia and Jane had not gotten to that part in the Nine Scriptures yet—assuming, of course, that the fragmented texts the Denomination held in their possession were real. Cinzia wouldn't be surprised if they were fake.

They had to be fake. This nonsense about the tiellans couldn't possibly be true.

"I preach what I know every day, by the pond," the Beldam said. "You can learn just as well there as anyone."

"I'm not sure it is wise to preach of the Nine Daemons, inciting such fear. But if you told us what you know, we might be able to offer something more than simply fear."

"Like what? Do you think you can actually offer protection? From the Nine Daemons?"

"We can," Cinzia said. It wasn't an outright lie, at least; she and Jane were hoping to find out more about how to fight the Nine Daemons.

The Beldam considered this for a moment. "Very well," she finally said. "If you truly think we can do something to protect these people..."

"One condition," Cinzia said.

"What is that, my dear?"

"You can't mention the tiellans in your sermons. You can't call them the children of the Nine Daemons."

The Beldam's bushy eyebrows rose. "Now you're starting to sound like the Denomination," she said. "Telling me what I can and can't say."

Cinzia's cheeks grew hot. "You want to protect these people? Then you will do as I say. You can speak of whatever you wish when you're alone, but we are going to protect these people. What you've been saying is harmful."

"I don't see it that way."

"I don't care how you see it," Cinzia snapped, surprised at her anger. "You will either stop, or we will take further action."

The Beldam frowned, her ancient eyes meeting Cinzia's. For a moment, Cinzia thought the woman might refuse.

But, finally, the Beldam nodded. "I will do as you say," she said. "If you truly think you can protect us."

16

Harmoth estate

KNOT LEANED BACK AGAINST the west wall of the house, watching the sun set into the ocean. To his right, from somewhere in the grounds on the northern side of the manor, Knot heard the buzz of the Odenites. Five more had arrived that day, a human family of four, and an older tiellan woman.

Jane and Cinzia were busy translating their book; he'd poked his head in earlier that evening. Jane had insisted that he not enter the room, only stand in the doorway, so as not to see the bloody tome they were translating. They were so protective of it. Wished he could say it had nothing to do with him, but that didn't seem to be the case anymore. Izet had changed that.

The sun was just above the horizon now, a red-orange orb. Knot heard footsteps and tensed. He turned to see Elessa approaching him.

"Sorry," Elessa said, "I didn't know you were here."

Knot shrugged. "I don't own the place. You can go where you please."

"That may be true, but if I'm… if I'm disturbing you, I can go."

"Ain't disturbing nobody," Knot muttered.

When she did not respond, Knot began to feel uncomfortable. He could leave, or get a conversation going. His choice surprised him.

"You arrived here a year ago," Knot said, recalling their

earlier conversation. "Told me it was a story for another time."

Elessa leaned against the wall next to Knot. She walked with a certain poise, something Knot recognized. There was nobility there, sure. But something else, too, a casual preparedness, a tensing of the muscles and fluidity in the step that bespoke combat training, though the woman carried no weapon that Knot could see.

"I suppose we could go into that story now, if you like," Elessa said. "There really isn't much to tell. I'm afraid it won't be as exciting as I made it seem."

"I've got low expectations," Knot said.

"Very well," Elessa said. "But I don't know you very well, Knot. I'd like to hear a bit more about you, too, being the Healed One and all."

Knot snorted. "I can tell you about me, but I asked first, darlin'."

Elessa smiled. "I came to Tinska one year ago because my parents died," she said, her eyes sad. "Before that I lived my entire life in Turandel, a city on the coast south of here. And then my parents died, and I… I had no reason to stay."

"Who were your parents?" Knot asked.

"My last name is Storonam," Elessa said, reluctantly. "My parents were Ingran and Faria."

Knot blinked. Ingran and Faria Storonam. Definitely sounded familiar. There was a strange itch in the back of Knot's mind. This was the sensation he needed to avoid, he knew, the one he'd felt when he arrived at Harmoth, just before…

"Sorry to hear they passed away," Knot said. He thought Elessa twitched at his words, but in the dying light he couldn't be sure.

"When my parents were taken from me, something…

changed. All the things that used to matter, no longer did. Reintegrating myself into the noble circles of Turandel as a newly orphaned woman did not feel natural. And, soon, I… I was impelled to leave."

Knot frowned. "Impelled? The other nobles pressured you?"

"No, it wasn't that. Well, it was, but that's not what I meant. I was impelled by other means." She met Knot's eyes. "Have you spoken with Jane about her visions?"

Knot chewed his cheek. He'd heard Jane speak of her visions. Never quite had a conversation with the woman about them. Religions concerned him about as much as governments. Or at least they had until Izet.

"I'm not saying I had a vision," Elessa said quickly. "I'm not anything like Jane. But I did receive an impression… a feeling, that I should leave Turandel, and come here."

Knot raised his eyebrows. He didn't care much what other people believed so long as it didn't affect him, but this sounded more than a bit crazy.

"If it was a feeling, how did you know to come here?"

"I… I can't say for sure," Elessa said. "I just know I ended up here. Where I am supposed to be."

Knot nodded, but it sounded bloody crazy. "You've spoken with Jane about this?" he asked.

"Not yet," Elessa said. "I've been meaning to, but she's been so busy…"

"I'll get you in to speak with her," Knot said. Despite his skepticism, Knot had one other thing in mind. Cinzia, supposedly, had experienced a revelation in Navone, a revelation they'd followed. That revelation had left Lian, Winter, and Kovac dead, and had nearly killed everyone else. Jane and Cinzia had informed them later, after Izet, that the revelation had not been from Canta. It had been from somewhere else, likely the same source of the being that possessed Kovac, likely the same source that had confronted Knot, Winter, and Astrid underneath the imperial dome. Oddly enough, Knot had never resented Cinzia for leading them astray. It did not seem to have been her fault. It'd been his idea to go to Roden in the first place, anyway.

"That would mean a lot to me," Elessa said. "Thank you."

If Elessa had indeed been influenced by a force of some kind, better for Jane and Cinzia to discern what it was before something bad happened again. And if what they had experienced was nothing, then perhaps Jane could tell them that, too.

Knot sighed. "Your parents," he said. "Their name sounds so familiar to me, but I can't quite place it." The itch was there, again, in the back of his mind.

"Have you ever been to Turandel?" Elessa asked.

"No," Knot said, "can't say that I have." The itch was there, taunting him. He might've been to Turandel before—or a part of him might've, anyway. "How'd they die?" he asked. And, as he looked into Elessa's eyes, he knew before she even answered.

"They were killed," Elessa said.

"Are you all right?" the woman said.

The woman, Lathe thought. Elessa Storonam. Daughter of Ingran and Faria Storonam.

"Knot, are you all right?" Elessa repeated.

Lathe stared at her, and then at the sun low on the western horizon, and had no notion of how he had got here. Or where "here" was.

One thing was clear, though. He had killed Ingran and Faria Storonam with his own hands. And his being here with their only remaining daughter couldn't end well.

Lathe jabbed his hand out, connecting with the woman's throat. She gasped harshly and clutched her neck. Lathe did not know why she was asking whether he was all right. Lathe did not know what was going on, except for one thing. He was not in control.

Lathe hated not being in control.

He turned, putting the ocean behind him. A large house lay before him. He must have been knocked unconscious when he… when he…

He frowned as he walked quickly around the side of the building, to the north. When he what? Lathe could not remember the last thing he had done.

He swore as he turned the corner and saw a large mass of people milling about. He ducked back around the side of the building. A few faces had glanced in his direction, he was sure. One person in particular had noticed him, a young girl in a cloak, but that didn't matter. The crowd hadn't seemed hostile in any way, although Lathe couldn't very well make that assumption, not when he had no idea what in Oblivion was going on. There had looked to be at least a hundred of them. A hundred people could cause problems for him no matter their intent.

Lathe turned and walked back along the ocean-facing side of the house. Elessa had collapsed against the wall, still clutching her throat and making small wheezing sounds. She reached out to him, but Lathe rushed past, and turned another corner so that he was shielded by the house. He looked over his shoulder to make sure no one had followed, and then strode south towards a formal garden.

The garden had once been well kept, but seemed neglected now. The shrubberies and arranged flowerbeds were covered with dead leaves and overgrown with weeds. To the east he could see what appeared to be a cemetery, but he couldn't be sure as the grounds were quite large. His best bet would be to slip into the woods on the far side of the cemetery and circle around to the road in the hope there was civilization close by. He was somewhere on the western coast of Khale, probably in the north of it. The sunset, the beach, the chilly weather gave that much away. Beyond that, he was lost.

"Where do you think you're going, nomad?"

Lathe stopped. "I don't have any business here," he said. "I just want to get home."

He turned around, slowly. A child had spoken to him. The same girl who had caught his eye in the crowd for those few seconds, heavy hood drawn up over her face.

"Who are you?" Lathe asked.

The girl laughed, and walked towards him. "Someone who cares about what happens to you. The more appropriate question is, who are *you* this time, nomad?"

Lathe frowned. This child knew him. Or thought she knew him, anyway. But that didn't matter. Perhaps he had been involved in some kind of deep cover mission here, which was why everyone was treating him like someone else.

If that's true, why can't I remember getting my orders? He remembered his home in Triah, he remembered Sirana, he remembered the Nazaniin. But he did not remember this place. He did not remember this girl. And he did not remember whatever in Oblivion had happened to get him here.

"I'm going to leave now," Lathe said. "But I'm afraid I can't have you running off and telling anyone." He began walking towards the girl.

Her eyes widened. "What are you going to do to me?" she asked.

"What I have to."

"Please," she said. "Please don't hurt me."

Lathe wouldn't hurt her, not too much, anyway. He'd tie her up, gag her. Leave her somewhere easily found. No use harming a child, not without reason.

"Please," the girl said again, backing away from him. The setting sun cast its orange rays across the garden, across her hood, leaving gray shadows everywhere else.

Lathe advanced towards her. If she screamed, he'd have to move quickly. He reached out, grabbing her wrist. He was about to place his other hand around the girl's mouth, when she twisted free of his grip. Lathe frowned. Was she trained in combat? Or in escape, at least. She had to be a noble to have trained so young.

Lathe lunged at her, but she dodged—faster than she had any right to. Lathe grasped nothing but air. He spun to face her just as she punched him in the face.

Goddess did it *hurt*.

Lathe blinked as his vision refocused. This girl was not what she seemed. Which meant this entire place might not be what it seemed.

"That's right," the girl said with a grin, her pleading helplessness all but disappearing, "asking *who* I am was the wrong question."

Lathe couldn't afford to waste time. He sprinted away from the creature, back towards the house. If he could lose her, he could skirt around the edge of the building and eastward, into the forest.

The girl slammed into him from the side, but Lathe rolled with the tackle, allowing her momentum to spin him and take them into the wall of the house. Lathe wrapped his arms around her and slammed her up against the wall.

The blow would have stunned any normal person, and perhaps done permanent damage to a child. As he always did when dealing with children, Lathe felt a faint undertone of regret.

This child, however, was not even fazed. Lathe held her up against the wall, and just as he reached for her throat she kicked him hard in the chest, and sent him stumbling backwards. Before he could recover she was on him.

"Asking *what* I am would've been far more appropriate."

Lathe deflected her first blow, but her second connected with his belly. He clenched his muscles but it still landed hard. He dodged her third strike, and her fist went past him, upsetting her balance. Knot gripped her wrist and twisted, at the same time rolling to get her off him.

The trick worked, and Lathe rolled to a crouch, facing the girl. She shook her hand limply in the air. That was a good sign—at least she could feel pain.

"You must be Lathe," she said with a grin.

Lathe didn't respond. None of this made any sense: a girl with unnatural strength and speed; no memory of how he came to this place, or why. He felt like he was in a dream, but everything was too real around him.

The girl rushed at him again, but changed her direction at the last moment and leapt onto the wall, using it as a springboard to launch herself at his face. Lathe spun out of the way and used her momentum to toss her out into the garden, just as the last rays of sunlight flickered into dusk.

Lathe was about to run when something made him stop. An instinct he hadn't used in years. Out in the garden, in the gray dusk where he had thrown the girl, he saw two glowing green lights.

"Vampire," Lathe growled.

"Right you are."

Lathe swore. Now that the sun had set, he stood no chance. He had never encountered a child vampire before, but if her daytime strength was any indication, her nighttime phase would be deadly, even for him.

She rushed at him, and Lathe braced himself. For the first time in many years—and again the odd emptiness of time in his head echoed, taunting him—he felt fear. This was a fight he couldn't win.

Just as the vampire was on him, Lathe connected with the Void. The process was easy, even after whatever had happened to get him to this point. He was in the black warmth of the Void, and he slipped two *tendra* off to the side, gripping a large rock with each *tendron*. He reached his remaining *tendra* in front of him, around the vampire, and tried to grip her clothing to restrain her. As a telenic, Lathe's *tendra* could only interact with inanimate objects. Rocks, weapons, and clothing were all game, but his *tendra* would pass harmlessly through the living—trees, animals, and of course people.

But his *tendra* were terrifyingly weak. He could barely lift the rocks, while all his remaining *tendra*—nineteen of them—barely slowed the vampire as she bore down on him.

She crashed into him, slamming his head against the wall. He should have known better. He should never have relied on psimancy to get him out of this, not when his memories seemed so… clouded. Empty. The vampire swept his feet out from under him, and Lathe collapsed to the ground, still reeling from the blow to his head.

"I knew your powers hadn't left you," she said. "You just need to figure out how to use them."

Lathe blinked as she rolled him over, grinding his face into the dirt. He felt his hands being tied behind his back.

What is she doing to me? He hadn't suffered a blow to the head that powerful in a long time, he knew that much. *What do vampires do to those they kill?* The bitch was probably preparing her next meal.

"Astrid! What are you *doing*?"

Two women approached, running around the corner of the house.

"Another episode," the vampire said. "Get over here now, before he figures out a way to escape."

"Hold him still while I heal him."

Lathe felt another pair of hands on him. He craned his neck to see one of the women, her face in shadows, gripping his shoulders, and the other woman, a blond, laying her hands on his head. *I know her,* Lathe realized. He struggled, but the vampire was far too strong.

"Don't struggle, idiot," the monster said. "We're helping you."

The blond woman had begun speaking, although Lathe couldn't understand any of the words. Her eyes were bright blue, even in the dusklight. He knew her face from an image transfer that one of the house acumens had given him. A potential contract. The party that had been considering them for the hit had never hired them before.

The Cantic Denomination.

This was a wanted woman. Not only wanted, but likely with a death price on her head. Lathe did not know how much time he'd lost, but surely enough for this contract to get through. Lathe was looking at a dead woman. It was only a matter of time.

And then, as the woman continued speaking, Lathe felt a strange sensation, as if he were falling asleep uncontrollably, fading away into darkness…

Knot woke with his face in the dirt and something pressing on his back.

"Feeling better, nomad?" Astrid's voice came from above him – she must be standing on him to hold him down.

"Another episode?" he asked, coughing.

Astrid stepped off him, and he rolled over to see Cinzia and Jane looking down at him.

"Another episode," Jane confirmed. "How do you feel?"

"Fine, now," Knot said. He stood, slowly, brushing dust from his clothes. "What exactly did I…" Knot hesitated, frowning. Then, he bent and vomited.

He heard Astrid swear, and Cinzia mutter something under her breath. Jane volunteered to get a clean rag, and walked quickly toward the house.

"My head," Knot said when he was finished, wiping his mouth with a sleeve. "What happened to me?"

"This was the one," Astrid said quietly.

Knot looked up at her. "Lathe?" he asked.

Astrid nodded.

Cinzia reached for Knot's head. "What are you talking about?"

"This is the episode we'd feared, since they first began a few weeks ago," Astrid said. "Lathe is one of the primary sifts in Knot's head. It's Lathe's body that Knot occupies now."

"And who is Lathe?" Cinzia asked, looking into Knot's eyes. "Oh, Goddess," she whispered.

"Lathe is a Nazaniin assassin," Knot said. Might as well get to the point.

"Knot..." Cinzia whispered, staring at him.

"My pupils are unequal sizes," Knot said, nodding. He had a concussion, then. Between his grinding headache and spontaneous vomiting, he'd suspected as much.

Cinzia turned angrily on Astrid. "What did you do to him?" she asked.

"I stopped him from getting away," she said.

"By giving him a bloody concussion?"

"Better that than him escaping to where we'll never find him again," Astrid said. "Or worse, hurting anyone else in the camp."

Knot's mouth went dry. "I hurt someone," he said. He racked his brain, trying to remember. "I was with Elessa," he said. "Is she all right?"

Astrid and Cinzia looked at one another without saying anything, and it was all Knot needed to hear.

"She'll recover," Cinzia said quickly. "But you did hurt her. She'll likely have trouble speaking for a while."

Knot shook his head. What was he thinking, staying here? This was Pranna all over again. He was harming those he cared about simply by being around them.

"Knot..." Astrid said, but he ignored her.

"Where is Elessa?" he asked. "Can I... can I see her?" He needed to apologize.

"I don't think that's advisable," Cinzia said quietly.

Knot nodded, the pit in his gut seeming to go on forever. Of course she wouldn't want to see him. He had nearly killed her.

"You need to rest," Cinzia said. She glared at Astrid once more. "You've been hurt badly. If you do not rest, it could get worse."

"Don't blame her," Knot grunted. "She did what she had to do." Cinzia was right. He had been hurt. "Grecetamin leaf," he said. "Should grow near here. I'll need some."

"I know what that is," Astrid said. "I'll get it." Before they could say anything she was running towards the forest.

"She feels bad."

Knot and Cinzia turned to face Jane, who had returned with an armful of damp cloths. She handed one to Knot. "Clean yourself up," she said. "You need some rest."

Knot turned to look after Astrid. She didn't deserve to feel guilt for what she'd done, what was necessary to protect others, and to save him from himself. Knot was the only person at fault.

"Does anyone else know what happened?" Knot asked. He did not know why, but he worried what the others might think of him. Jane's growing army of followers surely wouldn't call him the Healed One any longer if they knew what he'd done, although Knot wasn't so sure that was a bad thing. There were others, though. Cinzia's parents. Ader. He did not want them to fear him.

But, at the same time, there was no reason Knot could think of why they shouldn't.

"Not at the moment," Jane said. "And we intend to keep it that way. Although if Elessa decides to say something, we couldn't stop her. Or, even if we could, I don't believe we should."

"No," Knot said. "We shouldn't."

He wiped his face and dabbed at the vomit on his clothes.

"There's something else," Jane said.

Knot laughed without mirth. "Course there is."

"I don't exactly understand what is happening inside you, Knot. I have managed to heal you so far, by Canta's grace, but I'm not sure how many more times it will be effective. Your… *you* have been more difficult to find, each time."

"Why didn't you tell us this earlier?" Cinzia asked, her tone rising. "We could have done something sooner."

"I was not sure," Jane said. "But I am now."

Knot took a few deep breaths, then nodded. "I understand." He stood, slowly.

"Let me help you."

Knot wasn't sure which of the women had said that; it was getting dark, and he was...

Knot stumbled, and Cinzia and Jane both rushed to either side of him. "Come on," one of them said. "Let's get you inside."

Knot wanted to resist, wanted to do it on his own. He already had an idea of what he had to do growing in his mind, but that would have to wait. He would need to heal first.

"Yes," Knot said, locking his emotions away. "Let's get inside."

17

ASTRID SAT BENEATH AN awning on the north side of the Harmoth house, her hood pushed back. It was another sunny day—a rarity in this area, Jane had told her—and the second in a row. Tinska's climate should be agreeable with Astrid's proclivities, but not lately.

It was still chilly, being only the third month of the year. Most of the Odenites still wore cloaks and furs. The snow had all but melted, however, and greenery was showing itself.

Some glanced at her as they passed. There was talk of what Cinzia and Jane were doing; somehow, word had reached them of a new religion. Some were even asking for positions in the new religion, for Canta's sake. Greed never ceased to flow through human veins. Or tiellan veins, for that matter. If power was up for grabs, people wouldn't hesitate.

Astrid could see, in the distance, another crowd gathering by the pond. The Beldam was speaking again. The old woman drew more people each time she spoke. Astrid was about to get closer to hear what the Beldam was saying when someone spoke her name. Astrid turned to see Cinzia walking quickly towards her.

"He's gone," she said.

Astrid didn't have to ask what Cinzia meant. She'd feared this would be Knot's reaction, but had hoped he would at least have the sense to recover from a concussion before he skipped town.

"When did you see him last?" Astrid asked.

"Early this morning, sleeping in his room. Both Jane and I checked on him."

"Then he can't have been gone long," Astrid said. It was still a couple hours before noon. That was good. He couldn't have gotten far.

Astrid sighed. "I suppose you want me to go after him?"

Cinzia looked surprised. "We supposed you would want to," she said.

Astrid rolled her eyes. That's one thing Knot had over these women; he understood Astrid's sense of humor. Astrid glanced back at the Beldam. She would have to wait.

"I'll find him," Astrid said, hoping she was right.

Astrid knew Knot wouldn't have taken the road to Tinska. Too obvious; too many people might have seen him leave, might have wondered where the Healed One was off to. No, Knot still had Lathe's instincts. Just as Lathe had intended last night, Knot would have struck out in an easterly direction, straight through the forest.

The good thing about tracking someone through a wooded area was the plethora of potential signs one could leave. Finding the first sign was the difficult part. Forests were big. But all Astrid had to do was cross paths with Knot once, and she'd be on his trail.

Fortunately, it did not take long. Astrid came across some light bruising among the vegetation, and knew where to go from there.

For whatever reason, Knot had chosen not to cover his tracks. Astrid came across a variety of heel impressions in the leaves and dirt, broken twigs, and grass trails through clearings that clearly indicated where he was heading. Knot's instincts were better than that. Astrid couldn't think why he wasn't using them.

Then again, she had given him a significant head wound.

"What d'you think you're doing?"

"You circled around," she said, turning to face him.

Knot shrugged, sheathing the sword that had been raised towards Astrid. "Figured you'd follow me. Didn't seem to make sense to go to all the work of covering my tracks."

"You wanted me to find you," Astrid said. The thought made her hopeful, for some ridiculous reason.

Knot shrugged again. "I knew you'd catch me," he said. "That ain't the same thing."

Astrid rolled her eyes. Hope was such a stupid thing. "Come on, nomad. Back to the estate we go. You're in no condition to be traipsing through the forest."

"Ain't going back."

Astrid folded her arms. "That so? Your explanation had better be bloody impressive. Otherwise you're coming back, whether you like it or not."

Knot frowned at her.

"Don't make me give you another concussion."

Knot threw up his hands in frustration. "I'm putting them all at risk!"

Astrid said nothing. Best to let him get it out.

"I'm a danger to them all," Knot said. "To Jane, to Cinzia, to their family. I could snap at any moment, and who knows what Lathe will do the next time he finds his way out. Or someone worse." Knot stepped towards Astrid. "I'm a danger to you, now, too. Lathe might remember you, next time he wakes. If he does, he won't hesitate. And if you think it's me and not him..."

"I've already told you," Astrid said, "killing me isn't easy. You don't even know how to do it."

"Maybe," Knot said. "Doesn't mean that Lathe won't know."

Astrid considered that for a moment. The Nazaniin assassin Kali had known her way around killing vampires. Stood to reason that Lathe would, too, given they worked for the same organization. Astrid wasn't aware of any local stashes of nightsbane, thank the goddess, but even so. There were other ways to kill a vampire.

"So this is like Pranna all over again," Astrid said. "You're running away from your problems, and from the only people on this bloody Sfaera that care about you."

Knot was glaring at her, now. Good.

"Do you honestly still think you were right, leaving Pranna the way you did? You think Winter wouldn't have wanted to see you, after what happened on your wedding night?"

"I got her father killed," Knot said. "She wouldn't have wanted to see me."

"She did, though. She followed you, left her home for you. What does that tell you, nomad?"

No response this time. Idiot. Why wouldn't he just talk to her?

"Go ahead. Get angry. Tell me I can't talk about Winter. I know that's what you're thinking. You're running away because you don't want to lose the people you care about."

"You're right." Knot said it quietly.

"For someone who's always trying to do what's best for the people around him, you're damn selfish. You know as well as I do that Jane and Cinzia are targets. We know what kind of shit those people flocking to them are going to go through. We know, Knot. And you can help them. So just *stay*, all right? Stay."

Knot cleared his throat. "I already said it. You're right."

Astrid's eyes widened. "You did already say it, didn't you?" She laughed, relieved.

"You think she would have wanted to see me, after what happened in Pranna?"

Astrid blinked. Of course he was referring to Winter, but… what did Astrid really know about that? Only what they'd told her. "I wasn't there, nomad. I can't tell you what she was thinking. But if it were me, it's what I'd have wanted." *It's what I want now,* she wanted to add. "Come on," she said. "Let's get back. Before you have another bloody episode."

She started towards the Harmoth estate, but Knot did not follow. Astrid sighed, turning back to face him. "What?"

"I said you're right. Never said I'd go back with you."

Astrid felt a rush of anger course through her. "Don't be an idiot," she said. "What in Oblivion are you going to do?"

"I have to learn more about the sifts inside of me," Knot said. "I have to make them stop."

"And you think you can do that on your own?"

"I've got to try. I know you say this is like Pranna, but… I know what's wrong with me this time, and I'm going to face it."

Astrid needed to be careful. If she wasn't her head might explode with frustration. Although it would serve Knot right for being so *stupid*.

"What're you going to do when you have an episode on your own, out there?" Astrid asked. "Jane won't be around to help you."

Knot shrugged. "Don't know," he said. "But Jane already told me she can't heal me forever. I'll be just as helpless with them as I am out on my own, eventually."

Stubborn idiot. At least Jane would be around, at least she could *try*. "Where in Oblivion are you going?"

Knot chuckled. "Can't tell you that," he said. "Then you might come with me. Someone needs to stay in Tinska to protect Cinzia and Jane, like you said."

"What if I went?" Astrid said, an idea forming. "What if I searched for whatever it is you're looking for."

"I can't make you do that—"

"You're not making me," Astrid said quickly, "I'd be doing it *for* you. In the meantime, you could stay in Tinska. Recover a bit. Jane could heal you, should an episode happen again. It's far safer this way."

Knot hesitated, which was good. He was considering it. "What if Lathe breaks through again?" he asked. "You were the only one that could stop me before."

"I don't know," Astrid said, irritated. She hadn't thought this all the way through. "We can post guards on you at all times. Something like that. Make sure Jane is always at hand to heal you, should you need it."

"Jane has more important things to do than babysit me."

"Of course she does. I never said my plan was perfect, but it's still a whole lot smarter than yours."

"How would you know what to do, when you get to where I'm going?" Knot asked.

Astrid laughed. "What do *you* plan on doing?" she asked.

Knot was silent. Astrid smiled. She had him there.

"If you can improvise, I can, too," she said. "And… we may not be completely out of contact while I'm gone."

"What are you talking about?"

"There were voidstones in the pack you picked up in Tir." Astrid remembered seeing the small stones, roughly the size of a human thumb, polished and covered in runic marks. She recognized them easily; she had one of her own.

"What are you talking about?" Knot asked.

Astrid sighed. "Voidstones. You have some. They're a method of communicating through the Void, for those who can access it. You can access it, Knot. You're a psimancer."

"Not anymore. We've been over this."

"Ask Lathe," Astrid said. "He used telesis against me. *You* used telesis against me, while you were Lathe."

"He could access his *tendra*?"

"Sure could. They weren't full strength, though. Don't get your hopes up, about taking over the world with your *tendra*, because that won't be happening anytime soon. But he could use them. He could access the Void. That much was clear. If you imprint yourself on one of your voidstones, you can use it to communicate with me through the Void. I can report to you what I find. You can tell me what you think I should do. It's a far better idea than whatever you've dreamed up."

"You said these stones allow two people with access to the Void to communicate. You, then, have access to the Void?"

"Not the way a psimancer does, not that kind of willful connection. Mine is more… subconscious. Some would say I'm a creature of the Void."

After a moment Knot took a deep breath. "What if I can't imprint myself on one of these… stones…?"

"I'll help you. We'll go back together, now, and I'll make sure it happens. Then I'll leave. I'll go wherever you want me to go, Knot." Astrid cocked her head to the side. "By the way… where *do* you want me to go?"

"Turandel. It's a small city south of here, on the coast."

Astrid almost choked on her own spit. *Bloody Turandel? Of*

all places in all the bloody Sfaera, it has to be there?

"Sounds delightful," she said, smiling. "Why Turandel?"

"It's where Elessa is from."

Astrid blinked. "And?" What did Elessa have to do with anything?

"I wasn't entirely honest before. I do remember some of that last episode. I know that if I want to learn more about the sifts, about myself, then there are answers in Turandel. You go there, and I'll tell you what to look for, starting with House Storonam. Elessa's family."

Storonam. She hadn't known that was Elessa's family. Astrid had not heard that name in many years.

Knot sighed. "You're sure you want to do this? It could be dangerous."

"It's me, nomad. You can find danger in my afternoon shit."

Knot raised an eyebrow. "I didn't know your kind did that."

Astrid laughed.

The next day, Astrid found herself almost in that exact same spot in the forest. This time, however, she was alone. Knot had agreed to her plan; she would travel to Turandel to investigate House Storonam, while Knot stayed in Tinska where he could rest, heal, and protect Cinzia and Jane should any danger befall them.

Astrid felt a faint tugging on her mind, both a physical and a mental sensation, as if there were something attached to her brain, gently pulling at it. Astrid sighed, reaching into one of the sealed pockets of her cloak and pulling the voidstone out. Physical contact with the stone was necessary to make the connection.

Astrid placed her thumb on the dark, crimson-colored rune on the stone, and allowed her mind to enter the Void.

"What do you want now?" she asked. Why Knot could

possibly want to voke her three times in one morning was beyond her. Likely he was just excited that it was possible at all—or that he could access his *tendra* in the first place.

There was a pause at the other end, which was strange. There was no reason Knot would pause. After all, he—

This wasn't Knot.

"Hello, child."

Astrid swallowed, hard. "Hello, Mother."

Again, silence at the other end. The Black Matron would want an explanation of Astrid's impertinence when she answered the voke signal. Well, Astrid wouldn't give it to her. Not unless she expressly asked for it, anyway.

"It has been some time since your last contact," the Black Matron said after a few moments. Astrid did not know the Black Matron's real name; she had never even seen the woman. She only knew she must obey her.

"I know," Astrid said. She waited as long as she could between contacts with the Black Matron. The last time had been about a week before they arrived in Tinska. She wanted to relay as little information as possible. "I apologize," Astrid said. "There is not much to report."

"You are still traveling?"

Astrid cleared her throat. "No," she said. "No, we are near Tinska. We've met with the Oden family, and have chosen to stay at their estate."

"When did you arrive?"

Shit. Astrid could lie, say they arrived yesterday. But the Black Matron might already have contacts in the area; she might already know. It was impossible to read this woman. "A few days ago," Astrid said. Nine days, to be exact. "I know I should have contacted you earlier, but… but things have been a bit strange, here."

"Explain, child."

Astrid sighed. She hated the Black Matron, she hated the Denomination, she hated her obligation towards them both. But she had no way out of it. And she needed to give them something.

"People have begun to gather here," Astrid said. "Humans and tiellans."

"Gathered for what, exactly?"

"I'm not sure," Astrid lied, "but I think they're here for Jane. They think she is some kind of… prophetess."

There was a pause before the Black Matron spoke again. "And what does Miss Oden do with these followers?"

"They're calling themselves Odenites. And I don't think Jane knows *what* to do with them." Another lie. But she had to have something to tell her next time, especially if she hadn't yet returned to Tinska.

"How many have gathered?"

"Over one hundred," Astrid said. That, at least, was accurate. Or it had been, yesterday morning. People were flowing in almost every day, now.

"Could be worse, then. You will keep me informed on this topic, my child."

"Of course, Mother."

There was another pause. Astrid continued walking as they spoke; there was no need to stop when communicating this way. Some psimancers, she knew—acumens, like Kali—could communicate in more elaborate ways. They could see one another, even see through another's eyes a thousand miles away. Things were much simpler for Astrid. She could hear the person's voice from the other end; she could speak, and be heard. That was about it.

Astrid knew the Black Matron was waiting for her to

mention Knot—or Lathe, as the Black Matron called him. That was her duty, after all, her main reason for being here in the first place.

"What of Lathe?"

"You mean Knot," Astrid said. It was true, after all. Lathe as the Black Matron knew him had ceased to exist.

"Yes, so you keep telling me," the Black Matron muttered. "Have you discovered what sift is prominent yet? There must be one in charge of Lathe's body."

"No," Astrid said, feeling frustrated. The Black Matron had asked this question before. Astrid had tried to explain it to her. "He is none of these sifts… and all of them. As if a new person were created in Roden. He has his own personality, his own way of doing things. He remembers bits and pieces about those who make up his conglomerate sift, but nothing specific."

"Look into this further, child. Discover who this Knot really is. He says he has no memory of himself, of his life, up until a year ago?"

"A little more than a year, yes," Astrid said.

"Very well, child. Continue as you are. I'd appreciate your contacting me next time, though. Reaching out to you grows tedious. You're the one working for your own redemption, are you not?"

"Yes, Mother," Astrid said.

"Very well then. Until next time. Canta guide you."

Astrid let out a long breath. She hated speaking with that woman. She hated it even more since she had actually come to care for Knot. The Black Matron had informed her that she must follow this man—the man she had thought was Lathe Tallon—and learn about him. Easiest way to do that had been to join the man on his journey. The Black Matron hadn't been pleased, but even she had to admit the plan had worked out well. Perhaps too well.

Astrid knew one thing. As much as she liked Knot, there was something more important. Something that haunted Astrid, and wouldn't stop haunting her until her debt was paid, and she had found redemption.

18

CINZIA WATCHED AS JANE threw a pebble into the ocean. It sailed forward, skipping eight or nine times until it finally sank into the waves. The ocean was calm today, the swells gentle and rolling.

It was mid-morning, and the sky was gray, the sun only a bright patch in the east. The beach was wet; it had rained during the night. It was not cold, thank the Goddess, but neither was it warm. Cinzia had a shawl wrapped around her shoulders, but still shivered. She had not exactly dressed for this occasion, through no fault of her own; Jane had not told her where they would be going. "Out for a walk," was all she had said. Jane's pretentious vagueness was starting to grate on Cinzia. She didn't know how much more of it she could take.

"When did you learn to do that?" Cinzia asked. She and Jane used to try to skip stones when they were children. The rocks they threw always sank without a single bounce.

"I don't know," Jane said beside her. "A few years ago. Father taught me."

Cinzia felt a sudden, unexpected weight of jealousy settle within her chest. She had made the choice to go to the seminary. Jealousy shouldn't be a feeling she concerned herself with. And yet, the thought of Jane spending the past eight years with their father and mother, with their siblings, made Cinzia jealous.

"Cinzia, I'd like you to be my first disciple."

Cinzia looked back to the ocean. Somehow she had known this was coming. It was the next logical step in reviving Canta's religion.

"Is that why you asked me out here?" Cinzia asked, surprised at her own calm.

"You have to see the divine coincidence. You're named after one of Canta's Disciples. You were a priestess in the Cantic Denomination. Who better to be the first disciple?"

"I still *am* a priestess," Cinzia corrected her.

It was technically true; she had not yet received papers of excommunication. Of course, she would have been difficult to find in Roden. Now that the Denomination likely knew exactly where they were, Cinzia expected those papers any day.

Assuming a more severe judgment did not arrive first.

Then, Cinzia shook her head. "I don't think I can do it, Jane. I couldn't serve you faithfully."

"You wouldn't be serving me, sister, you would be serving Canta."

Cinzia relaxed a bit. She had meant her question as a test of Jane's humility. If Jane thought this was going to be some organization that she could exert her will over, Cinzia would have nothing to do with it.

"In fact, what you're saying actually tells me that you *will* serve faithfully. Skepticism, questioning, all of those things will be necessary in the coming days. I will need someone by my side who will not take every word I say as gospel."

Cinzia sighed. Damn her sister for actually making sense. "Do not play on that weakness to get me to do what you want. I will not be manipulated."

Jane nodded. "I understand. And I don't believe skepticism is a weakness. I need someone like you to keep me in line."

"That's a lot of responsibility," Cinzia said.

"It will be shared. You will not be the only one who shoulders it, sister. Trust me."

Cinzia looked down at the smooth pebbles at her feet. She bent and picked one up, hefting it in her hand. It was a dull brown color, and about half the size of her palm, oval in shape. She threw it, and watched the stone sail through the air before plopping anticlimactically into the waves.

"And if you can't trust me, trust Canta."

"Trust is a concept I take issue with, lately," Cinzia said.

"'Those who wish to see Canta's miracles will see them,'" Jane quoted. It was a line they had translated from the Book of Baetrissa. "'Those who do not wish to see them will see only accident, happenstance, and serendipity,'" Jane continued. "'For many of Canta's miracles will be invisible to all but those who believe.'"

Cinzia rolled her eyes. "How in Canta's name did you remember that?" she asked. "We translated it months ago."

Jane shrugged, tossing a pebble up and down in her hand. "I've been rereading our papers."

"When do you have time to do that?"

"I just find the time." Jane threw another pebble into the ocean. It skipped a half-dozen times before sinking.

Cinzia picked up another pebble and threw it, but once again it plopped into the water.

"You think I can't see Canta's miracles?" Cinzia asked.

"I think, at least sometimes, you may not wish to."

Cinzia bent to pick up another stone, this one wide and flat. As she stretched her arm back to throw, Jane caught her.

"Not like that," Jane said. She stretched her arm out beside her. "Throw it side-on, so the flattest section of the pebble flies parallel to the water. Make sure you get a good spin on it—use your wrist more than your arm."

Cinzia experimented, swinging her arm back and forth at her side. Then, winding up, she let the pebble go, flicking her wrist. The pebble sailed through the air, skipped twice, and then sank into the water.

"Well done," Jane said.

Cinzia was about to look for another stone when Jane spoke. "It's me, isn't it?"

Cinzia looked up. "What do you mean?"

"If you witnessed the kind of miracles you've seen from anyone else, would it be so easy to doubt?"

Cinzia did not have to think long about the answer. "No," she said. "I don't think it would be so easy."

Jane sighed. "I knew it. I—"

"I don't think it would be so easy to doubt," Cinzia continued, "but I think I would still doubt all the same. We have our issues, but my problem with faith does not lie with you."

Cinzia realized the words as she spoke them. A part of her, this whole time, had been blaming Jane for her lack of faith. The truth was, it had always been her choice.

Perhaps, now, it was time Cinzia began to choose differently.

"If I agree to be your disciple," Cinzia said softly, "who else will shoulder the responsibility?"

"I'm considering a few," Jane said. "But I wanted to get your input on them."

"Women, I assume?" Cinzia asked. She couldn't imagine a male disciple any better than she could imagine a male priestess. Or priest, she supposed they would have to be called.

"Of course," Jane said.

"Are all the women you're considering named after one of the originals?"

"Not necessarily."

"Cinzia was not the first disciple called by Canta," Cinzia said. "Elessa had that privilege." She made the motion, stone in hand, of throwing it as Jane had shown her. The movement felt unnatural to her.

"What does that matter?" Jane asked. "We are following in history's footsteps, Cinzia. We're not duplicating it."

"But shouldn't we duplicate all we can? Make it as close to Canta's original institution as possible?"

"Organizationally speaking, yes," Jane said. "Looseness in that area is one of the many reasons I think the Denomination has wandered so far from what it once was. But otherwise... I think we just need to do what we think is right. I think that will be enough."

"Enough," Cinzia repeated. A low bar to clear.

"Would you like to hear who I've been considering?" Jane asked.

"Good a time as any." Cinzia sat on the ground and began removing her shoes.

"I've thought about Mother, for one. She has always been a devoted Cantic, even if she was one of the last people in the family to believe me. Er... Cinzia, what are you doing?"

Cinzia had removed her shoes and stockings, and now sat on the beach, barefoot.

"I think I'm going to get my feet wet," Cinzia said. "And I don't think Mother would be a terrible choice. She *is* devoted. And unreasonably proud of you."

Jane sat next to Cinzia and began removing her own shoes. "But?"

Cinzia shrugged. She let her feet rest on the pebbles, felt the stony smoothness in contrast to the sand. She felt like a child again. "I don't know. Something about it doesn't feel quite right."

"No," Jane said, removing her socks now. "It doesn't, does it?"

"Who else?" Cinzia asked. She stood, her bare feet sinking into the beach.

"The triplets, of course, but they are very young."

"Too young. Perhaps one day, but… we are not forming the Church of Oden, Jane. This is the Church of Canta—or so you keep telling me."

"You see?" Jane said, stepping up beside her. "This is exactly why I need you." Then she giggled.

"What?" Cinzia asked.

"It's just been a long time since I've done this. Barefoot, on the beach."

Cinzia smiled. "Me too."

"That woman, from the camp on our estate. Elessa. She has come to mind."

Yes, Cinzia thought, although she couldn't tell whether she was reacting to Jane's statement or to how good she felt walking towards the water. The pebbles had given way to smooth sand now, cold but comfortable on the soles of her feet.

"The woman Knot attacked?" Cinzia asked.

"Yes," Jane said, walking beside Cinzia. They were approaching a line of darker sand, thoroughly wet from the water's constant massage.

"What do you know about her?"

"I know she's become something of a leader. She was one of those opposing the Beldam. People look up to Elessa."

Cinzia hesitated, momentarily distracted by Jane's mention of the Beldam. They had not yet invited the woman to share what she knew, and to speak more about what they could do against the Daemons. Cinzia feared that the longer they waited, the more dire the consequences might be.

She stopped just before they reached the tideline. "I don't know Elessa well, but the idea of her as a Disciple does not bother me."

"Yes," Jane said, standing next to Cinzia. "I feel the same way."

Jane looked at Cinzia with a nervous smile. "The water will be cold," she said.

Cinzia smiled back, and reached for her sister's hand. "I know."

Then, gripping their skirts, they stepped forward together.

THEY HAD SENT FOR Elessa more than an hour ago, but she had not yet come. Cinzia was sure the woman was wary of Knot—after what Lathe had done to her, in Knot's body, Cinzia couldn't blame her.

"If she doesn't come," Jane said, "then we have our answer."

Cinzia pursed her lips. She sat sideways in one of the large, overstuffed library chairs, her feet dangling over one armrest and her back resting against the other. Jane stood near the desk in the corner, shuffling through papers. Their translation of the Codex.

Just then, a brief, sharp knock echoed in the library. Cinzia sat up immediately, smoothing her skirts. It wouldn't do to look juvenile when the subject matter they were to be discussing was so significant.

"Enter, please," Jane called out.

The door opened, and Elessa walked into the library, her back straight, head high. She wore a light silk scarf around her neck, and Cinzia knew exactly what hid underneath. She had seen the angry violet bruise starting to form only moments after Elessa had been attacked.

"You asked to see me?"

Cinzia stood, unsure of what she should be doing. Was standing appropriate? Or should she have remained seated? She did not want to intimidate Elessa, but wanted to offer respect, too. One would have thought her training at the Cantic seminary would have come in handy in moments like this, but Cinzia's mind was blank.

"Yes, Elessa," Jane said, smiling and walking towards the woman. "We are glad you came. Please, sit down. Make yourself comfortable."

Elessa's eyes flickered from Jane to Cinzia, and then she moved to the armchair across from where Cinzia had been lounging. She sat down on the edge of the chair, back still straight, hands folded in her lap.

Cinzia smiled at Elessa, but the woman did not smile back. Cinzia sat back down. Jane glided over to the desk where she retrieved the matching wooden chair, and brought it over, so the three of them now sat in a triangle.

"How are you, Elessa?" Jane asked.

"As well as can be expected," Elessa said, eyeing Jane warily.

Jane reached out, placing her hand on Elessa's knee. "Again, we are so sorry about what happened."

"Is that what this is about?" Elessa asked. She stared at the hand on her knee, until Jane took it away. "Are you going to tell me what happened to Knot? One moment he was himself, and the next he was looking at me as if he had never seen me before in his life. No one has told me what that was about yet, despite my asking."

Cinzia exchanged a glance with Jane. This was not what they intended to speak with Elessa about, but they couldn't very well leave this woman hanging.

"Knot did not attack you," Cinzia said. "Or, at least, not the Knot you know. Knot is different from us, Elessa. For lack of a better description, he… he has different identities, floating around in his head. Sometimes one of these identities takes over, and he has no control over them when that happens."

"So… you're saying Knot is insane?" Elessa asked.

Jane began to speak, but Cinzia interrupted her. "Not exactly," she said. "Normally he is very sane, but he was not in control when he… when his body attacked you. It was someone else. That does not excuse what he has done, or what happened to you. We are terribly sorry for that, and if there is anything we can do to help you, or make you feel safe, we will do it. But we wanted to at least give you something of an explanation, before we tell you why you're here."

Elessa stared at Cinzia, her eyebrows knit together. Cinzia couldn't tell whether the expression was disbelief or derision. Either seemed likely.

"We can tell you more about it later," Jane said. "But please, let us talk to you about something else. You, and many others like you, have gathered here. Knot told us how you came to leave your home. I was so sorry to hear about your parents."

"It's fine," Elessa said. Cinzia couldn't read the woman's face.

"Knot tells us you've been here longer than almost anyone else, and that the reason you traveled here is… rather unusual?"

"I…" Elessa glanced at Cinzia once more, then back to Jane. "I'm not sure I can explain it. I felt I had to come here. And not just Tinska—I knew I needed to come to an estate south of the town." Elessa met Jane's eyes reluctantly. "Knot, before he attacked me, he said I should talk to you about these impressions. Why would he say that?"

And then Jane smiled. "Because I know exactly the feelings

of which you speak," Jane said excitedly. "That's how I came to be here, too. That's how all of this started."

Cinzia refrained from rolling her eyes, but she couldn't help giving a small sigh of exasperation. What, were these two going to bond over shared visions, now?

"What form did these impressions take?" Jane asked.

Elessa glanced from Cinzia to Jane once more. She seemed nervous.

"It is safe," Jane said, smiling. "You can tell us. We of all people will believe you."

Speak for yourself, Cinzia thought.

"Feelings, mostly," Elessa said, her face flushing. "There were a few moments where it almost seemed as if someone whispered in my ear."

Jane nodded. "Anything else? Visions, dreams?"

Elessa shook her head. "No, I'm sorry."

Jane's face fell. "Quite all right," she said. "It does not matter how Canta speaks to us, only that she communicates with us at all. And she does, as we both have seen."

Cinzia looked at Jane carefully. She seemed unusually disappointed by this turn of events. Had she thought there was someone else like her? Someone who actually had visions?

Cinzia was suspicious. She once thought she had experienced personal communication with Canta, only months ago. Turned out the being that had been communicating with her—*using* her—was not Canta at all, but something far more malicious. Cinzia did not know what proof there was that the same thing was not happening to Elessa.

"Have you heard my story, Elessa?" Jane asked, the disappointment on her face fading. Elessa shook her head. "Then it's about time you did. I was discontented with the Cantic

Denomination, and decided to ask Canta Herself what I should do if I believed the Denomination to be incorrect. There is precedent for communicating with Canta, as Nazira's writings explain. But the Denomination interprets that scripture to mean that Canta only speaks to her chosen servants; for anyone else to attempt such communication is blasphemy. I knew this, but felt it was the right thing to do."

The first time Cinzia had heard Jane tell her story, she had not been able to listen past the point where Jane described herself—a woman outside the priesthood—praying. It had been too disturbing.

"What happened when you prayed?" Elessa asked, her face still eager. "Did you receive impressions, promptings, just as I did?"

Jane took a deep breath. "Not exactly. What I experienced was more… it was something more tangible." Jane glanced at Cinzia. "But before I experienced Canta's communication, there was something else."

Something else? Jane had never told Cinzia of anything else that had happened during that first communication. Jane had prayed, and then Canta had appeared to her, had spoken directly to her.

"I knelt there, on Mount Madise, and prayed. But before I received an answer, something… something attacked me."

Cinzia's eyebrows shot up. This was *definitely* not anything she had heard before.

"Goddess rising," Elessa whispered. "What was it? Was it… was it Canta?"

"No," Jane said. "The force that attacked me was something else entirely. Do you know of the legend of the Nine Daemons, Elessa?"

"I thought it was just a bedtime story, until I heard the Beldam talking about them."

"It is no bedtime story," Jane said. "The Daemons are real. They have broken through into the Sfaera, after thousands of years of banishment."

"I… I don't understand."

"I know," Jane said. "All of this will take time, but that is one thing you must know immediately. We are not only being called and gathered to reform Canta's religion. We are being called and gathered to save the world from the greatest threat we have ever faced."

Cinzia stared at her sister with narrowed eyes. Was that what this was about? Was Jane making up a portion of her story to motivate others into action? The threat of the Nine Daemons was real; both she and Jane knew that well enough. But Cinzia was not sure they needed to lie to emphasize that threat.

"How do you know? How do you know it was the Nine Daemons?" Elessa asked.

"It was not all of them," Jane whispered. "Just one. Just the most powerful. You know him as the Fear Lord, but his name is Azael."

Cinzia squirmed at the name. She remembered Kovac's eyes, smoking in the dim light. It was strange; the sun was still up, in fact she could see the brightness through one of the library windows. The mere mention of the Fear Lord's name did not make this space any darker. But somehow Cinzia thought that it should, that the lamps should grow dimmer, that an eclipse should cover the sun at such a sound.

"How did you escape?" Elessa asked.

"His power stems from many things, but as his title suggests, he is first and foremost concerned with the fear of other beings. His attack was exactly that: Azael showed me the great horrors of my heart, those things I most fear more than any other. He showed them to me as if they were happening, as if I were living through them over and over again."

Jane was shaking. Cinzia stood and retrieved a blanket from one of the unoccupied chairs, then draped it around Jane's shoulders. A part of Cinzia was appalled that her sister would go to such lengths to tell a lie, when a truth would do just as well. What had happened in Izet was just as horrible as what Jane described now, or at least it had seemed so to Cinzia. And yet there was another part of her that wondered. Had Jane truly experienced this? If so, why had she not spoken of it before?

"Thank you," Jane whispered. "The darkness, the fear, seemed eternal. I thought that was my life; in the moment it seemed all I had ever known. The fear and the awful eternity of it all. But then, in the midst of the greatest darkness, there was a ray of light."

"Canta," Elessa whispered.

Cinzia pursed her lips. Why would Jane not get to the point, to why they had called Elessa here in the first place?

Jane nodded. "She appeared to me, Elessa."

"You mean you felt Her impressions, Her presence, as I have?" Elessa asked.

"No," Jane said, "for me, it was more than that. I *saw* Canta. She appeared to me, spoke to me. She said that the Denomination had indeed strayed from the truth, that while there were good people in the Denomination who sought to do well, there were also many others who did not. Canta instructed me, and informed me that I would be Her servant, to bring about Her will on the Sfaera once again, as Her Disciples of old had done. And that's why we called you here, Elessa. Because we have a duty for you, just as Canta has a duty for me."

"Me?" Elessa asked.

"Yes," Jane said. She had stopped shaking now, and sat tall, her back straight.

"What could you possibly want with me?" Elessa asked.

"Canta called Nine Disciples when She walked the Sfaera," Jane said. "Part of Canta's will for me is that I re-establish that order."

Cinzia watched Elessa's face carefully as Jane spoke her next words.

"You are to be one of Canta's nine disciples," Jane said. "You've been called to serve the Goddess."

Elessa blinked. She did not seem to have processed what Jane had said.

"You mean… you mean I am to serve as a priestess?" Elessa asked, proving that she, indeed, did not understand. In thc Denomination's hierarchy, the office of disciple was the very lowest calling. It made sense that Elessa would be confused.

"No," Jane said. "Forget what you know about the disciples in the Denomination. Remember the stories of Canta's original Nine Disciples. That is what you will be, Elessa. We are calling you to help form, found, and lead Canta's religion on the Sfaera."

Elessa stared at Jane, still expressionless. "You mean… why me?"

Jane gave a soft laugh. "I know this is confusing, and I know that you will probably not fully realize what this means at first. But Canta desires your help. You will do great things, great works on the Sfaera. You are one of Canta's children, and you've a role to play, as we all do."

"Do you accept this position, Elessa?" Cinzia asked. She knew the woman was overwhelmed, but they needed an answer.

The blank stare on Elessa's face finally gave way to a broken smile. "I… yes. Yes, I do accept," she said.

"Wonderful!" Jane moved towards Elessa, wrapping her arms around the woman, nearly knocking her off the chair.

Cinzia smiled, and realized she genuinely meant it. It would be good to have another voice among them. "Welcome to the fold, Elessa," Cinzia said.

When Jane finally released her, Elessa stood, and then it was Cinzia's turn to nearly be knocked over by an embrace.

"Thank you," Elessa whispered.

Cinzia patted the young woman's back, unsure of how to respond. But Elessa's gratitude felt good.

"Well, we have much to do, don't we?" Jane said. "I suppose we must begin at the beginning. In order to form Canta's religion, we need Her power. And as far as I know, only one of us currently holds that." She looked at Cinzia.

"What are you talking about?" Cinzia asked.

"You're a priestess in the Cantic Denomination, sister. You hold Canta's power within you; whether it was given to you through corrupted means matters not. You hold it, and you must now share it."

"*You* were a priestess?" Elessa asked, her eyes wide.

"I *am* a priestess." Cinzia resented the surprised way Elessa had said it. "Jane," Cinzia said through clenched teeth, "you never told me about this."

"I know, and I'm sorry," she said. "There is so much to keep track of, I… I forget things, sometimes."

"I can't just ordain you both to the priesthood," Cinzia said.

"Why not?" Elessa asked.

Cinzia stared at the young woman, about to give a dozen reasons why not. But, as Cinzia thought it over, the question sank in. There were reasons Cinzia *should* not, of course. A dozen reasons and more. But as for reasons why she *could* not…

"I will think this over," Cinzia said. "I can't betray everything I stand for so easily."

"Of course, sister," Jane said. "Take all the time you need. We have much to do, besides."

Cinzia's mind wandered out as her sister began explaining exactly what they would be doing. She was far too preoccupied. No matter how hard she tried to tread the surface, she was constantly being pulled deeper and deeper into all of this. She only hoped she wouldn't drown.

19

KNOT SLEPT FITFULLY. HE wished he could blame it on his injured head, but he'd had trouble sleeping ever since Izet. He opened his eyes and took a deep breath—a breath that immediately caught in his throat when he noticed the faint orange glow shimmering at the corner of his vision.

Fire.

Knot leapt out of bed and rushed to the window just as a panicked knock rattled his door. Outside, he saw a section of Odenite tents burning brightly against the night. It was the same area of the grounds that Cavil, Ocrestia, and the largest group of tiellans in the camp occupied. Knot cursed.

"Knot, we need you!"

He recognized the voice as Eward's, and the lad burst into the room just as Knot grabbed his blackbark staff and dagger.

"What do you know?" Knot demanded.

"Nothing, just that some tents in the tiellan section have caught fire."

"Ain't coincidence. Let's go." *Before it's too late.*

They ran down the stairs and out of the front doors. Wind whipped at Knot's clothing as he rushed across the grounds toward the flames. Knot found himself wishing he hadn't sent that damn vampire away after all. He'd have given his right hand to have Astrid by his side.

"There," Knot said, pointing at a group of Odenites gathered at a distance from the flames. As he drew closer, he realized they were all humans.

"Canta's bones," he growled. Then he raised his voice, shouting to get the attention of the group. "Where are the tiellans?"

Some of the humans looked at one another. Knot recognized Dannel, staring intently at the ground. Knot checked himself, taking a deep breath. Losing his temper wouldn't help.

Before any of the humans could answer, Knot heard a scream. He turned back to the flames, squinting, and could just make out a few forms running between the burning tents.

Some of the tiellans were still in that inferno.

"Goddess, why aren't any of you helping them?" Eward was demanding as Knot ran towards the scream. The fire had engulfed roughly a dozen tents, and spread to the branches of the large ash tree around which the tiellans had camped. A tiellan woman ran right into him, almost knocking him over. Knot stumbled back, but managed to catch the woman by the arm.

The woman cringed. "Don't hurt me! Please!"

Knot released her arm, not wanting to frighten her further. "Who did this?" But the woman ran off.

Her response confirmed Knot's fears. This was not an accident. It was an attack. Whether by other humans in the camp or Kamites from Tinska, Knot couldn't be sure, but it had to be one of the two. Knot rushed into the haze, coughing through the smoke. Two more tiellans ran towards him, but the moment they saw him they changed course.

Ahead of him, Knot saw someone lying in the grass. Turning the body over, he saw a tiellan man, eyes wide, face pale. Dead. Not from the flames, either—his abdomen was torn to pieces. Someone had taken an axe to him.

Knot heard a laugh. It was close, and getting closer. Following instinct, he darted between a pair of smoldering tents and swung hard with his blackbark staff at an oncoming figure.

The laugh caught in the man's throat, and he fell to the ground. Knot yanked him up roughly by the collar, and came face to face with the axe-wielding man with the Kamite tattoo who'd been the ringleader of Ocrestia's abusers.

The man's eyes widened when he recognized Knot. "Oh shi—"

Knot head-butted him. The man's head snapped back, his nose exploding in a burst of blood, and he dropped his axe. Knot was about to toss the man to the ground when he noticed a group of tiellans on the other side of the tents. Seven men on horseback surrounded them, herding them together. Knot heard screams around him, saw figures rushing through the haze. Angry shouts. There was the horrifying smell of burning flesh.

There was no doubt. Kamites from Tinska had set fire to the tiellan tents. The smell told Knot that at least a few tiellans had perished in the flames. Amidst the chaos of the smoke and flames, a battle raged within Knot. His cold, calculating self fought against an anger he had never felt before.

Knot growled, a guttural sound beginning deep in his gut, and then threw the man he held into one of the burning tents. The man screamed as he crashed into the blaze, his cries intensifying as the flames took him.

Knot focused on a figure running between the tents a row over. He snuck between another gap in time to grab the figure—a tiellan, he realized by the size and weight of the man—by the arm. The man shouted. It was Cavil.

Knot raised a finger to his lips, and Cavil's shout faded as recognition registered in his eyes, still wide with fear. Cavil was about to speak, but Knot cupped his hand over the man's mouth. "Stay behind me," Knot said.

Cavil nodded.

Knot handed Cavil his staff, drew his dagger, and stalked quickly through the smoke. Sparks from the burning tree limbs above him floated down. Knot caught another tiellan, sobbing as she ran, and directed her behind him. Cavil would have to help the woman.

He heard a cough to his right. Knot bolted in the direction of the sound, slipping up behind a tall man carrying a club. Knot wrapped one arm around the man's head, then drew the blade of his dagger across the man's throat. The man wheezed and fell, bleeding into the grass.

Knot kcpt moving, eyes stinging, and found another human dragging a tiellan child by the arm. Knot crept beside the man, grabbing the man's wrist and twisting. The man let go of the boy. Knot twisted the man's arm farther until it snapped, then slid his dagger in and out of the man's back once, twice, three times.

Knot looked around. No other shadows moved among the tents. He could see the group of tiellans huddled between the men on horseback clearly now. Seven men. He could handle seven men, even on horseback.

Knot turned back to Cavil and took his staff. "Get them to safety," he said, nodding towards the woman and boy.

He sprinted towards the nearest rider. The man's horse pranced away as he approached, but Knot caught up in time to swing his staff at the man's skull, knocking him to the ground. The riderless horse galloped away, and Knot lunged at the next rider, grabbing him by the belt and heaving him to the ground with a crunch.

The other men spurred their horses towards him. Knot threw his dagger into the nearest man's neck. He immediately fell from his saddle.

Between the fire and Knot's violent outburst, the remaining horses spooked. One reared up, throwing its rider. Another horse sprinted in the opposite direction, taking its rider with it. The other two men dismounted before their horses did the same. That left three men on the ground, each advancing slowly on Knot, a pitchfork and two axes between them.

Knot's lungs burned from smoke and exertion, but he didn't care. It could have been Winter these men attacked. It could have been Bahc, or Gord, or Lian, any of the people Knot had grown to love in Pranna. Men, women, children – these men did not seem to care when it came to tiellan life. He wouldn't forgive that.

Knot dodged an axe and swung his staff into the attacker's shins, tripping the man up, and kicked him in the face. He parried a pitchfork thrust and struck the assailant in the face, sending him stumbling backwards. The man he'd kicked tried to stand, but Knot kicked him again, just as the third attacker rushed forward with his axe. Knot stepped neatly out of the way and gripped the man's arm as he passed, twisted, and threw him into the ground.

Pitchfork Man charged again, but Knot extended his staff, thrusting it into the man's throat. He collapsed to his knees, choking, eyes rolling back into his head.

Knot drove his heel into the face of one of the men on the ground as he stirred, and then everything was still. No attackers remained. Cavil and the other two tiellans walked quickly to the group of tiellans the men had herded together.

In the distance, the giant ash tree groaned and creaked. Knot looked up, coughing, just in time to see one of the flaming branches collapse onto the burning tents below in a burst of sparks.

Hours later, dawnlight turned every cloud a shade of warm pink. Smoke mingled with fog and the mist of a new day on the estate, but no fires remained.

While Knot had been fighting, Eward had organized the human onlookers into a bucket brigade, carrying water from the pond. Fortunately the tiellan tents and the ash tree were rather isolated, and nothing else had caught fire. But only cinders remained where the tents had once stood, and the ash tree was a black skeleton.

Knot had jumped in to help as soon as he could, and only now found a moment to stop and take in the insanity of the previous night. Cavil walked up beside him.

"Thank you," he said.

Knot did not trust himself to reply. He wished he'd gotten here earlier, wished he could've somehow seen this coming.

"Your wife?" Knot grunted.

"Safe. She was in the group you saved. We owe you twice now. Thrice, I guess, if we're being accurate."

"I'm sorry for what happened," was all Knot could think to say.

"So am I," Cavil said, walking away.

Cinzia and Jane approached, still in nightdresses, faces caked in sweat and soot.

"How many dead?" Knot asked.

"Four died in the tents," Jane said. "Another two were killed by the men."

"And what are we going to do about it?" Knot asked.

"I don't know," Jane said.

"Ain't like you."

"Even if I'd foreseen it, even if I'd been prepared, I'm not sure I could have changed it. Or that I'd know what to do now."

"The tiellans have no homes. They'll need shelter."

Jane nodded. "That, at least, has already been seen to. As many as possible will stay in the house until we can find other accommodation for them."Now, more than ever, we need to band together. We will need the structure of Canta's Church to face what lies ahead."

"Think we'll need more than that," Knot said quietly.

20

Dungeons of the imperial palace, Izet, Roden

Winter stared at the ceiling of her cell, clutching the frost crystal. They had continued to give her the drug. Not often, but every few days, as far as Winter could tell. Unsure of whether there would be more, she had not been able to help ingesting the drug immediately the first few times it had appeared. But the last time she'd saved it, hoping that if she took it at a different time of day, the powers that blocked her would be gone.

Her hope had been misplaced.

Now she clutched another crystal, saving it less because she thought the same tactic would work, but because she savored holding it almost more than the idea of swallowing it. The moment she ingested it, it would be gone. But if she saved it, she at least had something to look forward to.

Three knocks sounded at her cell door. Immediately Winter released her mind, searching for who it might be. She sensed her gaoler, stoic and simple-minded. The other presence was...

A black skull, wreathed in dark flame, flashed in her mind.

Daval.

Winter knew him only by his absence. Once her father had shown her what he called an eclipse. The event had been horrifying. He and Winter had stood atop a hill near Pranna on a summer's day, looking up at a rare clear blue midday sky, when something impossible happened. A massive shadow raced across the plains toward them.It was many times the size of a mountain, and swept over the land faster than anything Winter could imagine.

Winter's first instinct had been to run, but her father put his hand on her shoulder, gently.

"You're safe," he had told her. "Wait, and watch."

It had taken every ounce of strength Winter had as she waited, nestled beneath her father's arm. The shadow had approached quickly, and Winter kept looking up at the sky expecting to see a massive dragon sailing through the air. The legendary creatures from the Age of Marvels were the only things she could imagine that could cause so great a shadow.

Then, not accompanied by a rushing sound as Winter had expected but rather by a stark, deafening silence, the darkness reached them, engulfed them.

"Look up," her father had whispered.

The sun was gone. In its place was a horrible black circle surrounded by a burning ring of white flame. Winter gripped her father's hand tightly.

"What does it mean?" she had asked.

"I'm not sure it means anything. Only that more time has passed."

Winter remembered that empty black circle, and the burning ring around it. The sun had been absent, and yet she knew it was there, it had been impossible to hide. The same was true of Daval. His mind was only blackness to her, but the workings of it were too bright to ignore. She couldn't see his mind, but she could see the burning ring around it.

"Bring her out to me."

The gaoler stepped into Winter's cell. "Up with you," he said, kicking at Winter's legs.

Winter stood, slowly, and walked out of her cell and into the brighter light of the corridor. Sure enough, Daval stood there waiting for her.

"My dear," he said, smiling at her. He spread his arms wide.

Winter blinked in the light. It took her a few moments to realize that Daval expected an embrace. Apparently it took Daval longer to realize that she wouldn't give him one.

He lowered his hands, his smile fading somewhat. "You should be happy to see me," Daval said. "I bring good tidings."

Winter said nothing.

"You know who I am, I assume?" he asked. When Winter did not respond, he continued with a shrug. "Whether you do or not does not matter. I know who you are, and I know that we require your services. We will pay you, of course. We can give you money, gold. New clothes. We would move you from this horrible accommodation."

Winter scoffed. "Help you? Why would I ever help you?" This man had to be mad if he thought she would—

"And we can pay you in *faltira*," Daval added. "As pure as it comes. As much frost as you could possibly want."

Faltira.

"What do you want me to do?" Winter asked, incredibly ashamed that she would ask the question, but overpowered by the idea that she could have unlimited frost.

Daval smiled. "I hope to soon receive a new title."

Winter knew exactly what he was referring to; thoughts of the succession were in everyone's head in the empire. Daval's mind might be hidden from her, but thoughts about him certainly were not. He was one of the top contenders for the imperial throne.

"But my power is still fragile. There are those who would

seek to stop me, and others who would seek to take it from me, once I get it. I can't have that happen."

"What do you expect me to do?"

"You, my dear, can cause others to fear me. That is what I need now, more than anything."

Her telesis, then. That was what Daval was after.

"What is to stop me from using my power against you?" Winter asked. And she certainly would. If she could get her hands on frost and not be blocked by one of those Ceno idiots, she would turn this entire city to ash and dust.

"I never said you would use your powers," Daval said. "I only need you."

Winter frowned.

"I see you don't understand, and I apologize. I have not been clear. Your powers, of course, are too dangerous to allow you access to them. But your presence would be more than enough. Rumors have spread of who you are, what you've done. Very strategic rumors."

"You spread them yourself."

"Well, not *myself*, no. I don't gossip. I pay people to do that for me."

"You want me at your side, to threaten those who threaten you."

"That's the gist of it, yes."

Winter wondered, for a moment, what it would be like to attack this man. To tackle him to the ground, claw at him, kick him, tear into his neck with her teeth, hurt him in whatever way she could. He deserved it. *She* deserved it.

Only the bright ring of fire stopped her.

And if she wouldn't kill him, not yet, then she had nothing to lose by taking his deal. Everything to gain. More freedom only meant more opportunities for those guarding her to slip, to allow her the room she needed. "Very well. Show me this new place, where you'll allow me to live. Show me the gold. Show me the frost. And I'll help you."

Daval's smile broadened. "Wonderful. I knew we would see eye to eye." He nodded at the gaoler. "You're relieved of your duties here. Take the day off."

The gaoler grinned, bowing. "Thank you, my Lord," he said, and walked briskly away down the corridor.

Winter was about to follow after the gaoler, but Daval stopped her. "One more thing I must tell you." He placed his hands on her shoulders. He was short for a Rodenese man, but he was still almost a head taller than Winter. "I love you, Winter."

Winter stared blankly at him. She had learned, somewhere along the way of her imprisonment, to not react to things immediately. And so, while a part of her laughed at the ridiculousness of what Daval had just said, and another part of her cringed in disgust, Winter's face remained calm, unaffected.

"So?" she asked.

Daval smiled at her. "I just thought you should know."

He turned and walked down the corridor, and Winter followed. Near the end of the corridor, Daval's guard captain, the tall woman Urstadt, waited for them along with two Ceno monks in dark green robes.

"Now tell me," Daval said with a smile. "Do you like whiskey?"

Keep Amok, Izet

An hour later, Winter found herself in Daval's study. Winter had never seen so many books in one place; they overflowed from the packed shelves that lined the room, they were stacked in corners and on tables. Daval sat at the large desk in the center of the chamber.

Daval had dismissed the monks, but his guard captain remained. Winter stood by the doorway, Urstadt towering next to her. There were two chairs facing Daval's desk, but Urstadt, motionless, did not seem interested in sitting down.

Winter shrugged to herself. If the woman wanted to be that formal, fine. But if Daval had meant what he said—that he was going to use Winter as a tool—then she was going to damn well do as she pleased in the meantime. She walked forward and slouched into one of the chairs facing Daval.

Daval smiled, although the expression did not reach his eyes. "Of course, make yourself at home, my dear. If we are going to have the long and fruitful relationship that I anticipate, I hope we can be comfortable around one another."

"What about your guard?" Winter asked. "She going to sit down?"

"Standing suits me just fine," Urstadt said.

Daval chuckled. "Please, sit down, Urstadt," Daval said, indicating the chair next to Winter. "Have a drink with us, why don't you?"

Urstadt did as requested, with all the excitement of a soldier obeying orders. Which was to say, very little excitement at all.

Daval stood and walked toward a cabinet. He returned carrying three glasses in one hand, and a bottle of amber liquid in the other.

"I'm proud of you, Urstadt." Daval sat down at his desk once more. "What we have accomplished with House Farady, and now the betrothal, will help a great deal, I think."

"Thank you, my Lord," Urstadt said, sitting tall in her chair.

Daval sighed, pouring two fingers of whiskey for each of them.

"Are you proud of yourself?" Daval asked, sliding one glass across the desk to Urstadt. He slid the other towards Winter.

Urstadt took the glass hesitantly, but did not drink. "Am I… Sir? I don't understand."

Winter raised the glass to her lips, and gulped. Her eyes widened, and she had to stop herself from spitting the stuff all over Daval's desk. Instead, she swallowed, the liquid burning all the way down her throat. This was not the pleasant burn of frostfire, however. This was pain without the pleasure.

"I mean are you proud of what you've done?" Daval asked, apparently heedless of Winter's spluttering. "What *we* have done, I should say." He turned to Winter. "We have made an example out of House Farady—a scheme that was almost entirely Urstadt's brainchild. My daughter and Girgan Mandiat are engaged to be married, and they will soon be the most powerful couple in the empire. The succession will be decided soon. And you, Winter, have now decided to join us. We have a lot going for us, it seems."

Urstadt fidgeted. Probably something to do with the fact that Daval was talking so much. Winter could relate.

"I think we might have the two-thirds vote required to win the succession," Daval said, musing to himself. "Between the eight minor houses we control, the eleven houses sworn to Lord Mandiat, and the houses we have won over by eliminating Farady… we might have enough. Thirty-five houses have pledged to our cause. There are almost fifty houses on the Lords' Council. Thirty-five should be more than enough, really. But matters of politics never turn out the way one expects. There will be changes, last-moment shifts. Some in our favor, but some not, to be sure. All this is to say that we have a great deal going for us, or so it would seem. But Urstadt still hasn't answered my question."

"I'm happy our house has succeeded in so many of our goals," Urstadt said. "But as for what happened to House Farady… I don't know if I am necessarily proud of that, sir."

Daval nodded, looking into Urstadt's eyes. "And why is that?"

Winter felt out of place. Why was she a part of this conversation? If Daval only wanted to use her as a tool, why did he care about bringing her into his plans?

"We have completely destroyed one of the houses," Urstadt said. "I know why we did it. But now they are gone, my Lord. I don't know what to think about that."

"You regret our actions?" Daval asked.

"No," Urstadt said quickly. "But I do question them."

Daval nodded. "I have many speeches for situations like this. The greater good outweighs the evil of what was done. That House Farady had it coming. Or that this is the way of the Sfaera: kill or be killed. But none of those arguments have ever rung true with me. The world is full of nuance, and nuance compounds choice."

"If you don't believe any of that," Winter asked, "what do you tell yourself?"

Daval cleared his throat. "That's why I have brought you both here, tonight." He nodded at a bookshelf to Urstadt's left. "There, on the second shelf from the top, is a book by Cetro Ziravi. *Poems and Verse*. Take it down, if you please." Urstadt rose and did so, then made to hand it to Daval, but he shook his head. "No," he said. "I'd like you to read a passage from it. Page seventy-nine, I believe."

"Sir, I—"

"I know you don't like to read, Urstadt," Daval said. "But I'd like you to read this."

"Very well, sir," Urstadt said. Winter was amused at the strange sight; this woman in armor, a warrior, flipping through the pages of an old book. "Page seventy-nine?" Urstadt asked.

"I believe so," Daval said. "What is the title at the top of the page?"

"'Wild Calamity.'"

Daval nodded, smiling. He sat back in his chair. "Read it for us, please."

I do not control myself,
I do not hold back, hoping my rage and power spare the deserving,
I do not weep through eternity, nor do I scrape my knees along the floors of time, atoning.
Because I love what I love, and I love all things.

I destroy all things,
Just as I create them.
I could not destroy that which I did not first love,
And so the circle spirals onward.

To destroy, I must first know love,
And to create, I must first know destruction.
And to love, create.
Meanwhile, the needing, the touching skin, the welding bodies, the connecting of every pair of lost children, soft in body and young in mind,
Continues my pattern
and life's wild calamity.

To destroy, I must first know love. Winter felt the chill of the words as Urstadt read them. She looked at Daval, who was sitting back in his chair, eyes closed.

"Do you understand, Urstadt?" he asked. "What about you, Winter?"

Winter only shrugged. The words intrigued her, but she would have to read them herself before she could say she understood them.

"Would you like me to help you?"

"I would, my Lord," Urstadt said.

Daval smiled and opened his eyes, looking at Winter. The man apparently wanted a verbal confirmation.

For the briefest flash of a moment, Winter was no longer looking at Daval. She was looking at the black skull, wreathed in flame, grinning across the desk at her. Panic shocked through her, but as quickly as the vision came, it fled, and she was looking at Daval once more.

Winter swallowed. "Sure."

PART II

THE DRIFT OF STARS

21

Harmoth estate

CINZIA PACED BACK AND forth, heart pounding. The Odenites had congregated in front of a makeshift wooden dais, hastily constructed by carpenters found among their numbers. They had constructed the dais in the shadow of the charred remains of the great ash tree on the grounds, and the Odenites—now numbering in the hundreds—had gathered around to hear their Prophetess. Cinzia was behind the dais on the side nearest the house, while the crowd gathered noisily on the other side. This was the first time Jane would address them as a whole. It was earlier than Cinzia and Jane had intended, but after the Kamite attack—they found Kamite tattoos on the bodies of each of the men Knot had killed—they knew they couldn't remain silent.

The address would inform the people of Jane's intent to rebirth Canta's religion, as well as counteract the teachings of the Beldam. While the woman had stopped preaching against the tiellans publicly, her words had still caused damage that needed reparing. And, according to Astrid, the Beldam still held secret meetings at night, preaching the same doctrine.

Cinzia still had not invited the Beldam to speak with her and Jane, and she wondered whether these secret meetings were a response to that slight. Cinzia had not purposefully ignored her deal with the Beldam, but she simply had not had time.

Jane stood nearby, smiling. Cinzia did not know how her

sister could be so calm. Cinzia had asked her what she planned to say, but Jane had been evasive. Cinzia couldn't understand such an attitude. As a priestess she had planned her sermons meticulously beforehand, knowing every potential citation or angle she might use.

Jane would be delivering the sermon today, but it was Cinzia who felt unprepared.

Jane waved for Cinzia to approach. "It's time," she said.

"All right," Cinzia said, strangely breathless. "I hope you're ready for this."

"I'm always ready when I put myself in Canta's hands," Jane said. "Things will work out the way they are supposed to, Cinzi. As always."

Jane walked up the steps to stand at the podium that had been constructed for her.

"My brothers and sisters," Jane began, and suddenly something threw her violently backwards. Jane's body twisted and she landed on her side with a thud, nearly sliding off the dais. Cinzia glimpsed a dark shaft protruding from her sister's abdomen as she collapsed. An angry streak of red was spreading around the shaft.

Cinzia's mouth worked wordlessly. She couldn't breathe. For a brief moment she remembered that day in Navone, watching her sister on the gallows, unable to help, unable to do anything. Screams rose up from the assembled Odenites as some turned to run, while others pressed forward towards the dais, towards Jane. Then, Cinzia felt someone push past her.

"Come on," Knot shouted, bounding up the steps. "We need to help her."

Jarred out of her stupor, Cinzia ran up the steps after him. Elessa was already kneeling over Jane. "She's been shot," Elessa said, looking up at them frantically. She was pressing the hem of her dress around the shaft of a crossbow bolt, trying to stem the bleeding.

"Oh, Goddess," Cinzia whispered, kneeling at her sister's side. "Jane?" her voice rose. "Can you hear me?"

"Cinzia..." Jane whispered, her voice weak. Slowly, she turned on to her back.

"It's all right," Cinzia said, not knowing how in the Sfaera it would ever be all right. "We're going to help you."

"Where did it come from?" Knot shouted, his head turned towards the panicked crowd in front of the dais.

"Someone near the front," a man shouted back. "We didn't see who."

"Were there other bolts? Is anyone else hurt?" Knot asked.

"I don't think so," someone said. Perhaps Elessa, but Cinzia was not sure.

"Whoever did this intended to kill her," Knot said. "And may be hanging around to finish the job." He looked to Cinzia. "Can you help her?"

Cinzia blinked. "Can I...?"

"Haven't you been trained?"

Cinzia looked down at Jane. Of course she had received medical training as a priestess, but...

"You need to help her," Knot said. "You're her best chance."

Cinzia nodded, knowing he was right. Blood pooled beneath Jane's body, which meant that the bolt had likely gone through to her back. Only a few fingers of the bolt below the fletching protruded from her stomach. Jane clutched at the wound with pale and blood-soaked hands.

"We need to remove the bolt," Cinzia said. "Help me turn her."

With Elessa's help, and that of another woman Cinzia did not recognize, they shifted Jane back onto her side. Sure enough, Cinzia saw the arrowhead protruding from her sister's back.

Was the shaft broken? she wondered. She gently tested it. It seemed intact. She hoped to Canta the thing had not shattered or splintered.

"I need a knife, a saw, something," Cinzia said.

Knot handed a serrated knife down to her, and Cinzia began sawing away at the shaft above the arrowhead. Jane groaned.

"I'm sorry, Janey," Cinzia said, cutting as fast as she could. "I know it hurts, but we're going to help you, I swear it."

In moments, the arrowhead fell to the dais.

"I need cloth to place on the wound on her back."

Elessa looked up at her, her face pale. "Where do I get—"

"Cut it from your dress," Cinzia said, trying to keep her voice calm. She was already tearing strips from her own skirt. When they had enough, Cinzia placed the ball of cloth Elessa had gathered on the wound on Jane's back. "Help me lift her," she ordered, and Elessa and the other woman helped as Jane groaned, and she wrapped the long strips of cloth she had made around Jane's torso, tying the bundle of cloth securely against the exit wound.

"Now, we need to pull the shaft out," Cinzia said. "I'm going to do it quickly. Immediately afterwards, you need to put pressure on the wound." She looked into Elessa's eyes. "*Immediately*, do you hear me?"

Elessa nodded.

"All right," Cinzia said. "I'm so sorry, Janey." Then, in one swift motion, Cinzia pulled the bolt from her sister's body. Jane screamed, her back arching. Cinzia tossed the shaft to the side, trying to ignore the streams of blood that poured through

Elessa's fingers as she pressed down on the wound, despite the cloth. Instead, Cinzia looked into Jane's eyes, holding her hand.

"It's going to be fine, Janey," Cinzia said, trying to smile. "You're going to be fine."

"Is there anything else we can do?" It was the woman Cinzia did not recognize.

"Not right now. In a moment we will take her into the house," Cinzia whispered, looking down at Jane. She had done what she could, what she knew, but with a wound like this…

She sensed motion above her, and turned to see the woman—her eyes suddenly narrowed and full of deadly focus—standing above her, a long dagger in her hand. Cinzia's breath caught in her throat.

Knot was moving before Cinzia could scream. He grabbed the woman by the head and twisted, sharply. The would-be attacker slumped to the dais, dagger clattering harmlessly beside her. There were more shrieks from those Odenites who hadn't fled.

"What—"

Knot swore. "She must have been one of them," he said.

"Goddess rising," Elessa whispered, her hands still pressing on Jane's wound.

"I don't recognize her," Cinzia whispered.

"Nor I," Elessa said.

Knot grunted something in response, but Cinzia ignored him. She was looking at Jane, whose lips were moving.

"Quiet, everyone!" Cinzia leaned in close, gripping Jane's hand tightly in her own.

"What is it, Janey?" Cinzia asked. "What are you saying?"

"Heal… me…"

"What did she say?" Elessa asked.

Jane pointed slowly at Knot. "The way… I healed… him,"

she whispered, her voice barely audible.

"She wants us to heal her?"

Cinzia nodded, slowly, feeling numb. What could she possibly do?

Jane squeezed her hand, so, so slightly. "Please," she whispered.

"I… I don't…" Cinzia felt Elessa's hand on her arm.

"I can do it," Elessa said. "I was there when Jane healed Knot."

Cinzia scowled at Elessa. What could this woman possibly know about healing? She had only known Jane for a few weeks. She couldn't possibly—

Elessa placed her hands on Jane and started to speak. Cinzia was too dazed to truly understand what Elessa said, but she was aware of the other woman praying, invoking, doing *something*. Cinzia's vision was blurry with tears but as Elessa spoke, Cinzia could have sworn she saw something. Light, perhaps. Color. A blur and shift.

As quickly as it began, the strange vision stopped. Elessa stepped back, and Cinzia felt hands on her own.

Jane's.

Cinzia sobbed as she looked down at Jane's face. Jane was smiling weakly.

Jane pulled lightly on Cinzia's hands, and Cinzia lifted them. She looked through Jane's torn dress, where the ragged, bleeding wound had been. In its place was a wound, yes, but one that had healed. A scab, on the verge of scarring over.

"Oh, Jane," Cinzia whispered, and she knelt down to hug her sister.

After a quarter of an hour arguing, of Cinzia and Knot insisting that Jane go inside to rest, to stay safe, Jane's stubbornness finally won out.

And now she stood, with Cinzia's assistance, on the dais where she had been shot only a short time ago, addressing her people.

Jane's speech was moving; it was well put together, articulate, and inspiring. She spoke of Canta's guiding hand in drawing them all to this place, together—and that more would arrive every day. She spoke of the importance of unity, and that Canta viewed all of her children—human and tiellan—alike and with love. Jane spoke of her visions, and Cinzia realized it was the first time she had shared her story publicly. Jane spoke of the Codex of Elwene and of their work in translating the sacred text. Cinzia blushed, unable to help herself, as Jane lauded her strength and level-headedness in the journey they had undertaken. And, finally, Jane spoke of the new religion—the Church of Canta, she called it—that they were planning to revive upon the Sfaera. Jane introduced Cinzia and Elessa as her first two disciples, and promised the imminent ordination of many more.

At the end, the Odenites did not cheer, but Cinzia did not think it was necessary. It was not a speech that invited cheering. It invited awe.

"Help me down, please," Jane said quietly, when she had finished. "I need to rest."

"Of course," Cinzia whispered. With Jane leaning heavily on her, Cinzia led her sister down the steps. Whispers began before Jane's feet had touched the grass. Cinzia couldn't hear what they were saying, but she could guess. Hardly an hour ago, Jane had been on the edge of death. Then, one of her disciples had placed her hands on Jane's head, and now Jane was healed. It was a miracle. It was a day people would whisper about for many years to come.

But Cinzia felt as if her soul were being torn in two. Elessa had healed her sister; Cinzia had not been able to do it. She had *chosen* not to step forward and try.

"Jane," Cinzia began, "I'm sorry—"

"It's all right," Jane said, breathing heavily. "Don't regret your actions, Cinzia."

"I just… I did not know if I could do what you asked…"

"It was as Canta willed it," Jane said, smiling. Cinzia could tell the expression was forced, but she thought it might be because of the pain rather than ill will.

Cinzia shook her head. "I failed." She thought admitting it would make her feel better, but it only made her feel worse. "Canta wanted me to heal you, and I couldn't."

Jane put a hand on Cinzia's shoulder. "I don't mean to sound rude, Cinzia, but… not everything is about you."

Cinzia stared at her sister, not sure how to respond. Given what Jane had just been through, Cinzia could forgive a little rudeness, but the comment stung nonetheless.

"Canta did not necessarily want *you* to heal me."

"But you asked me to do it."

"That was *me*, Cinzia. I do not speak for Canta every moment of every day. I was desperate, sister. It is just as likely that Canta wanted me to ask you because the Goddess *knew* how you would respond. She may have been trying to teach you something, knowing that Elessa would heal me all along."

"Yes…" Cinzia said slowly, "perhaps you're right." What Jane said made sense. But it did nothing to change the fact that Cinzia's faith had failed her once more.

22

At Cinzia's request, Knot had moved the body of Jane's would-be assassin to one of the house's empty rooms. The woman lay naked on a table, her clothing in a neat pile at her feet, ready for the body to be washed and laid out for burial. She was an older woman, her body lean and well-muscled, but her skin now had the pale, artificial look of death.

"What have you found?" Knot asked Cinzia, who had summoned him.

"Two things," Cinzia said, walking around the table. "This," she said, lifting a small parchment, "and something on her body."

Knot took the folded paper from Cinzia, examining it.

> Mark: Jane Oden.
> Location: Harmoth estate, outside Tinska, northwestern Khale.
> Description: 1.7 rods, 63 kels, blond hair, blue eyes.
> Known associates: Pascia and Ehram Oden (parents), Cinzia Oden (sister), Kovac Lothgard, Eward Oden (brother), five younger siblings (names unknown), Danica Cordier (tiellan), Lian Sorenhald (tiellan), Lathe Tallon, and a young girl (name unknown).
> Orders: Eliminate.

"Knot? Are you all right?"

Knot looked up from the paper, suddenly aware he had been staring at it for some time. Two words leapt out at him: *Danica Cordier*. They had neglected her middle name. The name she went by.

Winter.

"Fine," Knot muttered. "This is a mark order. Not uncommon, although sloppy business to carry it on her person. A professional would have memorized it, then destroyed it."

"Whoever sent the order has our names," Cinzia said. "All except some of my siblings, and Astrid's."

"What do you know of the seal?" Knot asked, pointing to the image at the bottom of the parchment. It looked like the Trinacrya, the entwined circle-and-triangle of the Cantic Denomination, but instead of the shapes being hollow, the entire image was inked in. It looked more like a black circle with three points emerging from it.

"I can't be sure."

"But you can guess?"

Cinzia nodded. "I can guess." She sighed. "The Denomination has many factions. The three main branches, of course: Revelation, Inquisition, and Priesthood. But there are others. Only rumors, of some."

"And what faction would this be?" Knot asked.

Cinzia shook her head. "I don't know. I can't say for sure. But based on what happened in Izet and what is happening now… it might be the Cult."

Knot raised his eyebrows. He had never heard of such a thing.

"Goddess, I can't believe I'm even suggesting this," Cinzia whispered. "The Cult is a rumor, a joke. Something priestesses at the seminary tell stories about late at night."

"But it is real enough for you to suspect that this may be them?"

Cinzia stared at Knot, unblinking, for a moment. "I think it might be."

Knot shrugged. "We knew the Denomination would come after us eventually." He looked up. "You said there were two things. What was the second?"

"Of course." Cinzia walked around to the body. "Help me turn her on her side. You need to see her back."

The woman had a small tattoo on her back, no larger than a clenched fist, but it was incredibly detailed. It was a seal of some kind, a perfect circle with a maze-like design within, hundreds of tiny intricacies and pathways jumbled together. The symbol meant nothing to Knot and he said as much.

"I don't recognize it, either," Cinzia said. "I just thought you might. It could have nothing to do with the attempt on Jane's life. But it was the only other thing about this woman that might be of any use."

Knot nodded. "It may have significance. If we could… if we could make a replica of this design, that would be helpful."

"Soffrena is a talented artist," Cinzia said. "I believe she could make an accurate copy."

"Good." He examined the parchment again. "There is something else."

"What?"

"This ain't a personalized mark order," Knot said. "It's a general one. There're likely other people out there with this order, too."

"You said this woman might be working with someone."

Knot shook his head. "Not what I mean. If someone was working with this woman, he would have received the same order she did. They'd be considered a single unit. I'm saying that orders like this one went out to other units."

Cinzia's eyes widened. "How many?"

"Impossible to say. Could be only a few, three or four. Might be a dozen or more." For the second time Knot wished he'd never sent that damn vampire away.

"What… what does that mean?"

"Means I can't protect you anymore. Not alone. We're fortunate we've gotten this far."

"But who else is there? Astrid is gone, and there's no one else…"

"We'll need to train guards," Knot said. "We have dozens of young, strong people out there. They won't make great warriors, not many of them, anyway, but we can at least give them some training, some discipline. Between protecting Jane, you, and Elessa I'm spread too thin. They can help."

"They might be of help with the Kamite attacks, too," Cinzia said.

"Might be," Knot said, although he wasn't as confident about that. What was happening with the Kamites was messy, unclear. He was not sure how to go about dealing with that. When it came to tactics, however, to guard duty and training and giving and taking orders, he could hold his own.

"I'll start recruiting tomorrow," Knot said. "With your and Jane's permission, of course."

"Of course. I'll ask her."

"We'll also have to investigate this," Knot said, nodding to the woman's body. "If she really was working with someone else, we need to know who, and whether he or she is still around."

"I can help you with that," Cinzia said. "I've got a talent for reading people."

She put her hand on Knot's shoulder. "Get some rest," she said. "Tomorrow we're going to have our hands full."

23

Keep Amok, Izet

"Hello?" Winter called out, knocking lightly on the door.

She was on the ground floor of the keep, where Daval had said she would meet her tailor. She had already met the rest of her personal servants—a half-dozen just for her—but apparently her tailor, whom Daval had simply referred to as "Galce," had his own quarters within the building, and she was to go and see him.

Winter had never owned more than half a dozen outfits in her life, let alone had her own tailor. Or servants. Or a room in a castle.

She wondered what it would be like if she simply lived this way. Serving Daval. It seemed she would have all of the money—and frost—she desired. What else did she have to live for?

You can live for revenge, a part of her whispered, angered at the idea that she would consider anything else. And yet, she *was*. This life would be comfortable. It might even be interesting. Assuming, once her usefulness expired, Daval didn't kill her.

"Enter, enter," someone said, and Winter slipped through the doorway into a small, well-furnished room. A set of large mirrors stood at the far end of the room, each facing inward to a small diamond-shaped pedestal. Dozens of drawers lined two walls, and two large doors led into what Winter assumed must be large closets.

She grasped a pouch in one of the pockets of her dress, a pouch that had been waiting for her when she entered her new chambers. It was full of *faltira*. Winter had immediately taken a frost crystal, just to make sure it was real. Then she had made herself promise that she would take them sparingly. Daval said he could get her a limitless supply, but Winter doubted that was the case. At some point, there would be a shortage, a catch, a price she couldn't pay. She needed to have a stash saved up for that day.

But until then, she was looking forward to getting new clothes. She now wore a loose, sky-blue dress, simple but elegant. It was not her style, however. Daval had informed her that none of her things—not her clothes, her bow, her *siara*—had been kept during her imprisonment. Winter was surprised at how devastated she was; the tight, form-fitting leather clothing she missed because it had represented the new her, the powerful Winter. The *siara* she couldn't care less about, but the bow had been a gift from her father.

Standing towards the back of the room was a short man, bald, with a significant belly and dark skin.

"Welcome," the man said. "I am Galce. You are Winter?" Winter nodded. Galce smiled, cocking his head to one side. "Ah, a tiellan. The emperor said you were a tiellan, but I almost did not believe him. I'm happy to see the rumors are true." Galce walked up to Winter, circling her, looking her up and down. "I have always wanted to design for the tiellan body, truth be told," he said. "You're so delicate, so elegant. I look forward to this very much."

Winter was surprised to hear Galce mention her heritage. None of her servants had—Daval must have ordered them not to, Winter realized in retrospect—and, after spending over six months in the dungeons, Winter had almost forgotten that Roden was a nation that had completely exiled the tiellan race.

Funny what one could forget while rotting in a dungeon.

"You're from Andrinar," Winter said.

"Yes I am," Galce said, smiling, looking into her eyes. Winter was surprised at his boldness. She wondered if this Galce knew who she really was, what she had done. Would he still look into her eyes if he knew?

"And how did you find yourself here, in Roden?" Winter asked. "I thought Andrinar was independent from the empire?"

"Not in so many words," Galce whispered, with an odd wink. "We are technically still under the empire's rule, though we all but run ourselves."

"Then why don't you leave it?"

Galce shrugged. "Things are good for us. We have all the benefits of running our own nation, and the benefits of the empire's protection and resources, meager as those have been of late. We have no conflict with Khale, but we have never been friendly with them, either. Until Roden completely withdraws their support, I don't think we will, either. You must take life as it comes, my dear. The only order is chaos. The only way to live is to let yourself go."

Winter blinked. How could there be order in chaos?

Galce pulled out a long tape measure. "But that's a discussion for another day. For now, we have much work to do. I must say, I have dozens of ideas for how to dress you, Winter. Dozens and dozens, I think. A black dress is a must. How chic you would look in a black dress, hugging your hips, in the fashion of my lord's young daughter. An innovative young mind, she has. Yes, a black dress, and I believe a light fawn color would go very well with your skin tone..."

"Wait," Winter said, putting up her hands. "I want something different."

Galce laughed. "Not a dress? My *garice,* you're now in Castle Amok, and I daresay you will be spending a great deal of time in the imperial palace itself, what else in the Sfaera would you wear?"

Winter shrugged. "You may make me dresses if you wish, but I won't wear them. I need something practical. Black leather, form-fitting, that provides a bit of protection and a lot of movement."

Galce blinked. "I don't think a dress will—"

"Not a dress," Winter said, "breeches and a shirt or tunic of some kind. Waistcoats work, too. A leather overcoat, perhaps."

Galce stared at her, and Winter could almost see his mind racing. "Yes," Galce said, quietly at first. "Yes," he said, this time a bit louder. "Yes!" he shouted. "This will be a challenge for me. Black leather can look very stylish, yes, but it can also be functional, and... yes, I believe I can do what you ask. Come, Winter, come to the measuring stool, we will see what old Galce can do for you, my *garice*."

Winter obliged. As she looked in the mirror, she felt nothing, could not share Galce's excitment. Dead, black eyes stared back at her, devoid of any emotion.

What have you done? she asked herself, but she couldn't bring herself to care enough to respond.

24

Turandel, western Khale

ASTRID PULLED HER CLOAK more tightly around her as she walked the streets. The sun was nearly setting; she had timed her journey so she would arrive as darkness fell. She wanted her first few hours in Turandel to be when she was at her strongest.

Turandel was a small city, but long, stretching parallel to the sandy beach just to the west. The place seemed no different than when she had left it. Five major roads—known as the Five Fingers—ran the length of the city, lined with shops and apartments. The nobles' quarter was to the south, easily recognized by its tower-houses, and of course Castle Storonam looming above them all. She thought of Elessa Storonam. She was the reason Knot sent Astrid here in the first place, although Knot had yet to reveal what his connection to House Storonam might be.

There were two Cantic chapels in the city, one in the south that served the nobles, the other in the north among the shops and other businesses. Astrid felt comfortable moving further south; her time in Turandel decades earlier had mostly been spent near the merchant's guild in the northern part of the city. The south, while not unfamiliar to her, felt far less threatening.

Why, of all the places in the Sfaera, did it have to be Turandel?

Astrid looked over her shoulder. She had made enemies here, years ago. Chance was those enemies had long since left to find other, more fertile ground. But Astrid was never one to rely solely on chance.

No one had followed her—at least that was a good sign. Astrid turned down a side street, just in case. She had been walking down the Sea Road, the road that ran closest to the beach, but the inn she intended to stay at was further inland, on the southern half of Crastan's Road, the fourth of the Five Fingers if one counted the Sea Road as the first.

The usual daytime bustle was drawing to a close, and many were in the process of closing down shops and stands. Many small alleys ran perpendicular to the Five Fingers, but they were for pedestrian traffic only. Astrid reached the Ring Finger Inn just as the last rays of light faded on the horizon. Her transformation had already occurred, but her glamour would allow her to get a room. As a vampire, Astrid had the limited capability to alter her appearance to others, which came in handy at night when she would otherwise frighten anyone she came in contact with.

Her glamour only worked so far, though; while she could calm the bright glow of her nighttime eyes, mask her fangs, and replace her elongated claws with normal fingers, she couldn't alter her appearance from what she already was—a little girl. She couldn't make herself look adult, or look like a boy. It was nothing short of an inconvenience.

But Astrid had found ways around that inconvenience. Astrid tore a strip of cloth from her dress. This was her traveling dress, and had seen much worse. She gathered her hair in a ponytail and tied the cloth around it in a bow.

The guard at the door to the inn looked down at Astrid as she approached. He was a large man, thickly muscled, wearing boiled leather armor and a short sword at his side. A long spear rested against the wall behind him.

"You all right, little miss? You lost?" the man asked, his voice kind. Astrid was unsurprised; she had become used to both extremes—people were either exceptionally kind to her, or sought to use her in whatever way they saw fit.

"No, sir, I believe this is the right place. The Ring Finger Inn, is it not?"

"That it is, that it is," the guard said, kneeling down so he looked at Astrid at her level. His face was round, his cheeks surprisingly soft and smooth-shaven given his muscled body. "What brings you here all alone? Have you lost your family?"

"No, sir," Astrid said, keeping her voice meek. Adults never liked it when she spoke to them as peers. "I'm supposed to meet my entourage here." She gave him a half-smile for good measure.

"Very well, little miss, in you go. The innkeeper will help you."

Astrid grinned. "Thank you, sir!" She almost skipped into the common room as the guard opened the door.

Astrid had been inside the Ring Finger Inn only once or twice before, nearly forty years ago. The place did not seem to have changed much. She remembered the name by happenstance only; she had never spent much time in this area of Turandel. The common room was similar to many others Astrid had seen throughout the years. A collection of rectangular tables running half the length of the room, surrounded by chairs occupied by a dozen patrons. A large hearth at one end of the room, a fire glowing merrily within. A bar with stools at the other, at which sat a woman and two men. Heads of stag, deer, boar, and even a black bear loomed outward from the walls. Those details seemed new, Astrid mused. She did not remember them from the last time.

Astrid walked up to the bar, pushing back her hood. It was particularly high, and she could barely see over it. She had adjusted her glamour so that, in addition to hiding her claws, teeth, and eyes, it also made her seem more refined. Her coarse, gray wool cloak would appear a bold forest green. Her hair, unwashed and relatively unkempt, would be a healthy golden color, and the rag that tied her hair in a ponytail would be a bright green bow.

"Excuse me?" Astrid asked, trying to peek over the bar. The innkeeper was at the other end, helping another customer. The innkeeper looked over his shoulder but did not see Astrid.

"Down here," Astrid said, waving her hand.

The innkeeper's gaze finally lowered to Astrid's level. She smiled up at him.

"Er... hello there..." He looked at Astrid, then looked up, around the room, no doubt seeking her parents. "Can I help you?"

Astrid nodded. "I need a room, please. A comfortable one. I shall likely be staying for a few nights. Arrangements should already have been made."

"And you are...?" the innkeeper finally managed, after a moment of staring.

Astrid scoffed. "Lucia Oroden, of course. You've been informed of my arrival."

The innkeeper's stare did not falter.

Goddess, if there were contests for staring idiots, this man would win them all.

"Er... I'm sorry... Lucia, did you say? My apologies, but we have not been informed of anything in your regard... um... Are your parents here, by chance?"

Astrid rolled her eyes. "My parents? Are you mad? I am *Lucia*

Oroden, for Canta's sake. You mean you've not heard of me?"

The innkeeper slowly shook his head.

"The famed child-scholar? The explorer? The genius, Lucia Oroden?"

The innkeeper's head continued to wag back and forth. Not surprising that he hadn't heard of Lucia Oroden—the girl did not exist. It was one of Astrid's aliases, whenever she had to travel on her own.

"What, have you been living under the sea for the past two years? Have you heard nothing of my education in Triah? Of my calculations in Cineste? My excursions in Maven Kol?"

"Er... I am sorry, Miss..."

"Oroden."

"Miss Oroden, but we have had no warning. Are your parents with you? Perhaps I should talk to them—"

"Oh, Goddess!" Astrid wailed, looking up to the ceiling. She raised a hand to her forehead. "Why must he bring up my parents? Taken so early from me, for reasons I know not. And now I, alone, travel throughout the Sfaera, masking my grief with adventure. Alone."

She could feel a tear squeezing out of one eye. Perfect. Folk like this loved dramatics.

"Er... Miss... Miss..."

"Oroden!" Astrid wailed.

"Miss Oroden! Please stop; I did not mean to bring up your parents. Er... I had no idea that they'd passed, anyway, is what I meant, you see..."

"Durian Bain!"

It was like the scream of an eagle skimming a lake. Everyone turned to look for the source, including Astrid, who had gone silent, mid-wail, hand still on her forehead.

"What are you doing to that child, Durian Bain? Explain yourself, this instant." A woman, thin and young, hair up, and wearing large spectacles, had barged down the stairs and into the common room. "I could hear her bawling up on the third floor."

"I… I wasn't doing nothing to her, I swear it."

But Astrid knew when to take a cue. She jabbed her finger towards Durian. "He kept talking about my parents!" she cried. "He wouldn't stop bringing them up! Everyone knows they're dead!"

The woman looked from Durian to Astrid. "Yes, well… that was terribly inconsiderate of him, wasn't it?" Her gaze settled on Astrid. "Now… who are you?"

Astrid paused, hoping she'd sown seeds in fertile soil. Sure enough, an older man who had been sitting at one of the long tables stood up. "She's the famed Lucia Ordonin!" he shouted, pointing his finger at Astrid.

"Oroden," Astrid corrected.

"She's the child-scholar, the girl-adventurer! Here, come to visit Turandel."

The woman looked at the man who had spoken, then back at Astrid, obviously perplexed. And for good reason. Astrid would have burst into laughter had she not been a good actress.

"I'm sorry, Lucia… who?" the woman asked. "There's a child-scholar?"

"Well, course there is," the man who had spoken up for her said. "Haven't you heard of her?"

"Aye, she's famous!" another voice rang out from the other side of the room. "She's been all over the Sfaera, and she's only… er… she's only…"

"She's very young!" another voice chimed in.

Astrid couldn't help the smile that crept across her face.

If she had been in one of the revivalist musicals, this would be when the inn would break into song about her adventures.

"Of course," the woman said, lowering her head to look at Astrid over her glasses. This woman wasn't entirely fooled, it seemed. She walked up to Astrid, holding out her hand. "Miss Oroden, it is a pleasure to have you here at our humble establishment."

Astrid accepted the woman's hand, smiling up at her. "Thank you."

"I am Sandea Bain. I run the Ring Finger. You've already met my husband, Durian." She nodded to the innkeeper. Sandea pulled up a chair for Astrid, and another for herself. She sat, indicating Astrid do the same.

Astrid did, not caring that she seemed smaller still when she sat. Most people viewed her size as a disadvantage, but Astrid had learned that power did not reside in body size or position. No, power had a very specific language, and Astrid had learned it in great detail.

"Now, what can we do for you, Miss Oroden?" Sandea asked.

"I need a room, please," Astrid said, wiping imaginary tears. "I have come all this way, and I have heard of this place, the Ring Finger Inn. I was told I would be welcome here."

The innkeeper leaned over the bar and whispered something in Sandea's ear. Sandea nodded, and looked back to Astrid. "You claim we should have already known of your coming," she said. "Yet we had no knowledge of it. Why is that?"

Astrid shrugged. "I don't know, Mrs. Bain. I sent one of my entourage ahead, to ensure we would find a place here. He did not arrive?"

Sandea looked back at Durian, who shook his head. Sandea

removed her spectacles, cleaning their lenses with a fold of her dress. "I'm afraid not, my dear," she said. "How many are in this entourage of yours? And where are they?"

Astrid looked up at Sandea, slowly allowing horror to leak into her eyes. "I… I…" Then, Astrid buried her face in her hands, crying audibly.

After a moment of this, she felt a hand on her shoulder. Astrid looked up, red-eyed.

"Miss Oroden, are you all right? What happened to the rest of your group?"

Astrid looked away dramatically. "They are dead," she said. "On the way here, we were ambushed by bandits. I escaped but everyone else was killed. Fortunately we were close enough to Turandel for me to get here by nightfall. And now I fear the same fate must have befallen the man I sent ahead."

"I thought you said you traveled the Sfaera alone," Durian the innkeeper said. Perhaps he wasn't as dim as he seemed. "Why were you traveling with an entourage?"

"Oh, that's just a saying," Astrid growled in her best upset little girl voice. "Of course I wouldn't travel the world alone; I'm a child! I always travel with people, but now… now I fear the myth will become reality…" For effect, Astrid buried her face in her hands once more, sobbing. She heard a whispered conversation between Sandea and Durian; Astrid's advanced hearing picked it up easily.

"Why did you ask that, idiot? No reason to antagonize her further."

"Sorry, she just seems… she seems odd, that's all."

"Of course she seems odd. She is odd. That doesn't mean that you need to be a fool."

"Fine, but…"

"Just shut up, let me do the talking."

"Er… Miss Oroden, I'm so sorry for your loss… losses. We do have a suite available. You can stay there tonight, without cost, to give you time to get your bearings. We can bring in Turandel's Watch and investigate these bandit attacks. Surely we can recover some of your—"

"No," Astrid said quickly, shaking her head. "No, it is too soon. I can't talk about that." She stood up straight. Time to shift approaches. "And while I appreciate your offer, I can't accept a room without paying. It wouldn't be proper."

Sandea cocked her head. "I fear propriety went out the window long ago," she said. "These are unusual circumstances, my dear. Let us help you."

"No," Astrid said, "I couldn't possibly—"

"I'm afraid we must insist," Sandea said with a smile. "Come, I will show you to the room myself. Have you any baggage?"

If only you knew.

Astrid shook her head. "Only what I have with me," she said, indicating her traveling pack.

"Very well. The third-floor suite will be large for you, but comfortable. Come with me."

Astrid followed Sandea to the stairs. She looked over her shoulder before ascending, and noted that, while most of the common room had returned to its business, there were a few eyes watching her, emitting varying mixes of pity and curiosity.

Good, Astrid thought. She already had them wrapped around her finger.

"Such a beautiful room," Astrid said, as Sandea showed her around. It was true, even if the real Astrid would never care to say it out loud. The furniture was expensive and the space was *huge*, appearing to take up at least half the third floor, and was divided into a bedroom area, a living space with a couch and a large armchair, and even a small library with a few dozen books.

"I'm glad you like it," Sandea said. "Please, make yourself at home. We are pleased to host the famed Lucia Oroden in our humble establishment."

Astrid caught the way Sandea said the word "famed," with a hint of sarcasm. No matter. Astrid had a feeling she would get to know Sandea quite well before her stay was through.

"Once you've settled in, please come down and join us for a meal. We would love to hear more about your travels, and it will likely do you good to spend time around others, after what you've gone through."

Astrid, her back turned to Sandea as she inspected the room, raised an eyebrow. Where did Sandea get off thinking she could give advice to someone who had just lost so many people? Or, at least, someone who was *pretending* to have just lost so many people.

Nevertheless, Astrid turned and gave a small nod. "Yes," she said, "that sounds nice."

Sandea smiled. "Wonderful. Please let us know if there is anything you need from us, Miss Oroden."

When Sandea was gone, Astrid immediately leapt onto the tall four-poster bed, and let the thick, soft quilts and the cushy mattress envelop her. She sighed. She hadn't expected them to give her their best room. That had been a happy accident.

Usually this particular ruse gained her enough sympathy for a room and a meal, but rarely on this scale. Of course, Sandea did not seem to have much trust in her, which was fine with Astrid. Astrid wasn't that trustworthy.

She reached into her pocket for her voidstone, pressed her thumb to the rune, and sent her thoughts into the Void. It was still a strange experience, even after doing it dozens of times. It was not a visual sensation—Astrid did not have that kind of power—but it was nevertheless tactile, and the experience so defined in her mind that, if she closed her eyes, she half-expected to see herself sailing through blackness, searching through hundreds of thousands of tiny points of light in the Void.

Because she had bonded her voidstone to Knot's, it was simple to find him; she was practically drawn right to him. She felt a tangential connection, a leash behind her connecting her to the Black Matron, too, but she ignored that connection.

"Astrid?" Knot's voice rang in the Void.

"I'm here," Astrid said. She stretched out on the bed, looking at the plain, plastered ceiling. Odd that the ceiling was so mundane when the rest of the room was so elaborate. Of course, most people did not spend much time looking at ceilings, Astrid supposed. "I just arrived in Turandel."

"You safe?" Knot asked.

Astrid scoffed. "I'm fine," she said. "I just wanted to check in with you."

"Just arrived? Where're you staying?"

"An inn."

"An inn without a name?"

"No sense in giving you the name, is there? What does it matter to you? I'm here, and I'm safe, and I'm wondering what to do next."

"Look, kid, the name of the inn should—"

Astrid sighed in exasperation. "It's the Ring Finger Inn, for Canta's sake," she said. "Goddess rising, like it even matters."

There was silence. Knot, she knew, was still getting used to this whole communication-through-the-Void thing, and she was obviously not making things any easier.

"Sorry," Astrid said. "It's just… it's just strange, traveling alone once more."

"Sure."

Astrid took a deep breath, calming herself. "Okay, nomad," she said. "What is the next part of the plan? You wanted me to come here. What now?"

"Find out about House Storonam," Knot said.

"Okay," Astrid said. "I presume this is something to do with Elessa. Anything specific?"

"Her family is not in power anymore. See if you can find out why."

"What does this have to do with your sifts, nomad? Why will this information be helpful to you?"

There was silence at the other end again. Astrid waited patiently.

"I'm not entirely sure," Knot said eventually. "I just… it's a place to start, I guess."

Astrid frowned. She'd been afraid of this. "And what happens when I find out about Storonam?" she asked. "That won't take me long." She had already ingratiated herself among the people at the inn. She did not imagine it would take that long to do so with the nobility.

"Ingran and Faria Storonam were killed a couple of years ago. See if you can find out the circumstances of their deaths."

Now it was Astrid's turn to hesitate. "They were killed?" she asked, after a moment. "By whom?"

"I have my suspicions," Knot said. "But I need confirmation. Find out, and get back to me. If you can't find out anything about the Storonams, see if you can contact the local Nazaniin *cotir*."

"I think the last thing we need is another bunch of psimancers—"

"They're the only ones who might be able to help me, if

Jane's healing really is starting to fail. Use them as a last resort, but use them if you have to."

Astrid sighed. "Very well, nomad. Your wish is my command."

Knot said nothing to that.

"How are *you* doing?" Astrid asked. "Any more episodes? Assassination attempts?" Knot had told her about the incident before Jane's speech—and the miraculous healing that had occurred.

"Neither."

"And your concussion? Are you up and about?"

"Doing well enough," Knot said.

Astrid frowned. There was something he wasn't telling her. "All right," she said. "Well. I guess that's it. Anything else?"

"Not from me."

"All right," Astrid said again. "I guess I'll talk to you later."

"All right," Knot said.

"All right," Astrid said.

Silence.

"Good talk," Knot said.

"Yep," Astrid said.

"I'm going now."

"Me too. Bye."

Astrid eventually made her way down to the common room, where Sandea was waiting for her.

"Oh my," Astrid said, "I hope you've not been waiting for me this whole time."

Sandea inclined her head. "Our only objective is your comfort, Miss Oroden. Please, let's have a meal."

Astrid obliged, following Sandea to the end of one of the long tables. There were a few more people in the common room than there had been before, but it was still far from full. A red-haired fellow was playing the lute near the hearth.

"Your lutist is good," Astrid said, nodding to the player.

"Thank you," Sandea said. "He's traveled here from somewhere very far away. It is not often we have someone of his talent at the Ring Finger. He has a strange name, though. I can't quite pronounce it."

Astrid nodded, watching the lute player. His fingers seemed to glide across the strings; the melody he played was both haunting and yet, somehow, lovely.

"We haven't got much on the menu tonight," Sandea said, taking the seat across from Astrid. "Just a veal stew, bread and cheese. I don't suppose you take wine?"

Astrid raised an eyebrow at the woman.

Sandea laughed. "I joke, of course." She signaled one of the servers, and ordered two bowls of stew and a cheese platter. "So, what brings you to Turandel, Miss Oroden? Someone of your fame can't have much to do here. Are you passing through?"

These were valid questions, for which Astrid had any number of canned responses. Knowing the right one to give was vital, but Astrid had not yet discerned Sandea's intentions, or what she thought of Astrid—or Lucia, rather—in general.

"Yes and no," Astrid responded. "I'm currently writing a treatise on Khale's western coast, from the Great Western Gulf to the Sorensan Cliffs."

"Is that so?" Sandea asked. She returned Astrid's gaze easily, without challenge. Without overt challenge, anyway. "It sounds fascinating."

Astrid nodded, although again she caught Sandea's sarcasm, just barely hinted at, beneath the word "fascinating."

"It *is* fascinating," Astrid said, somewhat defensively.

Although why she would be getting defensive about a fictional treatise, she didn't know. "Khale's western coast is full of unusual flora and fauna. The iridescent sea-life in the Great Western Gulf, the vicious eagles at Gurn's Point, and, of course, the giant coastal trees between Turandel and Tinska, to name only a few."

Sandea nodded, and for the first time Astrid thought Sandea might be impressed.

"Have you seen these coastal trees before?" Sandea asked.

Astrid had indeed seen them before, when she spent time in Turandel years earlier, but she couldn't very well tell Sandea that.

"I haven't," Astrid said. "Which is why I was so looking forward to this trip."

"And you've been to all the places they say?" Sandea asked. "Cineste? Maven Kol, even?"

Astrid laughed. She had, but it did no good to say so in this situation. "Cineste, yes. Maven Kol, no. I'm only thirteen, I can't have traveled that much. I haven't had the time."

"*Thirteen?*" Sandea said, her voice bordering on shrill. "I thought you were younger than that."

Astrid smiled, shaking her head. Of course her body was younger, but this was all part of her ruse. She tapped her head. "I know I look young for my age. What I lack in size I make up for with intellectual acuity."

"So it would seem," Sandea muttered.

Astrid nodded distractedly, but had lost all interest in Sandea, in anything else at all.

Olin Cabral had just entered the Ring Finger Inn.

Shit.

He was tall, smiling, and unnaturally attractive. The square jaw, the dark eyes, the smooth skin of his face practically glowing. Olin Cabral's beauty did not seem natural; Astrid had never thought so. His golden-blond hair was worn longer now, almost to his shoulders; the last time Astrid had seen him it had been cut short. But that only made him more pretty. He wore well-tailored clothing, not as elaborately decorated as a nobleman's, but clean and well made.

Shit, shit, Astrid thought. *How did he find me?*

A dozen greetings were called out at Cabral as he walked across the common room. Still popular. Still well liked.

This was not good at all.

Cabral walked right up to Sandea. He greeted her with a smile that could light the dark.

"Sandea, how are you, darling?" Cabral's voice, a high, melodious tenor, was almost as intoxicating as his looks. And the man could sing, too. Astrid had heard him do so, and the sound's beauty was potent enough to impregnate anyone who happened to hear it.

"Oman, welcome." Sandea smiled, standing, and she and Cabral kissed one another on both cheeks; the greeting was customary in southern Khale, and the nations of Alizia and Maven Kol. Strange to see it this far north, though. Another affectation Cabral had developed, apparently.

Oman? Astrid thought. A new name. She wondered how he managed such a thing, in the same city, so soon.

"Oman Cabral, this is the child-explorer, adventurer, and scholar, Lucia Oroden," Sandea said, indicating Astrid.

Astrid stood, smiling, though her eyes never left Olin—Oman, whatever he called himself now.

Olin's smile widened. "You don't say! The famed child-scholar, Lucia Oroden, in our humble city? What a day this is, indeed."

Sandea looked at Olin, her brow creased. "You... you've heard of this girl?"

Olin laughed, throwing his head back. "Have I *heard* of her? This is the girl who has traveled the Sfaera, seen things many men many times her age have never seen, with an intellect that rivals the sharpest minds in the Citadel!" Olin snorted, looking at Sandea. "Are you saying you haven't?"

Sandea was looking at Olin, eyes narrowed. As much of a problem as Olin's presence presented, Astrid was enjoying seeing Sandea forced to acknowledge the legitimacy of Astrid's false identity.

"Well, I... I mean, I may have heard rumors, but I never expected... I never thought..."

Olin laughed again. "You never thought they were true? Well of course they are; you can see for yourself." Olin knelt, taking Astrid's hand in his own. The touch sent a toxic rush through Astrid's body; it took every bit of control she had not to shudder at the sensation. Instead, she focused on Olin's eyes, looking into them intently.

"My lady," Olin said, kissing Astrid's hand. Astrid felt sick. "You must do me the honor of dining with me and mine. To hear your stories, where you've been, what you've done, would be a pleasure indeed."

"I..." Astrid was unable to continue. There was no recognition in his eyes, no sense of what had once been between them. There was a part of Astrid that wondered whether this was not the Olin she knew after all—perhaps it was some relative, or even someone else entirely.

But those dark eyes couldn't lie to her. And he knew Astrid's cover story too well.

"Oh, I'm terribly sorry," Sandea said, and Astrid felt the

woman's arm around her shoulders. "Lucia has been through some… some difficulties, lately."

"Oh no," Olin said, his face falling. He stood. "My condolences, little one." He rested a hand on Astrid's shoulder, and again Astrid had to resist the urge to shrug it off, to slither away from it as quickly as she could. "But you must come and dine with us," Olin said. "We absolutely *must* hear of your adventures. When will you come?"

Astrid swallowed hard. She was unsure how to respond. "I…"

Surprisingly, the relief came from Sandea. "As always, your kindness is greatly appreciated. We will get back to you about the dinner appointment. For now, I think this girl needs to rest."

Olin nodded, flashing his smile once more. "Of course," he said. "Please contact me as soon as possible. I will await your response." Then, with a twirl of his cloak, Olin turned and left the inn.

Sandea sighed, and sat back down across from Astrid. Astrid, waiting until Olin had left, until she was sure he was gone, eventually followed suit.

"I'm sorry about that," Sandea said, reaching across the table and putting her hand on Astrid's.

Yes, Astrid thought, *her view of me has certainly changed.*

"Oman Cabral, while generous and usually kind, can be a bit insensitive."

"You… you know him well?" Astrid asked, still watching the door.

Sandea snorted. "Better than I'd like," she said. "Oman is good for business, even his presence helps our inn. But there are things about him… things I don't trust."

Astrid found herself nodding. "Yes," she said quietly. "I feel the same way."

"Although the fact that he invited you to his residence is a great honor. Very few, other than those close to him, get to see the inside of Oman Cabral's home."

Astrid swallowed. Why could she not tear her eyes away from that door? "Must I go?" Astrid asked.

"I... I don't know," Sandea said, after a moment. She seemed surprised. "No one has ever refused an invitation from Oman Cabral. Not even a noble would do such a thing."

"Then I must attend," Astrid said.

"I would, if I were you," Sandea said. "As odd as he may be, he has done many good things. And he is well-respected; he is a helpful person to know."

"I'm sure he is," Astrid said. Finally, she tore her eyes away from the door. She looked at Sandea, who was staring at her.

"Are you all right?" Sandea asked.

Astrid cleared her throat. "No," she said. The moment she had seen that smile creep across his lips, Astrid had known. This was Olin Cabral. The vampire who had imprisoned her, tortured her, and manipulated her for decades.

25

Council chamber of the imperial palace, Izet

THE LORDS' COUNCIL CONVENED, as it always did, on the morning of the spring equinox. It met four times a year, once on each equinox and solstice. Looking out the window of the chamber, Daval could hardly believe the equinox had arrived already. Everything that had happened—Grysole's death, Daval's ascension to Tokal-Ceno and fusion with Azael—had only happened a few short weeks after the winter solstice. That such time had passed already seemed strange.

Daval met eyes with Kirkan Mandiat, seated at the head of the room. The Lords' Council convened in the same chamber as the Ruling Council, but the former had too many members to all be seated at one table, so the lords sat at a scattering of smaller tables. Front and center was the empty throne, and the large table where the members of the Ruling Council were seated. While they would have no vote today, their presence was nonetheless required at such an event.

Kirkan Mandiat, as the former emperor's First Counselor, would take charge of the meeting, but as a member of the Ruling Council he forfeited his vote, leaving Daval one vote behind. Hirman Luce, however, as Second Counselor, would remove one vote against Daval.

The rest of the Ruling Council—High Priestess Rowady, Watch Commander Kuglen, and Merchant Leader Dagnatar—

were all present. The high priestess was the only other member of the Ruling Council who opposed Daval's ascension, other than Luce. Rowady, of course, did not want the leader of the Ceno order on the throne. Daval couldn't blame her.

Kuglen was easily swayed, and had supported Daval's cause without hesitation. Mandiat had assured Daval that the merchant leader Dagnatar, after a series of long conversations and a series of even longer payments in gold, would support Daval's claim, too. The Ruling Council's support would be paramount. One couldn't lead without it.

But, for now, the situation was left up to the lords.

Unfortunately, no other people were allowed in the council chamber while the Lords' Council convened, other than a few appointed servants. Otherwise, Daval would have brought Winter. While her presence might not have been productive, he had a new toy, and he wanted to show it off.

Four sharp knocks pierced the low murmuring of those assembled. Kirkan Mandiat was holding the emperor's gavel in one hand. The hum quieted, and all eyes turned to him.

"Lords of the Realm and members of the Ruling Council," Kirkan said, "we have gathered on this day, the first equinox of the 172nd year of the People's Age, to answer the question of succession. Our late emperor left a void upon death. Our duty is to fill it, for the good of Roden and her people."

"*For the good of Roden and her people.*" The voices of nearly threescore lords rang through the hall, Daval's voice among them.

"We have no other business this day than to find a worthy successor to the throne," Kirkan continued. "We will first take nominations from the lords. Once we have attained a full ballot of three names, we will entertain discussion of the names listed, and vote. The process will repeat until we have reached a two-thirds majority consensus. Then our new emperor will be sworn in before the eyes of our Goddess, and a new age for the Azure Empire will begin."

Daval frowned at the mention of the Goddess. Including Cantic doctrine in their laws had been a mistake of their predecessors, Daval's own great-great grandfather having played an unfortunate part in that inclusion. They had shed the beliefs of their ancestors for the religion of their enemies, and not batted an eye. His seat in the Lords' Council was in the far corner of the back row. An unusual place for a lord with his power, but Daval had requested it, so he could have a clear view of those who spoke. This meant sitting among the less-powerful lords; in fact, the man with whom Daval shared a table, Dren Freysalt, was a lord in name only. He owned only a modest house, and had no bannermen of which to speak. His claim to nobility was heredity; his forefathers had once controlled a large percentage of the western farmlands, but had lost them to other lords in minor disputes. Dren was a smart man, but unmotivated, and had not done much better for his house than his recent ancestors. But Daval did not mind such company. Often, the gossip and secrets passed among the lesser lords were far more important than what was going on among the High Lords. It paid to have a foot in both circles.

"Let the nomination process begin," Kirkan said, striking the gavel on the table. "Are there any lords here who wish to nominate someone to the ballot?"

Gragan Vatster, a lord of middle rank, stood. "I nominate Hirman Luce."

Daval was not surprised. House Vatster had been a long-time vassal to Luce.

Another lord, also vassal to Luce, stood. "I second that nomination."

"The nomination has been seconded," Kirkan said. He looked at Hirman Luce, sitting at his right hand. "Lord Luce, do you accept this nomination?"

"I do," Luce said. The man seemed more sober than he'd been at Cova and Girgan's engagement ball, for the good of all present.

"Very well," Kirkan said, nodding. "We will now open this nomination up to discussion."

Silence weighed heavily in the room. Unsurprising. Luce was an obvious nomination; no one would be arguing his place on the ballot.

"Very well," Kirkan repeated. "With no discussion, we will take it to a vote. All in favor of placing Lord Hirman of House Luce's name on the ballot, so signify."

A forest of hands raised once more, accompanied by another chorus of "Aye." The vote was certainly not unanimous this time, but obviously still a majority. Daval rose his hand among them, voicing his consent. His rival on the ballot was inevitable; it was better to move things along quickly.

"And those opposed?"

A few hands raised, but not enough to contest the nomination.

Kirkan knocked the emperor's gavel on the table once more. "Let it be written that Hirman Luce has been nominated to succeed the late Emperor Grysole," Kirkan said. "His name shall be added to the ballot. Any other nominations?"

A lord in the back row, on the opposite corner of the room from Daval, stood and nominated Dren Freysalt, of all people. Daval sat back. He had instructed Danzel Britstein, Lord of the Island Coalition and one of his vassals, to wait until the third nomination.

Upon Freysalt's potential nomination, a number of other

lords balked, and an hour or so of discussion and counter-nominations took place. Daval was not particularly interested in who took the second spot. The final vote would be between himself and Luce, that much was certain. So Daval sat back in his chair, waiting for the nomination process to play itself out, when an unexpected name joined the list of potential nominees for that third slot: Danzel Britstein.

Daval sat up, eyes narrowed, looking at Britstein. According to law, once nominated, a lord could no longer nominate anyone else. Daval had other supporters that he was sure would nominate him, but Britstein had been chosen. He had been promised a place on Daval's inner council once he ascended to the throne. Surely Britstein wouldn't throw all that away for an infinitesimally small chance of…

"I accept the nomination," Britstein said.

Daval felt blood rush to his face. When the vote was already so close, losing any votes to Britstein would be disastrous. Britstein was publicly known as a supporter of House Amok; any votes they drew would likely come from other supporters of Daval and his house's claim.

Daval stared daggers into Britstein's back, but the lord did not turn to face him. Fortunately, there were at least five other names vying for the second ballot slot at this point, and Britstein's chances of actually getting through were slim. Britstein would face the consequences.

But as the discussion continued, it became clear that Britstein was the frontrunner. Daval could enter the discussion, of course, try to state why Britstein was not fit for the job, but his words would seem self-serving, spoken only to stop his potential votes from fracturing. And the lords supportive of House Luce had caught on; they were saying all they could to tout Britstein's qualities as potential emperor. Complete bullshit, of course. Britstein could hardly manage his own house, let alone the empire, but Luce's supporters knew how important it was to split Daval's vote.

The vote was called, and the Council nominated Britstein to the second slot.

Finally, Kirkan called for the third nomination. Daval clenched his jaw. Now, Daval had to rely on one of his other supporters. Surely they would realize the prestige and power that would be in it for them; surely they would see the opportunity, and seize it. Sure enough, Daval saw Lord Plade, one of Amok's vassals, standing.

But before Plade could speak, someone stood up.

"I nominate Kirkan Mandiat for the third and final slot on the ballot," the man said.

This is not going as you planned.

Daval froze. The Fear Lord's voice in his mind had been strangely absent, recently.

No, it is not, Daval admitted.

What are you going to do about it?

Daval didn't know, but he was not about to tell the Fear Lord that. His hands, restless on the table, found the voting stone in one corner, a small, polished, blue-painted stone half the size of a man's fist. He gripped it tightly in one hand.

There was silence as Kirkan Mandiat, his face pale, eyes wide, looked around.

Only three nominees were allowed on the ballot. If Mandiat accepted, and a vote was called for before Daval could be nominated, that would be it. Daval's chance to be emperor would be lost before it began.

You must be emperor, the Fear Lord's voice, dark and deep

and rolled in fire, whispered in Daval's mind. *That is how events must unfold.*

Daval met eyes with Kirkan Mandiat. Daval shook his head, ever so slightly. Kirkan looked at Daval a moment longer, before he finally nodded. He looked down. "Reluctantly, I must reject this nomination. It has been my pleasure to serve you as First Counselor, but I'm afraid I'm not the leader Roden needs for what we are to face."

Daval relaxed; he now did not regret telling Mandiat everything. That, surely, was the only reason the man rejected the nomination.

"I nominate Lord Daval of House Amok." Lord Pladc, finally.

The nomination was seconded, and Kirkan looked once more to Daval. "Do you accept this nomination, Lord Amok?"

Daval stood. "I do," he said.

Kirkan nodded, and looked around the room. "Is there any discussion on this point?"

Silence.

Good, the Fear Lord's voice echoed in Daval's mind.

"Then let us vote. All in favor of nominating Lord Amok to the imperial ballot?"

A chorus of "Aye" and raised hands. It was easy to see he had the majority.

"Very well." The knock of the emperor's gavel resounded once again. "The ballot has been filled. Hirman Luce, Danzel Britstein, and Daval Amok have been nominated to succeed our late emperor. We will now begin the vote, for the good of Roden and her people."

"*For the good of Roden and her people.*"

Daval spoke the words with everyone else, and felt an old,

familiar fire in his veins. It was the fire he felt when he secured his first vassal. It was the fire he felt when the Fear Lord had come to him, months ago.

"The voting will proceed as follows," Kirkan said. "Each lord will come to the front of the room, and declare the man for whom he will vote. Then that lord will place his voting stone in the corresponding repository."

A door opened at the side of the room, and three servants walked in, each carrying a clear glass container. There was a series of lines on each, indicating the number of stones needed for victory.

"Once one of the repositories has reached the two-thirds marker, the corresponding nominee will be sworn in as emperor. If, after everyone has voted, no repository has been filled to the two-thirds marker, we will allow for a brief period of discussion in which each of the nominees will speak, and then vote once more. We will repeat that process indefinitely, until we have chosen a new emperor. Let the voting begin."

Daval watched the vote, gripping his own voting stone in his fist. As a nominee, he would no longer be able to use it. So far the vote had been split relatively evenly between Daval and Luce. It seemed Daval had a few more stones, but the count was close so far.

The Ruling Council's duty was to observe the election. Though members could not vote, they would know which nominee each lord had voted for. They could use this knowledge to leverage the other lords against the emperor, all while maintaining an air of neutrality. It was a despicable part of Rodenese law, one that Daval himself abhorred. But it was law, nonetheless.

Most of the sixteen High Lords had voted, now, and none of the votes had been a surprise. It was not the High Lords who were the wild cards in these elections, it was the mid-ranking and lesser lords who carried the real power. Many had approached Daval with votes for sale, subtly broached. Daval was sure they had approached Luce with similar offers.

Lord Trask declared his vote for Daval, and put his voting stone in the container. By Daval's count, that marked nine for Daval and seven for Luce. As expected. Now for the lesser lords. Three more votes to Daval, three more to Luce. Lord Plade was the last of these, and his vote fell to Daval. Then Lord Gavrak walked to the front of the room. Gavrak was one of those who had approached Daval with an offer, but Daval's spies whispered that Gavrak had approached Luce as well. Gavrak was a wild card; his vote would be one of the deciding factors. Lord Gavrak held up his voting stone. "I cast my vote for Lord Britstein."

Whispers wove throughout the hall. Daval's eyes widened. That was certainly unexpected. There were, historically, one or two votes for the third candidate in any election, but Daval had not expected it from Gavrak. Gavrak's house was powerful but not wealthy; and while Gavrak sought gold rapaciously, his atrocious spending habits negated his income. Britstein's offer must have been generous, indeed, to buy Gavrak's vote.

Another vote was cast for Luce. But the next lord voted for Britstein. There were no whispers this time, but confused voices. There was even a shout of disbelief from among the High Lords.

"A subversion," Daval whispered. He spoke to no one in particular, but a few heads turned in his direction. Such a thing had been attempted before. The election of an emperor happened only rarely, when an emperor died with no living heir, but only once had a subversion been achieved, in which the lesser houses banded together to elect one of their own.

The next lord voted for Britstein, as did the one after that. And soon, when Britstein's receptacle was at equal measure with Daval and Luce's, Daval knew his suspicions were correct.

But, after a quick count of the votes that had already been cast, Daval knew this voting session would be inconclusive. Mandiat would call for another. There were forty-nine votes in total; thirty-three were needed for a two-thirds majority, but between Luce and Daval, twenty-one votes had already been cast. Even if every lesser lord voted for Britstein, they wouldn't reach their goal.

And, sure enough, that was what happened. Every lesser lord voted for Britstein. Even Freysalt, the lord with whom Daval shared a table.

"You can't win," Daval whispered to Freysalt as he sat back down. "Not while the High Lords are still split between myself and Luce."

Freysalt smiled. "Then we shall have to reconcile that split, won't we?"

Daval frowned. "This is not the time for subversion. This is the time for unity."

"I agree," Freysalt said. "And we should all unite behind Lord Britstein."

They do not understand the stakes, the Fear Lord whispered. *They do not know. They think they are doing good, but they are sowing their own destruction. You must stop it.*

"The final vote," Mandiat declared from the front of the room, standing once more with the emperor's gavel in hand, "is as follows. Ten votes for Lord Hirman Luce. Eleven votes for Lord Daval Amok. And twenty-eight votes for Lord Danzel

Britstein. As we have not reached a two-thirds consensus, we will now give each of the nominees a few moments to speak, after which we will vote again."

There was murmuring. If the first vote was inconclusive, the second almost always was, too. They could be in for a long day, perhaps even a long night.

The emperor's gavel silenced the murmurs. "Order, my Lords, order," Mandiat shouted. "We will do our duty, and we will be here as long as it takes." In a quieter voice he spoke to the servants stationed at the doors. "Bring us food and water, and be sure the cooks are alerted as to the situation. They will need to be on call for the day."

The servants left the room. Mandiat looked back out at the lords. "We will do our duty," he repeated, "until our duty is done. For the good of Roden and her people."

"*For the good of Roden and her people*," the lords repeated without enthusiasm. Daval felt it, too. This would be a long day. But the Fear Lord was right; Daval needed to find a way to bring the lesser lords to his side. For the good of the realm.

"Lord Luce, the floor is yours," Mandiat said, sitting down. "I advise you to be brief."

Daval shook his head. Brevity would be the last thing on Luce's mind.

Daval rubbed his eyes. The bodily enhancements endowed by the Fear Lord were significant, but even he was getting to the point of exhaustion.

They had been voting, talking, and voting for a day and a night and an entire day again without pause. The sky darkened once more outside the great glass windows, and still no consensus had been reached. At one point Daval feared the minor lords, and Britstein's eloquence, had won over enough High Lords to carry the nomination through. But then, nearly a day later, the vote had been split evenly once more.

Servants, looking equally as tired as the lords, walked between the tables, delivering food and drink. No alcohol was allowed during a vote, but Daval watched more than a few lords taking furtive sips from flasks stashed in their robes. As lords placed their votes once more—the twenty-seventh vote—Daval observed at least a half-dozen men drifting in and out of sleep.

As people's tempers shortened they would seek the easiest solution. Britstein still carried the majority, usually around twenty-five votes, while Daval and Luce split the rest between them.

There was an audible sigh of frustration. A lord had just cast his stone for Hirman Luce, ensuring that this count, too, would be deadlocked, though ten or so votes had yet to be cast.

You are all wasting valuable time. The Fear Lord's voice pierced Daval's mental haze like a dagger. *Your efforts are all better focused elsewhere*.

I am aware of that, Daval thought, wearily. *Do you have any suggestions?*

I have many suggestions. Perhaps I should connect with this Britstein, if his case for the throne is stronger than yours. Perhaps he was the better candidate all along.

Britstein is a faithful Cantic, Daval complained, unable to stop the panic rising in his chest. He had thought his own position was assured; he had thought he would be emperor.

You are dispensable, the Fear Lord growled. *You all are. Show me that you are less dispensable than these others, Daval. Prove yourself to me.*

I will do as you command, my Lord.

The last lord had cast his vote, and sure enough, no one had the two-thirds majority.

Mandiat tapped the emperor's gavel on the table with significantly less enthusiasm than he'd had when the meeting began almost two days ago. "We will hear from each of the candidates once more, and then vote afterwards." Mandiat tapped the gavel again. "Lord Luce, you're first. Speak."

Lord Luce stood, and there were more groans. The lords were tired of hearing empty promises. Even Britstein, who had begun his speeches with an astounding amount of charisma, was losing his touch. They were all tired, Luce and Britstein and Daval most of all, their voices hoarse from speaking.

Luce blabbered on about his same topics, his claim to the throne, his strengths as a leader. When he was finished, Daval was pleasantly surprised to see Britstein looking almost as lethargic. Britstein was making jokes, now, which would only move the crowd in the favor of the High Lords. No one wanted a childish man as their emperor.

"The best thing about the vote taking this long," Britstein said, shaking his head, "is that the longer the vote takes, the less likely it is that one of the lords will rise up against the others when the final vote falls. This might be the most peaceful ascension we've had in centuries, simply because we're so exhausted."

Daval smirked. It was true that in the past, lords had spoken against the new emperor following an election, and sometimes those words had led to violence.

Which was all the more reason for Daval to take the throne. Now.

Britstein took his seat. Daval observed more than a few heads shaking; the lords were not pleased with Britstein's nonchalance. This was Daval's chance. He stood, smoothing his robes. He had elected to wear the robes of the Tokal-Ceno's office in place of his lordly garb. The statement was clear; while Daval was one of the High Lords, he also had a calling still higher. It also made his absence from the Ruling Council that much more obvious.

Daval walked to the front of the room. He stopped, looking out at the lords, many of whom were ignoring him completely. Daval stood in silence for a few moments, and eventually all heads turned to face him. They were wondering at his silence.

Let them wonder.

In addition to his strengthened physique, Daval had received other gifts from the Fear Lord. He had been reluctant to use them, wanting to save them for the right time. No better time than now. He snapped his fingers.

A crack of thunder filled the room, and everything was engulfed in utter blackness. While Azael was the Lord of Terror, his domain of power spread far beyond fear. Darkness, too, was his to command, and as the Fear Lord's servant, Daval shared that power.

Shouts of frustration, anger, and confusion filled the room, but Daval was less interested in those shouts than he was in the whispers. The whispers of horror that roiled beneath the braying of those whose first reaction in times of danger and uncertainty was to shout their boldness to the world. But beyond those sounds was something else. A sound Daval recognized very well. It was indistinguishable from the other whispers, at first, hardly louder than a rush of air, but it was constant, and it was growing. It was the whisper of an empty seashell, but magnified, constant and terrible. It was the rush of nothing, and it grew to fill the ears of every lord.

Daval let the darkness and uproar continue for a few

moments, then snapped his fingers once more, and the dark veil lifted. The noise, however, continued, and it was now so loud that many of the lords were covering their ears, though little good such a thing would do them.

All eyes were on Daval. And, when Daval raised his hand, the terrible rush of the void around them collapsed, and the room was silent.

"This charade ends now," Daval said, his voice echoing in the chamber. "We have gone on long enough. Roden needs an emperor who will carry her through the times to come. Times that hold a danger for our empire that you don't yet know."

Daval turned his head to Hirman Luce, seated at the Ruling Council's table. "Lord Luce is a coward and a drunkard. His occupation of the throne would only send Roden into ruin." Daval glanced at each of the High Lords who supported Luce. "You all know this. Accept it."

Daval's gaze fell upon Danzel Britstein. "And Lord Britstein, who supported me until this evening, is a turncoat and a child. He will sell his loyalty—and Roden's—to the highest bidder. He is not fit to lead. Each of you know this."

Every lord that met Daval's gaze did so with terror-filled eyes. Daval knew that look well. None of them would look away; not until he was through with them.

"I am Daval Amok. I am a High Lord of Roden; my family have ruled their holdings for centuries, with a fair, just, and shrewd hand. That alone gives me a strong claim to the throne. But I am also the Tokal-Ceno. I have been chosen, in the ways of our ancestors, to represent the Scorned Gods on the Sfaera. For too long have we tolerated this nonsense," and here Daval waved a hand in the direction of the Cantic high priestess at the Ruling Council's table. "For too long have we embraced the religion of our enemies. It is time for us to take our rightful place, and to usher in the era of the Scorned Gods. I will lead us into that era. I will lead us against Khale, and against anyone else in the Sfaera who stands against us. I will be your emperor."

Daval took a deep breath, then walked back to his seat at the back of the hall. He was conscious of the eyes following him. Daval sat down, but the silence continued.

After a few moments, Mandiat stood once more. "We will begin another vote," he said. "Let us go about it quickly. For the good of Roden and her people."

"*For the good of Roden and her people*," the lords echoed.

Mandiat slammed the gavel sharply, and the voting began once more.

One of the High Lords who supported Luce was apparently swayed by Daval's speech; he cast his vote for Daval, giving Daval ten and leaving Luce with six. But Daval was not hoping to change the High Lords' minds; his success relied on who the lesser lords would now choose.

Daval's mood darkened as the first few still voted for Britstein, but then there was a change. One of the lesser lords, Grundst Odelins, cast his vote for Daval. And that, it seemed, changed everything. Every lord after Odelins cast his vote for Daval, and before Daval knew it, his receptacle was filled past the line.

Murmurs rippled throughout the hall; the lords seemed surprised that they had actually reached a consensus. Mandiat stood, but despite his disheveled hair and drooping posture, he was smiling. "My Lords, it has been a long night, and day, and night again, but the vote has been counted, and we have a successor. Lord Daval Amok, please stand."

Daval stood, feeling strange. He had dreamed of this day

for some time; he had wondered if it would ever really happen. Now that it had, he felt outside of himself. He felt as if he were watching another man accept the position as emperor of Roden. He felt as if—

Out of the corner of his eye, Daval saw movement. Suddenly soldiers poured into the room. Soldiers wearing the green and gold colors of House Luce. At the Ruling Council's table, Hirman Luce had stood up.

The lords around him let out exasperated groans. After such a long time spent voting, this was adding insult to injury. The final vote had not even been close; Luce, with his six votes, came in third behind Britstein and well behind Daval. This was poor form on Luce's part.

But the groans quickly turned to panic as Luce swept around the Ruling Council's table, pulling a dagger from beneath his robes, and stabbed Mandiat in the back, over and over again. Lords shouted in panic, called for their guards, huddling closer and closer together in the center of the room. More soldiers entered the chamber.

"The emperorship is mine!" Luce shouted, as Mandiat's body collapsed to the ground in front of him. Luce was splattered in blood from shoulder to knees, and held the bloodied dagger triumphantly above his head. Daval found himself fixating on a single red drop that had found its way onto the High Lord's nose.

"It should have been mine by rights," Luce said. "Amok was right about one thing: this vote *was* a farce. I'm going to make it right." He looked to his guards. "Kill everyone who voted for Amok or his bitch Britstein. But leave Amok and Britstein. I want to deal with them myself."

Daval was aware of the guards closing in on the huddled mass of lords in the middle of the room, himself among them.

Then he had a realization. He was emperor, now. And he wouldn't stand for this.

A pity I couldn't bring the tiellan girl.

With the strength given him by the Fear Lord, Daval leapt onto one of the tables so he stood taller than all in the room. He turned to Luce. "Call off your men," he said. "As your emperor, I command it."

Luce laughed. "You know the funny thing about all this?" he asked, spinning his bloodied dagger in his hand. That spot of blood on his nose was smeared, leaving a thin line of crimson. "You couldn't command a goat if you wanted to, and yet here you are, expecting *me* to obey your orders."

Daval turned to the soldiers around him. "I am your emperor," he said, his back straight, his voice firm. "I command you to stand down. There is no need for further bloodshed here. If you stop now, you will not face my wrath."

A few of the soldiers hesitated; if they had been outside in the hall, they had surely heard Daval's election to the office of emperor. And while they knew their purpose, while they knew they were here to mount a coup, many hesitated.

"If you bloody *kill* him, I'll be emperor, and you'll all be rewarded for your loyalty," Luce shouted from the front of the room. Daval could almost hear the man's eyes rolling as he spoke. He had not realized how insane Hirman Luce was until this very moment. A critical error on his part.

Those soldiers who had hesitated glanced at one another, at Luce, at Daval, and then advanced once more.

Daval sighed. He had already demonstrated his power once tonight. He supposed there was no harm in demonstrating even more of it. He snapped his fingers. There was utter and complete darkness. He heard Hirman Luce's deranged screams above the shouts of confusion and alarm.

"Daval, you son of a bitch! Your petty tricks will not stop me! You'll die for this, you bastard!"

Daval only shook his head. "These are not tricks," he whispered, although his voice was now magnified, filling the room, merged with another voice—a deep, rolling voice, wreathed in flame. "These are not petty."

And then, all around him were screams, and beautiful, unfettered terror.

26

Tinska

CINZIA EYED THE CITIZENS of Tinska as she and Jane walked through the main street of the town. She tried not to feel suspicious of them, but recent events had not made her very confident in how she or anyone from the Harmoth estate might be treated here.

First, there had been the men who had followed the tiellan woman Ocrestia back to the estate, pestering and threatening her. Knot had handled the situation, and sent the men packing. Then there was the nighttime attack, but so far no officials in Tinska had acknowledged the event, despite the men Knot had killed. Nevertheless, antagonistic feelings towards Jane's family and the Odenites had only grown since, and not just against the tiellans. Almost every one of Jane's followers who entered the town now complained of ill treatment by the townspeople—even those who had come from Tinska themselves. Most reports consisted of name-calling and rude gestures, but one man—a human—had been cornered in an alley by a group and beaten quite savagely. He had barely made it home.

Knot, upon seeing what had happened to the man, had wanted to go into town and find the people responsible. It had taken a great amount of coaxing from both Cinzia and Jane to remind him of his duty. He had reluctantly agreed, but Cinzia worried he still might seek out those responsible. There was a part of Cinzia that also wanted that revenge. But starting an all-out war with the population of Tinska would be disastrous on all fronts. It was one thing to defend oneself against violence; quite another to go on the attack.

"Here," Jane said, stopping in front of a dry goods store. Cinzia followed her sister inside, a bell clinking as they entered. They had nearly run out of parchment paper for their translation, and were running low on candles and ink as well. Cinzia had suggested that they ask someone to go into town for them—she did not relish the idea of facing persecution, especially when people might recognize them as Odens. But Jane had insisted they go. Just because they were leaders of the new Church did not mean they could take advantage of their position.

"Can I help you?" asked the young man behind the counter, a smile on his face.

Jane returned the smile, and proceeded to tell the young man the materials they sought.

Cinzia felt a pang of… what? She was not sure how to describe the feeling, other than to say that she missed being a priestess. She missed being recognized by the white-and-red and the Trinacrya. She missed being served, sometimes even feared. It was selfish of her and she knew it, but she did all the same.

The young man scribbled down a list of the items Jane requested: candles, parchment, bottles of ink, quills and a box of candies.

"What are the candies for?" Cinzia asked, one eyebrow raised, as the young man went off to fetch the items.

Jane shrugged. "I don't know, I thought the children might like them."

"The children? You mean Sammel, Ader, and the triplets?"

"Well, yes, but there are dozens of children on the estate, now. I mean all of them."

Cinzia nodded. She never would have thought to bring candies back for the Odenite children. Perhaps that's why Jane was the one in charge, Cinzia mused. Which was fine with her. She was not fit to lead, in more ways than one.

"Have you thought any more about my latest candidate?" Jane asked.

"I have," Cinzia said. Jane had suggested that the tiellan woman, Ocrestia, become one of the nine disciples. At first Cinzia had been shocked—a tiellan as one of the nine disciples? Tiellans were only allowed to be the lowly disciples in the Cantic Denomination; they couldn't hold any form of the priesthood.

But the more Cinzia thought about it, the more it made sense. They were not seeking to create another Denomination; they were seeking to create the Church of Canta the way She had meant it to be, something that harkened back to what the Goddess Herself created when She walked the Sfaera. Why not include the tiellans? Why not give them positions of leadership?

"And what do you think?" Jane asked.

Cinzia sighed. "I have some reservations. Some humans will not like the idea of a tiellan being called as a disciple, put in such a prominent position."

"If my disciples are to bring Canta's teachings to our followers, then yes, that is exactly what it would be," Jane said.

"There will be humans who don't take kindly to that. And if we are truly trying to build a following, I fear that might deter people from our cause."

"We are trying to build a following," Jane said. "But we are not trying to lure people in. If people choose to follow us for what we are, we will gladly take them in. We don't want those who can't embrace our ways wholeheartedly."

Cinzia nodded. It was the response she had hoped to

hear. "Then I think we should do it," she said. "If anything, her selection might help improve relations between the tiellans and the humans. Or, at least, show that intolerance is not acceptable."

"That is my hope," Jane said. "Then we shall speak with her as soon as we return, and ordain her if she accepts."

"Why the rush?" As the one who would do the ordaining, Cinzia had her reservations. She had reluctantly taken on that responsibility, acknowledging that no one else could, but it still weighed heavily on her shoulders.

Just then, the young man returned, his arms full. "Here you are, my Lady. We found everything except for the feather quills, but we should be getting another shipment of them in the next few weeks."

"Wonderful," Jane said. "And no matter about the quills; I believe we have enough to last until you get more. How much do we owe you?"

"Follow me," the young man said, nodding his head toward the counter. "My father will do the reckoning."

The young man walked to the counter where an older man now stood, having appeared silently while Jane and Cinzia were talking. The older man, who looked very much like his son—both had dark, thick hair, bushy eyebrows, and both were short, shorter than Cinzia—examined each item before passing it to his son, who packed them in a box.

"Very well," he said, looking up, meeting eyes with Cinzia and Jane. "Your total comes to..." His voice trailed off.

Cinzia swallowed hard. This couldn't be good.

"You're the two elder Oden girls," the man said. It was not a question.

"We are, sir," Jane said.

"You two and those ruffians you're attracting to your estate are causing a lot of trouble around here."

"I'm sorry," Jane said, "but the people gathering on our estate are not ruffians. They are normal people, like you and me. If they have caused any harm, it has only been to protect themselves."

The man snorted. "That's not what I heard," he said.

"I don't care what you've heard." Jane's voice was stern and Cinzia nudged her; they did not want to cause any more trouble than necessary. "Any trouble caused has been by *ruffians* from Tinska. We have done nothing to provoke them. I assume you didn't hear about the gentleman from our estate who was cornered in an alley and beaten within an inch of his life a few days back?"

The man glared at Jane. "No, I've heard nothing about that."

"That's no surprise," Jane said. "I don't know who is provoking the people of your town to hate us, or who is spreading misinformation, but I suggest you learn about us before you persecute us."

The man's eyes narrowed. "You're Jane, aren't you?" he asked.

Jane nodded. "I am."

The man's eyes turned to Cinzia. "And you're the oldest? Cinzia?"

Cinzia's throat was dry, but she managed to whisper a soft, "Yes."

The man's stern expression softened. "Bah. I remember you both coming here when you were girls. You were harmless back then." He met Jane's eyes. "Are you harmless now?"

And, just like that, Cinzia remembered the man, remembered the store. She had come here with her father as a child.

"I don't know about harmless," Jane said. "But we are the same girls you knew all those years ago. We have no ill intentions, let alone towards Tinska."

"I shouldn't serve you," the man said, gruffly. "If townsfolk knew I did, they wouldn't like it. Might be consequences."

Jane nodded, seeming to understand. "We don't want to cause you and your family trouble," she said. "While we may disagree with the reasons behind it, we will leave." Jane turned, and Cinzia made to follow her sister out the door.

"Wait."

Cinzia and Jane stopped, and Jane looked over her shoulder.

"I don't know what's going on, but I don't believe you mean us harm. Take the box and go, quickly."

"Thank you," Jane said, smiling. "We will not forget your kindness."

"I fear I might not, either," the man muttered. Jane paid him in silver coins. The son, wide-eyed, had remained silent and staring through the whole exchange.

"Good luck to you and yours," the man said as they left the store. "I hope all this dies down soon."

"As do I," Jane said.

That may no longer be a possibility, Cinzia thought.

27

Cabral residence, Turandel

Astrid looked up at the large double doors of Olin Cabral's tower-house, which sat on the Sea Road, just north of the Slice, the road that cut the Five Fingers in half through the center of the city, running west to the sea. The doors were heavy things, oak, painted black, twice the height of a man, and studded with vicious-looking iron spikes. Unnecessarily vicious, in Astrid's opinion. No one would be storming the city of Turandel any time soon, let alone an obscure tower-house. Cabral's little fortress was all for show. Of course, there had been a time at the beginning of the century where the people had begun to suspect what Cabral was. His residence had almost been stormed, then. Perhaps the spikes weren't completely superfluous.

Sandea had arranged the meeting. The woman had contacts in every corner and class of the city, and Astrid had spent her first few days in Turandel asking Sandea's contacts about the Storonams under the guise that the noble house had once been acquainted with Lucia Oroden's parents. But nothing she had found would lead her to the Nazaniin or anything that might help Knot. Finally, fearing her silence towards Cabral might offend him, Astrid had asked Sandea to arrange the dinner.

And, now, here she was. At Olin Cabral's doors. Astrid took a deep breath. She had hoped to find out something that would help Knot and get out of Turandel before her silence toward

Cabral became suspicious, but things hadn't happened that way. If she fled the city now, Cabral would likely find out and track her down. Astrid was fast, and good at covering her tracks, but Cabral had taught her much of what she knew, and had a few hundred years' experience more than her besides.

And she couldn't leave without finding something that might help Knot. Cabral might have information; if there was anything worth knowing in this city, Cabral would know it. Even though the information would likely come at a price.

Slowly, the doors creaked open, leading directly into the tower-house; there was not space enough in Turandel for anyone to have curtain walls, except for those surrounding Castle Storonam. Like the other tower-houses in the south of the city, Cabral's was a large stone structure, with thick walls, strong doors, and arrow slits, but Cabral's house was particularly large, taking up almost an entire block of the city, towering six stories into the sky, and the stone had been whitewashed and then painted black. The paint had chipped over the years, so while most of the exterior was dark, it was scattered with pale spots.

The whole thing was very extravagant, but if Cabral's business was anything like it had been when Astrid was last in Turandel, he could afford it easily. A successful merchant was often more wealthy than a noble these days.

Astrid peered inside the doors but saw nothing but darkness. Typical of Cabral; he would want her visit to be as disorienting as possible. She looked behind her, and noticed a few passers-by were staring at her. Based on their expressions, Sandea had been correct; Cabral did not have many visitors. Let alone the famed child-scholar, Lucia Oroden.

Astrid swept through the open doors, uncomfortably aware of how much like a gaping maw they seemed. The darkness within swallowed her, and the doors closed with a creak.

"Hello?" she called out into darkness. Astrid had very little trouble seeing things in darkness that would cloud a normal person's vision, but it took a moment even for her eyes to adjust.

No response came. She was in a hallway, grim and joyless, without paintings or tapestries. Cabral had not changed in that respect, it seemed. The arrow-slits were covered with dark cloth, blocking all light.

Hearing footsteps, Astrid turned to see a woman walking towards her, a candle cupped in both hands. She was dressed in fine clothes, soft silks that plunged in a deep neckline, exposing the skin between her breasts. And yet she curtseyed to Astrid with humility. A servant, then.

"You're the Lady Lucia Oroden?" the servant asked. Her smile was joyless, and Astrid saw she was young. Hardly a woman at all, no more than six or seven years Astrid's senior. There were ragged scars, across her neck and chest.

"I am," Astrid said. "I am to meet Master Cabral for dinner."

There's nothing you can do for her, Astrid said to herself, eyeing the girl's scars. *Not now, at least. You can't throw away the business at hand on a whim.*

"Follow me, please. I shall escort you to the great hall."

The servant girl turned at the end of the hallway, and climbed a curving stairwell. Astrid followed in the darkness. They emerged into another hallway as austere as the last, but now Astrid heard echoes in the distance—laughter, conversation, faint clattering. The girl led her to a tall archway, through which she could see the great hall.

It has been decades, she told herself. *You're not who you were then. Neither, probably, is he. You can do this.*

A hearth burned brightly at one end of the great hall.

Attractive men and women sat around a long, rectangular table, each of them dressed impeccably. Servants—young boys and girls, clad in expensive but rather revealing clothing, similar to Astrid's guide—were removing empty plates, serving food, and refilling bejeweled goblets. Astrid grimaced as her mouth watered involuntarily at the thought of what might be in the goblets.

Cabral sat at the head of the table, his combed, unfettered golden hair falling around his shoulders, his face smooth-shaven. The other diners seemed less bright, both in appearance and demeanor; the men were more rugged, their dark hair worn short, with stubble and beards. The women, even in their colorful gowns, were paler than Cabral.

"Ah," Cabral said, "my dear Lucia Oroden. I'm so pleased you could come. I'll introduce you to everyone."

"Thank you for the invitation," Astrid said, sitting at the chair on the opposite end of the table to Cabral. "And please, call me Astrid. No need for pretense."

The chair was massive, dwarfing Astrid's small frame, but she tried to make herself comfortable, putting her feet up on the dining table. Cabral's Fangs—at least that's what he had called his minions decades ago—gave her a few odd glances, and one of the servant girls almost poured one of the goblets to overflowing, unable to take her eyes off Astrid. The man whose goblet she was filling nudged her, and the girl stopped herself just in time.

Cabral's smile widened. "Astrid. Of course. I did not know whether you would be willing to forego your alias, even in closed company. But I'm glad you have. It's good to see an old friend."

Astrid returned his smile, shifting in the stupidly massive chair. "It is good, isn't it?" She lifted herself just a touch so she could peek at the plate of the nearest man.

"Well, what are we having?" she asked.

Cabral laughed. "Of course. My manners have truly deteriorated, haven't they? We have so little company these days, we forget ourselves." Cabral clapped his hands. "Mutton and veal for our guest, please. And to drink..." Cabral looked at Astrid, one eyebrow raised.

"The usual," Astrid said. "If you can remember it."

Cabral laughed again, harder this time. He seemed in a positive mood. "The usual! Let me see if I can recall... yes, yes, I believe I do." Cabral turned to a servant boy standing at his shoulder. This one, Astrid noticed, had no visible scars on his neck. Not yet, anyway. Astrid pitied the lad.

"A goblet of *sanguinar*, spiked with brandy," Cabral told the boy. He looked back at Astrid. "Am I correct?"

Astrid spread her hands out wide. "You remember, Olin. I'm flattered."

Cabral nodded to the boy, who glided away. Then he let out a long sigh. "Astrid, Astrid. It has been so long. How are you?"

"Well enough. I see the years continue to treat you kindly."

"They do, don't they? What of this alias of yours, Lucia Oroden? Do people believe you?"

Astrid snorted. "Of course they believe me. The question is how long they'll continue."

"The curse of our kind."

"I don't recognize any of the Fangs," Astrid said, looking at the men and women around the table. "Is that what you still call them? Or have you lost them all?"

"Oh, how rude of me. I've yet to make introductions. Yes, I'm afraid you won't recognize any of my friends here today. If you want to call them Fangs, I suppose you may. Although I have one out on a little errand of mine, who should be returning any day now. I'm sure you'll recognize him. You do remember Trave?"

Astrid's breath caught in her throat, just for a moment. If there was anyone she hated more than Cabral, it was Trave, Cabral's right-hand man. Cabral was cruel, but he was clever and at least had the pretense of manners. He could be reasoned with. Trave, on the other hand, was nothing but a monster.

"Ah, I see that you do. Perhaps he will return in time to chat with you. I'm sure you both have much to catch up on. Trave has… not been the same, since you left. As you might imagine."

Astrid forced a smile. "I'm sure we've all changed to some degree," she said.

"Now, as for these others…" Cabral proceeded to introduce the Fangs around the table. Astrid was surprised to note, as she looked at each of them more closely, that they had not all contracted the curse of the Ventus. Four of them had; the four that sat closest to Cabral, and only two of them had fully undergone the process. The other two were pale, sickly, their eyes a dull yellow color. They were in transition; whether they would survive was yet to be seen.

Cabral's unscarred servant boy soon returned, placing a plate of red meat and a goblet of even redder liquid before Astrid. The smell of the *sanguinar* was so strong that Astrid had to physically stop herself from downing the entire goblet in one go; instead, she lifted it slowly, and glanced at Cabral.

"To old friends," Astrid said, raising the goblet.

Cabral nodded. "To old friends," he repeated, raising his own. His eyes turned to the Fangs, who quickly followed suit.

"To old friends," they muttered.

Astrid took a sip of the *sanguinar*, the delightful liquid pouring down her throat, filling her with warmth and an essence she had not felt in years.

As Astrid ate, she engaged in conversation with Cabral. The others around the table remained relatively silent, occasionally whispering to one another but, for the most part, concentrating on Astrid. Their stares made her supremely uncomfortable; Cabral's company had changed as little as Cabral himself, it seemed. While none of the faces looked familiar, Astrid could almost see their direct counterparts in the gang that Astrid had known during her last visit.

"I see you still prefer your dour aesthetic," Astrid said, stuffing a forkful of veal into her mouth.

Cabral grimaced. "Dour? Quite the opposite, my dear."

"You still enjoy burning art, then?" Astrid asked.

"Of course I do. What else would one do with it?"

Astrid shook her head, and took another sip of *sanguinar*. She was trying to ration herself; she did not know if Cabral would deign to refill her cup, and she wanted it to last.

"Art is meant to be consumed, is it not?" Cabral asked. "I only consume it in a far more permanent way."

"*You* don't consume it, Olin," Astrid said. "I know you like to think you absorb it somehow, but all you do is destroy it. That's not as philosophical as you like to make it sound."

"I burn paintings and tapestries. I cause ancient sculptures to crumble to dust. I consume the artists that created them. What more could one want?"

Astrid shrugged. "I don't think much about it."

"An undecorated home is the best kind. The absence of decoration *is* the decoration."

Astrid took another bite of veal. "Too philosophical," she said, her mouth full. "Has the consumption of artists changed you?"

"I'm always changing, my dear. That's the beauty of living like we do."

Astrid snorted. "Funny. I always thought the horror of living like we do was that we never change at all."

Cabral laughed. "I've missed our little spats. Like an old married couple, are we not?" He looked around at his Fangs. "Can you believe she was once one of you?"

There was nothing but the sound of utensils scraping on plates for the next few moments. Astrid appreciated the break in conversation. Dealing with Cabral was exhausting; he was a difficult man to please, and impossible to predict. She finished her meal quickly, and just as she was scraping the last morsels off her plate, a servant girl appeared to take it away.

"Would you like more, ma'am?" The girl blushed. "I mean… my… my Lady… miss?"

The Fangs laughed uproariously. Astrid turned to the servant girl—the same one who'd nearly spilled *sanguinar* over one of Cabral's henchmen. Like the others, she wore revealing clothing, a jeweled necklace contrasting starkly with the scars on her neck.

"No more, thank you. I'm full."

It's all right, Astrid mouthed, but she was not sure the girl saw her as she took the plate and scurried out of the great hall. A smart move; best get out of sight before Cabral's henchmen made an example of her.

"Well," Cabral said, "now that we've shared a meal, let's get down to business. What brings you back to Turandel, my dear? When you left decades ago, I thought you would never return, unless it was to burn my house down."

"What makes you think that isn't my reason for coming?" Astrid said.

Cabral laughed. "Oh, Astrid. Tell me the truth."

"I'm helping a friend," Astrid replied.

Cabral's eyebrows rose. "A friend, is it? I'm surprised you've managed to make one of those. I assume he's a recent acquaintance? You've never been able to keep someone's company for long." Some of Cabral's Fangs snickered.

Astrid closed her eyes. "He is a recent acquaintance." She wouldn't let him get under her skin.

"And what business do you have on his behalf?" The snickers turned to chuckles. Astrid ignored them. Cabral always chose idiots to elect to his "inner circle." That would be the fool's downfall one day.

"I'm investigating the Storonams," Astrid said, testing the waters.

Cabral nodded. "Isn't everyone? I might be able to help you if you just told me what in Oblivion you were looking for."

"Can you blame me for not? You've never made the greatest confidant."

Cabral frowned. *Shit*. She had gone too far. "Even so," Cabral said, his eyes narrowing, "you should tell me anyway. I may be able to help, if I deem you worthy. But, if you don't, I can certainly make your life difficult."

Astrid lifted her goblet, downing the last of her *sanguinar*. Cabral nodded at another servant boy, who began refilling her cup.

Astrid looked up at the boy. "Just a touch more, please, but no more after this." As much as she craved the drink, she couldn't afford to lose her senses tonight. Not here, of all places. "Very well," she went on. "You're right, Cabral, I might as well tell you. I'm here to investigate the local Nazaniin presence."

A few of the Fangs whispered to one another. Astrid glanced at them, understanding. Vampires usually kept far away from Nazaniin triads. For good reason. When her gaze returned to Cabral, she had to flex every muscle in her body to keep from shuddering. He was staring at her, eyes narrowed, beginning to glow a horrible red color. The sun must be setting outside; where Astrid's eyes glowed green at night, those of most other vampires she had met glowed red. Astrid was not sure what caused the difference. For all she knew it was as trivial as hair color, and she just happened to manifest a particularly rare version of it.

"Who told you?" Cabral finally asked, after staring at Astrid for a moment, his eyes burning into her.

Astrid swallowed hard. She lifted her goblet, taking another sip. "Told me what?"

"Who told you about our issues with the Nazaniin?"

Astrid's eyes widened. "No one told me, Olin. If you have them, they are your own. My business with them does not concern you."

Cabral looked at each of his closest henchmen intently, his eyes burning. The eyes of the two who had made the transition to vampire had also begun to glow, while the two who were in the midst of the process remained pale and sickly. Each of the Fangs shook their heads.

"No," he said quietly, "none of you." He turned back to Astrid. "You truly have not heard what has been going on here?"

Astrid shook her head. "Nothing at all." She raised her goblet, once more draining the *sanguinar* from it.

"Curious," Cabral whispered. "Curious, indeed. But perhaps this is what we need. A mosquito seems to be buzzing in both of our ears at once, my dear. We can destroy it together, once and for all."

The servant boy walked up to Astrid to refill her goblet. "What are you doing?" Cabral asked sternly.

"I... I was just filling our guest's cup once more, Your Grace," the lad said. He was young, perhaps sixteen or seventeen.

"Did our guest *ask* you to fill her cup again?" Cabral asked.

Astrid swallowed. She knew the outcome of this exchange.

"I... no, Your Grace. She did not."

"What did she say the last time you filled it?"

The boy hesitated and Astrid tried to interject. "Olin, I don't care—"

Cabral held up a hand, and Astrid knew better than to speak further. "What did she *say*?"

"She said she did not want any more," the boy whispered.

Astrid looked around the room. The others at the table were glaring at the lad, their eyes burning with hunger. The other servants had all stopped what they were doing, empty eyes staring at their fellow.

"She did say that, didn't she? Why, then, did you go to fill her goblet again, my pet?"

"My Lord, I'm terribly sorry. I forgot. It will not happen again, I swear."

"I'm sure it won't," Cabral said, smiling at the boy. "Grendine, ensure that he won't make that mistake again, will you?"

One of the Fangs at the table, a woman sick with the curse but not yet transitioned through it, stood up, a smile stretching across her pale, sickly face.

Astrid trembled with anger and helplessness as Grendine strode up to the boy and struck him in the face. Astrid flinched. The lad spun with the force of the blow, landing on his hands and knees on the stone floor. Grendine kicked him, hard, in the abdomen, and pulled him up by the collar of his shirt with one hand, hitting him over and over in the face with the other. Then she drew a knife from her belt and nicked the soft skin of his neck, just below his jaw. Blood welled up. Grendine, still in the transition process, had no fangs or claws, but she needed human blood to survive, far more blood than a fully developed vampire; Grendine's hunger would be fierce and nearly insatiable.

"Grendine has proven herself time and again," Cabral said quietly, as Grendine closed her mouth around the boy's neck, drinking greedily. "She is a great ally, and will soon be one of us. We look forward to that day with anticipation. Her transformation should be finished by the next new moon."

"I do not need to destroy the Nazaniin here," Astrid said, changing the subject. There was nothing she could do to help the lad. "I just need information from them."

"Ah," Cabral said, nodding. "But you could get your information from them, and then destroy them, could you not?"

Astrid frowned. "I… I don't know, Olin. I know nothing about their presence here. Tell me, and I can give you a more accurate answer."

Cabral nodded, seeming to have made up his mind. "The Nazaniin have a full triad in Turandel. An acumen, a telenic, and a voyant. Two of them are actuals, one a variant. They have been investigating *us*, you see. They have taken an interest in my dealings, in my business, in who I associate with. They have their suspicions about me and if they find out the truth, our time in Turandel will come to an end."

"So why haven't you taken care of them yourself?"

"Let's just say that I've been waiting for the right moment. With you around, I might just have the manpower I need to mount the necessary attack."

The sound of Grendine drinking from the servant boy stopped. Grendine, wiping blood from her grinning mouth, walked back to her place at the table. A few servants rushed to the boy and took him out of the great hall. The boy was not dead; he was too valuable to be allowed to die. They would keep him alive, barely, until his next mishap.

Astrid shivered. She hated to make a deal with Cabral, knowing what he was. But this might work. If Cabral gave her information about the *cotir*, if he could get her close to them, she might be able to find out more about Knot. The Storonams were all but a dead end; the Nazaniin were her last hope.

"Can you do it?" Cabral asked.

"If I get what I need from them," Astrid said, "then yes, I will help you kill them."

Cabral smiled and sat up. "This would be very pleasing to me. We would have taken care of these Nazaniin annoyances long ago if it were not for my status in the city. This could be very beneficial to both of us."

At that moment a servant girl came rushing in. She moved quickly to Cabral's side and whispered in his ear. Cabral's mouth twisted into the most sinister smile Astrid had seen on him yet.

"How wonderful. It seems our friend is back from his journey. My dear Astrid, are you ready to see Trave again, after all these years?"

The blood froze in her veins. Her body was stiff, but inside her head a storm raged. "'Ready' is not a word I would use to describe my feelings at the moment," Astrid replied.

She turned at the sound of heavy footsteps, and looked up to see Trave stride into the great hall. When she had last seen him he had smiled almost constantly; while he ate, while he fought, while he raped. Now his expression was somber, his scarred face pulled downwards. Astrid remembered the scars, remembered staring up at them in anger and in sadness and in despair and finally in resignation. He wore a gray eyepatch over an empty socket, strapped around his long and unwashed dark-brown hair. While vampires could heal from most wounds very quickly, they couldn't heal from wounds suffered before they turned, or from the removal of limbs or other body parts when cauterized with fire, as Trave's eye had been. And, while they could usually recover from burns if they got out of the sun or fire quick enough, sustained damage often left scars. Long exposure meant a vampire would be burned to a useless husk.

Astrid flexed her left hand. The last time she'd seen Trave, her left hand had been badly burned. It'd taken nearly a decade to become functional again.

Cabral's voice boomed across the room. "Welcome, Trave. It has been too long. Your journey was successful, I trust?"

"Successful enough," Trave rasped, his voice as rough as Astrid remembered. A sudden resolve filled her. She couldn't hide from this man. She stood, planting her feet on the seat of her chair, and stared at Trave, back straight, head tall. Their gazes locked. Astrid glared at him defiantly, proudly. Trave's gaze did not leave hers, but Astrid saw the last emotion she would have ever expected in the man's eyes. Astrid saw fear.

Cabral laughed. "I knew this reunion would be too good to miss. Trave, you remember Astrid? And, Astrid, I know you remember Trave."

Astrid and Trave stared at one another, but to her surprise, Trave was the first to look away. He swept past Astrid without a word, and took his place at Cabral's right hand.

Cabral laughed. "So uncomfortable," he said, giving a mock shiver. "I'd hate to be either of you in this moment. Such a strange reunion."

Trave leaned close to Cabral, whispering something in his ear. Cabral frowned. "No, Trave. Not today. I need you here. In fact, an important task has arisen. The Nazaniin have been making threatening noises for weeks, now. Astrid has kindly offered to help us dispose of the *cotir*, provided she gets some information from them that she apparently needs… for a friend."

Cabral laughed again, another short bark. "Can you believe it, Trave? She says she has friends, now. Who could have predicted such a thing?" He looked at Astrid, his eyes glowing red in the hazy light of the great hall, brighter and brighter as darkness descended outside. "I can trust Trave to be stealthy in his actions. You two will take care of this Nazaniin threat together. You will then report back to me, and we will all be one happy family once more."

Cabral laughed again but Astrid felt none of his mirth. Killing a Nazaniin triad was difficult enough. Having to work alongside Trave… it was nigh on impossible.

28

Harmoth estate

KNOT CHEWED HIS CHEEK as he stared at the body, the second laid out in the Harmoth mansion in the last week. The first body had been that of a female assassin; this was a young man, a new Odenite who had only arrived a few days ago. Knot did not know the man's name. Not that he would recognize him if he did; the man's face was a bruised, broken mess, and his attackers had branded a cross and crescent into his forehead.

Cinzia and Jane conversed quietly, their parents Ehram and Pascia by their side. Elessa and Ocrestia, who had also been recently presented as one of Jane's disciples, stood nearby. Elessa had not yet met Knot's gaze, and he had made an effort not to look in her direction, either. He did not want to make her any more uncomfortable than she already was.

"Please, tell us what happened," Ehram asked. He spoke to a middle-aged woman, who sat in a chair next to the young man's body. Her eyes were wide and staring outward into nothing. The dead man's mother. Ehram placed a hand on her shoulder. "I'm sorry to make you go through it," he said. "But we must know what happened."

"We were passing through town," the woman said, "on our way to see the Prophetess." The woman's eyes flickered to Jane. "A group of men approached us. Four, maybe only three. They asked where we were heading, and we told them, we didn't know any better, we didn't know what they would do, Canta help us, we didn't know..." The woman trailed off. Jane moved to her side and put her arm around her. "We told them where we were going, and... and they laughed at us at first. They asked if we were elf-lovers. We did not know what they were talking about. They kept laughing, but then, they... they..."

The woman's voice choked into silence, and she reached out to the bed, where her son lay. "They started pushing my son," she said after a moment. "They started pushing him between them, laughing at him, calling him an elf-lover. And then one of them hit him. Hit him hard, and he fell to the ground. One of them picked him back up, and then they hit him again, and again... Canta rising, they just kept hitting him, and wouldn't stop. One of them had a medallion, with the cross and crescent, and there was a torch nearby..."

The men had branded the mother, too. The angry burned flesh stood out on her forehead. Knot couldn't imagine the pain the woman was feeling—and her brand was likely the least of it.

He turned and walked out the door, not sure what to say. He knew what that boy had faced; Knot had experienced a taste of that fear and prejudice in Pranna. He was no tiellan, so he could never know exactly what they felt, but he'd been called elf-lover and worse. But he had known how to handle himself. This young man had no such defense.

Knot leaned against the wall in the corridor, breathing slowly. After a few moments the door opened and the others joined him.

"Are you all right?" Cinzia asked, her eyes looking up at him with concern.

Knot eyed Elessa warily. He did not want to frighten her. "Fine," Knot said. "Just... just trying to handle some emotions."

"We all are," Cinzia said.

"This is not right," Jane said.

"No shit," Knot muttered.

"Of course it isn't right," Elessa said. "But what can we do about it? We can't control how they treat us, how they think."

"No, Jane is right," Cinzia said. "Something is off about how we are being treated here. Something is different."

"This isn't *normal*," Jane said. "I don't believe the people of Tinska would act this way of their own accord. To kill an innocent young man? I believe someone, or something, is affecting them."

"How do you mean?" Elessa asked. Knot had hardly heard the woman speak since he'd attacked her. *Since Lathe had attacked her.* But how could she tell the difference?

"The Nine Daemons are loose in the world," Cinzia said.

"Yes," Jane whispered.

Cinzia pointed at the window, towards Tinska. "You think one of the Nine Daemons is…" Elessa was nodding; Ocrestia was staring at Jane with dark, smoldering eyes.

"Is that possible?" Elessa asked. "Could one of them really be… influencing people?"

Cinzia glanced at Knot. "If what we experienced in Roden is any indication, then yes."

"It is more than that," Jane said. "They are among us."

Knot slammed his fist against the wall, perhaps with more force than he intended. Each of the women, with the notable exception of Ocrestia, jumped at the sound. Knot regretted it immediately, especially when he saw the way Elessa looked at him. "What in Oblivion are you all talking about?" he demanded.

"Jane thinks that one of the Nine Daemons is—"

"I know what you are *saying*, but what do you *mean*?"

Cinzia frowned at him. "You were there in Roden, Knot. You saw what happened—"

"Of course I *saw* it," Knot said, throwing up his hands. "But that doesn't mean I have the slightest clue what it was, what it *meant*."

"We have already discussed this," Cinzia said, shaking her head. "That man—that thing—that came through the portal, in Izet, was Azael. One of the Nine Daemons. He ushered in the Rising, allowing the Nine Daemons to once again walk the Sfaera."

Jane put a hand on his shoulder. "I understand you have questions," she said. "We have not been clear in our explanations, and for that I apologize. But we don't understand everything going on here, either. I've made many guesses about what the Rising means, what the Nine Daemons could actually be doing among us. None of them are based on fact."

"I just want to know what *you know*," Knot said. "I can't be of much help, otherwise."

Jane nodded. "Very well... but I'm afraid it is not much. Azael, the Daemon you encountered in Izet, is one of the Nine Daemons. Their leader, or so the stories say. By gaining entrance to the Sfaera, he opened the door for the other eight. We may not have seen them come through the portal that night... but they are here. They can influence us, certainly, and some of them may have already seized physical forms." She began moving down the corridor. "Come," she said. "Let us discuss this somewhere more comfortable."

Somewhere more private, Knot translated. He nodded to himself and, with the other three women, began following Jane up the large staircase.

"And what are they going to do, now that this door is open?" Knot asked.

"We can't be sure *exactly*. But we do know something of

their end goal. The Nine Daemons are of a world beyond our understanding. We speak of the Praeclara, where Canta dwells, and where each of us might dwell if we are judged worthy. We speak of Oblivion, the nothingness we will become if we are judged otherwise. And, of course, we currently dwell on the Sfaera. But…we never speak of the other place."

Knot grunted. "Always thought Daemons were from Oblivion."

"So the Denomination teaches," Jane said, glancing at Cinzia, "but, as in so many things, they have gone astray in their doctrine."

Jane ushered them into a large drawing room. A chaise longue, a couch, and three large stuffed chairs took up the center of the room, while other chairs, made of wood and intricately carved, lined the walls. A huge inglenook fireplace topped by a massive marble mantel slab took up one side of the room.

"Come in," Jane said, sitting down in one of the stuffed chairs. "Take a seat. Let us discuss this openly." Cinzia sat on the chaise longue, while Elessa took the couch. That left an armchair each for Knot and Ocrestia. They glanced at each other, then sat down.

"So the Nine Daemons are from another world," Knot said. "But they are not the only ones?"

"No," Jane said. "You know the other denizens of their world as Outsiders. I believe Astrid was the one to tell you that term."

Knot frowned, remembering what they'd faced in the imperial palace. He could still see their elongated, sinewy bodies, and oversized jaws with rows of dagger-like teeth.

"Whenever a portal opens to this other world," Jane said, "some of the Outsiders are inevitably dragged through it."

"But we are not dragged to the other side in return?" Knot asked.

Jane shrugged. "I don't think so," she said. "But I can't be sure."

"No one was dragged back in Izet," Knot said. "Not that we could see, anyway."

"And that is the only portal we know of," Jane said. "But, as I said, the other Daemons should have access to this world, now. Whether they have arrived in full form is yet to be seen. I'm not even sure Azael remained here physically."

"But you think one of them is in Tinska?" Knot asked.

Jane nodded. "I do. It is the only explanation I can think of as to why the people are acting this way. The Daemons would likely be able to sense where we are. Where *I* am. It would make sense they would send one of their own here… to me."

"You mentioned their end goal, but you never elaborated," Knot said. "What are the Nine Daemons here to do?"

Jane sighed. "It is simple, and yet it is not. The easiest thing to say would be this: they are here to destroy us. They are here to destroy our world, our people, everything we know."

"But there is more to it than that," Knot said.

Jane nodded. "There is always more to it than that… but the truth is, we know very little of them, or what they want."

Knot snorted, unable to help himself. "For all we know the Outsiders are perfectly agreeable folk? We just have no way to communicate with them, to understand what they want?"

Jane shook her head. "No," she said. "Surely your experience with Azael and the Outsiders in Izet has taught you more than that, Knot. Can you truly imagine they are agreeable? Can you imagine living in harmony with the embodiment of fear itself?"

He had to admit that he couldn't. Those things had driven Winter to overdose; they had ultimately killed her. The final Outsider that had emerged from the portal had been larger than any living thing Knot had ever seen, nearly as tall as the imperial dome itself. And the beast had displayed nothing but animosity and feral instinct. Nothing civilized at all.

The Daemon, Azael, was far worse.

"This is all well and good," Elessa said in a tone of voice that made Knot suspect it was anything but. "What are we going to do about Jane's suspicions? What about this Daemon that might be in Tinska?"

"Shouldn't we find out if the suspicion is even correct, first?" Ocrestia said.

Jane nodded. "Of course. Something is causing this change in Tinska's population; we need to discover whether it is one of the Nine Daemons or something else entirely."

"How do we even begin to go about it?" Elessa asked.

"Or," Cinzia added, "if it isn't a Daemon, what could it be? We have a responsibility—"

"Stop." All eyes turned to Ocrestia, who was now standing. "Do you even hear yourselves? Are you really that ignorant?"

"Ocrestia..." Cinzia reached for Ocrestia's hand, but the tiellan wrenched it away.

"Do you think what's been happening to the tiellans in the camp is *supernatural*? You truly think that humans couldn't be capable of treating us this way?"

"But they aren't just doing it to tiellans anymore," Elessa said. "That man down there was a human. They called him an elf-lover."

"That's true," Cinzia said. "When Jane and I were in Tinska the other day, we—"

Ocrestia laughed. "Do you even hear yourselves? The fact that *humans* are now involved in the violence is proof it's supernatural? Because, Canta forbid humans are ever violent against other *humans*. You think this is so shocking, but I know better. What happened to that boy happened to the men in my town all the time. The Kamite order has been around for centuries. Women I knew were raped by Kamites, by human men, just because they were tiellan. Terrible tragedies, but never surprising. And you shouldn't be surprised, now. This violence is not new. You've just been ignorant of it."

Ocrestia sighed. "I ain't saying that you're wrong, Jane," she said. "Might be a Daemon pulling strings in Tinska. But don't forget the violence that's been waged against my people for centuries. Don't blame it on some Daemon without real proof."

When Ocrestia sat down, she seemed very small. For a moment, the woman's slight figure and pointed ears reminded Knot of Winter. He saw *her* curled up on the chair. But Ocrestia's pale, silvery hair was very different from Winter's raven black, and while her eyes were dark, they were nowhere near Winter's twin midnight pools.

"Goddess, Ocrestia, you're right," Jane whispered. "Whether a Daemon is manipulating people in Tinska or not, the fact remains that humans have *chosen* to act. It was wrong of us not to acknowledge that."

Both Cinzia and Elessa whispered their own apologies. Ocrestia shrugged, sitting back in her chair. She glanced at Knot, who nodded to her. She nodded back.

"We have work to do then," Cinzia said. "A great deal, it would seem."

They stayed up talking through the night, and, listening to the women's plans, Knot felt hope for the first time in many days.

29

Turandel

ASTRID WAITED.

Trave had agreed to meet her in a narrow alley. It was dark, although a few hours short of midnight, and Astrid looked down at the alley as she clung to the frame of a window, her toes curled around the sill.

The conversation with Trave after her reunion with Cabral a few days before had been awkward. She had expected Trave to still be furious with her, but he had not seemed so at all—which only made Astrid more suspicious. Trave's emotions were dangerous, but he usually wore them openly. She didn't like that she couldn't read him. She was still baffled by the fear she had seen in his eye, like seeing a dog walk around on two legs.

Which was why Astrid was hiding above the alley. She was not about to throw herself into Trave's company without first assessing the situation.

When Trave finally appeared, his eye illuminated the alley ahead of him like a crimson torch. He was alone. That did not necessarily make the situation better, but at least she knew her odds. At this point she was relying on Trave's fear of Cabral to keep him in line, to keep him from betraying her, from… doing anything to her, really. She and Trave had a job to complete, and Trave would, she hoped, put off his revenge until it was finished. Then, Astrid feared, she might have a problem.

She dropped down silently from her hiding place, landing quietly in the street behind Trave. Trave turned. "Glad you showed up," he said, his voice gruff.

"Didn't have much of a choice," Astrid said.

"You and me both."

They stood staring at one another for a moment. Astrid felt her instincts tugging at her, pleading with her to get as far away from this man as she could. His whole demeanor threw her off.

"What the hell is wrong with you?" Astrid asked.

Trave frowned. "I don't know what you mean."

"You're acting so bloody calm. What in Oblivion are you planning, Trave?"

"I'm not planning anything. I am... very different than when we last met, Astrid."

"No shit," Astrid muttered. She eyed him warily.

"I'm not going to hurt you."

"The old Trave—"

"The old Trave is gone," he said. "He burned away years ago. He burned away when you burned me."

Astrid narrowed her eyes. That memory was still fresh in her mind, after decades. She feared it would never leave her.

"Cabral thinks he is torturing us by giving us this mission together. He thinks we are terrified of one another. But that doesn't have to be the case. Not for you, anyway."

Astrid stared deep into Trave's clear gray eye. "Let's just get the job done," she said.

Together they walked along the shadowy streets, careful to hide their faces—and the glow of their eyes—beneath their hooded cloaks.

"The telenic and the acumen are the actuals," Trave said.

Each class of psimancer was dangerous in their own way. Telenics, like Winter, used psimancy to move inanimate objects around them. Acumens, like Kali, used the power to manipulate the minds of others.

"You're sure?"

"Sure as I can be," Trave said. "Some of my men will lure them out. The acumen and telenic will investigate. We'll kill them, and find the voyant for you."

"The voyant won't see us coming?" Voyants were potentially the most dangerous of the three, but voyants were extremely rare. Somehow, voyants used psimancy to discern future events, but most of them were glorified soothsayers. Astrid had only encountered one or two whose power could be deemed formidable.

"The voyant will not be a problem."

"If he is as weak as you say, I might need another to question. We should take one of the others alive, too. The acumen, if possible."

They turned a corner. Supposedly Trave's men were luring the Nazaniin out of their headquarters right now. It would be a small ruckus, but the strike would be surgical, not enough to alert the town police.

"We are close," Trave whispered. "With any luck, my men have attacked and fled already, and—"

Trave and Astrid stopped. The street before them was wide, with buildings on either side, and a small tower-house that Astrid assumed must be the Nazaniin Turandel headquarters. The street was empty, save for the bodies.

Astrid counted six of them in a row, sitting up with their backs against the tower-house, their legs sprawled out in front of them. Each man had a large hole in his skull.

"Shit," Trave said.

"Yeah," Astrid whispered.

A man and a woman walked out of the shadows, into the moonlight.

"Welcome," the man said, a broad smile on his face. "We've been expecting you."

Trave threw something so fast Astrid did not even see what it was, but the telenic—the woman—swiped it away with her *tendra*.

"*Two* vampires?" the man, the acumen, asked. "Curious. We've been aware of the vampire activity in this city for some time, now, but we did not know how many of you there were. How many more of you are there?"

A ringing began building up between Astrid's ears. Fortunately acumens had far less power over vampires than humans; he could annoy them, but whatever powers made Astrid strong, fast, and deadly, somehow made her mind more resistant to an acumen's force. Especially at night.

What worried Astrid far more was the nightsbane herb she was sure both Nazaniin carried. She did not think they would have nightsbane-soaked blades, like Kali had done in Izet. They wouldn't have had the time or the warning, if this voyant was as miserable as his reputation indicated. But just the herb itself would be a challenge.

"Which one you want?" Trave rasped.

"I'll take the acumen," Astrid said. She'd prefer the telenic, as she'd had her share of battles with them. But she needed the acumen alive, and she did not trust Trave to hold back.

"Very well." And then Trave was sprinting forward, claws out, pointed teeth bared.

Astrid lowered her hood, watching the acumen. The man was middle-aged, short, but lean. Astrid did not know whether he was a graduate of the Citadel, but she wouldn't underestimate him. He had undergone Nazaniin training, and that was enough.

The man drew a sword, the familiar long, slightly curved blade of the Nazaniin.

And then, someone else stepped into the moonlight behind the acumen. Another man, this one taller, younger, bigger. The voyant.

"The voyant's here!" Astrid shouted, moving quickly towards them. The closer she got, the more the pain in her skull increased, and she began to feel sharp, burning pain coursing through her blood. One of them had nightsbane, although not a very large quantity. Kali had been in possession of a great deal, and had rendered Astrid immobile. If whatever this *cotir* carried touched her, that would happen again, but she believed she could fight them face to face, or at least make the attempt.

Trave certainly could. He swiped a claw at the telenic, but she dodged neatly, wielding a sword of her own and three or four other weapons with her *tendra*.

Astrid swallowed hard, ignoring the pain. She did not know how Trave was moving the way he did; she felt like she wanted to lie down and die.

Knot had better bloody appreciate this.

Then, Astrid charged forward.

The smoldering pain beneath her skin seemed to burst into flame, and then she was fighting the acumen, dodging slashes from his sword, trying to return her own with her claws. She was tiny, though, and he outreached her. A sword scraped against her back with the sound of steel on stone; her hardened skin resisted a great deal of damage, but Astrid felt a wound open. She cried out, thinking it had been one of the telenic's *tendron*-wielded weapons, but then saw the voyant standing behind her. She rolled to the side just in time to escape another attack.

He is no variant, Astrid realized. *He is an actual.* Her view of their battle completely changed. An actual voyant, one who could tap into his powers without the help of frost and wield enough of his power to fight, could be very dangerous indeed. Telenics were the most obvious threat, but rarely the most deadly. Acumens were often far more dangerous, and a fully functioning voyant was the worst of them all.

Astrid tore a cobbled stone up from the street with her claws and threw it at the voyant, but he stepped out of the way casually. With her advanced eyesight in the night, Astrid saw the reason why. The voyant's eyes were closed. He was smiling. He had seen the stone flying towards him before Astrid had even thrown it. She needed to separate the two Nazaniin. She couldn't fight them both at once. The voyant must have the nightsbane, she decided; the horrible screeching pain had been worst when he had slashed her.

Trave had the telenic on the ground, about to finish her, when the voyant turned to face him. This gave Astrid an open shot at the acumen. She charged at the man, running on all fours, then leapt. He slashed at her in mid-air, but Astrid turned and the blade missed her. She landed and immediately leapt back up, using the stone wall of the tower-house to vault herself even higher, above the acumen. He looked up, raising his sword, but did not move in time. Astrid kicked the sword aside and plunged her claws into the man's face. Her teeth followed, burying themselves in the man's neck, and Astrid tasted the sweet toxicity of blood on her tongue. But she couldn't feed now, as much as she longed for it. The acumen was down; the ringing in her head had stopped. She needed the voyant. He would be her best informant.

Astrid turned to see the voyant and the telenic closing in on Trave. He swiped at one then the other with his claws, but they had cornered him against the building. Astrid charged once more, aiming for the voyant. If his eyes were still closed, he would see her coming. Or so she hoped. Sure enough, he turned at the last minute, dodging out of the way as Astrid lunged at him.

Astrid heard a gurgle, and watched as the telenic's body slumped to the floor, Trave's claws in her throat.

Two down. Astrid only had to make sure that Trave did not kill the third.

The voyant backed away, his eyes closed, looking—but *not* looking—back and forth between Astrid and Trave.

"You can't defeat us both," Astrid said.

"You will not leave me alive, no matter what happens here," the voyant said, matter-of-factly. He seemed far too calm.

"That's not necessarily true," Astrid said.

"It is," the voyant said. "I've seen it."

Astrid shrugged. She glanced at Trave, who nodded. They had both fought voyants before. They had fought them together, in fact. Trave moved forward, snapping at the voyant, and Astrid did the same, lunging in with her claws. The voyant avoided Trave's teeth and deflected Astrid's claws with his sword.

There were three important things to remember when fighting a voyant. For one thing, they would anticipate your every move, so attempting to anticipate theirs was useless—they would always, *always* be one step ahead. Instinct had to take over.

Astrid and Trave attacked again, faster this time, lunging in and backing out quickly. The voyant continued to defend, but Astrid and Trave were dividing his attention; his parries and dodges were deteriorating, growing more desperate.

The second thing to remember was that there was strength

in numbers. Splitting a voyant's attention meant diminishing his ability to read how he could be attacked. One person could only divide his attention so many times.

Astrid lunged in, dodging around the voyant's sword, taking a swipe to her cheek there, a kick to her stomach there. The blows were the necessary cost of victory.

The last thing to remember was simple action and reaction—a voyant's advantage was only in reaction. Take away his ability to react, and you take away his advantage. Force him to act, and the ground becomes more even. Voyants had supernatural reflexes, but that did not mean they were infallible. If you attacked one quickly enough, if your onslaught was steady, the moves would blend together. The voyant would falter. So Astrid had to be *fast*.

She went after him in earnest, striking and retreating, faster and faster. Astrid kicked a leg out from under the voyant, but it was Trave who finally found the opportunity for a killing blow.

Which was exactly what Astrid didn't want.

Trave snarled, lashing his claws at the voyant's neck, but Astrid reacted just in time, shouldering her way into Trave's side while simultaneously slamming her fist onto the voyant's skull. The man dropped to the street, unconscious.

Astrid growled, glaring at Trave. "What in Oblivion do you think you're doing?"

"What I came here to..." Trave's voice faded, as did some of the intense red light from his eyes, leaving only a soft glow. Then he nodded.

The fact that Trave was so willing to back off was one more surprise Astrid could add to her growing list. She had thought she would have to fight him, to force him to let the voyant live for her to interrogate him. Instead, he had conceded the man to her willingly, helping her carry the voyant into the Nazaniin headquarters. Then he returned to the street to clear up the bodies.

Astrid couldn't even begin to guess his motivations. But she had more pressing concerns. She reached out and gripped the voyant's forearm. The man's name was Ferni. He'd been very forthcoming about that; she'd hardly had to torture him at all. But she needed to know a lot more.

Astrid tightened her grip and felt bones crack. Ferni screamed, or made the best attempt he could given that he was gagged. Astrid placed the index finger of her other hand, caked with drying blood, on the voyant's lips.

"Shhhh," she told him. "Shhh." Ferni's screams turned to choked sobs. "There, there," Astrid whispered. "It's all right. I imagine that hurt worse than the slivers of wood under your fingernails, but I promise that pain will return soon, too."

She crinkled her nose. Ferni had shit himself almost an hour ago, and pissed himself more than once by the smell of things. They were in what Astrid assumed was Ferni's office, the place strewn with scrolls and books. Ferni was strapped to a chair, his arms tied in front of him, resting on a desk.

"Look, Ferni," Astrid said. "I don't want to be here any more than you do. Give me something helpful, and this can all end." Ferni stared at her, eyes wide. Sweat soaked his brow. Cold sweat, Astrid imagined. She sighed, sitting back. "I can't imagine the horror of being a voyant and being tortured. You see everything I do before I do it, don't you? Or, at least, you have the option to see it. I know *my* curiosity would get the better of me. I wouldn't be able to help myself. Do you know what I'm going to do next?"

Astrid ran her hand up his thigh, and Ferni let out a light

squeal around the gag. "No, that's not where I'm going. Not yet." Astrid's hand slid back down Ferni's leg, finally resting on his knee. She rubbed the kneecap, smiling at Ferni.

"Do you see it, Ferni? Do you know what I'm going to do next?"

Ferni shook his head, whimpering.

"Are you sure you don't want to look?" Astrid said. "It might prepare you for the pain."

Ferni shook his head again.

"You could always just tell me what I want to know. Then all of this would go away."

Ferni shook his head, this time closing his eyes. Then, Ferni squirmed mightily, letting out a scream through the gag.

Astrid laughed out loud. "You peeked ahead, didn't you?" She gripped Ferni's kneecap between her fingertips and squeezed. Lightly at first, then squeezing harder and harder. Ferni's squirming and screaming grew more and more frantic, until the bone shattered between Astrid's fingers, and Ferni's screaming commenced in earnest.

Astrid waited a few moments for Ferni's cries to weaken into sobs. Then she slammed her fist down on the desk. "Ferni!"

Ferni jumped, or whatever the equivalent of a man tied to a chair and table jumping looked like. His eyes shot toward Astrid.

"Are you going to talk now, or what?"

Ferni looked at her, eyes wide, tears streaming down his face. Then, slowly, Ferni nodded.

Astrid grinned. "Wonderful," she said. She reached out, and Ferni flinched. "Now, now, I'm just removing your gag. I've got to be able to understand you, otherwise I'm afraid you're only in for more pain." She untied the gag, and Ferni gasped in a breath. "Now, what do you know about Lathe Tallon?"

Ferni took another deep, ragged breath.

Astrid sighed impatiently, leaning forward. "If you're not ready to talk, I'll—"

"No!"

Astrid raised her hands, leaning back. "Very well then, Ferni. Talk."

"All right," Ferni said, and his face scrunched up tight like he was about to sob, but he fought it. By the Goddess, the man fought it. "All right," he repeated. "Lathe Tallon."

"That's right," Astrid said. "I know he was a member of your order, Ferni. Tell me what you know about Lathe the agent of the Nazaniin."

"He was one of our top agents," Ferni said. "He was in the High Echelon."

"What's the High Echelon?"

"The Triad's favorite psimancers, their generals. The most talented and dangerous psimancers in the world. Lathe was… everyone in the organization knew his name."

Astrid shook her head. "Is that all you have to tell me? Because if so, I…"

"I've seen him," Ferni said. "Twice. Years ago, he was sent on a mission here to assassinate… to assassinate two members of the nobility."

"The Storonams," Astrid said.

Ferni's eyes widened, but he nodded. "Yes," he said. "Lord and Lady Storonam. He was sent here to kill them."

"Why him and not you?" Astrid asked.

"Local agents never handle local jobs," Ferni whispered, leaning his head back against the chair. "We always bring in outside help for that."

Astrid nodded. "To keep your cover?"

"Among other things."

"You saw him a second time. When was that?"

"Almost two years ago, before he disappeared. He was on his way to…"

"Where?"

Ferni looked at her, eyes twitching.

"Canta's bones," Astrid muttered. "I'll hurt you more if you don't tell me, Ferni. Confidentiality be damned. Tell me what he was doing."

"Going to Roden," Ferni said. "He was going to Roden, for a job. I don't know what it was, I swear."

Astrid nodded, considering this. The story tallied with what Knot said had happened, with what she had heard about in Izet. But still, none of this seemed helpful. "Who do you report to?" she asked.

Ferni's eyes widened.

"Who is it?" Astrid asked again. "Ferni, I don't have to keep encouraging you, do I?"

"No," Ferni whispered, hanging his head. "No. I report to Rune. A member of the Triad."

"A voyant?" Astrid asked.

"A voyant, yes."

"And you report to him via voidstone?"

"Yes."

"Where is it?"

"Oh, for Canta's sake—"

In one smooth motion, Astrid's hand snapped out and clamped itself on Ferni's mouth. With the other, she drew out her claws, and pointed one long, knife-like claw a hair's breadth away from Ferni's open eye. "Where is it?" Astrid asked again. Ferni squirmed, screams muffled by Astrid's hand. "Will you tell me?"

Ferni nodded vigorously. Astrid released her hand from his mouth, but kept her claw close to his open eye. "In a pouch, near my cloak," he said.

Sure enough, she found the stone in a pouch. She held it up. "This is the one?" she asked.

"Let me see it."

Astrid held it up to him, showing Ferni the rune on the smooth stone's surface.

Ferni nodded. "That will get you in touch with Rune."

Astrid looked at the voidstone, turning it over in her fingers. Then she looked back at Ferni. "Transfer it to me," she said.

With a sob, Ferni's head bowed. "I already have," he said. "I began it the moment you asked where it was."

Astrid nodded. What the man said was true. She could feel the voidstone bonding to her. This might be what could truly help Knot. This might be what they had both been looking for.

You only had to torture a man to get it.

Astrid banished the thought. What was done was done. She could help this man, now. "Thank you, Ferni," she said. "You've been a great help. I'm sorry for what I have done to you."

Astrid reached out and drew one claw across Ferni's throat. She did not stay to watch the blood flow.

"Did you get what you came for?" Trave asked.

"I did. Did you take care of the bodies?"

Trave nodded.

"Good," Astrid said. "Then let's get the hell out of here. I would *love* to never see this city again."

"I know what you mean," Trave said, and as he said it Astrid caught the hint of something in his one eye—what was it? A flicker, perhaps of the fear she had sensed in him days ago, perhaps of the anger she had known before. She could not read him.

They walked out of the Nazaniin tower-house together, into the early morning darkness.

There waiting for them was Olin Cabral and what appeared to be all of his Fangs.

"What is this?" Astrid asked, looking at Cabral.

"You've done me a great service, Astrid," Cabral said. "It is now my turn to repay you."

"I have what I need," Astrid said. "I don't need payment." She knew what Cabral considered payment; she wanted none of it.

Cabral sighed. "I was afraid you would say that. And I'm afraid I must insist." He nodded to Trave.

Astrid turned to Trave just in time to see his face. He did not look triumphant. If anything, his face showed… sorrow?

"I'm sorry," Trave said. Then they descended upon her.

151st Year of the People's Age, Cabral residence, Turandel

Astrid scrubbed the floor, watching the blood fade from the stone. Another servant dead. Another one of the silly human girls who thought they could gain something by associating with Olin Cabral. And Astrid was cleaning up the mess.

Behind her, the Fangs laughed and drank. Cabral had been gone for almost a week; no one would say where. That had made the week difficult. Without Cabral, the Fangs were unruly. Without Cabral, the Fangs were unafraid.

The smell of sanguinar *reached Astrid's nostrils, and her mouth watered. They let her have the drink only on occasion. When she was a good girl, they said. She had to resist the urge to lick the blood from the floor, suck it from the cloth. They would beat her for drinking it. They would break her bones, only to let them heal, and then break them again. Astrid knew that from experience.*

The other servants, all older than Astrid, the fools who thought there was something to gain from being here, attended the Fangs, seemingly oblivious to the blood on the floor.

The sound of a bottle shattering reached Astrid's ears, the sharp crack and sprinkling of glass, and the Fangs laughed harder. One of them laughed so hard that he began choking on his drink. Astrid turned, hoping it was Trave. She was disappointed; it was only Fuud, the buffoon who made an idiot of himself once an hour or so. One of the Fangs shouted something, but Astrid ignored them, hoping she could clean this mess and go back to her quarters without any trouble.

It wasn't until she heard the shout a third time that Astrid realized it was directed towards her. She immediately turned, her face growing pale.

Trave was staring at her, red-faced. "What did you say, girl?" Trave rasped. Astrid had heard many stories of what happened to Trave's voice. Some said that, before he turned, Trave had suffered from some disease. Others said he'd growled his throat raw while running through the wilds like an animal. Still others said Cabral had once forced him to eat hot coals as punishment. Astrid did not know which was true, if any of them were.

Astrid stood, head bowed, facing Trave. "Nothing, sir. I didn't say nothing."

Trave laughed. "If you didn't say nothing, then you said something, girl. What did you say?"

Astrid swallowed. Sometimes they fell for the poor-child routine, the child who couldn't speak properly. Other times, they did not.

"I am sorry, sir. 'Fraid I misspoke. I did not say anything, sir."

Trave frowned, glaring at Astrid with those horrible, dead eyes. The now-silent Fangs glared at her with contempt; the other servants stared at her with indifference. Astrid had never gotten along with either—the Fangs thought her inferior, even though she was one of them, and the servants viewed her as one of the Fangs but worse: not just a monster, but an abomination that had taken the soul of a child.

"Very well," Trave rasped. He sat back down, chuckling. "Back to work, bitch."

Astrid nodded, swallowing hard. She had barely knelt down when she felt strong arms lift her back up.

No.

The Fangs laughed as they carried her across the room. Trave smiled as Astrid was brought to him. She returned his gaze, too afraid to look away. That only made things worse.

The two men set her down in front of Trave, still seated at the head of the table, where Cabral normally sat. Trave had grown bolder, lately; there was once a time when no one would have dared sit there.

"Our little Astrid," Trave whispered, leaning forward. "You've never quite learned to behave, have you? Never quite learned to obey your betters."

A few Fangs, Fuud included, chuckled at this. Astrid knew the routine well. She would find no friends here. The best thing to do was submit. But that did not stop her mind from pleading against what was about to happen.

"I am very sorry, sir," Astrid said.

"You aren't sorry," Trave rasped. Then, in one smooth motion, he stood, and punched her in the face. Astrid's head snapped back, her neck cracking. She lifted it just in time to see another blow pound into her gut. Astrid's body tried to double over in pain, but the Fangs held her up. Night had fallen a few hours ago, and the vampires were at their strongest. This included Astrid, but she was by far the weakest vampire present, nighttime or not. Being punched by Trave was like a human child being punched by a human adult.

Astrid endured a few more punches, hoping that would be the worst of it. But, when Trave ordered the Fangs to hold her down, she knew it would not be.

"Fetch me the Songbird," Trave rasped.

No, please, Goddess.

The Fangs hurled Astrid roughly to the table, crushing china and sending silverware and goblets flying. The tangy fumes of sanguinar *filled Astrid's nostrils, but she had neither time nor energy to crave it. Four Fangs now held her down, one on each limb. Astrid raised her head as much as she could, staring at Trave through a swollen eye. Her heart pounded in her skull, her eyes were blurred with blood and tears. One of the Fangs arrived carrying a small, silvery hammer. The thing looked tiny in Trave's large palm.*

"Do you know why I call this one the Songbird?" Trave asked, grinning down at Astrid.

Astrid shook her head, unable to stop the tears streaming down her face. Of course she knew why Trave called the hammer the Songbird; he had told her dozens of times, and insisted on retelling her, every time.

"Because it makes people sing like little birds," Trave said, laughing and laughing. Then, his voice grew hard. "Hold her hand down."

Fangs slammed her palm onto the table, and Astrid knew from experience that if she did not spread her fingers wide, she would face worse.

Trave laughed. "Such a good little girl," he said. "You know the routine so well." Then, with a sharp crack, Trave slammed the Songbird down onto the tip of Astrid's little finger.

Astrid shouted, her shout quickly fading into something between a cry and whimper.

"Ah, just like a songbird," Trave said, and smashed the little hammer down on Astrid's ring finger.

This time she screamed, her scream deteriorating into sobs, and Trave continued, shattering the bones in each one of her fingers.

"I grow tired of this," Trave said, having finished with her left hand.

"Want the Minstrel?" one of the Fangs asked.

The Minstrel was a normal-sized hammer. The bones Trave crushed with the Minstrel were much more difficult to heal. Astrid took a deep breath. She could handle the Minstrel. As long as he didn't—

"Bring me the Diva," Trave said, tossing the Songbird aside. "I'm in the mood for a real performance."

No, no, no, Goddess please, no!

Astrid tried to stay calm, but fear raked at her chest, made her shiver. Best thing to do was stare at the ceiling and wait for it to be over. But with the Diva, she couldn't do that. Trave would break her legs, her arms, her ribs, everything he could with the massive sledgehammer. Astrid couldn't endure pain like that again. She would not endure pain like that again.

And then, something within her snapped—she almost heard whatever it was break apart in her mind. She looked from side to side, at the Fangs who held her arms. Gardin to her left—he was too strong for her by far, and her left hand was all but useless. Fuud to her right. Fuud. He was drunk, and he was a fool. Fuud was the one.

Astrid twisted her right arm so she could grip Fuud's forearm, and then squeezed with every ounce of strength she could muster. She felt the bones of Fuud's forearm break. Fuud screamed, and the crunch of bones filled Astrid with elation.

But her right arm was free, and between Astrid and Fuud, lying on the table, she saw salvation: a long knife, meant for cutting fish, slightly curved. Astrid swept the knife up in her hand, raised her head, and stabbed Trave in the eye.

Trave, who had just taken the Diva up in one hand, looked out into nothing for a moment, his mouth agape.

Astrid did not know why, perhaps from the shock of what had just happened, perhaps because of an act of some god or goddess that had a brief fraction of a moment of pity for Astrid, but the Fangs who held Astrid's legs suddenly let go.

Only then did Trave begin to scream.

Astrid twisted, brought her knees to her chest, and then kicked with all her strength. Both feet connected with Trave's torso and sent him flying across the room like a stone from a sling, crashing into the wall above the fireplace. Trave fell, part in and part out of the fire, and before Astrid could even register what she was doing she had leapt across the room and was beating him, beating Trave's head into the coals of the fire, blow after blow raining down on him, feeling the flames lick up her arms but not caring. She tore the knife from his eye and began stabbing him, again and again in the chest. She laughed, sick with herself for what had been done to her and for what she had done, but now too far gone to stop herself, and with her injured left hand she reached into the fire for a glowing orange coal.

She held the coal before Trave's face for a fraction of a second, the skin of her hand burning, acrid smoke rising into the air. Then she thrust the coal into the bleeding hole where Trave's eye had been.

"Do not ever touch me again or I will kill you," she wanted to say. But all she could do was scream into Trave's face, scream and scream until her throat was raw. Then she pulled herself away.

Everyone in the room was staring at her, eyes and mouths wide. None of the Fangs made any move to approach her. No one made any move at all.

So Astrid limped away, felt the burning heat and crushing pain of her charred left hand, the raw soreness in her throat. She fled Cabral's great hall, already feeling her body heal, already wondering whether her soul ever would. At the entrance of Cabral's tower-house she ran. She ran and ran, until she left Turandel, until she left everything and all of it far, far behind.

30

Imperial palace, Izet

WINTER STOOD TALL NEXT to Daval, the fire of *faltira* burning in her veins. She couldn't help but try using her *tendra*, but—as always—she was blocked. No matter. She would find a weakness one day; that was why she needed to take the *faltira* so often, now that she had a limitless supply. She needed to take it to test the blocks on her power.

They were in the Lords' Hall, meeting with the Ruling Council. Daval sat on a throne at the head of the long oak table. He had recently appointed his new son-in-law, Girgan Mandiat, to the position of First Counselor—the position the young man's father had occupied until he'd been killed at the succession vote. Girgan sat on Daval's immediate right, Hirman Luce next to him. Daval had allowed Luce to remain Second Counselor, even though Luce had tried to mount a coup against him. Winter couldn't fathom why he'd been chosen to serve on the Ruling Council. Luce, Winter realized, was likely one of the enemies she had been hired to intimidate.

To Daval's left sat Watch Commander Borce Kuglen, merchant leader Arstan Dagnatar, and High Priestess Jemma Rowady. His daughter Cova, as the new crown princess, sat opposite him on the other end of the table.

Each of the members of the Council eyed Winter warily; this was the first time Daval had deigned to display her in public. The stares of fear and distrust brought Winter a great deal of pleasure.

Daval's retainer of Ceno monks stood near the doorway, while Winter and Urstadt flanked the throne. Winter wore a dark tunic and a black leather overcoat, the hem of which reached her thighs. The overcoat was padded and studded, but still surprisingly light. She also had tight leather breeches, similar to those Kali had given her, but more comfortable and useful. Galce knew his business; the breeches had hidden pockets for blades and other weapons. She carried a dagger and a small knife, and the fact that she had no knowledge of how to use them, other than for hunting and fishing, was something no one else needed to know.

"It is time we recommence Grysole's work," Daval was saying, looking around the table. "Grysole was building our power, preparing to attack Khale. It is important that we continue what he started."

"Your Grace," High Priestess Jemma said, smiling, "with all due respect, are there not more appropriate actions to take at this point? We must rebuild after losing an emperor and a... a major public figure in such short time. The palace sustained such damage..." Jemma's eyes flickered to Winter as she trailed off.

Bloody right, Winter thought. *I destroyed your dome, and the abominations that you'd brought into the Sfaera with it.* But her smugness dissipated as she remembered the monsters she'd faced. She suppressed a shiver.

Girgan Mandiat laughed. "Of course you would want to hold off on our offensive against Khale, High Priestess. The Denomination wouldn't want the seat of its power threatened."

"The Denomination is *neutral*, my Lord," Jemma said, her voice stern. "We don't take sides in such things. We prefer peace, of course, and that's always what I would advise."

"Neutral my ass," Arstan Dagnatar muttered. The table erupted in shouts and accusations, the nobles and leaders yelling at one another in anger.

"*Order!*" Daval shouted above the chaos. "I will not have my Ruling Council behaving like children. We will discuss this civilly, I command it."

Borce Kuglen leaned forward. "I'm sorry, Your Grace, but I must agree with the high priestess. Our forces in Izet were greatly diminished during the..." he too glanced at Winter, "the disaster. Rebuilding is necessary, I'm afraid."

"If we are constantly rebuilding, we'll never accomplish anything of our own," Dagnatar responded. "We live in a new age, a time where the Sfaera is open to us. I say we seize every opportunity we can."

Kuglen shook his head. "If you had any military experience at all, you'd know that an offensive move is folly when there is unrest at home. We must take care of the inner vessel first, before we look outwards."

Winter knew next to nothing about these people, only what little her servants had told her. Daval had remained silent about the business aspect of these meetings; he only wanted her there for intimidation purposes. She considered, not for the first time, entering the minds of some of these people to discern what their true intentions were. But she did not know if she could stop herself from slipping into the strange place of star-lights, as she'd done before. And she couldn't risk her acumency being discovered.

Hirman Luce, who had been silent up until this point, raised his head. "I'm surprised you're willing to consider an offensive against Roden at all, Your Grace," he said, spitting out the last word with derision. "You've taken one of their own, a tiellan, as your pet. How do we know you don't mean to sell us out to Khale, or worse, allow the tiellans a place in our society once more?"

All eyes turned to Winter. There was animosity, fear, and distrust on everyone's faces.

"Winter is now my private bodyguard," Daval said, "that's all. As for her status as a Khalic citizen and a tiellan, I have granted her amnesty as long as she serves me."

Dagnatar leaned forward, speaking more quietly, as if doing so would mean that Winter couldn't hear him. Winter was quickly placing the merchant leader solidly in the idiot camp. "Can you really control someone of such… such power?" he asked.

"Of course not," Daval said, inducing a bout of nervous shifting around the table. "I couldn't possibly control her. But why ask me? Why not let her speak for herself?"

"I have sworn to serve Daval Amok," Winter said. "And by association, the good of Roden." It was much easier to say than she had thought it would be. She wanted vengeance against those who had slaughtered her loved ones but vengeance was exhausting. And she simply did not have the resources to mount such an offensive. It did not seem to satisfy the others, but it wasn't meant to; her unpredictability was as important to her intimidation factor as her reputation of power.

"I assure you, my Lords, my Ladies, my devotion to Roden is full," Daval said. "That's exactly why we must press forward with our offensive against Khale."

"We could do both."

Winter watched, almost with disappointment, as all eyes turned to Cova Amok.

"What do you mean, daughter?"

"We can rebuild here and begin our offensive simultaneously."

Kuglen laughed. "I'm sorry, princess, but we don't have the resources for such a—"

"I'm sorry, *Kuglen*, but I wasn't finished."

Winter smiled. She liked this girl already.

Cova continued. "We need to put effort into rebuilding here, that much is true. So why not involve the citizens in the effort? They can rebuild the dome. We don't need the Watch or the army to do that, nor do we need them to increase morale."

"Without a sense of security," Kuglen said, "we can't increase morale. My forces provide that security."

Cova rolled her eyes. "We wouldn't take *all* your forces, Kuglen. We would leave sufficient for the needs of Izet, but we could use a number of your cohorts to bolster our Imperial Contingent. We can marshall the forces of Andrinar and the Island Coalition, but I'm afraid that will not be enough. Besides, what more would increase the sense of security, and the morale of our citizens, than a successful offensive?"

Other heads nodded slowly around the table. The high priestess remained silent; it seemed she did not think it worth the effort to voice her concerns further. Rowady was the odd one out in this group. Winter wondered how much longer the Denomination could expect to have any influence in Roden.

"I believe the princess has the beginnings of a solid plan," Girgan said, smiling at his wife.

"It sounds feasible to me," Dagnatar said.

Daval, too, smiled. "It does, indeed. Cova, would you mind drafting a proposal, showing us the details?"

"Of course, Father."

"Have it ready for us within the week, and we can vote on the motion. I believe it will be for the best of Roden."

The meeting progressed, but the items of business grew

less and less interesting, and Winter found her mind wandering. She was vaguely aware of some of the Council members staring at her, but she did not care. *Let them stare,* she thought. *Perhaps, in the near future, I can give them even more reason to do so.*

When the meeting had ended, Winter and Urstadt escorted Daval through the corridors of the palace. Winter was fully aware that her presence was nothing but a formality. Urstadt was the only one who could really defend Daval. A part of Winter hoped something might happen, just to see Urstadt in action. Winter had heard many things about this warrior in people's thoughts as she traveled through them during her captivity. She felt the same curiosity, the same draw that had drawn her to Kali: Urstadt had strength. Winter wanted what Urstadt had.

"That was a productive meeting, don't you think?" Daval asked as they walked.

"I suppose," Winter said.

"Your response was perfect, I must say."

Winter nodded. She was still not sure how to act around this man. Was she his captive? Just a weapon? Surely he did not think of her as his equal?

"That is what you expect of me, then?" Winter asked. "To stand by your side and look intimidating?"

"Close enough," Daval said. "People fear what they don't understand and can't predict."

Yes. She wondered, momentarily, whether such a tactic might even work with Daval.

"Luce is a problem," Urstadt said.

"Luce is a controlled problem," Daval muttered. "The only reason I've let him live is to set an example for the others."

"An example of what, Your Grace? I would think swift

justice would have been the most effective response."

"But not the most effective," Daval said. "I have other plans at work." He glanced at Winter. "What do you think of that poem we discussed—'Wild Calamity'?"

Winter shrugged. Daval had explained it to her, something about the process of creation, and how love and destruction were inherent parts of that process. It all sounded like nonsense to her.

"I find it interesting,"Winter said. *Might as well play the part.*

"Consider those words as we prepare to take action against Hirman Luce. I think you will find them invaluable."

I doubt that.

"How would you feel if I were to grant you the use of your powers?"

It took all of Winter's control to hide her excitement. She cared far more about psimancy than silly poems. She stared at him, trying to keep her face expressionless. "How do you know I wouldn't use them against you?"

"It is a simple thing for me to drop the blocks I've placed on you," Daval said. "And just as simple for me to raise them up again. I would grant you temporary access, but if you used your powers against me, you'd lose them again. Permanently."

Permanently. Winter was not so sure. Daval didn't know she had access to acumency. She doubted he knew enough about her to take away her psimantic access completely.

And yet.

She craved the feel of using telesis again almost as much as she craved frost. Frost was not the same when she couldn't use her powers. It would feel so *good* to feel powerful again.

"What do you want me to do?"Winter asked.

Daval smiled. "I want you to make an example of Hirman Luce."

* * *

Hours later, when the woman has been shown her new quarters in the imperial palace, she finds herself lying on her bed—her new bed, stuffed and covered in smooth sheets and thick quilts, in the middle of her new room, modest by the palace standards, she is sure, but larger than any room she has slept in before. Two pouches lie on a carved table. One is filled with gold, the other with *faltira*. The woman ingested one of the frost crystals only moments before, and now lets herself drift with the sensation. As she lies on her bed, looking up at the canopied top, her mind leaves her body, and she finds herself jumping from mind to mind once more.

This time, however, the woman almost immediately finds herself in the place of drifting star-lights. The transition to this place of darkness, interspersed with millions of tiny lights, was much easier this time. In fact, what she realizes as she walks through the darkness, each step sending ripples of light out into the black, is that the lights around her feel very similar to the minds in which she travels. Each of the lights, she thinks, might be one of those minds. Perhaps she has been traveling through this space for some time, but is only now beginning to see it.

While this place of darkness and stars holds a certain wonder, she is not sure what she could, or should, be doing here. Then she hears sound where there wasn't sound before. Voices whispering in the dark. She can only make out a word or two.

Murderer.

Harbinger.

The voices echo in her mind, but she ignores them as best she can. Eventually, just like the last time, she sees the figure. A shape formed of the darkness between lights. This time, her fear is less pronounced.

Who are you? the woman asks.

The figure does not respond.

Tell me who you are, the woman says again, making the voice that emanates from her mind firmer. *I demand it.*

The figure stops advancing. The shape of shaded darkness stops, blending in with the stars, and the woman suddenly wonders whether it is there at all.

Who are you? she asks.

Winter?

The woman's eyes open wide. *Yes,* she says. *Who… who are you?*

The figure draws closer once more, and for the first time the woman discerns details. The figure's shape is thin, feminine, with long hair.

The woman's hand immediately moves to her neck, looking for a black stone necklace that is not there. *Who are you?*

Winter, the figure says, getting closer and closer. The woman can now see ripples of color spreading through the blackness from the figure's footsteps.

And, as the figure approaches, the woman can finally see. The figure has long blond hair, she is small and lithe. Then she is taller, with short black hair and eyes the color of a clear winter sky. Then she is someone different altogether, someone the woman does not recognize.

"Welcome to the Void, Winter," the figure says, not in the language of the mind but with words, words the woman can hear, and the figure smiles a smile that remains constant, despite her shifting features. A smile the woman remembers.

"Kali," the woman says.

The figure's smile broadens. "I've been waiting for you."

Interlude: Into the Void

Six months ago, Izet

"Who are you?" Lathe asked.

Kali laughed. "Of course," she said. "After all this time, you do not know. My name is Kali."

Then Lathe was rushing towards her, sword drawn. In a fraction of a moment she knew.

She was about to die.

Lathe's elbow slammed into her nose, snapping Kali's head back in a burst of pain and dark color, and his sword quickly followed, burying itself in her chest. Kali looked up at Lathe in surprise. Her mouth worked, but nothing came out. She tried to breathe, but could only gurgle. Time moved slowly, and Kali knew what she needed to do. She had her sift prepared and ready to send. She only needed a receptacle, a lacuna. The boy elf might do, his mind was malleable enough. If she only had more time…

Kali snapped her hand up, the hand holding the dagger, hoping to buy herself a few more moments as she reached out with her *tendra* toward Lian. But Lathe ducked, and Kali felt a burning tear as the sword was yanked from her chest.

"Lathe," Kali rasped, falling to her knees, frantically reaching out with her *tendron*, the *tendron* that carried the precious package of her life, the way she had resurrected herself three times before, searching for Lian.

"I'm s-sorry… I was only… following…"

"My name," Lathe said, raising his sword, "is Knot."

Then he lunged, and Kali's vision faded, her *tendron* still extended, fading, extending, fading, extending into darkness…

When Kali awoke, she could not breathe. She tried to fill her lungs, but felt nothing. She was in darkness, and she was darkness, and she was nothing at all.

She could not breathe, but she did not need to breathe. Kali tried to stand, but nothing happened. Was she paralyzed? She tried to remember, tried to think of the last thing she had seen. Something about a fountain. Nash had been there. And Lathe.

Kali, remembering, raised a hand to her neck. Lathe had stabbed her. Twice.

She should be dead.

She remembered reaching out a *tendron* with her sift, towards Lian. But she did not remember reaching him. And besides, Lian had not been wiped, so the results could have been disastrous. She should be dead. Her body had died, her sift had not found a new receptacle.

And yet, here she was.

Kali's first instinct was to reach for the pocket at her breast, for that slip of paper. Then she remembered how that paper had been lost in Navone, but even more worrying was the fact that she couldn't feel her body. She looked down but it was too dark to see anything. She moved her hands frantically, trying to find her face, her neck, her chest, her legs. She swiped her arm through where her head should be, where her vision should begin, and there was nothing.

This is a nightmare, Kali thought. *This is not real.*

She screamed a silent scream, and only the darkness heard her silence.

She had been in the darkness for what seemed like millennia. She felt nothing, could see nothing, seemed to *be* nothing.

But it was not a nightmare. It couldn't be. No nightmare lasted this long. No nightmare had such vivid sensation, and yet no sensation at all. And no nightmare was this constant. That, Kali knew more than anything.

This is death. Kali could remember, could almost—*almost*—feel the sharp stab that seared through her neck, killing her. That *must* have killed her.

But, if she was dead, why was she here? She was in darkness, but she was *not* here. Perhaps, Kali considered, she was in Oblivion.

There are worse things than Oblivion.

Then she noticed, in the distance, a tiny green light.

A light was good. A light was not Oblivion. Kali moved towards the light, surprised to find that she could indeed move, although not in any way that made sense to her. She did not walk but somehow shifted through the darkness towards the light. The closer Kali got, the more lights she saw. Hundreds, then thousands, and then beyond number.

The Void, Kali thought, a hint of hope blossoming somewhere in her—where? Her heart? Her mind? Neither seemed present, neither seemed able to house any sort of feeling, and yet there it was, blossoming in the space she occupied.

She was in the Void. The countless star-like lights around her blinked and burned, illuminating the darkness. One light in particular, a light that was somehow both a light and a pit of darkness at once, drew Kali towards it. This was a light she had never seen before. It was a dark, immolating mass, black and pulsing. She did not know who or what it was, but it pulled Kali towards it, as if she were caught by an ocean riptide.

Kali smiled, or at least she felt the way she would feel if she had been smiling. She did not know how she got here. She did not know why, or how she had become incorporeal. But she was not, it would seem, dead. She had hope. Perhaps she could find a way out of this place, make it back to another body. Another lacuna.

Kali eyed the dark-light warily. She would have to find out about that. But she was alive, in a manner of speaking, and she would do anything she bloody had to do to survive.

Four months ago, in the Void

Later, the amount of later Kali couldn't possibly comprehend, her hope had begun to fade. She had tried visiting other lights, had tried reaching *tendra* into them, had tried prying into their minds, their bodies, had tried using them as tools, but she felt powerless. She was nothing but a shade.

The dark-light was the only thing she felt a remote connection to, and that connection was *powerful*. Kali resolved that her only option was to explore the phenomenon. Moving towards the dark-light was easy; Kali only had to remain still, and the thing drew her towards itself. And it seemed that many of the other lights were drawn to the dark-light too.

The closer Kali came to the burning mass, the faster she moved. She moved so quickly she felt as if she were expanding, as if she were elongating past a point that made rational sense. When she finally reached the dark-light, the size of which Kali couldn't possibly determine—in one moment it still seemed the size of a pin-prick, then the size of a mountain—she felt herself pulled *into* the thing, bit by elongated bit.

And yet Kali was not afraid. She felt curiosity more than anything, a need to understand the dark miracle within the Void.

Quite suddenly, everything shifted around her. The color of the star-lights in the distance, the immolating dark of the thing that had Kali in its grasp, all swirled together, and she felt herself shifting, moving, coalescing.

Kali opened her eyes. Eyes that were real, eyes that could see. She raised her hand before her face, saw her fingers, long and slender. She tried to touch her face, but felt immediate disappointment. She felt nothing. But at least she now had some idea of herself.

As her eyes focused, Kali realized she was floating, looking down on something. Someone. Kali was in a cell. And below her, lying in the straw, was a figure Kali knew well. So well she swore, in rage and confusion and elation and triumph, in question and in wonder and in jealousy and in love.

The Harbinger.

Three months ago

Kali had watched Winter lying in her cell for only moments, and then she'd been jettisoned. Kali couldn't describe the experience otherwise. It was as if she had been on the tip of a massive whip that had lashed forward, cracked, and was then flung rapidly back into the Void.

And yet, that brief moment in Winter's presence had changed Kali. She was still incorporeal, but she could now move about the Void more easily, and, most importantly, she could now interact with the other star-lights. While she still had no *tendra* to speak of, she could approach the lights, see shadows of what they saw, hear fragments of conversations that they had, even discern whispers of their thoughts.

The Void, Kali had come to understand, was organized geographically. Distant lights, when she drew closer to them, usually expanded into great clusters of thousands of tinier lights. Cities. There was a cluster in Cineste, in Maven Kol, in Alizia, and many, many others. The biggest cluster of all, of course, was in Triah. But Kali found herself occupying the cluster of Izet. That made sense; that was where she had died.

Had *nearly* died. Didn't hurt to be optimistic about things.

But Kali had grown bored of Izet, of the overheard conversations. Other than the dark-light of Winter—a force Kali now realized she understood far less than she ever thought she had—she had no reason to stay.

She was going to escape. She would find a new lacuna, a new body to inhabit, and enter the Sfaera once more. But Izet was a dead end; she needed to make her way to Triah. She doubted she would be able to contact anyone in her current state—she was not that naive. But she could, perhaps, discern what the Nazaniin were up to, what their intentions were. After all, it seemed other things had happened, things beyond the scope of what Kali had ever expected. She heard whispers about Daemons returning, and the Scorned Gods of Roden.

And there was something else off about the Void in Izet, in all of Roden, besides Winter's strange dark-light. There was a presence, or an absence, or something affecting the darkness. Whether it was new to the Void since Kali had made her transformation, or whether it was something she could only notice now, she couldn't say.

Traveling through the Void towards Triah was quick work; once you began moving in a direction, you gradually accelerated as long as you stayed on the same trajectory. Unusually, Kali felt resistance, although she was still able to travel easily enough to slip through the darkness like a ship cutting through calm water, and soon she saw Triah's cluster ahead of her. It was a bright pinpoint of light from a distance, but as Kali approached it expanded into a million points of light.

Kali knew her way around Triah better than any other place in the world. She focused her attention on the center of the cluster, where she knew all of the important lights would be: Parliament, Canta's Fane, the Citadel, and beneath the Citadel the Nazaniin headquarters.

The lights were brighter here, although no theorists had yet been able to determine why the consciousnesses of people of great power or influence shone more brightly than others. Some said it was simply their effect on others; they influenced and commanded other lights, and thus drew light from them. Others said it was more of an innate power, shining from within their own potential. Kali did not care. She found such debates tedious, unless they could help her better understand how to use the Void. They had not been effective in that sense, so far.

As Kali searched through the lights, she imagined herself descending the tower of the Citadel, moving down through the floors, beneath the school for gifted and powerful children and finding herself in the headquarters of the Nazaniin, moving further underground still, until she reached the Heart of the Void, the central meeting place of the Nazaniin.

And there, in the Heart, she saw two of the lights for which she searched. She would recognize them anywhere, brighter than almost any other individual lights she had seen.

"They failed." One of the lights flashed as Kali heard the words, and an image began to coalesce before her, like a reflection in a lake settling after a light rain.

She saw a woman form from the other light, her red hair—longer than Kali remembered—tied back in a ponytail. Sirana. "Just as you predicted," Sirana whispered, her light flashing simultaneously as she spoke.

Kali could barely make out the two figures standing at opposite ends of the map table in the Heart of the Void. Sirana on one end, and on the other, Kosarin, bespectacled, bald, and stroking the circle beard he wore cut short.

"It was a necessary sacrifice," Kosarin said. Kali watched him adjust his spectacles. "For the good of the Sfaera."

"We already knew she was the Harbinger. Was it necessary to sacrifice Kali and Nash?"

They knew, Kali thought. *They knew all along that Winter was the Harbinger.* She fought her rising anger.

"It was the final test. You know the girl had to face them, in order for us to know for certain."

"Our sources say it was Lathe who did most of the work. If the girl didn't even participate, then the whole thing tells us nothing."

They were not certain, then? Kali frowned. Winter had to defeat her and Nash, in order to prove herself the Harbinger? That did not make sense. Sirana was right; Lathe—Knot, now—had done most of the work.

And then Kali understood. Sirana seemed to have the same realization. She leaned forward. "You killed them because they were a threat," she whispered, her fingers brushing a wooden chip representing a battalion of the Khalic army.

Kali noticed the bracelet Sirana still wore, a bracelet of voidstones that formed a ward, protecting her from an acumen's delving, Kosarin's included. Even if Kali had her powers, she wouldn't be able to discern Sirana's thoughts.

"You had them killed because Kali was growing too strong," Sirana said, quietly.

Kali was surprised at the pride she felt swell within her. She had always considered Sirana a rival to eliminate. But to hear such praise from Sirana—and, in a way, from Kosarin—pleased her. The feeling was almost as strong as the anger she felt towards Kosarin for what he had done to her.

"I did what was necessary for the Nazaniin," Kosarin said, his voice hard. "You're in no position to argue. You should be thanking me, Sirana. Kali had her eye on your position."

Sirana laughed softly. "Kali couldn't have my position. She was an acumen. If she took anyone's place, it would have been yours."

She's right about that, Kali thought.

"I did us both a favor. I suggest you stop worrying about it; what's done is done."

The faded, shimmering image of Sirana clenched her jaw. Kali could understand the woman's anger. If Kosarin had betrayed Kali, when would he betray Sirana? It seemed only a matter of time.

"If you're thinking I'm going to do the same thing to you, don't worry," Kosarin said, sighing. He sat back in one of the wooden chairs around the table. "I need you, Sirana. I have always needed you. That has not changed."

Sirana remained silent. For a brief moment, Kali felt the slightest hint of pity for the woman. After all, she had ordered her own husband, Lathe, on what she must have thought was a suicide mission into Roden. When the mission met its inevitable failure, she had called off the rescue operation. When someone matching her husband's description had shown up in Pranna, she had stepped aside and allowed Kosarin to send Kali and Nash. And, when the prophecies called for it, she had remained silent when Kosarin had called for Lathe's death.

Sirana had been following orders, for all the good it did her. Kali could respect that.

Kali suddenly realized she was drifting. She was being drawn slowly… somewhere. It did not take long for her to figure out where. She was being drawn backwards, back towards Izet.

Back to Winter.

Was the girl's pull really that strong?

"What of the events in the palace?" Sirana asked.

Kali struggled to remain where she was. Did the Nazaniin know what had happened in Roden? Had they some knowledge of what others were calling the work of the Nine Daemons?

"The ritual was successful."

"And what of the Ceno? What of this new religion?"

"Old religion, technically. Their leader is dead, but I'm sure they will regroup. They will be more of a threat than we realized, if they truly can block psimancy. We will have to be careful around them."

"It seems we have other, larger problems to worry about," Sirana said.

Kosarin nodded. "That we do. We live in an unprecedented time. The Nine Daemons will walk the Sfaera again."

Kali regarded Kosarin in surprise. She had not expected him to be a believer, of all people.

"You're still certain it was necessary?"

"For the Harbinger to reach her greatest potential, she must face the most powerful foes."

The way Kosarin and Sirana were speaking made it seem like they had something to do with what happened in Roden after Kali died. After her transformation, rather.

Kosarin removed his spectacles and began cleaning them with a small cloth. "Now that the Rising has begun, we're going to need to keep control of the Harbinger. The death mark on Lathe's head is officially repealed, and anyone who can bring him home will be rewarded."

"We need to be careful about who we send to bring them in," Sirana said. "It needs to be someone we trust."

"We'll send Code."

Kali laughed to herself. Code was the wrong choice. People said he was powerful, but Kali had strong feelings about that kind of thing. *Never send a variant to do an actual's business.* If Kali couldn't handle Lathe, there was no way Code would be able to. She tried to move closer to Kosarin and Sirana, but she was drifting away, the pull growing stronger.

Sirana shook her head. "He's on assignment in Alizia. Won't be back for weeks, at least. Cymbre just returned; shall we send her instead?"

Kosarin nodded. "She will do. Have her form her own *cotir*, and leave for Roden as soon as possible. We've received a recent contract request that might coincide nicely with their search for Lathe."

"And if Lathe doesn't want to come back?"

They still did not know what happened to him. Or, at least, they had not believed Kali's reports. They did not understand that Lathe was no more.

Kali could still remember the man's last words to her. *My name is Knot.*

Kosarin sighed. "You know the consequences, Sirana."

Kali did well enough. Death.

"Canta rising, we've got a lot of shit to do now," Kosarin

grumbled. "I'm going to sleep. Tomorrow begins a new age. It's up to us to determine whether it is humanity's last, or not." Then he stood and walked out of the room.

Sirana remained, looking at the map pinned to the large table before her. She pulled her knees up to her chest, wrapping her arms around her legs.

Kali watched Sirana for a moment longer, but the pull on her was so strong now that it seemed to take all of her energy to remain where she was. Reluctantly, Kali let herself be drawn back to Izet's cluster in the Void and the burning dark-light that now fully controlled her.

Two months ago

Kali found that she couldn't venture far from Izet for long without Winter's pull dragging her back. But the longer she stayed in Izet—the longer she stayed close to Winter—the more interesting things became.

Winter, it seemed, had gained access to acumency. Such a thing was unheard of; there was no record of anyone having more than one psimantic power in the history of the psionic arts. But Winter was the Harbinger. And, based on the strangeness of her dark-light star, she was an exception to the rule.

Winter's dark-light did not seem to function the way normal lights did in the Void. During her observations at the Citadel, Kali had seen acumen lights in action. Normally, an acumen light moved from place to place, interacting with other lights through *tendra*. Winter's star remained completely stationary, but drew other lights to it—*through* it—and interacted with them directly, with no *tendra* whatsoever.

It was a fascinating process to watch. Winter would jump

from mind to mind, would draw those lights *through* her in the Void. Kali had no idea what it meant, but it was certainly new.

There was another phenomenon she noticed, one light that was not actually a light at all—or, rather, it seemed completely covered by darkness. Kali couldn't discern who or what this light was, and Winter did not seem able to do so either. Although Kali had noticed, just barely in the corners of her vision, that when she was able to discern this dark object, it had some connection to something greater, something almost like a *tendron* that connected it with a larger force.

Mysteries filled the Void, more than ever before.

One month ago

Based on what she learned from eavesdropping on Kosarin and Sirana, Kali had a new set of ambitions. Kosarin had considered her a threat; that was why he had ordered her into a situation that got her killed.

Not quite killed.

A sense of urgency stalked her, as constant and nagging as the pull of Winter's immolating darkness. Which was why she had resolved to show Kosarin what he was truly up against. Kali had threatened him before; she would find a way to do it again, and make him understand what the feeling truly meant.

Unfortunately, Winter's pull was more and more difficult to escape. Kali could now only move away for short periods at a time, and could rarely find any conversations or lights worth investigating. She was beginning to understand how fortunate that first trip had been.

In Kali's most recent attempt to find Kosarin, Sirana, or even Rune, she managed to stay in Triah for what felt like mere moments before Winter's pull exerted its inevitable weight. But for those few moments, Kali recognized something odd. That same uneasy feeling, that same strange quality that affected Izet was now present in Triah, too. In Triah it was different, if only slightly, and because it was different it was almost easier to detect. It was as if a shroud had enveloped the Triah cluster, barely visible but detectable nonetheless. It was a misty film, of a faded, mostly transparent, purplish hue. What it meant, Kali didn't know. But she was beginning to suspect it had something to do with what had happened in Roden—with the ritual that Kosarin and Sirana had mentioned.

As she was pulled back from Triah, Kali noticed another phenomenon. She passed a small light, what she was sure would be a tiny cluster if she drew closer to it, covered by another shroud, similar to what ensconced Triah, although this one was blue rather than violet. What these colors meant, Kali could not even begin to guess.

And, when she returned to Izet once more, she finally saw what had been bothering her the entire time. Perhaps it was because she had noticed the shrouds around Triah and that place in between, or perhaps it was something else, but as Kali approached Izet she saw it. Another shroud, like that around Triah, but this one was so black that it was almost invisible, blending in with the Void. And, if Kali had to venture a guess, she would say that the strange darkness, the light that was completely covered, was connected to this shroud in some way through that strange *tendron*.

Kali realized she'd been reaching for the paper in her pocket once more. Old habits died hard.

* * *

Three weeks ago

Winter's pull was getting stronger. Kali could still travel with some effort, but she was not sure she would be able to make it all the way to Triah again. She resigned herself to observing the strange dark-light pulsing, occasionally going through periods of cycling through a half-dozen or a dozen lights, drawing them in, processing them for a moment, and then sending them back out.

It was during one of these cycles that the dark-light grew into a blur; it had been a tiny point of existence in the Void, but then it began to change. The dark-light grew.

And then Kali was no longer staring at the dark-light. Instead, she was staring at Winter.

Kali immediately moved closer, but as strong as the pull had been before, something had replaced it. A repulsion emanating from Winter kept Kali at bay. She struggled to approach the girl, speak to her, but to no avail.

This is it, Kali thought, *this is my opportunity. This is what I need to regain control.*

Kali pushed against the force that repelled her, pushed with all the urgency she had felt during her time in the Void, now accumulated and compounded and crackling all around her. She strained, watching as Winter—a corporeal, tangible Winter, eyes and hair dark as the Void around her—walked through the Void, her footsteps sending ripples of color out into the black.

As Kali fought her way closer to Winter, she began to sense herself, her body, forming.

Winter looked first afraid, then confused, and finally curious. But, just as Winter started to move in Kali's direction, just as Kali was moving through whatever force restrained her, Winter looked up, and seemed to look directly at Kali.

Kali cried out, tried to communicate with the girl, but she did not hear her. Instead, Winter's eyes widened, flooding with terror.

Kali cried out again. Winter took a few steps backwards, colors echoing beneath her, raising her arms to shield herself.

What are you? Winter asked, her timid voice echoing within Kali's consciousness.

Kali! Winter, it's me, Kali! Answer me, tell me you can hear me! For the love of Canta, answer me!

Then Winter was gone.

Yesterday

Kali had been drifting, letting the expanse of the Void wash over her, thinking of nothing, when the familiar pull of the dark-light shifted once more into resistance. Immediately Kali's awareness heightened. She looked around, and sure enough saw Winter timidly stepping through the Void, trailing ripples of color.

Almost immediately her eyes fixed on Kali.

Who are you? she asked.

Kali. I am Kali. Winter, you must hear me, you must remember me, Kali shouted, all the while fighting her way closer and closer. Her body was once again forming around her, solidifying in the Void.

Tell me who you are, Winter said again, her voice more hard, now, strained. *I demand it.*

Kali stopped. The resistance was gone. And, as she looked down at herself, she *saw* herself. Her body. Her feet, making ripples of color of their own.

Winter?

Winter's eyes opened wide. *Yes. Who… who are you?*

Kali took a tentative step forward.

Who are you? Winter repeated.

Winter, Kali said, smiling despite herself, delighting at the ripples of color spreading from her footsteps, delighting at the feeling of her hands, the taste of her tongue, the weight of herself.

"Welcome to the Void, Winter," Kali said, no longer in the language of the mind, but with words they could both hear, with the mouth she did not have before.

"Kali," Winter said, realization dawning on her face.

Kali's smile broadened. "I've been waiting for you."

And then, once more, Winter blinked out of existence, and with her, Kali's physical body. But Kali did not mind. She knew Winter would be back. It was only a matter of time.

PART III

ACHING FAITH

31

Imperial palace, Izet

"I WISH YOU WOULDN'T write on our bed, dearest. You'll spill the ink."

Cova glanced at the papers scattered around her, and the bottle of ink perched precariously on a stack of books on the bed. *Dearest?* When had Girgan started calling her that? They'd only been married a few weeks.

"Where have you been?" Cova asked, keeping the bottle of ink where it was. "You disappeared after dinner without a word." It was not the first time Girgan had done so. Cova understood that he was not particularly sociable, but that didn't mean he could avoid *her*.

Girgan sat next to her on the bed. "I'm sorry, I should have told you. I've been at the library."

Cova rolled her eyes. "One of these days you'll have to tell me what you're reading that takes up so much of your time."

"One day, I will," Girgan said. He reached for the bottle of ink. "Now, please, let's just move this..."

Cova slapped his hand. "I'll not move a thing. I've been writing in bed since I was a child and I haven't spilled once." That wasn't exactly true, but what did Girgan know? "What I really need is help with this proposal. I can't get it to sound quite right. Will you help me?"

Girgan sighed. "You realize you're advocating war?"

"A war with *Khale*. The nation that has robbed us blind and pounded us into the dirt for centuries."

"I hate to remind you, but own actions were not quite spotless."

"Only in response to Khale," Cova said, even though she knew it was a rote response.

"Of course that's what you've been taught; you're a member of Roden's high nobility; Roden's reputation and yours are the same. I'm just saying there are other ways of looking at things."

"And this is what they teach you at the Citadel, I take it? They teach you indifference to country and emperor?"

Girgan shrugged. "I'm not indifferent to Roden. I love this place. But I don't mind questioning how we do some things."

"They teach you to question your own nation's history?"

"Is there harm in acknowledging Roden's flaws as well as its strengths?"

Cova had to admit, she did not think there *was* harm in such a thing. But she did not like how Girgan acted about it.

"So what would you suggest as a course of action?"

"Certainly not war with Khale," Girgan said quickly. "We may have had a few good years recently, mainly thanks to Andrinar and the Island Coalition, but that does not mean our resources match that of Triah, let alone the whole of Khale."

"Our resources don't have to match theirs; we only have to defeat them in battle."

"Do you *really* think we can do that? Does our army compare to Khale's in size or training? Do we have a general that can compare to Riccan Carrieri?"

"With Andrinar's legions, our army technically outnumbers theirs," Cova said. "Roden's standing army can field twenty thousand troops; Andrinar could contribute more than double that number. That isn't even counting our militias. Khale's standing army consisted of thirty or forty thousand at most."

"And if Khale calls in *their* militias? What then?"

"We have a more powerful navy," Cova said.

"That's true. But our navy will only get us so far."

"We focus on Triah itself. We lay siege to the Circle City, forget the rest of Khale. We surround it with our armies, and besiege it with our navy. If we can choke Triah, the rest of the nation will kneel."

Girgan nodded. "A direct assault on Triah is perhaps the only strategy that would work."

"You think that would work?" Cova asked, surprised. *Whose side is he on, anyway?*

"I think it is the most appropriate strategy. But just because a strategy is the *most* likely to work does not mean it will."

"So you still think the idea is folly?"

"I think there are much better things we can do with our time and resources."

"Such as?"

"*Forget* about the empire. We could build up our own nation. Do we want to follow a false hope, for Roden's temporary glory, only to be destroyed? Or do we want to set up a lasting legacy that wouldn't fade with time?"

Cova shook her head. "We can't just forget about the empire. Even if we could… how can we have a lasting legacy without it?"

Girgan said nothing, instead staring off across the room.

"Girgan?"

He shook his head and his eyes refocused. He cleared his throat. "There are ways," was all he said. "I believe there are ways."

"That don't involve conquering Khale?"

"I believe so."

"I'm open to hearing them."

There was another pause. "I... I don't know," Girgan finally said. "I need to make sure I'm right about them. But I will tell you when I am, I promise."

Cova had not expected Girgan to be such a dreamer. That was fine, but there were things she could do *now*. That was all that mattered.

"You're still going to make the proposal, aren't you?"

Cova shrugged. "Better that someone actually presents an achievable plan than the Council arguing over a worse one."

"But what do you expect to *accomplish* from all of this?" Girgan asked. "Conquering Khale... think of the logistics. Khale is at least ten times larger than Roden; just the sheer landmass would be completely unmanageable."

"We don't have to conquer them," Cova said. "Not like that, anyway. We only have to earn back our respect."

Girgan nodded, but didn't say anything. Cova wondered if she had struck a chord with him; perhaps he had experienced problems at the Citadel because of his Rodenese heritage.

Girgan sat on the edge of the bed and placed his hand on hers. "You don't even know the Council will accept your proposal. Even if it is achievable."

"That's how it's always been. I can't do anything about what they do and don't accept, only the emperor can override the Council's decisions."

"Or the empress," Girgan said.

Cova laughed half-heartedly. "Who knows how long that will take? My father seemed old a year ago, but apparently he's found his youth again. He's more spry than I remember him being in years. He won't be leaving the throne anytime soon."

And why should she want him to? He might seem different, but he was still her father.

"Is that for the good of Roden, though?"

Cova looked at Girgan sharply. "What are you talking about?"

Girgan raised his hands defensively. "You've told me he seems different to you, lately. Since he became the Tokal-Ceno."

"I'm sure you changed quite a bit during your time at the Citadel."

"I did," Girgan said. "But changes that occur in people in power must be monitored carefully. You've heard the rumors about what happened at the succession. You've heard what people are saying."

Of course she'd heard the rumors. People said her father used some kind of dark magic to convince the other lords to vote him in as emperor. Cova did not know if she believed it. She had never heard her father mention dark magic, let alone seen him use it.

And yet, he *had* been acting differently. How could she explain that?

"Between those and the rumors surrounding the destruction of the imperial dome, it certainly seems to me—"

Cova held up a hand. "Wait. What rumors?" She hadn't heard anything about the dome.

Girgan hesitated. "I… I assumed you'd heard. They involved the tiellan woman."

"Winter?"

"And about the Ceno order and what really happened under the dome. Some claim that there weren't just human bodies in the rubble."

Cova narrowed her eyes. "What do you mean?"

"People claim there were monsters buried in the rubble,

along with the emperor and the old Tokal and dozens of Reapers."

"Monsters? Girgan, what are you talking about?"

Girgan stood, and began pacing the room. "I don't know. It could mean anything. They could be completely made up, or someone could be exaggerating whatever it was they found. Burned corpses, stone figures in the rubble. But they could be something else entirely. There's a reason Roden outlawed the Scorned Gods all those years ago, you know. It wasn't just the Denomination's influence. People did not like what the Ceno order was producing."

"That was then," Cova said. "Things are different now."

Girgan sighed. "You've said yourself that he is no longer the man you knew. Can you really trust him?"

"He's my father," was all Cova could say. She knew she wasn't answering his question, and the fact that she couldn't bothered her.

"What about the woman he brought to the meeting today? The tiellan, the *Khalic* woman? The tiellan who killed our previous emperor and the Tokal-Ceno."

Cova said nothing. Winter's presence at the meeting had come as a surprise to everyone.

"That woman is dangerous, Cova. Everyone knows it. Why would your father risk even *trying* to control such a creature?"

Cova took a deep breath. "I... I don't know. Perhaps he has a good reason. Perhaps she was a slave-warrior for Khale, perhaps Father has set her free..."

"Your father is now emperor *and* Tokal-Ceno. This girl supposedly killed the previous occupants of both positions. And now, your father seems on rather good terms with her."

"My father did not orchestrate that," Cova said quietly.

"Do you know that? Can you say that with certainty?"

Cova shook her head. But her doubt was there, and it had been there before Girgan had said anything about it.

"I'm just saying that we should keep our options open. We have a duty to Roden."

"And I do fear that the power may be affecting him," Cova said slowly. "Goddess, I can almost hear it working its way through him."

"You agree with me, then?"

Cova thought long and hard before answering. "Absolutely not," she said, finally. "My father has yet to do anything reprehensible, anything that would make me question his ability to lead."

"But you yourself have remarked on how different he is."

"Different does not mean dangerous."

"Cova, I'm not saying that he should be removed, necessarily, but—"

"Then what *are* you saying?" Her husband was dancing around a line terribly close to treason.

"I just… I just think we should be wary of him. Monitor him, even. The events of the past few months have been too conspicuous to ignore."

Cova sighed. "I could just *talk* with him, you know."

Girgan's eyebrows knit together. "Are you mad? How would you have that conversation? 'Excuse me, Father, I just wanted to ask whether you're a madman that killed the previous emperor and Tokal-Ceno. And did you cover up the fact that there were horrifying monsters buried in the rubble of the Imperial Dome? Also, you've taken the tiellan woman responsible as your bodyguard. Care to elaborate on that decision?'"

Cova hesitated, breathing deeply. It would do her no good to lose her calm. "You're operating under the assumption that my father is unreasonable. He isn't."

"Has your father told you why he wanted to be emperor

in the first place?" Girgan asked.

"I..." Her father had told her virtually nothing of his own motives. Cova had just assumed he wanted the throne. What High Lord in their right mind wouldn't? "No," she said.

"My father told me something before he was killed, when he and your father were plotting to take the throne. And what little he did tell me... it was impossible, Cova. Somehow your father convinced mine to believe something impossible. And if he could convince my father, he can convince others."

"What exactly did he tell you?" Cova asked.

Girgan looked away. "I can't say."

Cova scowled. She stood, walking around the bed to face him. "What do you mean *you can't say*?"

"I... I swore to my father I wouldn't tell anyone."

"Including your *wife*?"

Girgan nodded, the movement almost imperceptible. "Including my wife."

Cova stepped forward and shoved Girgan, hard. He stumbled backwards. "Do not ever swear that again, Girgan. We must have no secrets between us."

"I... I'm sorry," he said.

Cova couldn't tell whether he meant it or not. She'd caught the flash of anger on his face when she'd shoved him. She shouldn't have done that. "I hear what you're saying," she said. And she did. Some of Girgan's accusations were outrageous but... some had made her wonder. "But you have to promise me that you will not do anything without consulting me. Is that clear?"

"Very well," Girgan said. "But if it becomes clear that he is not fit to rule—"

"Then we will do something about it," Cova said. "You have my word."

32

Cabral residence, Turandel

"WELCOME BACK, MY DEAR. I hoped you would join us once again."

Cabral's men opened the doors to his tower-house just as the morning light of dawn began leaking hues of blue and gray into the city.

"I'm so pleased to see that you and Trave got along on this little excursion," Cabral said.

Astrid did not struggle against the vampires who held her. She did not stand a chance against them. She should have known he would attempt something like this; she had provided far too much entertainment for Cabral all those decades ago for him to let her go that easily. She needed to make sure he knew that keeping her around wouldn't be so bloody easy.

Astrid did not look at Trave. This was what she had expected of him. Whatever that shit was about being afraid of her or sorry for her was a ruse. She had known it all along.

"I've had your old quarters cleared out for you," Cabral continued as his men dragged Astrid inside the tower-house and along the corridors to the great hall.

"Just go along with them," Trave whispered in her ear.

Astrid turned her head sharply.

"For now," he continued, and then took his place at Cabral's side.

What in the deepest expanse of Oblivion is going on here?

"I thought I would ask you, my darling. Why don't you join us? Why don't you become one of us, as you were so long ago?"

Cabral's men set Astrid down in the middle of the great hall, while Cabral himself leaned back against the long dining table.

"We have an opening or two," Cabral said, spreading his hands wide. "I'm running rather short on experienced vampires."

Astrid stared at Cabral, but said nothing.

"Of course, it is completely your choice," Cabral said. "You can join us, work in harmony with Trave as you did last night—you two make such a good pair—or, you can… not. You can be our slave. You can exist to entertain us when we are at our worst. You know exactly what that is like, I'm afraid." Cabral smiled, arms wide open.

Astrid looked at Trave, who nodded almost imperceptibly. Astrid clenched her teeth. She'd be damned if she was going to fall for more of Trave's shit.

"I'd rather die."

Cabral frowned. "Oh, Astrid, no. Please don't disappoint me so. We would genuinely love your company."

"I'd rather have my head stuffed up a horse's ass." *Easy,* Astrid thought. *Don't need to go too far.* She half-feared Cabral would say something along the lines of "that can be arranged."

Cabral laughed. "Don't tell me you've turned over a new leaf. You can't really think you're *better* than us? Didn't you just spend half the night torturing someone?"

Astrid looked down. Cabral was right. She *had* thought she was better than them. Her quest for redemption, her time spent with Knot, must have clouded her mind. She had been trying to put on a brave front, but the more she thought about it, the more she realized the full implications of what this would mean for her. She was stuck here for years, last time. Who knew how long it might take her to get out again. If she got out at all.

Suddenly, joining up with Cabral's crew did not seem like the worst idea.

"I'm truly sorry to hear that," Cabral said. "I wish we had your old rags to give you to wear, but I'm afraid we'll just have to make do with what you've got. I'm sure those clothes will become rags in no time, my dear."

Fear gripped her. She was afraid of what they were going to do to her, now that she was back. She was afraid of Cabral.

And, most of all, she was afraid of Trave.

Late that night, while Astrid rested in her "quarters"—what amounted to little more than a closet where she could barely lie down—she heard a sound outside.

Astrid immediately sat up, the chains that held her bolted to the wall clanking.

She had thought it miraculous how she had escaped her first day without a beating. But this sound did not bode well. During the time she spent in Cabral's company thirty years ago, daytime beatings were always preferable to nighttime visits.

Astrid sat up, but her chains wouldn't allow her to stand. She could only crouch, cowering in the corner of her cell, and wait to see who had come to call.

Trave, his stubble and burned skin glowing in the red lights of his eyes and the green of Astrid's, looked into her cell.

It could not have been worse.

Astrid was speechless as Trave approached her, unable to move at all or defend herself. She remembered this helplessness. Astrid cowered against the wall. She couldn't do this again.

To her surprise, Trave did not pull her to him, nor did he strike her. Instead, there was a soft clinking sound, and

Astrid's shackles fell from her wrists.

Astrid stared at Trave. "What… what do you want from me? Does Cabral want to see me?"

"No," Trave rasped. "Come with me."

"Where are you taking me?"

"You'll find out soon enough."

Astrid was too stunned to argue.

"You should have listened to me," Trave whispered. "You should have accepted Cabral's offer."

"Why?" Astrid asked. "You'd just end up breaking me anyway."

Trave said nothing to this. Instead, he pulled a lever near the wall, and there was a mechanical whirr. A gaping black doorway yawned open before them.

"What is this?" Astrid asked. She had heard of hidden passages in Cabral's tower-house, but had never actually seen one.

"Just get in," Trave said.

Astrid was about to protest, but apparently Trave could tell. She felt his boot on her back as he kicked her into the darkness. She stumbled down three or four steps, but sprawled flat as the ground leveled off. Behind her, Trave entered the passageway, and closed the secret doorway behind him. Now, they were bathed in blackness, save for the dim glow of their eyes in the dark.

"Get moving," Trave said gruffly, but the way he shoved her was almost… gentle. Astrid obliged; whatever in Oblivion was going on, she knew one thing for certain: right now, it was only herself and Trave. She would take those odds any day or night against all the Fangs.

She tried to keep track of her surroundings; how many turns they made, when the ground sloped up or down. They soon reached a spiral staircase, going downward for at least four or five stories, and then the ground leveled off. They walked for a long time in darkness and in silence.

The corridor had a musty smell to it, like wet earth, and sure enough the ground beneath Astrid's feet was packed dirt. The walls on either side alternated between patchy earth, chipped and crumbling stone, and tree roots and wood beams. Eventually, Astrid felt a light breeze graze her skin. And then, quite suddenly, she was looking out at the stars and roiling ocean.

She and Trave stood at the tiny mouth of the tunnel through which they had been walking, in the middle of a set of tall, dark cliffs. Below Astrid saw nothing but rocks and pounding waves. The cliffs were sheer, impossible for a man to climb. The drop below them was deadly. For humans, anyway. A vampire could make the jump into the ocean with some injury, but would heal quickly, especially at night. And, if the timing was right, Astrid suspected a vampire would be able to find enough footholds in the cliffs to their way back up to the tunnel.

"Take this."

Astrid turned, and he shoved a bundle of cloth into her arms. It was her cloak—and, inside, her three voidstones; one for Knot, one for the Black Matron, and the one she had taken from the Nazaniin.

"Now jump," Trave rasped. "And don't ever come back."

Astrid turned, completely confused. "You're… you're letting me go?"

"I have debts. One is owed to you."

"Cabral will suspect—"

"Cabral will listen to whatever I say to him. He may take some convincing, but your escape will be entirely believable."

"Cabral knows about this tunnel?"

"Of course. Only he and I. And now, you."

"Why are you doing this?"

Trave met Astrid's gaze, and once again she saw that flicker in his eyes. Fear.

"What I did to you was... wrong," Trave said. "I'll never atone for it. But this is something, at least."

"What about the others?" Astrid asked. "The servants. Why don't you help them, too?"

"Cabral will only find more. The fewer that suffer, the better."

Astrid looked out at the ocean, then back at Trave. "If you truly wanted to change, to make up for what you've done, you'd—"

Trave slammed his fist against the rock wall with such force that dust tumbled from the ceiling.

"*Go,*" he growled, above the crashing of the waves. For a moment, Astrid saw the anger, the madness in him she remembered all too well. But, then, his shoulders slumped.

"If I came back, would you help me free them?" Astrid asked, immediately horrified that she would ask such a thing. Why in Oblivion would she ever want to return here? Why would she ever want to see this man's face again?

Because at some point you decided to try being a good person. That shit'll be the death of you, girl.

Trave stared at her for a moment, his eyes seeming to pierce through her. Then he walked back down the tunnel without looking back.

"Thank you," Astrid whispered, surprised she was even saying it. Then she jumped.

33

Council chamber, imperial palace

THE RULING COUNCIL DID not take the princess's proposal well. Cova wanted to conserve funds and an adequate Watch force for Izet while also funding a naval campaign to strike at the heart of the Circle City itself—Triah. Winter, standing beside the throne, observed the other Council members and attending lords in the chamber shaking their heads, frowning, even snorting in derision as Cova presented her plan. Unfortunately for the princess, there were more lords present than usual.

Frost flowed through Winter's veins. She had been more careful taking the drug since her encounter with Kali, if it was truly Kali at all—she still had not returned to the Void to confront the strange figure. But Daval had not specified when Winter was to make an example of Hirman Luce, so she had taken frost before the Council meeting just in case. If there were this many lords present, it might happen today. Luce only had to provoke her reaction, although so far he had remained silent through Cova's presentation. Cova, to her credit, continued her proposal with poise. When she was finished, however, the circling sharks attacked.

"You really think we stand any chance of victory against Khale by waging only a naval campaign against them?" Watch Commander Kuglen asked, his brows knit together in a scowl.

"Our navy is far more powerful than theirs," Cova said

calmly. "We stand the greatest chance against them with our ships. A land force would never get past the Blood Gate."

Dagnatar, leader of the merchants, leaned forward. "But why attack only Triah? Why not use our ships to get troops around the Sorensen Pass, and then mount a multi-pronged campaign?"

"We want to surprise them," Cova responded. "They will not expect a direct attack on their capital city."

Kuglen shook his head. "Surprise won't matter when our ships are going up against God's Eye."

Cova laughed. "God's Eye is a relic. You really think some tower built decades ago can channel the power of the sun? It's just a symbol meant to scare off attacks—and it seems to be working on you."

"It isn't just a tower, it's the tallest tower in the history of the Sfaera. And there are historical accounts of the Eye burning through ships in seconds."

"Whatever functionality it might have is limited by the weather. Girgan has seen it; he knows this is true."

All heads turned to Girgan, who nodded. "God's Eye can certainly be dangerous, but only in the right circumstances, which are impossible to create on a whim."

"You're willing to bet our empire on the weather, then?" Kuglen demanded.

"No," Cova said, "but if you listened, you'd know I have components to my proposal that—"

"I'm still not convinced we need to wage war against them at all," High Priestess Rowady chimed in. "Why risk it? Why not rebuild here, first?"

Winter glanced at Daval. She'd thought the man might be more protective of his daughter, but he only sat back on his throne, fingers steepled beneath his nose, observing.

Hirman Luce slammed his fist on the table. "This is folly," he said. "All of it."

Winter felt a rush of excitement. This could be the moment where he stepped out of line for the last time, and she could access her power once more. Guilt wisped within her at the thought; she was pining after an opportunity to kill a man just to use her power.

Cova glared at the lord. "Please, Lord Luce. Enlighten me as to my 'folly.'"

Luce did not answer Cova. Instead, his eyes bored directly into Daval at the head of the table. "You can't seriously be considering this, Daval."

Winter's palms were sweating, but she strode forward. If she did not appear confident, she would fail. She leaned down and met Luce's eyes. "You will refer to our emperor with the correct honorific, my Lord. You will call him Emperor, or Your Grace."

Luce glanced at Winter, his eyes wide at first, then narrowing as his face grew dark. For a moment Winter thought he would answer her. Instead, he turned back to Daval.

"Your daughter can't handle a simple proposal, Daval."

"Your Grace," Winter corrected again.

"How do you expect her to rule when you're gone? She can hardly put forward a plan of action, how do you expect her to lead our empire to war?"

Dagnatar raised a finger. "Hold on a moment, Lord Luce. Her proposal may be rough, but her plan itself was actually quite—" Luce continued talking over the merchant leader. As Luce's voice grew in volume, Winter felt more and more sure of herself.

This was it.

"You want to eliminate Canticism from our nation," Luce

continued, "but you disregard the fact that the majority of our citizens are still faithful Cantics. The Ceno order hardly has a presence outside of Izet, let alone in Andrinar or the Island Coalition. Daval, I recognize my mistakes. I think you need to start doing the same. If you don't—"

"*Your Grace*," Winter said, more emphatically this time. Frost rushed through her veins. She bored her eyes into Luce, daring him to acknowledge her. Daval had said he would release her blocks. At this point, Winter did not care what she had to do to feel her power again.

"And *her*." Luce jabbed his finger at Winter. "You've kept an elf alive in our empire, against all of our laws. And not just any elf. This… this *abomination* destroyed half the imperial palace, killed Grysole, killed the Tokal before you. You're keeping her like some kind of pet. It isn't right, Daval."

There. Winter sensed it instantly; her blocks were gone. While she always felt good when taking frost, without access to her *tendra* she did not feel the same elation, the sense of invulnerability. But now, Winter felt that power. Four of her *tendra* snaked out, lifting Luce by his robes.

Make an example of him, Winter remembered Daval saying. *Make sure they never forget how you killed him. They will never challenge us again.*

Winter had no mind for games or long-drawn-out spectacles. Instead, she pushed Luce backwards, simultaneously reaching out with a half-dozen of her other *tendra,* snatching swords and spears from the unsuspecting guards in the chamber. She slammed Luce into the wall upside down, stone cracking with the force of it, and before the man could scream, the weapons zipped through the air and buried themselves in his flesh.

The chamber fell silent as Winter relaxed. She had not moved—the entire event had only taken a few seconds—but every muscle in her body was tense. Now, she sat back in Luce's vacated chair, crossing one leg over the other, and gave the slightest hint of a smile. Someone vomited, the sound loud and tearing into the silence. All eyes slowly shifted from Luce's body to Winter. She recognized the looks. She had seen them in the Circle Square of Navone. She'd seen it on Lian, when he'd realized what she'd done.

Girgan Mandiat, however, was not looking at her. He was glaring at the emperor, his face red. Winter took note of that. The Counselor obviously had some sort of grievance with Daval, and that information could be useful.

Winter heard a dripping sound, and looked back at Luce's body, pinned to the wall. Blood flowed from a dozen wounds, his mouth agape, eyes wide open.

At the head of the table, Daval cleared his throat.

"I granted Hirman Luce leniency after his betrayal at the succession," Daval said, his voice quiet but still carrying easily in the silence. "That was a mistake. If it was only me he did not respect, I could let that go. But he did not respect the office of the emperor, and he did not respect our beloved empire. For that, he died."

Daval stood, his voice louder. "I *am* the emperor. I have been chosen. I have the power of the Scorned Gods at my back." He smiled down at Winter. "And other power, besides. Luce called this girl my pet. You can see how wrong he was. We are entering a new era. You're free to join me, and witness Roden's coming glory. Or you're free to rebel, and die."

Daval sat down, clearing his throat again. "Now," he said, Luce's blood *drip-dripping* in the background, "where were we?"

* * *

Afterwards, Winter and Urstadt walked on either side of Daval, escorting him back to his chambers. The three of them had been the first to leave the meeting, the other Council members and lords staring in silence at Luce's corpse. Winter was still reeling from what she had done. Her *tendra* had come to her so quickly, as if they'd never been blocked. But once Luce was dead, they were taken away immediately.

She had killed someone, just for a few seconds of using her power. This bothered her, but not in the way it should. She felt guilt, but it was not the suffocating heaviness that plagued her after Navone. It was a slight pull, nothing more. She had killed many more people than Luce in Navone, after all. She had killed people less deserving of death, too. Why she should feel guilt, even the slightest nudge, at killing Luce... confused her.

"Shall I send for servants to clean up Luce's remains, my Lord?" Urstadt asked.

"Leave him," Daval said. "Instruct the servants to get him down before the next Council meeting. I don't want to smell him. But for now, let him serve his purpose."

The ridiculous thought occurred to Winter that she did not know *how* the servants would get Luce down. The walls in the council chamber had to be four rods high at least, and Winter had pinned the man closer to the ceiling than the floor. Did the servants have a ladder that would reach that high?

"What are you thinking about, Winter?" Daval asked.

Winter almost laughed when she glanced at him. She wondered, briefly, why she did not always see the flash of the dark skull when she saw his face.

Winter shrugged. "Nothing of consequence."

"You just killed a man. Do you not feel remorse?"

"I stopped feeling remorse a long time ago."

Daval pursed his lips. "Is that what Ziravi teaches us?"

I don't much care what Ziravi teaches us, Winter wanted to say. But she knew such words wouldn't get her anywhere with Daval. He was obsessed with the ancient poet. Winter couldn't say the man's work was without merit, but she was not convinced they were words to live by.

"'Wild Calamity' says nothing about remorse," Winter said. Daval had asked her to read it every morning, and she'd obliged. For the most part.

"Doesn't it?"

Winter hesitated. Obviously it didn't. What more did he want from her?

"'To destroy, I must first know love,'" Urstadt recited. "Those words imply remorse. How can we not feel remorse when we destroy something we love?"

Winter couldn't tell if Urstadt was trying to prompt her, or simply trying to show off her own reading of the poem.

"But if I don't love something, I don't need to feel remorse," Winter said. Which would explain why she felt so little of the feeling, lately. She had so little left to love.

"You're missing the point, my dear. If you don't love something, you shouldn't be destroying it in the first place."

Winter rolled her eyes. "You *asked* me to make an example of Luce. To *kill* him. How could I possibly have loved the man? I did not even know him."

"How you come to love is your own business," Daval said. "I can give you orders. I can dictate who you kill and who you do not. I can't tell you how to feel, Winter."

"And you expected me to love Luce? In the matter of a few days, without even speaking to the man?" *Not to mention the fact that he hated me.* Winter was the sole tiellan, as far as she could tell, in all of Roden, and Luce had not been quiet about the fact that she disgusted him.

"I had hoped that you would come to that yourself," Daval said, "without my prompting."

"It seems that was a misplaced hope." Winter felt her face growing warm. Why she felt shame she did not know. She should relish every chance to disappoint this man.

They reached the doorway to the emperor's chambers and Daval turned to her. "I don't believe my hope was misplaced at all," he said. "Learning this lesson takes time, my dear. Everyone is capable of love, just as everyone is worthy of love, even for the smallest of reasons."

Winter shook her head. *Not everyone is worthy of love*. "I'm not sure it's a lesson I'll ever learn. Hypocrisy does not become anyone; I'm no exception."

"You see this as hypocrisy now, but you will understand soon enough."

"So if I love someone, that gives me the right to destroy them? That's what this is all about? Finding excuses to kill people out of 'love'?"

"We never have the right to destroy someone, Winter. That is always a choice we make. But, if we love what we choose to destroy, we at least know fully what it is we are going to do."

Since Winter had discovered she could use psimancy, she had thought of using her powers, even to kill people, as a necessity. A way to protect those she loved at best, or a compulsion to obtain more *faltira* at worst. But that was not right. Winter could admit that. Her actions had always been her choice. Or, at least, she had chosen to give up her right to choose.

If Daval was right about that, could he be right about loving what you wished to destroy?

"Urstadt will manage my protection for the rest of the day," Daval said after a moment. "I suggest you retire, and think about what we have discussed. You've much to learn, Winter. I hope I can help you, before it is too late."

Later that evening, Winter was once more at the door to the emperor's chambers.

"I need to see him," Winter told the two Reapers guarding the door. They had been instructed to accommodate her requests, but they frowned at her even as they ushered her into the antechamber. She resisted the urge to fiddle with the daggers at her waist as she passed them. She did not want to seem fidgety; she had a reputation to uphold. The daggers were useless things, really, but Daval insisted she wear them. Said it aggrandized her factor of intimidation. Winter thought they were pointless. She doubted she could hold her own against even a newly trained soldier. If she ever truly were to protect Daval, he would have to lift her blocks again.

Which was why she was here.

The guards were not Daval's only line of security—Urstadt was standing in the antechamber. "The emperor ordered you to take the rest of the day and think," Urstadt said. "I don't think he will be happy to see you."

"He'll see me anyway," Winter said. Her relationship with Daval was still difficult to define. He provided her with anything she wanted, but for all intents and purposes she was still a prisoner. She couldn't leave the palace. She was constantly blocked from using her *tendra*, even if she had all of the frost she could ever want. And yet, within the palace, she was given more freedom than most. Very few people could request an audience with the emperor at nearly any time of day and be granted it.

"I suppose he will," Urstadt said. "But the emperor is with someone. You must wait."

Winter sighed and began to pace the antechamber. It was lavishly decorated, with wide windows along one wall, and an ornate desk and chair along another. An elaborately patterned rug extended almost the full length of the floor, and various paintings hung on the walls. At the far end was the door that led to the emperor's inner chambers. Urstadt stood near the table, glaive leaning loosely in one fist, in full armor.

"Have you been thinking about the Ziravi poem?"

Winter stopped. Outside of what was necessary, these were the most words Urstadt had spoken to her since they'd first met. "I… I suppose so," she said, cautiously. Of course, Urstadt could be asking out of necessity, as well. Daval might have ordered her to.

"I did not think I would care for the poem. I don't much care for poetry in general."

Winter said nothing. Did Urstadt expect her to carry on a conversation?

"But the more I think about Ziravi's words, the more I am convinced of their truth. There is a reason the emperor adheres to them."

Winter walked to the chair. If Urstadt wasn't going to sit, she would. "They're one man's words. I don't see what genuine value they could really have."

"Is that truly what you think?"

"So Cetro Ziravi thought it was important to love people. He apparently advocates destruction as well. What of it? His experience isn't mine. And from what I've seen, there aren't many people out there worth loving. And, more often than not, the ones you do love don't make it very far."

"You've lost people?"

Winter hesitated. She hadn't realized what she'd been saying until she said it, and now she was not sure she wanted to have this conversation with Urstadt.

"Ziravi lost people in his life, too," Urstadt said after a moment. "Lost his parents when he was young. Two of his sons as an adult. A sister. He was not unfamiliar with loss."

Winter narrowed her eyes. "I thought you didn't care for poetry. How do you know all this about Ziravi?"

"I may not care for poetry, but I *am* thorough. I do my research."

Winter shrugged. "It doesn't matter. Ziravi responded in his way. I respond in mine."

"Ziravi *chose* to respond. You choose, too, Winter."

Thankfully, the door to the emperor's chambers burst open just in time to save Winter from that bloody awful conversation.

Cova rushed out of the room, her normally composed face contorted. If Winter did not know any better, she'd think Cova was about to burst into tears. She rushed through the antechamber and out into the palace beyond.

"Do not hate me for what you don't yet understand, daughter!" Daval shouted from the emperor's chambers. But Cova was already gone.

Peculiarly, Winter was jealous. It was their relationship she coveted, she realized. They were father and daughter. They might disagree, but at least they had one another. Winter felt a tiny grain of compassion for Daval. The man was cruel, a murderer. But he was also a father.

Urstadt smiled at Winter. "The emperor will see you now."

Winter took a deep breath, shoving whatever seed of compassion she felt for Daval back into the recesses of her mind.

She stood and walked into the emperor's chambers. Daval did not seem in a good mood. Winter did not know what had just transpired between him and his daughter, but it had obviously left them both unhappy. This was not the ideal time for Winter to be asking for favors. But she was here. Daval had told her to see him any time.

Winter wasn't sure she could have stopped herself anyway. Feeling the power of her *tendra*, even for just a few moments, made her want more. She craved it, almost as much as she craved *faltira*.

The emperor's chambers were divided into several rooms. The emperor's bedchamber, a study, a massive closet, a garderobe and bathing area, the emperor's personal armory, and a common area connecting them all. The combined space was larger than most Cantic chapels Winter had seen. They were surprisingly austere: simple rugs and curtains, and no art or decorations to speak of. The anteroom was more ornate, in fact.

Daval stood at one end of the common area, his hands clasped behind his back, facing away from Winter and out a large square window into the night. Winter could see the lights of Izet beyond the window, and felt her imprisonment even more keenly.

"What do you want?" Daval asked.

"I… I came to speak with you."

"I told you to take the rest of the day to think about what we had discussed."

"That's why I came," Winter said, her mind working quickly. If she told him what he wanted to hear, perhaps he would grant her what she desired.

Daval turned. The moment she saw his face, the horrible image of the black skull wreathed in flame flashed in her mind.

Winter shut her eyes, but the image seemed burned into her memory. The skull stared at her, grinning, motionless.

"You've had a change of heart, then?" Daval asked.

When Winter opened her eyes, the skull was gone, and it was only Daval who stood looking at her. His eyes were in shadow, sunken back in his head, his mouth stern.

"I… I think I may have," Winter said.

"Tell me."

"I grew up happy," Winter said. She had to spin the correct lie to really convince Daval. Starting from the beginning would give her time to form it. "For a tiellan, in a small coastal village, I grew up happy. I never knew my mother, she passed away giving birth to me, but my father… my father was a good man, and he raised me well."

Daval said nothing, but remained motionless in front of the window.

How easy it would be to just… push him out of it. But the thought was ludicrous. Daval was strong—for an old man, he was incredibly strong—and Winter had no power to speak of around him. Not unless he granted it to her first.

"But my happiness was not without difficulty. I watched family after family of tiellans leave our village because the persecution became too great for them to bear. I watched my father lose business and lose friends. I've seen tiellans—men and women both—beaten to the very edge of life. But when Knot came, and when we… when we grew close… I thought all of that might change. For the first time in my life I thought that what little happiness I had to begin with might grow instead of fade."

Winter looked down. "I couldn't have been more wrong. My father was killed on our wedding day, by men sent from Roden. Knot left me. I followed him, and discovered psimancy along the way. But I discovered the addiction that accompanies it, too, and I've never been able to escape it. I've killed people, just to satisfy it. When we arrived here, I thought it all would finally end. And it did—but not the way I wanted. I thought we'd go home, our adventures over. Instead, my husband and friends were slaughtered. And I was left to rot in a prison cell."

"What are you saying, my dear?"

"Everything I love has been taken from me. Can you blame me for finding it difficult to love anything else?"

Daval's mouth turned down. "If that is your conclusion, then—"

"Let me finish." Winter stopped herself, realizing she had interrupted an emperor.

"Go ahead," Daval said, his voice like iron.

"I just wanted you to understand why I thought the way I did," Winter said. "And how, despite everything that's happened to me, I… I believe you're right."

When Daval didn't respond, Winter continued. "I've been contemplating love, and Ziravi's poem. My whole life, I only loved people that I thought deserved my love in the first place. But now… now, I think I might see another way. I think… I think the point is loving people even though they *don't* deserve it. None of them do. Canta knows, I don't."

Winter knew she was making up the words as she said them, and yet somewhere, deep down, she wondered what exactly it was she meant. *The whole point is loving people even though they don't deserve it.*

"Once I realized that, I realized the importance of 'Wild Calamity.' I thought it was all about learning to love in order to destroy, but I had it wrong. Love is the end goal, not destruction. I think that's what the last few lines are referring to."

Love is the end goal, not destruction. Winter wanted to believe the words, but they weren't true. They might even be true for others. They would never be true for her.

Winter tried to keep calm when she saw a slow smile spreading across Daval's lips. His eyes were still sunken in shadow, but the smile was a good sign—wasn't it?

"Very good," Daval said. "I think you might be beginning to understand after all."

They stood there in silence for a moment, looking at one another. Winter was not sure what else she should do. Should she ask about her *tendra* now? Was he in a better mood?

"I'm glad you're making progress, Winter, but the hour grows late. If there is nothing else—"

"There is," Winter blurted out. "What else do you want me to do for you?"

"What do you mean?"

"I made an example of Hirman Luce today. When would you like me to do something else… like that?"

"You mean when will I lift your blocks again?"

Of course that's what I mean. "What I mean to say is… I appreciate all you've done for me. All that you're doing. And I want to know when I'll next be able to repay you."

Then, Daval laughed. The sound was strange, slow and halting, and before Winter could process what such a strangled, horrible laugh might mean, it was accompanied by another sound.

A thump of thunder that vibrated in Winter's chest and shook the very foundations of the imperial palace itself.

And then Winter was in blackness. At first she wondered if she had slipped into the Void, but quickly realized this was very different. There were no lights, no little stars of color. Here, there was only darkness. A darkness at once familiar and unknowable, and more terrifying than anything she could imagine. A darkness thick and oppressive, like a great cold blanket that was too heavy and offered no warmth, no protection. A darkness she had experienced once before, months ago, when her friends and her hope were still alive.

And the Voice.

"*Welcome back, little one.*"

Deep, booming, and folded in flame.

"*I am delighted to see you once more.*"

A figure was walking towards her. Winter could hear the footsteps echoing, echoing infinitely in the dark. Winter's nose caught the faintest hint of cinnamon.

"You can't fool him," the figure said. "Don't try."

"Mother?" Winter felt a terrible sense of repetition, as if she had had this conversation before.

"He knows you're lying," her mother said. "You had better not try it again. You're only a tool to him, girl. A weapon."

Winter shivered in the dark. "Mother, how…?"

"Don't speak, child. You're lucky I've come to you at all."

Winter's body shook, and she sobbed, once, but held the rest in.

Her mother laughed. "Weak. How a weak thing like you killed me, I'll never know. But it doesn't matter now, does it? I'm dead. And you killed me."

"*Murderer.*"

In a flash of light, the darkness retreated, and Winter was back in the emperor's chambers. She blinked, squinting in the torchlight, suddenly brighter than she remembered. Daval's laugh still echoed in the chamber.

Winter shivered, unsure of what had happened. Had she imagined what she had just seen and heard?

"You're clever, girl," Daval said. "You can read people. Tell them what they want to hear. That's a useful talent."

Winter was speechless. The stark terror of what she had experienced in the blackness still echoed endlessly inside of her. She wrapped her arms around herself to keep from shivering.

"You will next serve me when I am ready. When I ask it of you. No sooner. That's all you need know."

"Yes," Winter whispered, unable to do anything but agree.

"Very well. Be gone. Other matters need my attention."

Winter walked quickly out the door, feeling another chill run up her spine as she turned her back on Daval. She walked past Urstadt without a word, and into the corridors of the palace.

Daval was more powerful than she had imagined, and more intelligent by far. She couldn't outthink him. He was the emperor. He was her master. He was a daemon.

And he is a father.

Winter blinked at the thought. Again the seed of compassion came to her, seemingly from nowhere. How she could feel anything resembling sympathy for Daval, for that monster, was incomprehensible.

Winter walked back to her room, trying desperately to think of anything but Daval, darkness, and the harsh words of her own mother.

34

When Astrid finally made it back to the Harmoth estate, she was surprised to see how much things had changed. The constant influx of people, tiellan and human alike, had certainly not let up. Even in the fading light—Astrid was already able to walk about without her hood up—she could see hundreds of people in the grounds. But there also seemed to be more order to what had once been all but complete chaos. There were distinct rows of tents, fires spaced evenly throughout, and at one edge of the grounds was a clearing where a group of people were milling about in the blue-gray light of dusk. And, strangely, one of the giant trees toward the center of the grounds was now nothing more than a charred skeleton, the earth beneath it scorched and blackened.

Astrid wondered what it was all about. Her most recent contact with Knot had been brief, only informing him of her success in acquiring the Nazaniin voidstone. She had not yet told him about Cabral and Trave, and he had not yet told her about whatever was happening here.

As Astrid maneuvered around a group of people firing arrows at a line of straw targets and past men and women sparring with wooden swords, she began to get some idea of what was going on. This was a training ground. And there, shouting orders, stood Knot.

Astrid walked up to him silently, hoping to surprise him. But Knot, ever aware of his surroundings, must have noticed her. When he turned to her, his eyes were bright, cheeks raised in a rare smile. He rushed to her and Astrid leapt into Knot's arms. She did not know whether she was more surprised by the fact that Knot made the gesture or that she went along with it. Either way, Knot seemed genuinely happy to see her, and Astrid couldn't even begin to describe the way that made her feel. After everything she had been through in Turandel, after all the violence and excavated memories, this was a welcome change.

"What took you so long, girl?" Knot asked, gruffly, setting her down.

"Oh, you know, here and there. Out and about, and all that."

"Good to have you back."

Astrid smiled. "It seems you've some news of your own. What's all this?"

"More than you know," Knot said. Then, he nodded to a young man next to him.

"Form up!" the young man shouted. "Training exercises end now! Form up for inspection, and then it's off to dinner for you scum!"

Astrid raised an eyebrow. *Scum?* she mouthed to Knot.

Knot chuckled, shaking his head.

The people who had been training—Astrid counted about three dozen, human and tiellan, male and female—formed in a line, and the young man, Knot's sergeant it seemed, went down the line, inspecting the sweaty, dust-crusted bodies. Then, Astrid recognized the young sergeant. It was Cinzia and Jane's brother, the older one. What was his name?

Knot turned, and beckoned for Astrid to follow. "Eward can handle the rest."

Eward. Of course. The lad had taken well enough to command.

"Come on," Knot said. "Let's talk."

As Knot told her about the events of the past few weeks, they elected to walk around the grounds rather than head back to the house. As darkness fell they kept to the land behind the manor, where fewer Odenites ventured, so that others wouldn't see the eerie glow of Astrid's eyes.

On her way back to Tinska, Astrid had resolved to tell Knot everything that had happened. Or, at least, almost everything. Telling Knot about her fight with the Nazaniin, the voyant, and the voidstone she had procured was easy; telling him about Cabral, and especially about Trave, was not. There was no need for Knot to know details about her past with Cabral and Trave, about what had transpired between them.

Knot seemed to take it relatively well. "So you'd been to Turandel before?" he asked, after Astrid had told him most of her story.

She nodded tentatively. "Decades ago. I'd hoped Cabral and his Fangs had moved on, or been killed by now."

"Didn't mention that to me before."

Astrid shrugged. "Didn't think you needed to know."

Astrid felt his hand on her shoulder. "I... I am sorry for what you went through," Knot said quietly. "What happened to you shouldn't happen to anyone."

Astrid looked away, hoping Knot wouldn't see the tears in her eyes.

"Now what has been going on here?" she asked, anxious to change the subject. "This place is very different."

"A lot of things," Knot said. "After the Kamite attack, and

then the assassination attempt, we made a few changes. Cinzia and I oversaw an investigation, but nothing much came of it. We did implement a census, however, so we have a better idea of exactly how many people are here, and who they are. You've noticed the guard force we're training."

"I noticed," Astrid said. "Your investigation didn't yield any results? You told me the woman you killed couldn't have been working alone. You still don't know who she was working with?"

"We found a few of the tents empty, abandoned one morning," Knot said. "We think they might've already fled."

"But they might still be in the camp."

Knot hesitated. This was obviously a sore point for him. "Might be," he finally said.

"Surprised you haven't been able to find them, someone of your talents."

"I've had other things on my mind."

"More important than finding the rest of these assassins?"

"There are too many important things, these days."

"Things *have* been changing around here," Astrid muttered. So much, in barely two weeks. "What's the population at now?"

"Almost four hundred. Three hundred and ninety, according to the records."

"Our very own census. Who's running that operation? I can't imagine you and Cinzia are doing that, too."

"A young woman Cinzia met has taken charge of the census. Arven. A sharp one, if a bit... eccentric."

They continued walking for a few moments longer, the darkness encroaching upon them. Astrid found it comforting. But there was business to attend to. She pulled out the voidstone, holding it up to Knot.

"That's it?" he asked.

"This is it," Astrid said. "This is our connection to the Nazaniin. Shall we?"

Knot looked around. "Now?"

"Might as well get it over with," Astrid said.

Reluctantly, Knot nodded, and Astrid let herself slip into the Void to make the connection. While psimancers could hold a voidstone conversation internally, within their own minds, others that were connected to the Void—like Astrid—had to speak aloud, and the voice from the other end was heard audibly from the stone. That was normally an inconvenience, but at least this time, with Knot present, he would be able to listen to the conversation.

After a moment, she heard a man's voice, quiet and calm.

"*What's taken you so long to report?*"

Astrid and Knot looked at one another, unsure of how to proceed.

Perhaps this wasn't the best idea, Astrid thought.

Fortunately, Knot took the reins. Given the nature of Astrid's connection to the voidstone, his voice would be heard on the other end as well.

"This is Knot," he said.

"*Knot? Who? How did you come across this voidstone? Where is Ferni?*"

"You know me as Lathe Tallon."

Then, silence at the other end.

"*Lathe. Of course.*"

"Who am I talking to?"

"*You sound… different. I'm sorry I didn't recognize you. You are speaking to Rune, of course.*"

"Are you in charge?"

"*Am I in… am I in charge? What do you mean?*"

"I need to speak with whoever is in charge."

"*The rumors are true, then. You've lost your memory.*"

"Are you in charge or not?"

"*Well, Lathe... or Knot, however you prefer to be called... I'm a member of the Triad. Along with Kosarin, and... you really don't remember?*"

"None of your business," Knot said. "Are you going to tell me what I need to know?"

"*That depends, Knot, on what you want to know.*"

"Why are you after me?"

"*Strictly speaking, we aren't, at the moment.*"

"But you were. Why?"

"*We thought you had defected. A simple mistake on our part. We are sorry about that.*"

A "simple mistake" didn't begin to describe what had happened with Nash and Kali. Astrid wondered why this man—a voyant—couldn't have seen that in advance.

Then, she realized, she had not told Knot everything. She had not told Knot that the man he was communicating with would most likely be a voyant.

She mouthed the word to Knot, but he was not paying attention to her. She kicked him sharply in the shin, which certainly got his attention. Knot scowled at her.

"He's a bloody voyant," Astrid whispered.

"*Ah, someone else is there with you. Who else am I addressing?*"

Knot frowned at Astrid, his jaw clenched. "You're a voyant, aren't you, Rune? Why don't you figure it out?"

"*Ah, yes. Either you're remembering, or you have a very helpful friend. Either way I have some bad news. For whatever reason, my powers have been blocked from you since you, er, became as you are now. I can't see you, not in any way that makes sense. And as for whoever is with you... ah, yes. A vampire."*

Astrid and Knot looked at each other. Astrid shrugged.

"*From your silence I take it that I am correct. I usually am—a shame you don't remember that. But... what has happened to you fascinates me. We want you to return. We have many questions.*"

"Ain't letting you experiment on me, if that's what you mean."

"*Our view of you has changed. We think you could still be a great asset to us. And while our experiments might be... vigorous, I promise you they would not last long. We would find out any information we could about what happened to you, and then send you on your way.*"

"I'm not coming in," Knot said flatly. "You can forget about that."

"*I thought you would say that. Even without true sight of you, I have some semblance of who you are. Very well. What is it you want of us then, Knot?*"

"Leaving me alone would be at the top of my list."

"*I can guarantee nothing in that regard. But if it is information you want... I could send the nearest* cotir *to help you. The acumen in Tinska is of reasonable strength.*"

Astrid frowned.

"How did you know we were in Tinska?" Knot asked, voicing Astrid's question.

"*Just because I can't see you does not mean I can't locate the voidstone you're using. Simple psimancy, my friend.*"

Astrid shook her head. Another *cotir*? The psimancer groups had been nothing but trouble to them; she didn't relish the idea of facing another one.

"*If it's information you want, they could provide you with better material than I have.*"

"Can they tell me what happened to me?"

"*I can't guarantee anything, but as I said, the acumen is reasonably powerful. If anyone could tell you more about your... condition... it would be him. Unless you want to visit us in Triah, of course. But I must say... I am the wrong person in the Triunity with whom you should discuss this particular subject.*"

"Who should I be talkin' to then?"

Rune cleared his throat. "*It's 'to whom,' Knot. There really isn't much of Lathe left in you at all, is there?*"

"The way I speak ain't your concern," Knot said.

"Ain't? *Canta rising... Well, Knot. Let's make a deal. Meet with our* cotir. *We will give them some information about you, about who Lathe was. They may be able to tell you more about what happened to you as well.*"

Knot was looking at Astrid, eyebrows raised.

What could she say to him? It was his decision, ultimately. She shrugged.

"And what do you want from me?" Knot asked.

Astrid nodded. What Rune was offering was certainly not going to be free.

"*The same thing we're giving you: information. What happened in Roden? My sight can't discern it. Help us understand what happened, and we'll help you understand who you are.*"

Astrid watched Knot as he considered this.

"Very well," Knot finally said. "I'll meet with your *cotir*."

There was a pause on the other end, and Astrid was not sure, but she thought she heard voices in the background.

"*Splendid*," Rune said, after a moment. "*The leader of this* cotir *is named Cymbre. Don't worry; she is far more pleasant than Kali was.*"

"We can meet them in Tinska," Knot said. "Just tell us where."

Rune laughed. *"I can send them directly to you at Harmoth, Knot. I knew I'd be sending a* cotir *to Harmoth weeks ago, but I didn't know why until now."*

Rune started to say something else, but Knot gave a signal to Astrid, and Astrid severed the connection.

"What do you think?" Astrid asked, looking up at Knot.

He shrugged. "Hard to say."

"When do you think this Symbol person and the *cotir* will arrive?"

"Cymbre. And I don't know. If they're from Tinska, they could arrive any day."

Astrid shook her head. "I don't like it. We have no control over this. Cymbre and the *cotir* may help you, but what if they don't? What if they arrive with a *dozen* bloody *cotirs*? We might be able to handle one, but more than that..."

"We will have to prepare for that, then," Knot said.

"That's all you can say? That we'll have to 'prepare for that'?" How in Oblivion are we going to prepare for an army of psimancers?"

Knot began walking, and Astrid followed him. "There wouldn't be anything we could do if they sent an army, anyway. But now we might have a chance to reason with them. Negotiate with them, even learn from them. They seem willing to cooperate. Apparently I might have information that they value, too."

"They told Winter and Lian they were willing to cooperate. Look where it got them."

"If you don't agree with what I've decided, what do you think is best?"

"It's not that I don't entirely agree, it's just that I don't know if it was the best idea, I—"

"Then what *is* the best idea?"

Astrid frowned. The words of the Black Matron echoed in her mind. *Get him to Triah. He needs to be here. We need him.*

"We should go to Triah."

Knot laughed. "Why in Oblivion would we go to Triah?"

"To find the Nazaniin where they live. Rune said that was an option."

Knot shook his head. "If you're worried about facing a Nazaniin army, I think Triah is the last place you want to be."

"Or, if we're going to face one either way, we might as well surprise them."

Astrid looked up at Knot, watching him. He did not suspect anything of her. He couldn't. And yet she wondered.

"You're serious about this." Knot was frowning.

"I am. I think it would be best."

"And what about Cinzia and Jane? What about what is happening here?"

"What about it? It's none of our business. We have our own problems, we don't need to be bogged down by theirs, too." Astrid hated herself even as she said it. She had come to enjoy their company—or at least Jane's company, anyway—and having seen what she had seen in Roden, having seen Knot be healed of his episodes time and again, she figured there had to be something to what Jane and Cinzia were doing.

But, ultimately, that did not matter. Astrid had debts to be paid, and she had her own salvation to worry about.

Nothing could be more important than that. Nothing.

"You really think we could just leave them?" Knot asked.

Astrid did not want to seem completely ruthless. But if she could instill some of that ruthlessness into Knot…

Do you realize what you're trying to do? You're trying to turn this man, this man who wants to be better, who doesn't want *to kill, into the exact thing he does not want to be.*

The thought came with sharpness and fire, but Astrid couldn't let such thoughts dictate her actions.

"Goddess rising, if you really want us to go to Triah… I'll think about it, Astrid. But it won't happen anytime soon. We have far too much to do here. *I* have far too much to do here, even if you do not."

Astrid glowered at the ground as they walked back to the house, saying nothing.

35

The Void

When Winter finally returned to the Void, it was by accident. One morning shortly after moving to her new bedroom in the palace, Winter found herself in the dark expanse, and she had no idea how she'd gotten there. She had been sleeping, and dreaming, and Winter's dream had not been her own dream, but the dreams of dozens of other people. Winter had seen faces she did not recognize, heard plans and desires and fantasies that she had never known or cared about. And now she was here, in the Void.

Accessing acumency in her sleep. Winter shivered.

The blackness surrounded her, a blackness that at first Winter had difficulty distinguishing from the terrible darkness that Daval had shown her. But while Daval's darkness was terrible, threatening, this emptiness was nullifying and indifferent. The numberless lights stretched out before her. A part of Winter wanted to leave before she saw Kali again. The woman was supposed to be dead. What could she possibly want with Winter?

But why not stay? she thought. See what happens. Nothing wrong with a little chaos.

Sure enough, within only moments, a shape coalesced before Winter's eyes; the same dark, indescribable something began to shimmer and take color into itself, slowly forming a figure in the darkness. The figure, becoming more and more tangible the closer it came, made ripples of light in her wake, and then Winter found herself face to face with Kali.

The face shifted, just as it had before. Sometimes it was an older, wiser woman with graying hair, other times the woman Winter had met in Cineste, tall and dark with frosty eyes, and other times the girl Winter had watched die in Izet, slight and blond. Winter saw hints of at least one other woman there, too, and Winter wondered what relationship existed between what Kali had been doing—procuring multiple bodies for one sift—and what had happened to Knot—multiple sifts crammed into one body. If she had seen Knot in the Void before he died, Winter wondered what he might have looked like, shifting back and forth between his many sifts.

"Hello, Winter," Kali said, smiling just enough for her shifting eyes, from blue to green to gray to brown and then a frosty blue once more, to sparkle and reflect the thousands of lights in the Void.

"Hello, Kali," Winter said.

"You recognize me," Kali said.

"Well enough. Looks like you've invaded more bodies than just the two I knew you in?"

"*Invaded?* That is too strong a word, but, then again… it might not be."

"Why are you here, Kali?"

Kali looked Winter up and down. "You've changed, Winter. You're different."

"I'm no longer a victim of your lies, for one."

Kali raised an eyebrow and paced around Winter, her footsteps rippling with color. "Not exactly the change I think I see in you, but true nonetheless. How is that frost addiction going, by the way?"

Winter's cheeks grew warm—she didn't know that could happen in the Void. "Just fine." *I have all the frost I could ever want and more*, she wanted to add, but knew it would be silly to admit. "You didn't answer me before," she said. "Why are you here? We thought you died in Izet."

"You mean when Knot killed me in Izet," Kali said sharply, stopping in front of Winter.

"So you're dead?" Winter asked, a strange hope blossoming deep inside of her. "Do… do dead people come to the Void?"

Kali sniffed. "Dead people don't go anywhere," she said. "Let alone the Void. When I died—when your *husband* killed me—I tried to send my sift out again, into another body. But it all happened too quickly; something went wrong and I found myself here."

Winter smiled. The idea of Kali failing so spectacularly was almost joyous.

Kali's face darkened. "It seems you've changed a bit too much for my liking," she muttered.

"I can't tell you how happy that makes me," Winter said.

"We have our differences… but you looked up to me once, did you not?"

"Before you betrayed me, yes."

"I was following orders. I don't expect that to make you feel better, but it's the truth. If I don't follow orders, what—"

"Orders are for fools. Going against them is so much more fun." Winter almost laughed. She had never said anything like that before.

"I don't wish to argue, believe it or not," Kali said. Winter realized that Kali was reaching for something in her breast pocket, but she couldn't find what she was looking for. She seemed to realize what she was doing, and stopped immediately.

"I believe I can help you. I think we can help each other, to be more accurate."

Winter laughed. "You'll have to explain that to me."

"You are using acumency," Kali said. "Who better to teach you, to help you hone your skills, than one of the most skilled acumens to have ever lived?"

That certainly got Winter's attention. She wanted to ask how Kali knew she was using acumency, but she had a feeling that it had to do with the Void.

"Even if what you say is true," Winter said cautiously, "what do you think I can do for you?"

Kali looked down at herself, spreading her arms wide. "In the spirit of being honest, I'll tell you this: I don't seem to have corporeal form here, except when you are present. I don't know why. I have never experienced anything like this before, nor heard tell of it from other psimancers. It is uncharted territory. But… there is some power within you that makes this," Kali patted her chest with one hand, "possible. I want to understand it. And, maybe, if I *can* understand it, I might be able to figure out a way out of this place and back into my body."

Winter narrowed her eyes. "Back into *your* body?"

"Or *a* body, if you want to get technical."

Winter shook her head. "How do I know you won't choose me as your host?"

"Even if I wanted to, I don't think I could," Kali said. "It may take you some time to believe me when I say that. I suppose you may *never* believe me. But I have no ulterior motives, here. I'll eventually find another body to inhabit, yes. But it will not be yours."

"I have no idea how I could help you," Winter said. Kali was making it seem like this would be a trade, that Winter would have some information or power to give her in exchange for training in acumency. If that was the case, Kali would be sorely disappointed. Winter had nothing to give.

"I don't either," Kali said. "But I've learned to trust my instincts, and right now they tell me that you're my best chance."

"I could just leave you here," Winter said. Looking at Kali, especially at the blond version of her, the one that had confronted them in Izet, she couldn't help feeling angry. "For trying to kill me. For trying to kill all of us. I could just leave you here and never return."

"Could you?" Kali asked, one eyebrow raised. "Once you experience the Void, it is… difficult to stay away. I believe you already know this. But… I'll freely admit that if you somehow did find the strength to stay away, even just to spite me, I would deserve it."

Winter scoffed. "You really think that?" The Kali she had known would never have been so subservient.

"You don't understand what it's been like," Kali said, her voice suddenly soft, almost… almost *weak*. Winter had never seen Kali show vulnerability. "My pride, my vanity, even my obsessions over duty and orders and whatever else in Oblivion I cared about… none of that matters any more. It's all silly, compared to my desire to get out of this wretched place. Long ago all I wanted to do was spend time in the Void. Now, I would do anything to get out and never come back. And if you can help me do that, I am at your service."

Winter stood there, her feet planted in the Void, considering. Really, her decision came down to one question: was she willing to learn acumency or wasn't she? It seemed the same dilemma she had faced on the outskirts of Cineste, what seemed like years ago, when Kali had first told her she was a telenic. And, in that moment, the answer had been obvious. Of course Winter needed to learn all she could, to become as powerful as she could, to protect her friends. To protect and help those she loved.

And look where that had gotten her.

But, now, she was somewhere different. She was in a different place, and whether she liked to admit it or not, Kali was right. She was a different *person*. There was no one left to protect. But the idea of power, of becoming an acumen like Kali, drew Winter. And there was something Galce had said, something that she had not been able to get out of her mind.

You must take life as it comes, my dear. The only order is chaos. The only way to live is to let yourself go.

"All right," Winter said. If the Sfaera was giving her this opportunity, why not take it?

Kali smiled. "Wonderful."

What seemed like hours later—Winter couldn't be sure, she was not clear on how time passed in the Void—things were not going as well as she might have hoped. Kali's experience with acumency seemed to be nothing like Winter's.

"Surely you've sensed your *tendra*," Kali said, shaking her head.

"No," she said flatly. It wasn't the first time Kali had asked the question. "I haven't."

Kali looked at Winter, her eyebrows knit together. "Are you sure?"

"I think I'd know if I used *tendra* of any kind. Telenic, acumenic, whatever. But I haven't."

"But you've accessed acumency?"

Winter shrugged. She had certainly experienced some

strange things, moving from mind to mind, things she suspected were acumency, but she had no way of proving it. And the fact that Kali thought acumency required the use of *tendra* made Winter doubt what she'd been doing this whole time.

"I've never experienced what you're talking about. These *tendra* don't make any sense to me."

Winter stopped when she saw Kali grinning. "What in Oblivion are you smiling for?"

Kali began moving off into the dark. "Follow me," she said over her shoulder.

Winter had no choice but to follow Kali's rippling footsteps. As Kali moved away, she became more faint, less tangible. But, as Winter followed and moved closer to her once more, Kali's form solidified.

Kali approached a cluster of lights glowing in the darkness.

"Can you recognize what these are?" Kali asked.

Winter looked at each of the lights, and shrugged. "People, I guess." Kali had told Winter that each of the lights in the Void represented a person on the Sfaera; as many people as lived in the world there were lights in the Sfaera, and then some.

Winter had asked about the "and then some" part, but Kali had been reluctant to talk about it.

"Yes, but who *are* they? You're in the Void, Winter, you have the power to see these people, who they are, even what they are doing at this very moment."

"Kali, I don't know how."

"Watch me, then."

Tendrils of smoke seeped from Kali, reaching out of her. But they weren't smoke, Winter knew that the moment she saw them; they were something very different, because these tendrils were *light*. They gave off their own glow in the darkness, pulsing slightly as they extended out from Kali's skull. The tendrils were different colors, one pink, another yellow, another bright blue, and another a dark red. They reached out and connected with the small cluster of lights before Kali—four of them. Winter knew this image would be burned into her mind. Kali, standing amidst blackness, light rippling from her feet, wearing a shifting dress that flowed in the darkness around her, not as if by a breeze but rather as if she were underwater, and Kali's hair moving in the same way, flowing all around her face and shoulders.

"This is a family," Kali said quietly. "A mother and father, merchants. Two sons, one barely old enough to walk, the other not much further along. They are dining together, and the younger of the sons does not like what he is eating. The father looks on him with affection, the mother with annoyance, but an undercurrent of love. Rather picturesque."

Kali turned to face Winter, the brightly colored *tendra* still stretching, flowing from her mind into the lights around her. "Would you care to observe with me?"

"How… how do I do it?" Winter asked. Seeing Kali there, so majestically surrounded by light, Winter realized that she *wanted* that ability.

"You already have a knowledge of *tendra* as a telenic," Kali said. "These *tendra* should be similar. Telenics often think of their *tendra* as extensions of their body. Think of these *tendra* as extensions of your mind, Winter. As you see me doing now."

Winter nodded, and tried to release mental *tendra* the way she would release telenic *tendra* from her body. "Nothing's happening," she said.

And then, another *tendron* snaked outward from Kali's mind, floating lazily, meandering through the darkness, towards Winter.

Winter took a step back, and noticed Kali's figure fade ever so slightly. "What are you doing?" Winter asked. She did not trust this woman. Did she need to remind herself of that?

"I'm only trying to help," Kali said. "If you let me connect with you I might be able to see what blocks you."

"I don't think so," Winter said, shaking her head.

The *tendron* hung in the darkness before Winter, waving back and forth lazily. Winter could almost sense the thing's desire to get inside her head, and instinctively took another step back.

"I'll leave before I let you do that to me."

Kali and Winter held one another's gaze for a few moments. Then, quickly, the *tendron* receded back into Kali's head. "Very well," she said. "I don't want to pressure you. As I said before, I'm only trying to help."

"And help yourself while you're at it," Winter said, looking at Kali through narrowed eyes. "Don't forget that part."

"Goddess, if you'd just let me teach you I think you'd realize that—"

"I'm letting you help me," Winter said. The desire to learn was there—she felt almost as giddy as she had when she was first learning telesis from Nash. That compulsive desire to learn more about whatever power lay dormant within her. "Just on my terms."

36

Harmoth estate

Knot stood on the training grounds, watching as Eward ran the trainees through another exercise. The young man was a fast learner; Knot had taught him and the other first recruits a few exercises, but Eward had already learned them well enough that he could direct the trainees without Knot's help. The trainees—currently numbering almost forty—had been split into teams and were currently making their way through an obstacle course of sorts, including a portion at the end where a team had to draw and fire dummy arrows at another advancing team.

"They seem to be doing well," Cinzia said, watching the recruits from Knot's side.

"Still green, all of them," Knot said.

"Surely they are better than nothing."

Knot grunted in response. Truthfully, he was pleased with their progress. They were eager, he'd give them that, and determined, too, and he couldn't ask much more of them.

Cinzia lowered her voice. "I never expected Eward to take so easily to this sort of thing. He seems a natural at giving orders."

"It's one thing to give orders on a training ground," Knot said, "and another to give them on a battlefield."

"Good thing we're not planning on taking them into battle, then. Guard duty should be all they need to worry about."

Knot wasn't so sure about that. The growing animosity from

Tinska—from the Kamite order—worried him. If they attacked again, he wasn't sure how well their little force would fare.

"It's time we started putting more of them on guard duty," Knot said. "And we need to assign bodyguards to you and the other disciples, as well as Jane."

Cinzia cocked her head. "Is that really necessary? Jane needs the most protection out of all of us, surely."

"She does, but that don't mean we shouldn't protect you too. Two bodyguards to each disciple will be enough for now." They currently had four accompanying Jane wherever she went.

"Disciple Cinzia!"

Knot turned to see the young girl Cinzia had recruited to help with the census, Arven, approaching, waving her hand in the air.

"Yes?"

"I've been thinking," Arven said, and then stopped.

Knot and Cinzia stared at her, waiting for her to continue. The girl was an odd one. He couldn't quite place his finger on it, but her mind didn't seem to be quite all there. Course, that was something he could relate to.

"What have you been thinking about, Arven?" Cinzia asked.

"I've been thinking about—well, I've been thinking about—" Arven glanced at the guard recruits. "Is there going to be a battle?" she asked.

Knot exchanged a glance with Cinzia. Then he shook his head. "No, miss. No battles here. Just training some folk to guard the Prophetess."

So you're calling her that now, too? Knot was surprised by how easily the word left his mouth.

"Now tell us what you've been thinking, Arven, we both have other duties." Cinzia's tone was firm but her smile was warm; it seemed she'd figured out the best way to deal with the girl.

"Of course, Disciple Cinzia, of course. I've been thinking—would it be helpful to invite everyone into the house, just once?"

"That is an interesting idea, Arven, but I don't think everyone would fit."

"Not all at once, of course not all at once. But in groups, we could do… we could have formal meetings for the Odenites, invite them in a few at a time, to get to know you and the Prophetess and…" Arven glanced at Knot. "And everyone else."

Knot raised an eyebrow.

"Arven, that's an interesting idea, but…" Cinzia paused. "Perhaps I will bring it up with Jane."

"As you wish, Disciple Cinzia," Arven said with a smile. She was about to leave when she spun back around on one heel to face them once more.

"I almost forgot!" she said. "Your parents wanted both of you to go to the drawing room. They're with your guests."

"My guests?" Cinzia asked.

Arven shook her head, then pointed at Knot. "No," she said. "*His* guests."

The Nazaniin. They had already arrived. Rune hadn't been lying—he really *had* sent a *cotir* from Tinska.

"Knot?" Cinzia asked, turning to look at him. "What is going on?"

Knot swore under his breath, ignoring the looks that both Cinzia and Arven gave him.

"In the drawing room?" Knot asked.

Arven nodded. She seemed about to say something, but Knot did not wait to hear it.

* * *

All eyes turned to Knot as he barged into the drawing room, jaw set.

Astrid sat with her legs curled beneath her on one of the large overstuffed chairs. Jane, Elessa, and Ocrestia were there, along with Ehram, Pascia, and Ronn. None of them concerned Knot, however. His gaze fixed on the three people standing under the huge marble mantelpiece at the opposite end of the room, goblets in hand.

"Get out," Knot whispered, walking towards the group. One of them, a tall older man with gray hair, held his hand out to shake Knot's. Knot deliberately pushed past, until he was standing with his nose only inches from—and slightly below—him.

"Lathe Tallon, I presume?" The man dropped his hand. The other two with him—a woman, only a few years Knot's junior with brown hair and brown eyes, and another man, quite young, perhaps not even older than Eward—turned to look at Knot.

"I told them it wasn't a good idea to come in," Astrid said. "Said you wouldn't be happy about it. They didn't believe me."

"You should have believed her," Knot said, glaring at the man, who he'd decided was the one in charge. "Get out. I won't say it again."

The man placed his goblet down on a nearby table, raising his hands. "We don't mean to intrude. I had hoped you would be more accommodating, but if this is how it is going to be, I won't argue. This is your home, after all." The man paused, looking around the room. "Or… is it your home? Now that I think about it, doesn't this house belong to the Oden family, who have so graciously offered us their hospitality?" He picked up the goblet once more, and took a sip.

Ehram stepped forward. "Sir, we did not know Knot would receive you this way. Had we known, we might not have been so eager to… to welcome you."

"Told *them*, too," Astrid muttered. "Didn't believe me, either."

The man bowed his head toward Ronn. "If our gracious host asks us to leave, we will of course oblige. But where we are does not change the fact that we have business with Lathe, or Knot, or whatever you call him."

"Meet me outside," Knot said. "You shouldn't be in this house."

Knot turned to leave the room, but was stopped by Pascia. "I'm so sorry, Knot, these people said they were your friends—"

Knot placed a hand on Pascia's shoulder. "This is not your fault," he said. "I should have warned you."

Knot made for the door. He looked over his shoulder at the *cotir*. "Coming?" he asked.

Knot led them out behind the house, where there were fewer wandering Odenites that might overhear. As he walked out under the gray sky, he became keenly aware that this was the last location where he had experienced an episode; he had become Lathe here, only a few weeks earlier. He had not experienced any episodes since, but he was sure another would come, sooner or later. Meeting with the Nazaniin could help him avoid that.

"You're a cautious one," the man said, once they were outside.

"Course I am," Knot said. "As I'm sure you would be, in my place." He eyed each of them. He inclined his head towards the tall man. "You're Cymbre?"

The man smiled, but shook his head. "No, I'm afraid not."

Knot frowned. "Rune said I'd be met by a *cotir* led by Cymbre. Who are you?"

The man chuckled. "I am not Cymbre, but my companion,

here, is." The tall man smiled at the brown-haired woman, who was inspecting Knot with bland eyes.

Is this how people feel when I look at them? Knot wondered. The woman's eyes did not bore into him; that was completely the wrong word. Her eyes were expressionless slabs of brown, and Knot felt almost as if they were pressing him backwards, up against a hard wall, crushing him against it.

Cymbre said nothing. Knot's frown deepened. If this was the woman in charge, it did not seem she was very keen on communicating.

"Who are you, then?" Knot asked wearily, looking back at the tall man.

"My name is Jendry," he said. He extended his hand, but thought better of it—perhaps remembering Knot's earlier reaction—and quickly retracted it.

"And who's this?" Knot cocked his head towards the young man.

"Wyle," the kid said. "I'm the—"

"He's new," Jendry said.

"At least he speaks," Knot said, looking at Cymbre.

"Aye, he does at that. A bit too much, if you ask me. Now, let's get down to business. First off, what do I call you?"

"Knot."

The man nodded. "Figured as much. Lathe is truly no more?"

Knot shrugged. "I can't say. I just know who I am, and it ain't Lathe."

"Is Lathe dead, then?" Wyle asked.

Jendry shot Wyle an irritated glance, but Knot didn't mind. "Might as well be," Knot said. *Unless he decides to make another appearance.*

"Why do you want to know more about Lathe, anyway?

What do you care, if he's dead to you and all?" Jendry asked.

"He's still part of me," Knot said. "I need to understand who I am." *Before I lose myself.*

"But he's still in there somewhere, isn't he?" Cymbre asked. Her voice was low and raspy.

Knot frowned. "I take it you're the acumen, then?"

Cymbre did not respond, but continued looking at Knot with her dull, flat eyes.

"Actually," Jendry said, "she's the telenic."

"And you're the acumen?" Knot asked.

Jendry laughed. He looked at Cymbre. "If Lathe's in there, he's buried deep. He would've had us pegged the moment he saw us. This one thinks I'm a bloody acumen."

Knot couldn't help raising his eyebrows just a bit. "You're the voyant?" He glanced at Wyle. "And he's the acumen?"

"Now you're getting it," Jendry said with a grin.

"Lathe's in there," Cymbre said. "But he *is* buried deep."

Knot frowned at the woman. She didn't seem to be talking to him. Fine by Knot. He looked at Jendry. "If she isn't an acumen, what in Oblivion is she talking about?"

Jendry sighed. "Our Cymbre thinks she *knows* people. Thinks she can see into them a bit better than others."

"She's right," Wyle said with a shrug.

"She is at that. Doesn't claim it to be any kind of power, just good at reading people." Jendry nodded at Knot. "You wanted information on Lathe," he said. "We have it."

"Rune said you want to know more about what happened to me in Roden," Knot said slowly.

"Yes," Cymbre said. "If you please."

"Why?" Knot asked. "What are you going to do with that information?"

"I don't think that's your concern," Wyle said, leaning forward.

Cymbre put a hand on Wyle's arm. "We know so very little of psimancy," she said, slowly. "It is a science, an *art* of which we are just scratching the surface. Every bit of knowledge helps."

Knot frowned. He was suddenly unsure of this entire exchange. What information were they really able to give him? Could he trust it? And what would they do with whatever Knot told them about what had happened in Roden?

At the edge of his vision, Knot saw the door to the house open. A small form slipped out and walked towards them. Astrid.

"What is it?" Jendry turned, following Knot's gaze. "Ah, the vampire."

"We need to continue this conversation later," Knot said. He moved towards Astrid, but felt a hand on his shoulder. Jendry. The grip was far stronger than Knot would have expected.

"What about your end of the deal," he said, his voice devoid of his earlier levity. "You owe us."

"You'll get what you're due," Knot said. "But you interrupted something of a crisis we have on our hands. You'll have to wait."

"But your end of the—"

"I'll make good on it," Knot said, "when you make good on yours. Right now I got bigger issues." Between the assassination attempts, the Kamite order, and training a new guard force, Knot had his hands full. He tore out of Jendry's grasp, and walked towards Astrid.

She smirked as he approached. "I knew you wouldn't like them." She nodded at the *cotir* behind Knot. "Looks like they may not be willing to take no for an answer."

Knot turned to see the *cotir* coming toward him, Cymbre leading the other two.

"Look," Knot said, "I'll cooperate, I just have to deal with some things first."

"We believe we can help you," Cymbre said.

"I know you do, but I have other things to attend to before—"

Cymbre shook her head. "You misunderstand. We believe we can help you with your current… issues."

Knot stared at the woman as the words sank in. "I… how do you know about our current *issues*?" he asked.

Wyle waved his hand, grinning. "Wasn't too hard to glean from that ex-priestess's mind. It was all she was thinking about. Even if I can't read you, I can—"

Before he knew what he was doing—with the instinct that'd been with him since the day he woke in Pranna, the instinct that made him so dangerous—Knot lunged forward, grabbing Wyle by the throat.

"You don't delve my friends," Knot gritted. "You don't even touch them with your powers. That clear?"

He heard Astrid's voice behind him. "Um, Knot?"

"What?" Knot growled, glaring at Wyle. Wyle's eyes were wide, with surprise, mostly, but yes, Knot saw fear there, too. That was good.

"I don't think you're in the best position to make threats at the moment."

Knot turned his head, but stopped the moment he felt a cold blade at the base of his chin. Jendry had a dagger at Knot's throat.

"That knife's the least of your problems. I wouldn't look up if I were you."

Knot looked up, taking care not to nick his throat against Jendry's dagger. Above him was a huge stone, three or four times the size of his head, floating in midair.

Knot cursed. He let Wyle go, who gasped and collapsed to his knees.

Slowly Jendry withdrew his dagger, but the boulder remained, levitating above Knot.

Knot turned, being sure to do so slowly. He'd grown attached to his skull; getting it crushed was not something that particularly appealed to him.

"Get that damn rock away from me."

Cymbre stared at him. "Very well," she said after a few moments. There was a *whoosh* above Knot, and then a thud in the distance.

"We're willing to help you, but you need to treat us with respect. No more threats," Cymbre said.

"I'll only make that promise if you make a similar one. No using psimancy on any of my friends."

"Fair enough," Cymbre said. She looked at Jendry, who nodded, and then at Wyle, who was slowly climbing to his feet.

"Sure, whatever," Wyle said, coughing as he waved off Jendry's offer of help.

Knot blinked. He had not expected them to agree so easily. Of course, agreeing to it was one thing; whether they would stick to it was another entirely.

"Now," Cymbre said, "let's talk about these problems of yours."

PART IV

THE ONLY ORDER IS CHAOS

37

Harmoth estate

CINZIA WALKED UP THE stairs to one of the large first-floor rooms where Knot, Arven, and the Nazaniin *cotir* had set up a temporary base of operations. A wide window gave them clear view of the grounds to the front of the building and most of the people who had settled there.

"What have you found?" Cinzia asked.

"Nothing," Knot grumbled. He was standing at the window, looking out over the grounds. Arven sat at a desk, poring over stacks of paper, and the three members of the *cotir* lounged on chairs, chatting quietly.

"Nothing at all?" Cinzia didn't bother to mask her disappointment. "Arven, what progress have you made?"

Arven looked up, and a wide grin spread across her face. "Disciple Cinzia!" she exclaimed. "I did not see you enter." She stood, bowing. "I apologize for my bad manners."

Cinzia motioned for the girl to sit back down. "The work you're doing now is far more important than silly courtesies. What are you doing right now?"

Arven sat back at the desk. "A few days ago, as you asked, I took a census of the Odenites. I asked everyone's name, where they were from, what brought them here. Of course, I didn't do it alone, that would be ridiculous, it would have taken me weeks—"

"I know about the census," Cinzia interrupted, trying to

keep hold of her patience. "I would like you to tell me what you're doing *now*."

"Yes, yes, of course. What I'm doing now. Well, I'm looking through the census documents trying to find information that matches the descriptors Knot has asked me to find."

"And you've had no luck?"

"Well, I wouldn't say I've had *no* luck; I have not cut myself on this paper yet, and I haven't gotten a stomachache, either. So I suppose I'm lucky in that sense. But as far as finding any matches, then I would agree that there has been very little luck. In that area."

Cinzia nodded, not sure how to respond. She turned to Knot. "What are these 'descriptors' you asked her to find?" And, stepping closer to him, she said much more quietly, "Is she organized enough to do this kind of a search?"

"Attributes that would be most common to the type of people we are looking for," Knot said. And, sotto voce, "She's more organized than any three people I can think of combined. Easily distracted, but she has a good system. The issue is that there are almost four hundred names to sort through, backgrounds to check, and so forth."

"I see." Cinzia looked back at Arven, already poring over more documents. Then she nodded to the *cotir*. "What of them? What are they doing?"

"Wyle's the one that can really help at the moment," Knot said. "He's the acumen, and he's been delving into people's minds. He has a good vantage point from here, but it isn't easy to delve so many people, especially when there is no accurate way to keep track of who he has and has not delved without letting them know explicitly what is goin' on. His *tendra* can only reach so far, too."

"Delve?" Cinzia asked. It was not a word she was familiar with.

"Wyle is an acumen," Knot said. "He uses psimancy to connect with the minds of others."

"That much I remember," Cinzia said. Knot had explained what each of the three branches of psimancy did, roughly—people who could manipulate physical objects, people who could manipulate the minds of others, and people who could… the third one had not been as clear to Cinzia. Interpret prophecies? Make prophecies? Predict the actions of others? It did not seem to fit with the other two, although the concept had intrigued her. She was a seer, according to Jane. Did that mean she had some sliver of this psimantic power? Or was what she did, translating the Codex, words no human on the Sfaera could understand, something different?

"Just tell me what delving means."

"He's discerning the thoughts of the Odenites, listening for anything suspicious."

"He can do that? With anyone?"

"Essentially, yes. But he has to decipher a person's sift first, and that's not always easy. It is a lengthy process. Wyle is moderately powerful, he can discern three or four at a time, but he can't do so indefinitely. He is already tiring. It is difficult when he is so far away from them; *tendra* have physical limits."

"Could he discern my thoughts? Or Jane's?"

"He could, but I've ordered him not to."

"And he'll obey your orders?"

Knot hesitated. "Wouldn't be a bad idea to guard your thoughts around him."

Guard my thoughts? Cinzia wondered. *How in the world am I supposed to do that?*

Probably not by talking to yourself.

Cinzia shivered. The thought of Wyle having free access to her mind made her feel queasy.

"I'm not sure this is the right way to go about our investigation," Cinzia said quietly. "We are invading people's privacy."

Knot's face remained expressionless. "We are," he said. "You need to ask yourself whether that's something you're willing to do to protect your sister, and, ultimately, everyone here."

"I have a feeling Jane would disagree with it," Cinzia said.

"She asked you to lead the investigation," Knot responded. "You can confer with her, or you can make your own decision."

"You think I should lie to my sister?"

"Don't think you should lie. Just ain't sure you need to tell her exactly what it is we're doing."

"Do you think it is worth it?"

"I know what I saw in Izet," Knot said, grimly. "I know what we're up against. I know, somehow, that you and Jane are some of the only people that give us hope against what's coming. I think protecting you at all costs is necessary."

Cinzia pursed her lips. She would need to think on this. Was this something she was really willing to do? Condone the violation of the privacy of hundreds of people?

You could trust in Canta. That's what Jane would do.

But what of the tools that Canta provided Cinzia? Where was she to draw the line? Cinzia needed to take action to translate the Codex; she couldn't just sit back and "trust in Canta" that it would get translated on its own. Where was the line between what she could do, and what she couldn't? Could Wyle be another instrument of Canta?

Cinzia shook her head in frustration. "He's just choosing

people randomly to decipher? That's how he's going about this?"

Knot shrugged. "We don't have much else to go on at the moment, not unless Arven finds something."

"There's got to be a better way." Then, Cinzia had an idea. "Arven," she said.

Arven looked up, smiling at her. "Yes, Disciple Cinzia?"

"What was that idea you brought to me the other day? Something about meetings in the house?"

"Yes, Disciple Cinzia, of course. I brought them up while we were at the practice yard—"

"I know when you brought them up, Arven. Explain them again."

"Yes, of course, Disciple Cinzia. I proposed that we invite the followers to come into the house, to get to know the Prophetess and her disciples. Also, it would be an opportunity for me to get more accurate records of everyone."

Cinzia looked to Knot. "And could it also be an opportunity for our acumen to delve minds at closer quarters, with more organization? Root out those who mean us harm—if that's what we decide to do, of course," she added quickly.

Knot's eyes narrowed, and for a moment Cinzia thought he might object. "That might actually work," he said instead. "It would certainly be more efficient."

Cinzia nodded. "It certainly would be."

"Is everything all right?"

Cinzia and Knot turned to see Cymbre walking towards them. The woman's eyes reminded her of Knot's when she had first met him. Strange that when Cinzia looked into Knot's eyes now, that deadness was gone. She couldn't tell whether it was something in Knot that had changed, or something in herself—perhaps both.

"Hello, Cymbre," Cinzia said. "Tell Wyle to stop… delving. We're taking a new approach."

Cymbre raised an eyebrow. "You don't wish for our help?"

"We think we could use you in a far more efficient way. Knot and I are going to organize meetings at the house. A series of inductions, as it were. The Odenites will stay for a half-hour or so, Jane will address them, and they will meet us in person."

"And you want Wyle to delve the people in groups," Cymbre said, nodding. "It's a good plan. Better than what we're doing now." Cinzia wasn't sure, but she thought she noticed the woman's eyes flicker towards Knot.

"I agree. Please, tell Wyle to save his energy. I'm going to speak with Jane and Arven, and get this organized. How long are you and your friends allowed to stay?"

"We're here to serve you, and get what we came for." This time, her glance at Knot was unmistakable. Cinzia did not think she meant it to be missed, either. "How long it takes is irrelevant."

Cinzia nodded. "Very well. If the sessions had thirty or forty people in them, how many do you think Wyle could do in a day?"

Cymbre considered that for a moment. "It is difficult to say. Five or six, but that's an arbitrary number. I'll speak with Wyle."

"Do it, and tell Knot if you come up with something. With any luck, we can begin these sessions tomorrow."

"Luck?" Cymbre asked, raising an eyebrow. "I did not think that would be a word I would hear around this crowd."

Cinzia snorted. "Because we are religious?"

Cymbre shrugged, but when Cinzia did not respond—she wanted to hear what this woman really meant—she sighed and said, "Yes, I suppose that's what I meant."

"Luck and faith are not mutually exclusive," Cinzia said. "Faith is a belief in something unknown, or something yet to come. Faith is active and it is part of our being. You've faith that if you take a step, your foot will support your weight, just as we all have faith that the sun will rise, just as I have faith that there is a loving Goddess out there who wants to take care of us, and has a work for us to do. Luck… luck is passive. While Canta has all power, She chooses not to control all things. Thus the actions of others, or the weather, may not go in my favor. That is luck. Sometimes Canta steps in to influence things, sometimes She chooses not to."

That, perhaps, was her answer, Cinzia realized. Cinzia needed to have faith. But if luck placed an instrument such as Wyle in her hands, one that would help her protect her sister, protect this movement, why would she not take it?

"But why would She ever choose not to do so? If She loves us, as you claim, and if She has all power, why not make everything go according to Her will?" Cymbre asked.

"That is getting into another discussion entirely," Cinzia said. "Canta's love for us is perfect, and She is therefore willing to let us make our own choices; She wants us to be and do what *we* want. She encourages us, guides us, but she does not constrain us." Cinzia smiled. "But you did not come here for a sermon on Canta's attributes. I apologize."

Cymbre did not seem to mind the lecture. "Is that what the Denomination teaches about Canta? Or is that what your sister teaches?"

Cinzia cocked her head. "It is what I believe," she said. And she meant it. That fact brought more pleasure to her than she had felt in a long time.

"Well then," Cymbre said, looking from Knot to Cinzia.

"I'll inform Wyle of our new plan. We will stay in touch about the logistics, I suppose?"

"Yes, we will let you know."

"Very good. Thank you, Cinzia. You are… you are an elegant woman, and someone I'm happy to work with."

Cinzia blinked in surprise. "Thank you," she said, getting a hold of herself. "Not only for the compliment, but for your help. It is appreciated. As you can see, we are in great need."

Cymbre inclined her head, just slightly, and then turned to walk back to her *cotir*.

"Was that…?"

"Strange?"

Cinzia nodded.

Knot snorted. "Strangest thing I've seen all day. And I see a lot of strange shit." Knot cleared his throat. "Pardon my language."

Cinzia shrugged. "Forget it," she said. "I'm going to talk to Jane. Can you ask Arven to organize the Odenites into groups that would make some semblance of sense?"

"I'll see what she can do," Knot said.

"Thank you," Cinzia said, and was about to go find Jane when she paused and placed her hand on Knot's arm. "I mean it," she said, looking into his eyes. "Thank you for your help. We couldn't do this without you."

Knot cleared his throat. "Just doing my duty."

You're doing far more than that and you know it, Cinzia thought.

38

The Void

"ACUMENCY IS DEPENDENT UPON deciphering your subject's sift. Once you figure that out, you can learn to rearrange things."

Kali sat cross-legged, facing Winter in the Void, delighting in the feel of a physical body once more. This was the third time Winter had come to learn more about acumency, and things were... progressing. But, unfortunately, Kali had gotten no closer to figuring out what it was about Winter that made her physical body appear when the tiellan was around, and certainly no closer to figuring out if she could use it to get out of the Void.

"What do you mean, 'rearrange things'?" Winter asked.

"You can affect them in all manner of ways, from how the subject thinks to whom the subject has feelings toward and what those feelings are, to the subject's control over its body, and more. But that affectation is the result of *rearranging* on your part. You have to know a thing before you reorganize it."

"To destroy, I must first know love," Winter said.

Kali cocked her head. Those words sounded familiar, but she couldn't quite place them. "What do you mean by that?"

"Nothing." Winter shook her head. "Acumency sounds much more difficult than telesis."

Kali shrugged. "I'm sure it is, in many ways. But once you make those first connections, once you decipher and rearrange your first sifts, it becomes easier. Intuitive. Now, are you ready to try accessing your *tendra* again?"

"I don't know," Winter said quietly, looking off into the distance.

"I can't truly begin to teach you *how* to use acumency until you access them, Winter. Knowledge helps, but not unless you can put it to use." It took all of Kali's discipline to not force the girl. If Winter only *knew* how patient she was being, perhaps she would give Kali the benefit of the doubt.

The two sat for a while, coasting in the Void. Kali did not feel the same pull to Winter herself as she did to her dark-light. While the ebbs and flows of the Void nudged and pulled at them gently as they sat facing one another, neither Kali nor Winter moved very far. The darkness flowed around them, the effect of the Void's aether causing their clothing to shift gently, their hair to expand and flow in all directions. The underwater effect, Nazaniin scholars called it. Winter's long black hair twisted and writhed above her head, almost as if it had a life of its own.

"What is a Harbinger?" Winter finally asked.

Kali blinked. That, of all questions, was not one she had expected. "Where did you hear that word?" She had been careful not to discuss the Harbinger with Nash whenever Winter had been around to hear.

"I… I don't know. It's in my dreams, sometimes, and in the air here, it seems. Between us. What does that word mean?"

"In the aether," Kali said, absentmindedly. The girl could sense that concept *in the aether*?

"What's the aether?"

Kali peered at Winter, fighting the compulsion to delve this girl immediately, while she still had *tendra* to do it, to find out what in Oblivion was going on in her head.

"The aether is the chief substance of the Void. The stuff between stars."

"The darkness?"

Kali shrugged. "Not exactly. It's like the air we breathe on the Sfaera, but different."

"How do you know it is different than air? Have you tested it?"

"*That* is a discussion for another day. As far as the Harbinger is concerned..." Kali hesitated. She couldn't think of a reason to hold back. Might as well tell the girl. "There is not much to say. The Nazaniin prophecies say that the Harbinger will be a powerful psimancer—perhaps the most powerful to ever live. Her—or his—title implies she will be the forerunner of something, but the prophecies are not clear on what."

"You have no theories?"

Kali laughed. "Everyone in the Nazaniin has theories about the Harbinger. Some say she will usher in the Rising, the era of the Nine Daemons—or that she has something to do with Canta. Others think her presence is not so significant, that she will simply herald a new era. A few think she simply brings death."

"Death?"

"The end of all things."

Winter stared off into the Void for a moment. Kali couldn't blame her. That last one had always sent chills down her spine.

"And you think it's me."

"What makes you say that?"

"You do. You think it's me."

Kali shrugged. "I don't think anything. But I know the Triad thought it was you."

"Thought?"

Kali sighed. "Yes, and I'm quite sure they still do. I overheard them talking a few months ago."

"How could you have overheard that? You've been in the Void."

"Traveling is not difficult here. Once you move in a direction, you keep going at an accelerated rate until you choose to stop. It's actually much easier to travel through the Void than it is the real world. There are no obstacles, no mountains or rivers or storms to weather."

Kali thought, just for a moment, about telling Winter about the strange shrouds she had seen: the violet one in Triah, the blue one somewhere along Khale's western coast, and the dark one around Izet. But she thought better of it. Best to keep some information to herself. Until she knew what those shrouds were, it mattered little.

"I..." Winter's form flickered. "I'm sorry, Daval is calling for me. I need to—"

And then Winter was gone.

With Winter went Kali's physical form. She would have sighed if she had a body to do it with. She anxiously awaited each visit Winter took into the Void, if only because it granted her physical form temporarily.

Kali began moving, though it took a great deal of effort. Winter's pull was strong. She had seen the shroud in Khale up close, and she saw the shroud around Izet all the time, but she had only seen the one on the western coast in passing. Perhaps, if she investigated it a bit more, she might find some clue as to what it actually was.

She spotted the strange form easily from a distance, and directed her motion towards it. It appeared larger than when she had last seen it, on her way back from Triah. It was an opaque shade of light blue, and it encompassed a large area that Kali realized, as she approached it, was likely the town of Tinska. She had been through it before, but never taken more than a passing interest. It was not a large town; why one of these strange shrouds would be focused on Tinska of all places was beyond her.

As she approached the shroud, Kali slowed her movement. She yearned to see how the shroud would interact with her when she had her body, when Winter was around. The shroud did not change at all as Kali passed through it, and once she was inside the veil, not much was different, other than everything acquiring a faint bluish tint. Kali passed in and out of the shroud a few times for good measure. Still no effect. The edge of the phenomenon shimmered and waved, sometimes bright and glowing, other times barely visible against the aether. Up close, however, the shimmering waves of the shroud appeared more like tiny wisps of light, like the stars of the Void but infinitely smaller.

The shroud was odd, indeed. But looking at it closely, Kali saw no difference from the other two shrouds she had encountered, and thus nothing new to learn.

Like the Triah and Izet shrouds, this one was roughly spherical in shape. The veil bubbled outward, covering thousands of stars that made up the people of Tinska in the real world. The stars abruptly stopped at a location Kali knew to be the western coast of Khale. Beyond that was only ocean. If the border of the shroud told her nothing perhaps she might find something at the center; Kali began moving in that direction.

As Kali moved inward, keeping track of the veil borders around her, she realized that the city of Tinska wasn't exactly in the center of the shroud, as she had presumed. As she moved through the town, star-lights passing all around her, she saw the center was a bit south of the town, in a cluster of a few hundred stars. Kali did not know what this was—a gathering of some kind? She did not remember a settlement this large to the south of the town.

Kali stopped moving.

There, in the midst of the crowd of stars to the south of Tinska, was something she had never seen before. The stars of the Void, each representing a person, were simple things. Each represented a very complex being, and each had its own beauty, but appeared as nothing more than a colorful point of light.

What she saw now was certainly not that.

Kali could see a rose-colored star that seemed to be right at the center of the veil around Tinska, but this star was different. Around the point of light buzzed layer after layer of small spherical shrouds. She had searched for such a thing in Izet, but had found nothing. Nothing like this, anyway.

There was only one thing to do now. Slowly, Kali stretched one of her *tendra* out to the rose-colored star. It was time to get some answers.

Kali delved into the strange star with her *tendron*, and gasped. An image of a face blurred into her vision. A man, walking through grass. A man whom Kali recognized. She knew him as Lathe, but, as he had emphasized so intently before he killed her, his name was now Knot.

Kali withdrew her *tendron*. She stared at Knot's star in the Void for a few moments, dumbfounded, until she made her decision. Quickly, she began moving back towards Izet, Winter's immolating darkness helping to draw her back.

She did not know whether Knot's star was the source of the strange shroud or not. It did not seem to be. His star and the shroud were not even the same color, for one. Psimancers still knew very little about what each color in the Void represented, but there appeared to be latent relationships between certain colors. Knot's star was a pink, rosy color, while the shroud around Tinska was blue. Even so, Knot's potential relationship to the shroud couldn't be ruled out. It was odd that Kali had not found anything similar in Izet; she wished she had looked for something at the center of the shroud in Triah, too.

But the relationship between Knot and the shroud, if there was one at all, did not matter at the moment. Knot was alive. Winter thought he was dead. This was information Kali could use, it was leverage. This was something that could help her.

If she could, Kali would have smiled the rest of the way back to Izet.

39

Harmoth estate

CINZIA SMILED AS THE group of Odenites filed out of the house, waving as they left. She could tell that they appreciated being invited into the Oden home, and even more so meeting Cinzia, Elessa, Ocrestia, and of course the Prophetess herself in person. It was what they had come here for, after all, and Cinzia could sense their gratitude. Which was why she felt more than a little guilty about her true motivation for the invitation.

She had discussed her misgivings with Jane beforehand, of course, and to Cinzia's surprise, Jane had reassured her. What had gone unsaid, and what Cinzia still thought now, was that while saying they were doing this for *the Odenites* was all well and good, Cinzia couldn't shake the feeling that she was betraying them.

When the last Odenites had left, Wyle shook his head, as he had for the previous groups.

"Nothing?" Cinzia asked, disappointed. It was silly to have such high expectations after every session, but she couldn't help it. If they *didn't* get any information, the violations would be in vain.

"Nothing of note," Wyle said, "and certainly no assassins."

Cinzia sighed. "Are you all right?" she asked. "Have you rested enough after yesterday?" This was the first session that morning, but he had delved through five groups the previous day.

Wyle smiled. "I'm just fine. A good night's rest does wonders, even for a drained psimancer."

Cinzia smiled hesitantly in return, not sure what to say to that.

"I'm sorry," Wyle said, "am I making you anxious? I don't mean to."

"It's just... I did not expect you and your friends to be so... so open about your magic."

Wyle laughed. "We aren't, normally. But Knot knows about us, as does the vampire. And while we don't like sharing information with representatives of the Cantic Denomination, it doesn't look like you'll be reporting to them anytime soon."

The words hurt more than Cinzia would have expected. She looked at the ground. "No, I'm no longer a part of the Denomination, though I have not received my papers of excommunication yet."

"Oh, Goddess, look, I... I'm sorry. I'm just trying to make conversation, I did not mean to bring up something uncomfortable. I should have realized."

Cinzia shook her head. "No, don't blame yourself, it is something I should have dealt with by now." She wondered whether it really *was* something she should be over by now, but it sounded nice when she said it. "But," she added, "I have to admit it is hard to trust a man who could potentially discern my thoughts at any moment."

Wyle nodded. "That, I can understand. But I did make a promise."

"You made it to Knot, and he is not yet convinced of your commitment."

"Then I'll make another one to you, right now. I promise, I will not delve you or any of your family. No one except who

I am told to delve. I might've been flippant with Knot, but that was before… that was before I really understood what was happening here."

Cinzia looked at Wyle through narrowed eyes. He seemed sincere. But did that mean Cinzia could believe him? She was having enough trouble trusting Canta. How could she trust one imperfect man?

"Look, Cinzia… do you mind if I call you Cinzia?"

I don't know what other name I could go by anymore. "Sure," Cinzia said.

"I admire what you're doing here. I'm not sure about Canta, never have been. And my particular vocation makes it difficult to associate with the Denomination in any way. But… I think what you're doing is brave. Standing up against the Denomination, *leaving* it, for Canta's sake, and supporting your sister. That takes a lot of courage."

Cinzia blinked, looking up at Wyle. "I… thank you," was all she managed to say.

"You're incredibly beautiful, Cinzia."

Cinzia's eyes widened. She took a deep breath. "Wyle, you're very kind, but I should go find Jane, make sure things are ready for the next group…"

Wyle took a step closer to her. He was smiling, and Cinzia did not sense any overt threat from the man—although she was suddenly very aware of how much larger than her he was—but… she was not sure how to describe her feeling, other than her insides squirming together all at once. In sort of a good way.

"I know that priestesses can't have intimate relationships, but… you aren't a priestess anymore, are you?" Wyle looked down. "I hope I'm not being too bold."

"No," Cinzia said, her mind racing. "You're not being too

bold." She had always had her Trinacrya to shelter her from the advances of men, but now... now she had nothing to hide behind.

Cinzia did not like that thought.

"Actually, yes," Cinzia said. She raised her chin, looking up at him once more. "I think you're being too bold, Wyle. I appreciate your attention, but this is neither the time nor place. I have work to do, as I said, and so do you. Now, if you'll let me find my sister."

Wyle nodded, and Cinzia was surprised to see his face turning red. Not from anger, though. He seemed genuinely sorry. Embarrassed, even. He was a handsome man, with a strong frame and jawline. His hair, thick and brown, hung loosely over bright green eyes.

"I did not mean to overstep my bounds. You will not hear such talk from me again, Cinzia, forgive me."

"It's... it's fine," Cinzia said. He had not really done anything offensive, had he? He was interested in her, that was all, and truth be told Cinzia did not mind that.

You let him off just fine, Cinzia told herself. *You were kind, but firm.*

"Er... Cinzia? Are you all right?"

Cinzia looked up, realizing she had been lost in her own head. "Yes! Yes, thank you, Wyle. Thank you for the report. I shall speak with you again soon."

Cinzia turned and walked away, until she realized she was heading toward the kitchen. Jane was in the opposite direction. She turned and retraced her steps, giving Wyle an awkward smile as she passed by him again. She made her way to the drawing room where Jane was waiting for her, along with Elessa, Ocrestia, and Knot.

"Anything?" Knot asked, raising his head.

Cinzia shook her head, her eyes on Jane. Part of her wanted to take her sister aside and tell her all about what had just happened. She wanted to tell Jane that a man had just approached her with… what? Cinzia had no idea what, but telling her sister felt like the natural thing to do.

Jane, a man just made an offer of courtship. To me. *And it was Wyle! Can you believe it? What was he thinking? What was I thinking? It had not even crossed my mind that this sort of thing would happen when I left the Denomination, I do not even know how to handle this…*

"No assassins? Nothing else of note?"

Cinzia blinked at Knot. Her conversation with Jane would have to wait. If she could ever have it at all. "No assassins. Nothing else of note."

Knot nodded. "Very well. The next group should be coming in any moment. Is everyone ready?"

The sessions had run in a relatively uniform fashion so far, with Cinzia welcoming the Odenites into their home. Ocrestia would then address them briefly, speaking of her faith in Jane and Canta. Her speech was relatively similar in each session. Then Jane would address the people, but to Cinzia's surprise her sister's address was different every time. In one session she had spoken of how difficult it must have been for all of them to come so far, and how Canta would bless them for their efforts. In the next she had spoken of some passages from the Codex they had translated, and how important that work was. And in yet another she had spoken of mending family ties that were coming loose, or that had been broken. Cinzia had asked Jane why she chose to speak on different topics, and Jane had only laughed and said that she was glad Canta guided her and that she did not have to think of them herself.

To end the session Elessa would offer a prayer, after which the people were allowed a few moments to speak with Cinzia, Jane, Elessa, and Ocrestia, and then were ushered out the door to make way for the next group.

"Have I been doing my part well?" Ocrestia asked. "I know I say basically the same thing every time… Do you think the people accept me?"

"If they don't, they need to learn," Jane said.

"From what I've observed," Cinzia said, placing a hand on Ocrestia's shoulder, "you impress them. They certainly accept Jane as their Prophetess, and seem to accept you as a disciple quite readily. They may have their misgivings, but as Jane said, let them. Those feelings will change as they get to know you—and if they do not, they will have to answer to Canta."

Ocrestia nodded. She could relate to her feelings, at least on some level. While she had no idea what it was like to be tiellan, she knew what it was to be in a position of power and feel inadequate. Cinzia was quite young when she graduated the seminary, and was younger than most when she became a priestess. She remembered feeling very self-conscious during her first sermons—her first few *dozen* sermons—and knew the power expectations and fear could have.

"You're doing wonderfully," Cinzia said, squeezing Ocrestia's shoulder. She looked at Elessa. "You both are."

The four women looked at one another, and Cinzia felt quite suddenly a wave of affection for them. Not just for her sister, but for Elessa and Ocrestia, as well. They had a connection, and they had work to do together. She wondered who they would find to fill the six remaining discipleships. Who else would be called? Would they fit in with the four of them?

Underlying it all was the question that ran through Cinzia's mind almost constantly: would any of this really work? *Could* it?

But, for once in her life, not having the answers did not bother her so much.

Cinzia did not notice that something was wrong until partway through the next session, but once the feeling settled she could think of nothing else.

Jane and her disciples faced their audience from the front of the drawing room. Ocrestia had just finished her speech. As Jane stood, Cinzia felt a strange sensation in her chest, like her ribs were constricting, squeezing her insides, her heart.

Cinzia's eyes found Knot first, leaning against the mantel over the huge fireplace. Astrid sat in the front row, looking up at Jane—only Cinzia's family, Knot, and the *cotir* knew what she really was, and they hoped to keep it that way for as long as possible. Not just for security purposes—Astrid made a perfect undercover guard—but because if the Odenites realized Jane was friends with a vampire, what would they think? What would they do? Their new Church would surely lose a great many followers.

It took Knot longer than Cinzia would have liked to meet her eyes. When he finally did, he seemed *bored*, of all things. His gaze drifted through the thirty or so Odenites crammed into the room, resting every few moments on one face or another, but he did not seem to be on his guard. When his eyes finally met Cinzia's, they widened slightly.

Danger? Cinzia mouthed, not sure what else to do or say. Knot's eyes narrowed, and he shook his head.

Cinzia frowned. Did that mean there was no danger? Or that he had not understood what she had said? She nodded forcefully—but as subtly as she could—towards the audience.

Knot shook his head again, and then his eyes drifted away from Cinzia's to the group once more.

Cinzia wanted to swear. She looked around for Wyle. He was usually standing near the back of the room, acting as an usher at the door. Sure enough, his wide frame was visible near the back, but he was… what was he doing?

Wyle was walking to the back right corner of the room. It was the signal they had agreed upon. The assassins were here.

Cinzia's heart froze. She wanted to help, but what could she do? Cinzia glanced back at Knot, who by now was also looking at Wyle. She scanned the Odenites, but no one had moved. Time slowed around Cinzia for a moment. There was an old tiellan man, in the middle of the back row, scratching his head. A woman to the right of the room shifted in her chair. Someone to the left cleared his throat. A head in the middle of the crowd turned upward, looking at the ceiling, whether in prayer or supplication or boredom, Cinzia could not tell. She looked up at Jane beside her, who was speaking of the trials necessary for faith, but her voice was odd, lower than normal, and she spoke very slowly.

Then, in the back, a man slowly stood up. In his hand was a knife.

She did not have time to think about how he obtained the weapon. Knot's guards had done their best to make sure that none entered the house. Perhaps it had been planted.

Cinzia moved before she even knew what she was doing. She rose from her chair quickly, or at least wanted to, but she felt oddly sluggish, just as the man seemed to, just like Jane, whose voice sounded so lethargic.

Cinzia looked around. Knot had seen the threat, but he was moving even more slowly than Cinzia, as if walking through thick snow.

Goddess, Cinzia pleaded, *what would You have me do?*

In that moment, something clicked in Cinzia's brain. If anyone was going to stop this, it would have to be her. Canta had put it in her hands. Cinzia had to trust that Canta had done it for a reason.

Cinzia picked up the chair she had been sitting on. It was a simple thing, polished wood, solid but not particularly heavy. Cinzia had never considered herself a physically powerful person, but even she could lift the thing over her head with some effort.

People were starting to murmur, but the sound was slow and laborious just like Jane's speech, rising from the depth of the room like the beginnings of an earthquake. Cinzia heard the whispers start, heard people beginning to cry out, slowly, in low, drawn-out breaths.

Cinzia stood behind Jane with her arms either side of her sister, holding the chair out in front of them both, the seat and legs of the chair pointed out towards the audience. Her body was pressed up against her sister's back. Jane was turning her head to look at Cinzia, confused, but Cinzia did not care. She looked back out at the man who had extended an arm towards Jane. He no longer held the knife.

It took Cinzia a moment to realize that something was moving through the air towards them, slowly rotating like a windmill in the slightest breeze. A dark shape spinning towards them.

Then everything returned to normal. Voices picked up in pitch, the screams that seemed to have been beginning for moments suddenly quickened, filling the room.

Cinzia felt something slam into the chair she held, the force of the impact reverberating down her arms. She stumbled backwards, taking her sister with her. Jane landed on top of her, knocking the air from Cinzia's lungs.

"Cinzia, what's happening?"

"Assassin," Cinzia rasped, pushing Jane off her roughly only to then cover her sister with her own body.

Her lungs burned. She looked over at the chair she had used as a shield. A large, strangely shaped knife had pierced the seat, buried up to half its length.

Jane followed Cinzia's gaze, and then her eyes widened.

More people were screaming, some were shouting that they wanted to get out, but Cinzia knew that wouldn't happen. The protocol they had decided upon if such a thing were to happen was to shut the doors and let no one leave—finding the assassins was too important. All she could see was commotion, people stumbling over each other, trying to move towards the back of the room. The dozen guards tried to enforce order, but panic was thick in the air.

"Ladies and gentlemen!" A shout rang through the air, cutting through the panic. "Brothers and sisters!" the voice cried again, and Cinzia saw that it was Ocrestia, standing on her chair, trying to get everyone's attention. Slowly, the panicked Odenites turned towards her.

"Do not be alarmed. There is an assassin here, but we are going to take action. Please, be calm. Canta guides us, and she will guide you, too. Let our guards do their jobs."

Miraculously, the mood immediately calmed. Even Cinzia felt her breathing ease a little, the strain in her lungs fade. She rose to her knees, motioning for Jane to stay down.

Suddenly there was a commotion by the door. She was not surprised to see the knife-thrower at the center of it. He thrashed about, pushing people left and right, but Knot was already there. Knot moved quickly, so fast he seemed a blur, and the assassin crumpled to the floor. Cinzia felt a wave of satisfaction. She looked to Wyle. There might be more; she hoped he would know if that was the case. But Wyle was gazing into the crowd, his eyes clouded in concentration. *He must not have finished*, Cinzia realized. *He must still be delving the people.*

"Are you hurt?"

Cinzia blinked, surprised to see Astrid standing beside her. "I… I don't think so," Cinzia said as she rose to her feet. To her chagrin, Jane followed suit.

"You need to stay down," Cinzia whispered to her. "There may be more of them."

"That may be, but I will not cower on the ground."

"Astrid, can you stay with Jane, please?" As Cinzia said the words, she realized that Astrid was staring at her, a strange expression on her face.

"Of course," Astrid said.

"I need to speak to Wyle," Cinzia said, but Jane grabbed her hand.

"Thank you," Jane said. "You saved me, Cinzia. Thank you."

I don't think it was me who saved you, Cinzia wanted to say. She still remembered the strange sensation of everything slowing around her, Jane's voice as it lowered in pitch, the knife as it rotated through the air towards Jane. It was decidedly not normal.

"You're welcome, Jane," Cinzia said. "Now, please, stay with Astrid."

Cinzia squeezed Jane's hand, and then moved away. Ocrestia still stood atop her chair, comforting the Odenites. Cinzia was surprised at how easily she made her way through the throng, the Odenites backing away from her.

"Did you see her move?" someone asked.

"I almost didn't, she moved so quickly."

"Like lightning."

"She is Canta's servant, what do you expect? She has Canta's power."

As she approached the back door, she saw Knot standing beside Wyle. The man who had thrown the dagger was slumped against the wall beside them unconscious, his hands and feet bound.

"Has Wyle discerned anyone else that might be a threat?" Cinzia whispered to Knot.

Knot shook his head. "Not yet." He was frowning, but his eyes met Cinzia's. "That was a brave thing you did."

Cinzia laughed, unable to help herself despite the humorlessness of the situation. "I'm not sure brave even begins to describe it. What do we do now?"

She looked over at Wyle, who was scanning the crowd intently. He normally did not look so... intimidating, when he delved, but she suspected he was working harder now that they needed to get through this group as quickly as possible.

"We wait for him," Knot said, nodding towards Wyle. "He finds anyone else connected with either assassination attempts, we take them in."

"How?"

"By whatever means necessary."

"I've got one," Wyle said after a few moments. He leaned close to her and pointed in the direction of a group of Odenites. Cinzia found herself uncomfortably close to him. The memory of what he had said to her earlier was suddenly very clear in her mind. "The woman there. Blond hair, dark-blue dress. She's connected with this man, and she's looking for a way to escape."

Cinzia followed Wyle's gaze and saw a young woman, younger than Cinzia would have expected. "What do we do about it?" Cinzia asked.

"Might still be others," Knot said. "We risk them doing something more drastic if we show our hand."

"But if we don't take her now, she may find a way to escape."

"How many more people are left for you to delve?" Cinzia asked.

"Six."

"And that will take you how long?"

"A few minutes."

Cinzia nodded. "Then we wait until you've delved the rest of them."

Wyle nodded, and Cinzia settled back to wait, keeping her eye on the woman he had pointed out.

She did not have to wait long. Before Wyle had finished, another commotion broke out, but not around the young woman. A middle-aged man grabbed an older woman, wrapping one arm around her neck. In the other hand he held a metal tool of some sort, pressed up to her temple. The man moved towards the door, his back against the wall.

"Let me out of here!" he demanded. "I need to get out or this woman dies. I can't stay here any longer!"

Cinzia, eyes wide, looked at Wyle. He was shaking his head. "I… I already delved him. No signs of danger or any strange associations. He's just panicking. But he's not bluffing. He *will* kill that woman."

Beside Cinzia, Knot muttered a string of curses.

"Knot, can you stop him?" Cinzia asked.

"I can."

"Do it." Knot immediately began moving towards the man. "Wyle," Cinzia said, "continue delving the others. I'll keep an eye on—"

Cinzia stopped. The young woman was gone. She glanced

around frantically. They couldn't let her go. They had this woman in their grasp, they couldn't afford to—

And then Cinzia saw the woman approaching a window. The window was thick glass, not meant to open, but the woman was already hefting a chair, and Cinzia could guess what she was going to do next.

Cinzia moved quickly, or as quickly as she could, suddenly feeling very slow compared to how she had felt when saving Jane only moments before. The woman raised the chair above her head and threw it at the window, shattering the glass.

The Odenites, already panicked by the man who had taken a hostage, began to scream.

Cinzia sprinted towards the woman. She did not know what she would do when she reached her, but she knew she had to stop her somehow. Cinzia bellowed, surprised at the low growl that came from her throat. The woman turned to face Cinzia, her eyes wide, just as Cinzia lowered her shoulder and plowed into her, ramming her against the wall.

Cinzia stumbled away, her head spinning, but before she could regain her senses she felt a sharp blow to her stomach. What in the Sfaera had she been thinking charging a dangerous person like that? Something struck the side of her head. Cinzia's vision exploded in flashes of bright light. When she opened her eyes she realized she was lying on the floor, staring up at the female assassin. The woman turned, going for the window, but then stopped. She looked back at Cinzia, and their eyes met.

The woman muttered something that Cinzia did not understand. Then a small dagger appeared in her hand. Cinzia blinked. Where had the weapon come from?

Cinzia had been so focused on making sure that she did not escape, that she had forgotten that this woman was an assassin, sent here to kill Jane. But not only Jane, Cinzia realized, as the woman lunged towards her; anyone who was associated with Jane, and certainly Jane's sister, once a priestess, now her first disciple.

Cinzia knew, in that moment, she was going to die.

Then something blurred across her vision, colliding with her would-be assassin, sending the woman sprawling. A small form picked the woman up, slamming her head against the wall, and the assassin slumped to the floor, still.

Astrid walked toward Cinzia. Cinzia stared at Astrid's hand as the girl extended it down to her. The hand was small, but not as small as Cinzia would have thought. Cinzia had a sudden very vivid memory of looking at herself in the mirror when she was about Astrid's age. Cinzia had gone through what could only be described as an ugly phase—and that was being kind—around her ninth and tenth summer. Cinzia remembered looking in the mirror and being disgusted at how her hands and feet seemed so much larger than they should have for her skinny, boyish body. "You'll grow into them," her mother had said. "It's natural, dear." And her mother had been right. But now, as Cinzia looked at Astrid's hand, she had a very clear memory of looking into her looking-glass at that age. Astrid was at that same stage of growth, her tiny, boyish frame disproportional to her slightly more feminine, but certainly larger, hands.

She will never grow out of this, Cinzia realized. *She will be stuck staring at this form in the looking-glass until the day she dies.*

A sudden wave of crushing sadness descended upon Cinzia. Cinzia felt something very tangible for this girl, for the life she lived.

"D'you want me to help you up or what?"

Cinzia blinked, and then nodded, grasping Astrid's hand. As she moved, she became very aware of the warm wetness on her thighs and her undergarments. She felt her face turn hot.

"Pissed yourself?"

Cinzia's eyes widened as she stared at Astrid. "A little," she said.

A little?

"Don't worry," Astrid said, helping Cinzia to her feet. "Happens to the best of us when shit like this goes down. No one will care. No one will even notice. I'm just a bit more sensitive to smells."

As Cinzia stood, she realized, thankfully, that it *had* only been a little. She looked down. No wetness was visible through her dress. Still, the discomfort she felt was horrible, as if everyone in the room were staring at her.

But Astrid was right about one thing—it did not matter. Cinzia squeezed Astrid's hand.

"Thank you."

Astrid's hand slipped out of Cinzia's quickly, waving her off. "Don't mention it," she muttered.

"I mean it," Cinzia said, but the vampire had already turned back to the unconscious assassin. Cinzia took a deep breath, smoothing her skirts, careful not to press where the wetness might show through. She nearly jumped out of her skirts, wet or not, when a voice spoke behind her.

"You all right?"

Cinzia turned, hair on end, to see Knot standing behind her. "Fine," she said, looking over Knot's shoulder. "What of the—"

"We contained the incident," Knot said.

Behind him, Cinzia saw a few people from the crowd around the woman that the crazed man had taken captive, comforting her. The man himself was unconscious, slumped against the wall, next to the first assassin they had caught.

"Good," Cinzia said, with a sigh of relief. If that woman had been harmed, she did not know how they would have handled the situation.

"I'm amazed," Knot said, "at how quickly you went from doing something brave, to doing something stupid."

Cinzia's cheeks, which had not yet cooled down from her earlier embarrassment, now only grew hotter once more. "I know. I just… I couldn't let her get away."

"She could have killed you."

"She would have, if it weren't for…" Cinzia looked at Astrid, who was currently binding the female assassin.

"I know," Knot said.

"How does she do what she does?" Cinzia found herself asking, as she stared at Astrid. "How does she… how does she…"

"How does she live?" Knot asked.

Cinzia nodded. The great weight of sadness she felt for this girl—vampire or not—pressed down on her.

"She's strong."

"She is," Cinzia whispered.

"What are you two jabbering about?" Astrid had finished binding the woman, and was now approaching them.

"What to do next," Knot said.

"And what's that?" Astrid asked.

Knot glanced at Cinzia, who nodded. "We make sure Wyle has finished with the rest of them, and then we take these two into our care."

Astrid snorted. "Care. That's a nice way of putting it."

"How else would I put it?"

"Oh, Goddess," Astrid moaned. "You've a lot to learn about what's about to happen."

The three of them walked over to Wyle. The concentrated

expression had faded from his face. Cinzia hoped that meant he was done; these people needed to get out of here.

"She pissed herself, you know."

Cinzia nearly choked on her own tongue. She glared down at Astrid, then looked around herself frantically, hoping no one had heard the girl. No one seemed to be paying them any attention; Ocrestia, it seemed, had once more captured the room's attention. Cinzia was happy to see Jane, smiling proudly up at Elessa, seated nearby.

"Yeah, so?" Knot shrugged.

"You know too?" Cinzia glared at Astrid. "You said no one would notice."

Astrid shrugged, chuckling. "What do I know? That's never happened to me before."

"But you said—"

Knot and Astrid were both laughing, now, and Cinzia was surprised how little she cared. They had accomplished what they had set out to do. Cinzia felt good.

That evening Cinzia and Jane sat on the two overstuffed chairs in the library together, sipping tea. Jane had insisted that they continue with the meetings, despite having apprehended two assassins. Cinzia hoped that was all of them, but Knot was reluctant to think so. There would be more, he said. The attacks wouldn't end just because they caught a few people.

That realization had struck Cinzia with force. The threats, the violence, might not end.

"Cinzia," Jane said. "We need to talk about what happened today."

Cinzia closed her eyes. "Can't we just sit here in silence, for a moment? Enjoy one another's company?"

"We can. But eventually we are going to need to talk about what we *didn't* talk about with everyone else."

"What do you mean?"

Jane pursed her lips. "What you did today, sister."

"Ah," Cinzia said, eyes dropping to look into her teacup. "Yes."

"I mean to thank you," Jane said.

"You're my sister. I would do anything to save you."

"And I'm glad you did."

Cinzia waited, sure Jane would ask how she had moved so quickly to block the assassin's knife. But Jane remained silent.

"Is that all you wanted to say?" Cinzia asked after a few moments.

"That's all I wanted to say."

"You're not going to ask me how I did it? You just said we needed to talk about it."

Jane laughed. "I did, didn't I? Well, that is for you to tell me, if you wish."

Cinzia raised her eyebrows. She was of half a mind to change the conversation, just to spite her sister. *You won't get anywhere with that attitude,* she reminded herself. Pettiness did not become her. And besides, she *wanted* to talk about what had happened. She wanted reassurance.

"I think it was Canta," Cinzia said quietly.

Jane sipped her tea, listening.

"You know I have been struggling," Cinzia continued. "I experienced something wonderful on the rooftop in Izet, but... but I have had difficulty reconciling that with everything that has happened since. Kovac. Our movement. The abilities you and the other disciples are manifesting. I have wanted proof, I have wanted to experience the powers myself before I trusted. You asked me, weeks ago, why I needed to know before I trusted, and that question stuck with me. But I think, today, I finally let it go. I trusted first, and..."

"And you saw a result," Jane finished for her.

"Yes. I think I did." Cinzia looked up at her sister. "But I was scared today. When I chose to put my trust in Canta, I was *frightened*."

"What is faith without fear?" Jane asked. "If we have nothing to fear, what reason do we have to exercise faith?"

"So I can never have faith without fear? I could barely do it today. How am I supposed to take that leap again?"

"Because you saw the result. You will remember that next time, and it will get easier. The trust will come as you begin to realize that Canta will not leave you."

"So there will always be a result to my faith, like there was today?"

"I wouldn't necessarily say that," Jane said. "Faith is not something we do in the hope of a reward, but rather in the hope of becoming something better than what we are."

"And faith helps us become something better?"

"When placed in the right source, I think it does."

Cinzia shook her head. She wanted to believe what Jane said, but it was not easy. What if she trusted, one day, and no one was there to catch her?

"Do you really think it was Canta who guided me?" she asked after a few moments, surprised at the tears burning in her eyes.

"It was," Jane said with a smile. "I'm sure of it."

Cinzia took a long, deep breath. "How? You said as much in Navone, when..."

"Navone was a mistake," Jane said quickly. "On my part. I made a guess, when Canta's light had temporarily left me, and I was wrong. This is different."

"How is it different?"

"Because I know that it is," Jane said simply.

"Goddess, this faith business is maddening," Cinzia muttered.

Jane laughed.

"What about you?" Cinzia asked after a few moments. "Do you have that power, too?"

"I have whatever power Canta chooses to give me. So do we all, as Her disciples."

Cinzia thought carefully about her next question. "Could you have used it, in Izet? Did you let Kovac die, when you could have saved him?" A growing knot of resentment and anger formed in Cinzia's stomach.

"It is not that simple," Jane said.

"But it was a possibility," Cinzia said. "You could have, and you didn't."

"*No*," Jane said, with more force than Cinzia expected. "I can't use this power as I please. Nor anyone else on the Sfaera. Canta gives us whatever power She sees fit, when She sees fit. I... I am sorry, Cinzia, but it was Canta's plan that Kovac die in Roden."

Cinzia stared at the floor, unable to look at Jane's face. She knew her anger was irrational. If Jane couldn't control this power, how could she have chosen to let Kovac die? Not to mention the circumstances surrounding Kovac's death—for all Cinzia knew, the Daemon might have negated Canta's power. Nevertheless, the anger was there, writhing in her gut.

"I'm sorry, Cinzia."

Cinzia closed her eyes. "No one is to blame as much as I am," she whispered. She was the one who put the dagger through his eye, after all.

When Cinzia opened her eyes, she could look at Jane once

more. "So you're saying that the power that allowed Elessa to heal you is the same power that allowed me to save you today."

"That's what I'm saying."

"And the same power that lets you heal Knot?"

"Yes."

Cinzia's curiosity was piqued. "What else?"

"I know that Canta's power must only be used to help others. It must never be used for one's own personal gain or benefit."

"Is that even possible?"

"I'm not sure," Jane said with a shrug. "I have never tried."

"What else?" Cinzia asked.

"The closer the bearer of this power works in conjunction with Canta's will, the more significant her power will be."

Cinzia blinked. "I… I am not sure I understand."

"It's a bit complicated," Jane sighed. "Canta bestows her power on whom She chooses, when She chooses. In turn, those people are then allowed to choose how to use that power. But, if someone uses Canta's power for something other than what Canta intended, the power is weakened. If someone uses it exactly the way Canta intended it, that power is magnified."

Cinzia was nodding, but still not sure she was getting it. "So it's a guessing game?"

"Let us take what happened today as an example. Canta bestowed Her power on you today. You felt it, you knew you had it. At that point you had any number of options; you could have chosen to save me with it, as you did, or you could have chosen something else. You could have decided to attack the man with the knife instead of defending me from him."

"In other words, I wouldn't have been using it to help others, I would've been using it to *harm* someone."

"Exactly," Jane said. "Had you attempted to attack the

assassin directly, your power would have been less significant. You wouldn't have been as fast or as strong."

"Is that what Canta wanted me to do, then? To help you?"

"It is difficult to be sure," Jane admitted. "There may have been a higher action you could have taken, something closer to Canta's will, that would have granted you even more power."

"So how do we know if we are doing Canta's will?" Cinzia asked, confused.

Jane smiled ruefully. "We don't. The Codex gives some direction, and we may receive promptings, but this is where we come back to faith. We must press forward knowing that what we are doing is Canta's will. If we do, the blessings will come, and we will know afterwards."

Cinzia thought about that for a moment, although the thought still left a sour feeling in her mind. There was still the potentiality of not receiving a response or a confirmation. "Are there any other aspects to these powers?" she asked, not really wanting to pursue the faith topic any further.

Jane nodded. "Because Canta's power is inseparably connected with the Praeclara, and our mortal forms are unused to such power, Her power will take a great toll on us. That is why, I think, you are so tired today."

That actually made sense. Cinzia was exhausted. "How do you know about these powers?" she asked. "We have translated nothing of them in the Codex."

"Canta has revealed them to me," Jane said.

"And She revealed to you that what I did today was under Her power and direction?"

"She did," Jane said. "After a fashion. She rarely speaks to me in specifics."

Cinzia rolled her eyes. "I have about had it with Her

obsession with faith. She expects us to trust Her so much; you would think She would put a bit of trust in us."

"I think that's exactly what She does when She asks us to have faith," Jane said. "She trusts that we will choose faith over the alternative. And while I *do* think it has to do with faith, I... I think there may be something else going on as well. During a few of our conversations, She has almost seemed frustrated that She couldn't say everything that She wanted to say. As if She *had* to speak in generalities."

Cinzia looked up from her teacup. No one ever spoke of Canta being limited; She was all-powerful, and all-knowing. There was no limit to what She could do. And yet Jane was suggesting there was.

"This is not the first time you've said such a thing," Cinzia said, leaning forward. "In Roden, you said something had been blocking your ability to communicate with Canta. Is this something similar?"

"I can't be sure," Jane said. "But in Roden, I thought the problem was on my end, that I had done something to make me unworthy to hear Canta's voice. But, having had further conversations with Her, I... I am beginning to think that may not have been the case."

Cinzia, eyes still wide, attempted to process this. Something wrong with Canta? What in the Sfaera could that possibly be? "Has that barrier been there the whole time?"

"I think so," Jane said. "I did not know any better at first, but now... now, when I look back at our communication, it seems obvious. I truly believe that a portion of what She says is intended to draw me to a greater faith, to help me make decisions instead of simply relying on what She tells me to do. But... but She has *never* been clear with me, do you understand? She has always been vague."

"Have you asked Her about it?"

"Of course I have," Jane said. "But She ignores those questions. I think… I think She ignores them because She literally can't answer them. She has answered everything else, in one way or another."

Cinzia shook her head. "What power is there that could possibly limit *Canta*?" They were both silent for a moment, but then Cinzia remembered something. "Do you remember what happened when we spoke of this last time? When you told me that you thought something was blocking you?"

Jane took a deep breath. "It was the night… the night Kovac died."

"The night Kovac was possessed," Cinzia added. "The night Azael introduced himself."

"I have considered that," Jane said. "Of course it could be a possibility."

"Why would it not be Azael?" Cinzia asked. "He is obviously at complete odds with Canta."

"It just seems… it seems too simple. And Azael, while he may be the leader of the Nine Daemons, he is still just a Daemon. Canta is a Goddess, Cinzia. What power could he possibly have over Her?"

Cinzia sat back. That much was true. Azael and the rest of the Nine Daemons had been created by Canta's peers; how could they possibly have power over the gods? They were terrifying, to be sure, and their power was great, but… what could they really do? "But if you're right," she said. "If someone, or something, really is exerting power over Canta…"

"I fear it might be something more powerful than even Her," Jane said quietly. "Nothing else makes sense."

Cinzia supposed it was possible—they had learned from the

Codex that Canta was the firstborn of Ellendre and Andara, and that the two High Gods had raised their Daughter up to be like them. The two sets of triplets that followed Canta, the Brother-Gods Emidor—Irit, Orit, and Erit—and the Sister-Gods Adimor—Irali, Orali, and Arali—were powerful, too, but had never been on the level of the First Three. It did not seem possible, let alone likely, that Canta could lose her position in that Trinity.

"I think we had better get some sleep," Jane said after a while.

Cinzia nodded. She was exhausted; sleep would do her good. Especially if they were to finish the meetings with the Odenites on the morrow. Just because they had found some assassins did not mean that they could deny the rest of the Odenites a chance to meet the disciples.

Jane stood up, and Cinzia followed suit. It was almost midnight; she still had time to get a good seven hours of sleep in before the first meeting tomorrow morning. They started for the door, but after only a few steps, Jane stopped.

"What do you think about releasing the assassins?" Jane asked.

"Goddess," Cinzia moaned. "It is too far into the night to confront me with an idea that ludicrous. You want to *release* the people who tried to kill you? To kill *us*?"

"Why not?" Jane asked. "We know what they look like, now. They couldn't infiltrate our camp. Knot and Astrid, our guards, wouldn't let them near us."

"And if they are working with others still in the camp?"

"They aren't," Jane said.

Cinzia rolled her eyes. "Let me guess. You know this because Canta revealed it to you."

"No," Jane said, glancing away. "I know because I asked Wyle to find out for me."

Cinzia's eyes widened. She had thought her sister would be against the use of acumency. How could her sister, someone supposedly chosen by Canta to lead a new religious movement, to champion good in the Sfaera, invade the privacy of others so callously?

"We will hold them for a few more days," Jane said, resolved. "But after that, I think… I think we will release them."

"Why don't we just have Wyle *change* them," Cinzia muttered, "if you've already gone to the trouble of invading their minds so completely."

When Jane did not respond, Cinzia's blood ran cold. Was that what her sister had already done?

40

Imperial palace, Izet

"Ah, my *garice*. I'm so glad you've come. And I can hardly contain my excitement to finally make a gown worthy of your beauty!"

"Beauty?" Winter asked with incredulity. "Your empire drove my kind out decades ago. How can you possibly think me beautiful?"

"My empire has done many things with which I don't agree," Galce said. "The empire was wrong to remove your people from its borders. I think the empire is worse because of it."

Winter looked in the mirror. What could she say to that? Thank you? That did not seem remotely appropriate.

"The emperor's inaugural ball will be a wonderful event," Galce said, motioning for Winter to step onto the pedestal in front of the mirror. "I imagine you're excited to attend?"

Winter snorted. "I do as Daval commands, and he commands that I attend this ball. In a dress."

Galce laughed as he pulled out a measuring tape. "You are unique, *garice*, I will say that. But I wouldn't call the emperor by his first name if I were you; people have been executed for less."

"I call him Daval to his face," Winter said, not without some pride. "He doesn't seem to mind."

Galce's eyes widened, as did his smile. "Impressive, girl. You've gambled, and Chaos has ruled in your favor. For that I commend you; Chaos is a fickle master."

Galce continued working, measuring Winter's arms, hips, around her thighs. The measuring seemed excessive, but it was the same process Galce had used for the black leather clothing she now wore, and she had to admit it fit her perfectly. If he could make her a gown that fit the same way, Winter might actually want to wear it.

"You've mentioned chaos," Winter said after a few moments, her mind mulling over Galce's words. "More than once..." How to put this delicately? "What are you talking about?"

Galce laughed again, the sound rising up from his belly. "Chaos rules the Sfaera," Galce said. "Chaos is my master, just as it is yours. There is no escaping it, and no manipulating it. Chaos simply is."

"That seems a bleak way to look at the world," Winter said. Though she was one to talk.

"Quite the contrary," Galce said. "Chaos is a comfort, *garice*. Could you find more comfort in Canta? Chaos will guide us every step of our path; has your goddess done that for you? Have the Scorned Gods done that for Roden?"

"Canta is not my goddess," Winter said.

Galce merely nodded, and continued measuring.

"So... Chaos is your religion, then?" Winter asked.

"Chaos is Chaos. It is what it is. One does not worship Chaos, but we do live our lives according to it. Everyone does, whether they know it or not. Those who believe, like me, simply acknowledge and embrace it. We are all leaves on a great river. Sometimes we flow along easily on smooth waters; sometimes we encounter rapids and barely make it through—or not at all. Sometimes we find eddies and a moment of brief reflection; other times low-hanging branches catch us, we find ourselves stuck in rocky outcrops, and our progress stagnates."

"And Chaos is the river?" Winter asked.

"Chaos is *everything*. The river, the rocks, the trees and the weather. Chaos is the leaf itself, it is *us*, and all things around us."

"If you're a leaf on the river," Winter said, "how do you make any decisions? How do you do *anything* in life?"

"We do as Chaos directs."

"But what does that *mean*?"

"It means we live our lives, and trust," Galce said. "If an opportunity arises, we take it. If that opportunity pans out, we continue. If it does not, we return to what we were doing before or take the next opportunity."

"What you're describing doesn't sound very much like freedom."

"What is freedom other than what we want from it? If I feel free, if I have all I need, what more can I ask?"

"But there has to be something you do when you make decisions. Some kind of system. What if more than one opportunity presents itself?"

"Forgive me, *garice*, I'm being somewhat facetious. We do have a system. You see, as much as we see Chaos operate and work outside of ourselves, each of us has Chaos inside us as well. It is only a matter of looking inward, and we find the guidance we seek."

Winter frowned, unable to hide her disappointment. "That's it?" she asked.

Galce laughed. "That is only the beginning. Chaos manifests itself differently within each of us, but it is impossible to define, and that's the point. Everything we know, everything our world has become, began with something very simple. We call it the Prime Order."

"Chaos began with order?"

"Absolutely, *garice*. Chaos is not random, though it may seem that way to us, because we can never have a perfect knowledge of the Prime Order—the way things were in the very beginning. Because we can't have that perfect knowledge, we can't know anything. No matter how much history I learn, no matter how much I study the mind and how we make decisions, I can't *know* how you will respond to what I say or do, let alone how the world will respond. That is why we give ourselves over to Chaos." Galce jotted down one more measurement, and then put his measuring tape away. "You may get down."

Winter stepped down from the pedestal and Galce placed his hands on her shoulders. "What I'm about to tell you is something special," he said. "We don't often speak of this to people outside of the creed."

Winter stared at him. Then why was he telling her?

"You are right, *garice*. Sometimes, we are faced with decisions. But there is always a way to give ourselves up to Chaos, and to trust that Chaos will lead us to the best possible choice. Now, close your eyes."

Winter, overcome with curiosity, did so.

"Envision a perfect sphere, its surface smoother than anything you could imagine. It is large, it encompasses your whole vision. Now… what color is it?"

"Black," Winter said, without hesitation.

"Ah… that is unexpected. Black, then. That is your Chaos, Winter. This sphere can be two colors—black, as you see it now, or white. It can only be one color at a time; it can never be both. All you have to do is close your eyes, and you will see it. The color manifested each time you see it will indicate what you are to do."

Winter opened her eyes, more than a bit skeptical. "I just

imagine that sphere, whenever I need to make a decision?"

"Call it Chaos, *garice*. Give it the deserved respect."

"Of course," Winter said. She doubted it would work. It seemed the sphere—Chaos—would manifest itself as black every time Winter saw it in her mind. That was how it was conceived—how could it possibly change? Or what if it appeared blue, or green? Confining choice to two options seemed needlessly limited.

But Winter did not have to tell Galce that. He had been kind to her, and apparently revealed to her something very dear to him. "Thank you," she said. She truly meant it.

"You are welcome, *garice*. I can tell that you are an agent of Chaos. I can tell that you will use this gift wisely."

Later that night, after taking a frost crystal, Winter traveled to the Void. It was time to search for her *tendra* once more.

Kali was waiting for her.

"I'm ready," Winter said.

Kali grinned—no, she'd already been grinning, the moment she materialized in the Void. The grin looked strange on her shifting face.

"No small talk? You don't want to ask how my day went?"

Winter scoffed. "Don't much care. Let's find my *tendra*."

"As you wish," Kali said, still smiling.

"What do you want me to do?"

"Relax," Kali said. "We'll do what we tried before. Remember, this will not be exactly the same process as when you found your telenic *tendra*. You're a variant telenic, but an actual acumen. There are differences, so reset your expectations now."

Winter nodded and closed her eyes. She steadied her breathing—if she was even breathing in the Void, she wasn't sure—and relaxed.

The moment she shut her eyes, the dark sphere was there, looming in her mind's vision.

Winter's eyes snapped open. She had not been asking for the sphere—for Chaos. She had not even encountered a decision she had to make, yet.

Winter took another deep breath. It didn't matter. Chaos was not important to her right now. Her *tendra* were. She closed her eyes, ready to—

"For Canta's sake." Chaos was there once more, waiting for her, black as pitch and smooth as silk.

"Are you all right?"

"Fine," Winter said, too quickly. "I just—tell me what to do. What am I doing?"

"Concentrate. You've obviously been using your acumenic *tendra*, somehow. You just need to *see* them. What happens when you've 'sent your mind out,' as you've stated?"

"I just... I just..." Winter closed her eyes again. Chaos could not be there again, there was no reason to—

The black sphere waited for her in her mind.

Fine, Winter thought, to Chaos. *You obviously think I need to make a decision. Fine. I'll make it. Just leave me alone so I can do this, it's important.*

When Winter opened her eyes, Kali's stupid smile had finally faded. Instead, her mouth was open, jaw slack, eyes wide as she stared at Winter.

Or, more accurately, as she stared at Winter's *tendra*—dozens of them, luminescent, multicolored tendrils of smoky light, branching out from her.

"Is this... is this normal?" Winter asked, looking around herself in awe.

"This many *tendra* are not normal, no," Kali said, her eyes flickering around Winter. "But you aren't exactly a normal psimancer, are you?"

A few of Winter's *tendra* snaked their way towards Kali. Winter was about to stop them, when the thought occurred to her. Why not? Why not see what she could see in Kali for herself? At least then she might know for a certainty whether Kali was lying or not—what her true motives were. In time, Winter realized, she might even be able to shape Kali's motives herself.

To destroy, I must first know love.

Winter frowned. Could she ever love Kali? Someone who hated her race, who had tried to kill her and her friends? To love someone was to know them, accept them. Perhaps, if she could delve the woman, learn more about her, Winter might be able to accept Kali.

"What are you doing?"

Winter's *tendra* stopped moving. "What do you mean?"

"What are you doing with those?" Kali asked, pointing at the *tendra* that had been moving towards her.

"I need to practice, don't I?" Winter asked. "I need to learn how to use them, to learn how to delve, or whatever it is you call it. Shouldn't I practice on you?"

Immediately, five or six *tendra* appeared from Kali. They moved towards Winter's *tendra* and sliced directly through them, evaporating them instantly.

"Hey!"

"You will *not* start with me. We start with others. We start with some of those," she said, indicating the stars in the Void.

Winter nodded. Kali was right. Winter wouldn't have wanted Kali to delve her, so why should she expect Kali to let Winter invade her mind?

And yet... when Winter closed her eyes once more, Chaos

was still waiting for her, black and foreboding. That was that, then. Chaos dictated.

With all the strength Winter could muster, she sent her *tendra* towards Kali.

Kali reacted quickly, and her *tendra* sliced through her attack, but Winter just sent her *tendra* again. The woman obviously had fewer *tendra* than Winter did, and the sheer volume of the onslaught pushed Kali back. Winter saw panic in her eyes.

"I'd like to know what's really behind these efforts of yours," Winter said, trying to sound as calm as she could as she sent attack after attack towards Kali. "I suppose I have the means of finding out, don't I?"

"You don't know what you're doing," Kali said through gritted teeth. Kali was straining, too. That was a good sign.

"You've taught me well enough," Winter said, sending another volley of *tendra* towards her. "I can figure out the rest."

"You would betray me, Winter? You would do exactly—what—you feared—I would do." Each phrase was accented with another defensive slash from her *tendra*. Each time one of Winter's *tendra* was severed, a haze of color burst in the Void.

"I only fear it," Winter said, more *tendra* springing forth from her mind, "because you've already betrayed me once before. Now, I'm returning the favor."

Kali's first instinct had been to attack Winter's *tendra* at the source, but she quickly decided against it. She still needed Winter; she did not want to destroy this girl's potential.

And as Kali's *tendra* interacted with Winter's, she felt something she had never felt before. A connection—not with the girl, but with the *tendra* themselves.

An image flashed through Kali's mind: Winter, lying prone

on a large bed, eyes rolled back in her skull. But it wasn't just an image, Kali realized. It was real; Kali was seeing Winter's form as if she were actually in the room with the girl. It was a connection, Kali realized, to the Sfaera.

Kali logged the information away. No, she couldn't destroy this girl. She might be Kali's only hope of getting out of the Void. But Kali had had about enough of Winter's petty attack. The girl had insane talent with her *tendra*—and an insane amount of them—but she was not a fighter, not yet. And Kali had been trained by the best in the world.

Kali stopped her retreat and stepped forward in the Void, dodging and parrying a few of Winter's attacks with her *tendra*. Then, she punched Winter in the side of the head. Winter stumbled backwards, her onslaught temporarily over. Before Winter could recover, Kali punched her again. Winter fell to her knees.

"Attacking me was a bold move," Kali said. "But it was foolish, too." She reached out with one of her *tendra* and jabbed it into Winter's brain. Only too late did she notice Winter's doing the same, moving towards her.

Immediately, Kali was back in the room—a large bedroom, by the looks of it, with expensive-looking wooden furniture, dressers and a mirror and desk, at one end. A room in the imperial palace. This time, Kali was lying on the bed, looking up at the canopy above her with her own eyes.

Kali was in the real world.

Then, just as quickly, the real world was gone, and Kali was back in the Void, Winter cringing at her feet.

"What was that?" Winter asked.

"I... I don't know," Kali lied. She wasn't sure, but she might've just unlocked a clue on how to get herself out of the

Void. But she wouldn't tell Winter. Not right now. Just like she wouldn't tell Winter that her husband was still alive. After Winter's betrayal, it was something Kali might never tell her.

"We are done for today," Kali said. She needed to think on what had just occurred.

Without a word, Winter's figure blinked out of existence, and Kali was incorporeal again.

At least now, however, she had new information to keep her going.

41

Harmoth estate

"ASTRID, COME OUT OF there! The ceremony is about to begin!"

Astrid moaned, rolling over in bed. She did not sleep—or she did not need to, anyway. But that did not mean she didn't enjoy being a lazy little girl from time to time. What was Ader doing knocking on her door so early, anyway?

"Just a bit longer," Astrid muttered into her pillow.

"We don't have any longer! If you don't come out now, Jane said I have permission to come in there and get you."

Astrid's eyes snapped open. Quickly, she leapt up from the bed. It wouldn't do for Ader to come in and see her room like this. No, it wouldn't do at all.

The blood was the first thing to cover up. Astrid had fed recently; she had not been able to resist the urge any longer. She'd made the mistake of bringing the remains of her meal up to her room, and now one corner of the floor was stained a dark reddish-brown color. Astrid grabbed a rug from the foot of her bed and threw it over the stain. It was an odd place for a rug, but she figured Ader wouldn't notice. He was certainly less likely to notice a strangely placed rug than he would a giant bloodstain.

"I'm coming in if you don't say anything!"

"Just a moment, I'm not *decent*, Ader!"

Next were the weapons. Ader still had no idea who Astrid was—*what* she was—and she was not about to be the one to spoil things for him. That meant the daggers, the throwing knives and *shurikas*, the armor-piercing hammer, and the short curved sword resting on the end table had to be hidden. While Astrid had her claws, they only came out at night, and even then only offered her limited range. She liked to be prepared.

She swept the weapons to the floor with a series of clangs and clatters. Astrid swore.

"Are you all right in there?"

"Fine, I'm fine! Just knocked my toe against one of the bedposts, that's all."

With a few kicks, Astrid pushed the weapons under the bed. Then she took a deep breath, looking around. She did not think anything else would be too conspicuous. She exhaled.

"All right, Ader. You can come in."

The moment Astrid said it, she realized she was completely naked.

"*Shit*."

Astrid whipped the sheet off her bed and wrapped it around her, just as Ader walked into the room, a wide grin on his face. The grin faded the moment he saw her, and his face turned bright red.

"Uh… I… I thought you said you were decent… I'm so sorry, I…"

Astrid cleared her throat. "Um, yes, sorry, I… I forgot… I forgot I wasn't quite decent…"

Ader stared at the floor as if his life depended on it. Astrid could have laughed if she were not so nervous about completely traumatizing the boy. His ears were more red than the blood Astrid had drunk the night before…

Astrid's eyes widened. She saw that one of the daggers she had kicked underneath the bed had slid a little too far and now protruded from the other side—now in Ader's view as he looked at the floor. Astrid edged around the bed awkwardly, careful to not get the sheet tangled in her legs. Unfortunately this meant she was edging closer to Ader, too, who glanced up at her, his face even more red than before, and then back down at the floor quickly.

Ader took a step back. "I think I should leave, until you're decent."

Astrid finally reached the dagger and kicked it back underneath the bed.

"What was that?" Ader asked, looking up at her. He immediately looked back down.

"What was what?" Astrid asked.

Ader shook his head. "I'll see you later." He walked out of the room and closed the door behind him.

Astrid fell back on the bed with a deep exhalation. She liked Ader. He was a nice kid, and not boring, which was a quality Astrid always appreciated. But she and him had about as much in common as a rose and a wild boar, and Astrid knew exactly who the wild boar was in that comparison.

She had indulged him up to this point, but this encounter made her realize how silly the game was she'd been playing. Goddess, she had not even realized she was naked until he was practically in the room. Ader was a few years her senior, physically speaking, and he wasn't likely to take that sort of a thing lightly if he was like most twelve-year-old boys she knew. She didn't know many, admittedly, but still. Astrid sighed. Sometimes she wondered what in Oblivion she was doing here, with this batshit-crazy family.

Then she heard the tug on her mind that told her she was being voked. "Oh, for Canta's bloody sake." The Black Matron.

No one else had reason to voke her anymore. Astrid reached to her bedside table and picked up her voidstone.

"Yes," she said.

"You're still in Tinska, aren't you?"

The Black Matron had ordered Astrid to bring Knot to Triah. Astrid had not yet been successful.

"It is proving more difficult than I'd hoped," Astrid whispered. She kept her eyes on the door, on the light that shone through the crack underneath. She watched for shadows; she wouldn't be caught again. Or nearly caught—she thought back to Brynne, when Knot had almost discovered her.

"Then I expect you to overcome those difficulties. Get him here, *immediately*."

"Why do you need him anyway?" Astrid asked, and immediately winced. That was exactly the type of question she should have learned not to ask.

"That is not your concern," the Black Matron said. "Getting him here *is*. If you want any hope of salvation, of shedding your immortal coil and embracing death and forgiveness, you will redouble your efforts. Failure is not an option, girl."

Astrid breathed slowly and deeply. *Death and forgiveness.* The one she deserved, the other she did not. But the Black Matron promised her both.

She had grown fond of Knot. She couldn't deny that. But she had longed for death for far longer, and the Black Matron promised her absolution from her sins. If she did what they ordered her to do, Astrid would obtain forgiveness.

"I will not fail," Astrid whispered.

"See that you do not." The Black Matron severed the connection.

Astrid closed her eyes. She was not a fool. She knew that

following the orders of someone called the "Black Matron," who operated in secret and tortured her if she did not do what was asked, couldn't be in the service of anything good. And yet what the Black Matron had shown her had been *real*. The forgiveness they offered was tangible. A new beginning; a clean ending. But that did not change the fact that Astrid hated herself for every moment she spent in the horrible woman's employ.

She rose from the bed and found her smallclothes, and her favorite dark-green dress—the most fancy item of clothing she owned, made of thick, soft cloth and trimmed with gold. Fake gold, anyway, that was more of a faded yellow now than gold, but it had once been a pretty dress. Astrid blinked, looking at the garment, realizing how long she had owned the thing. Longer than she cared to admit.

But it was the nicest thing she had, and today seemed a day to wear something special.

This morning, Jane was continuing the work of establishing the Church of Canta.

Knot watched as Astrid made her way towards him, her cloak drawn up over her head. The girl was late. She should have been here long before the speeches started. That was the consequence, Knot conceded, of allowing Ader to wake Astrid up.

She was here now, though, and that was all that mattered. Knot chewed his cheek. He still, after all this time, couldn't shake the feeling that the girl was hiding something. She was likely hiding many things, though, as most people did.

"What'd I miss?" Astrid asked, stepping beside Knot.

"Nothing yet, lucky for you."

She looked around. "Where's the *cotir*? I thought they'd want to witness this."

"Got called back to Tinska on business. Should be back tomorrow or the next day." As relieved as Knot was to be rid of the *cotir*, their presence had become oddly comforting.

"I bet you're—"

"Astrid," Knot said firmly, "get to your post."

"Fine, fine."

Astrid leaped up onto the dais, taking her place just as Jane stood to address the crowd. A dozen of the guards Knot and Eward had trained stood at the base of the dais, the blackened remains of the ash tree rising above them, while the others had been scattered throughout the audience. Knot was not taking any chances.

Today was, officially, the first day of the new religion: the Church of Canta.

"We thank you all for gathering to hear us speak this morning," Jane said, her voice loud and clear. Knot was once again surprised at how much volume Jane could muster; even the Odenites on the fringes seemed able to hear her. Their numbers had almost reached six hundred according to Arven's ongoing census.

Now that the people of Tinska were refusing service to the Odenites, they were facing an imminent food crisis. Jane was aware of the issue, but insisted the foundation of the Church took precedence. Why that took priority over feeding her followers, Knot couldn't say.

"We thank you for the sacrifices you've made to be here with us," Jane continued. "We know many of you have left homes, families, friends, and fortunes. Some of you arrived here with all you had, which was not much to begin with. Others left almost everything behind. To each and every one of you, we extend our thanks, and Canta's blessing. You will begin to see Her hand in your lives as you continue to follow this path, I promise you.

"We have gathered you here today in the name of transparency. Many of you call me a prophetess. I reluctantly accepted that title, not only from you but from our Goddess Herself. At Her behest, I have called three disciples so far, and six more will follow. My sister, Cinzia, was the first. The others, Elessa and Ocrestia, were chosen from among you.

"We are in the process of reviving a religion—the same institution that Canta intended when She graced this world. We will go about things the way She intended them to be."

A few dozen shouts rose from the crowd, mostly along the lines of "Praise Canta" or "Goddess be thanked."

"That is not to say that there is not truth out there already," Jane continued. "I speak, of course, of the Cantic Denomination. I want to be clear. That organization is *not* evil, contrary to what I have heard many of you say about it. We have no quarrel with the Denomination; this must be understood. Especially in light of what else I'm about to tell you."

Knot was surprised. He had always assumed that Jane and her Odenites would be at odds with the Denomination. Apparently Jane advocated a different path.

"In order to fully realize our Church, as Canta meant it to be, we must leave this place," Jane continued.

Knot had heard nothing about leaving the Harmoth estate. He glanced at Cinzia, whose wide eyes and reddening face betrayed her surprise, too.

"We must return to the place where it all began, where Canta was at her most powerful, and at her most vulnerable, too. We are going to travel to Triah."

The Odenites' murmuring elevated into loud whispers, a

few shouts rising above the noise.

Cinzia's face was now completely pale. Knot knew that she had spent seven years of her life in Triah studying at the Cantic Denomination's seminary and serving as priestess to a congregation there. She had left all of that behind to help her sister. Knot could understand why this news would be less than welcome for her.

Jane raised a hand high above her head, and the crowd hushed almost immediately. "I know this comes as a shock to many of you, and I will remind you all of one thing, something we have tried to make clear since you arrived here. You're all free to choose. If you disagree with anything we do, if you want no part in it, that's your right. We will respect that decision, and if you don't wish to accompany us on our exodus to Triah, so be it. We will part ways with joy and friendship. But we hope that you *will* come with us. We will need the support of each and every one of you on this journey, as we establish ourselves in the heart of Khale, in the heart of the Sfaera. The entire world will hear about what we do there, and we will all witness miracles. That much I know to be true."

That mollified the audience somewhat. Knot could still hear many people whispering, but the shock and indignation at Jane's announcement had dissipated.

"One thing I do know," Jane said, with a bold light in her eyes, "is that we will face danger. The path to Triah will not be an easy one. But we *will* get there, and we will be stronger for it. I have seen it."

A movement caught Knot's attention, a shifting in the distance, at the top of the hill. He squinted. The sun shone brightly at his shoulder, and the road to Tinska was a fair distance away. As he narrowed his eyes, he saw what looked like a few figures on horseback cresting the hill. New Odenites, most likely, arriving just in time to hear Jane finish her speech.

Knot turned back to Jane, who was talking now about Cinzia, Elessa, and Ocrestia as her disciples, something about how they were extensions of Canta's power. But further movement drew his attention back to the hill.

More figures on horseback. Knot couldn't count them accurately from this far away, but he estimated there were at least fifty. Knot's chest tightened.

"I want to thank each and every one of you," Jane said loudly, a smile on her face, "for participating in the meetings we held in the house. It was a pleasure to meet each of you, to hear many of your stories. We are so grateful you're here."

Jane did not seem to have noticed the growing threat atop the hill. Knot glanced at Cinzia, who was still staring at her sister, white-faced. But the moment his eyes met Astrid's, he knew she *had* noticed the men. Her sight was sharper than any human's; she would be able to discern far better than he how many men there were, perhaps even who they were.

"We leave for Triah in two weeks," Jane said. "We have that time to prepare, to pray, and to continue serving one another. We will need to band together and forget our differences for this journey to be successful. You're all tools in Canta's hands. She will use you, hone you, polish you until you are prepared for Her express purposes. The process can be difficult, even painful, but I give you every promise that it is worth it. Thank you again. Now, let us prepare, and pray."

Jane stepped back, and Elessa stood to say a prayer. Knot slipped along the dais until he came to Astrid.

"Can you tell who they are?" Knot whispered.

"Not of a certainty," she said. "But they're armed."

Knot swore. "They're keeping the high ground. Are they in uniform?"

"No," Astrid whispered. "No uniforms. Their weapons are not exactly professional, either. Swords and spears, but I see a lot of pitchforks and clubs. Looks more like a militia."

"Or a mob," Knot said. Kamites. He was sure of it.

"How many of them?"

"A little over fifty so far," Astrid said, "but still more coming up the hill."

Elessa finished her prayer, with an audible "Imass" from the Odenites.

"Come with me," Knot said, motioning for Astrid to follow him to where Cinzia and Jane stood. Their plan had been to walk among the crowd after the speech, but Knot could tell that Cinzia was itching to speak with Jane. Understandably, if the idea of traveling to Triah came as much as a surprise to her as it had to Knot. But, at the moment, they had more pressing matters.

"A force is gathering at the top of the hill," Knot said quietly as he approached the two women. "Armed and on horseback. Ain't professional soldiers, but they look to be from Tinska."

Both Jane and Cinzia turned to him, eyes wide.

"Kamites?" Cinzia asked.

"Not sure. Both of you should get back to the house. I'll go see what they want. Might be able to turn them away." Not likely, but worth a try.

Then he heard Astrid swear, and shouts behind him. He turned to see his fears confirmed. The horsemen were charging down the hill, directly towards the Odenites.

Jane's announcement about Triah echoed in the back of Cinzia's mind, but as she saw the horsemen advance, she knew there were more pressing matters.

Her heart skipped a beat as Knot sprinted forward, shouting orders at the guards, Eward running to his side. She had been proud of her brother for taking charge of the guard force, but seeing him rush into danger made her wonder what in the Sfaera had ever made her think it was a good idea. There had to be over a hundred men on horseback coming down the hill; their guard force couldn't field half that many.

Knot and Eward were taking action. Cinzia needed to do the same.

"*Everyone who is not a guard, retreat!*" Cinzia shouted, surprised at the volume she could muster. "*Into the house!*" It wouldn't take all the Odenites, but getting them to retreat as far away from the advancing horsemen as possible was better than nothing.

Immediately, the people obeyed, but they were moving too slowly. Cinzia needed to get them out of the way so the guard force could form up before the horsemen broke into them. She looked at Jane, Elessa, and Ocrestia. All three women were staring at the charging force.

"*Help me*," Cinzia hissed. That jarred them into reality, and immediately they took up Cinzia's cries, herding the crowd towards the house, as far away from the enemy as possible. She was about to rush forward to start ushering people back, when a small form stopped her. Astrid.

"I need to get the four of you inside."

Jane, having finally gotten a hold of herself, shook her head. "Not until we get everyone else back. We need to give Knot and the guards room."

Astrid growled. "I'm staying with you, then. And as soon as the crowd is clear, we're getting all of you back inside."

"Fine," Jane said. "But no sooner."

"*Back to the house!*" Cinzia shouted again, hoping they could give Knot enough time.

"Spears!" Knot shouted. "Every guard with a spear, form the front line!"

The men and women did as asked. They were scared—Knot knew they had to be—but they obeyed orders. That was perhaps all that kept them from panic. They formed a line as they'd been trained, twenty spears across. His handful of archers formed up behind them.

"Spears on the ground!" Knot shouted. The front line obeyed while Knot turned to his archers.

"Fire at will," he ordered. "Break the charge!"

Arrows hissed overhead. He heard horses scream, saw the charging line falter as some horsemen went down, only to be trampled by those charging behind them.

Twenty spears against a hundred horsemen; behind the spears, roughly the same number of swordsmen. Eight archers, already firing into the horsemen. It would have to do.

Before Knot could turn back to the hill, he heard the rumbling.

"Brace yourselves!" Knot shouted. The guards stared at the charging enemy. In that moment Knot could see the terror on their faces.

"Hold!" Knot shouted, drawing his sword, already seeing some of his men itching to take up their spears. The horsemen were nearly on them, pitchforks and clubs and spears raised, expressions of utter detestation twisting their faces.

"Hold!" Knot shouted again, raising his sword high above his head.

Then, as the horsemen reached the flat at the bottom of the

hill, Knot lowered his sword swiftly. "*Now!*"

His guards took up their spears, and the enemy had nowhere to turn but directly into the sudden barrier of barbs that confronted them. Horses screamed, people screamed, Knot heard a loud choking sound that could have been animal, man, or even himself echo in his ears.

One of the horses charged directly at him, and Knot dodged the stab of a pitchfork, grabbing the wrist of the man on its back. With a sharp twist and a crunch, Knot brought the man to the ground, breaking his wrist and shoulder in the process. The man's horse scrabbled away.

"Regroup!" Knot shouted, fighting his way between two men on horseback. He nearly cut the leg clean off of one with a slash of his sword. The man fell to the ground screaming while the other rider's horse stumbled over him. Knot stabbed upward, and his sword slipped between the other rider's ribs.

All of his guards had engaged the enemy. Knot couldn't believe how many people—some of them his own guards—lay screaming, twisting, dying. It seemed seconds since the horsemen had charged, and there were already dozens of wounded. Knot shouted for his guards to form up around him once more. If they could stay together, they stood a chance.

Then, to Knot's horror, he saw a large contingent of horsemen run straight past his small force, bearing down on the retreating Odenites. Knot couldn't imagine what those would do to Jane's followers. But his priority was to get his men and women through this alive before helping the others.

Knot ran quickly to a group of his guards. One of them lay on the grass, not moving, blood pooling beneath him. Another fell as a club cracked sharply against her skull. Knot slipped his sword up between the shoulder blades of the man wielding the club. More men on horseback wheeled to face Knot, and as they did so the guards attacked, bringing the men down.

"What now, sir?" asked one of the guards.

"Form up," Knot said. There were pockets of people fighting all around them. Less than half of the enemy had remained to fight Knot's forces. The others galloped after the retreating Odenites. Already Knot could hear screams from the direction of the house.

He swore. "We need to defend the others. Come with me." He stalked forward, his eye on a group of men that had descended from their horses and were now surrounding four of his guards. "Come on," Knot repeated, and as he did, he suddenly remembered…

"Come on," Lathe said, leading his men to…

To where?

He was in a battle. Men and women were fighting, though hardly any seemed trained soldiers. He was holding a sword covered in blood.

A man, shouting at the top of his lungs, charged him with a sword. Lathe stepped out of the way, flicking his sword across the man's hamstring as he charged by. The man fell to the ground, writhing in pain. Lathe slipped his sword in and out of his neck and stepped over the body.

"Sir?"

Lathe turned, sword raised. Four people looked to him, eyes wide as they stared at his sword point.

"Who are you?" Lathe demanded.

He'd already deduced that he was in roughly the same location as the last time. The large house was behind them in the distance, the ocean to the west. No sign of the vampire, though, or the two strange women who'd shown up later. Other memories, blurry and undefined, pushed up through his consciousness. He remembered fighting men in the dark, amidst flames and smoke, near the burnt remains of a large ash tree in the middle of the estate grounds. He remembered that, but… but it was not himself he remembered fighting.

What in all Oblivion is going on?

"Sir," one of the men said, approaching Lathe with hands up, "my name is Eward. We are the guard force you've been training. You told us you might forget where you were, why you were here. We are fighting a battle, sir. We need your help."

Lathe turned at the sound of galloping horses in time to see four riders bearing down on them. "Spread out," he said. "I'll take center with Eward, the rest of you split to either side."

The men and women did as ordered, spreading out to greet the advancing riders.

Lathe instinctively reached to where he kept his daggers, and slipped one out of a sheath, hefting it. Good enough for throwing. He flung the weapon at the nearest rider, but the man turned at the last second, and the dagger buried itself in his shoulder rather than his neck. Lathe swore, but the riders were already on them. He slashed at the legs of an oncoming horse with his sword and the animal went down screaming, the rider falling with it as Lathe's supposed comrade—Eward—descended on him.

Another memory came as he wove forward, dodging the thrust of a pitchfork—a *pitchfork* for Canta's sake, what kind of battle was this?—and took down another horseman. He remembered meeting a *cotir*, one of whom he even recognized. Cymbre. They had spent time at the Citadel together. And yet… and yet, again, Lathe knew the memory was not his own.

Lathe turned to see that the soldiers had taken down the other horsemen, although one of his men lay on the ground, bleeding. He knew he had two options. He could stay, see this battle through to the end. He did not know what they were fighting for, but they could clearly use his expertise. Apparently he was their *leader*, for Canta's sake.

His other option was to leave. He did not know these people. His last memory—his last *true* memory—of being here was not pleasant. He did not relish the idea of encountering that vampire again.

"I'm sorry," Lathe grunted.

Eward turned to say something to him, but Lathe was already running towards the forest.

Astrid sprinted out of the house, her cloak flapping about her in the wind. She tightened the drawstring around her neck and face, cursing the sun as she did so. Why did it have to be sunny on this day, of all days? In a part of the Sfaera where the sun rarely deigned to show its face? She'd made sure Jane and the disciples had made it back to the house safely, as she'd been ordered to do, but no one ever said she needed to stay with them. She needed to fight.

Odenites flocked to the house, but there was no way they would all fit in. Men on horseback were already beginning to overtake the edge of the crowd. Astrid couldn't see what they were doing, but the screams, and the increasing panic with which the Odenites ran towards the house, gave her a pretty clear idea. At the base of the hill more of the attackers fought Knot and the guard force. It was too far away, and the action too convoluted, to see anything specific.

If Astrid could make it to the guards, she would. If she

couldn't, she could at least take out some of the men pursuing the followers.

Ahead of her, she saw Arven, leading the group towards the house.

"Arven!" she called out, and the young woman turned to look at her. Arven grinned.

"Astrid! We are running from the men attacking us."

"Yes," Astrid said, "I can see that. Where's Knot?"

Arven shrugged. "I haven't seen him. I can look around for you?"

Astrid shook her head frantically. "No! No, you've done a wonderful job, Arven. You're very brave. Please, keep them moving. As far away from these men as possible."

Astrid sprinted off, fighting through the crowd until she reached the stragglers at the back. All around her people were bleeding, wounded, dying. Astrid suddenly felt a craving so powerful that she almost forgot what was going on around her. The steely tang of blood filled her nostrils; she craved its bittersweet taste more than anything.

Astrid stood still for a moment, fighting the craving. She couldn't give in to it, not now. Not here. She had the ridiculous compulsion to get down on her hands and knees and lick some of the blood off the grass. Instead, she looked up, kept her focus ahead.

Right in front of her, a group of men were attacking two Odenites, both older men. As Astrid watched, one of the Kamites—what else could they be?—drew a dagger and stuck it through one of the men's ribs.

Even in broad daylight, Astrid was as strong as the strongest man, as fast as a trained warrior twice her size. She did not have her claws, but that was why she'd brought the short sword at her side. Astrid drew it as she approached the group. The man who had stabbed the Odenite laughed, saying something about how the old man was an elf-lover, and stabbed him again. Astrid broke into a run and leapt into the air, swinging her sword. The laughing Kamite collapsed, his head separated from his body.

The other men turned to look at her, anger red on their faces. But, when they saw who had killed their comrade, some of that redness faded, giving way to wide eyes and gaping jaws.

"Who in Oblivion are you?" one of the men asked.

"Why don't you ask when you get there," Astrid said under her breath, and lunged at the man, stabbing him in the groin. The man's eyes bulged and he buckled over, hands between his legs, blood spurting between his fingers.

Astrid swung her sword, severing someone's leg, and dodged around someone else's attempt to grab her, flipping through the air and kicking one of the men behind her in the face. She stabbed up into someone's abdomen, parried an attack and then slashed at another man's groin. Then, all was quiet. The only people standing were the other Odenite and one last Kamite, staring at Astrid in horror.

"You're a daemon," he whispered.

"To you, yes," Astrid said, licking her lips. She tasted blood and leapt upon him, unable to stop herself. Even though she'd just fed, the smell was too strong, on the ground and on her sword. She ripped his neck open with her teeth, and drank greedily.

When she looked up, the old man had fled. Good. She had no explanation for him.

The blood invigorated her, made her more powerful. She quickly turned back to the battle at the base of the hill between the horsemen and Knot's guards. She needed to free them, and then, she hoped, they could push back the rest of the attackers that now preyed on the Odenites.

Astrid ran towards them, twirling her sword in her hand, ready for more blood.

CINZIA STARED OUT THE window in horror. "They're getting slaughtered," she whispered. Jane, Ocrestia, and Elessa stood beside her. The rest of the Oden family stood at the back of the room in hushed silence.

Many of the Odenites had made it to the house; some had found their way inside, others had run past it into the woods. But others, the not so fast, and the not so fortunate, were left behind, and now fell by the dozen to the hideous men on horseback. Cinzia could not understand what would push these men to do such a thing. They were monsters.

She turned to her sister. "We have to do something. We can't let those people die for us."

"They are not dying for us," Jane said quietly.

Cinzia slapped Jane hard. "They are dying for *you* then!" Cinzia screamed at her sister. "We can't allow it!"

"They are not dying for me," Jane said, and Cinzia noticed the tears streaming down her cheeks—one cheek now bright red from Cinzia's blow. "They are dying for Canta, Cinzia. They are dying for their Goddess."

"You think that matters, who they're dying for?" Cinzia gestured outside, at the people who had gathered in Jane's name, the people who looked to Jane as their protector.

"I do," Jane whispered.

Cinzia could not contain the rage that welled within her. "We have to do *something*!"

Jane stepped forward, and suddenly Cinzia found herself wrapped in her sister's arms. She struggled at first, then melted into her sister's embrace, sobbing. She felt the anger leaving her, replaced by an overwhelming sense of despair.

"There is something we can do," Jane whispered, still holding Cinzia.

Cinzia pulled back. "The only people we have that can fight are out there doing it. We have no more weapons, no more fighters. We wouldn't stand a chance."

"We're not going to fight them," Jane said.

Cinzia watched as Jane walked towards the door. "Disciples, come with me," she said.

Their mother grabbed Jane's arm as she stood at the door. "Jane," Pascia whispered, her eyes misty.

"It's all right, Mother," Jane said, smiling. "All is according to the will of the Goddess."

ASTRID DUCKED AS SOMEONE swung an ugly-looking club at her. She pivoted in a crouch, clipping her attacker's shin and heel with her blade. The man shouted and fell, and Astrid buried her sword in his chest.

She wiped blood from her face and licked her lips, tasted the sickening sweetness of it, but had no time to dwell on it. She had drunk her fill from the man she had killed earlier; she had many more to kill today before she could allow herself to drink again.

"Gather to me!" Astrid shouted. She pulled her hood farther over her face. Fighting with a hood was difficult; it severely diminished her vision, and the constant threat of her face being exposed to the sun required her to adjust it constantly.

A dozen guards gathered around her, fighting in formation. She saw fear etched deeply on their faces, but they fought on nonetheless. She could see other guards trying to reach her, but there were still many Kamites to fight through. Astrid had asked where Knot was, but the men had shaken their heads solemnly. None of them had seen him since the first charge.

Astrid led the guards around her to another group of three in the distance, hacking at men left and right of her, snaking between people and under horses' legs to get the upper hand. The men behind her followed, taking down the Kamites that Astrid had injured.

The three guards had noticed Astrid's fight towards them and were now trying to close the distance, but there were a good dozen Kamites between them. The three wouldn't last much longer. She broke into a sprint. Those three were some of the last guards standing, and they were also her only hope of finding out what had happened to Knot—assuming he was not dead.

The Kamites saw her coming, but that didn't matter. Astrid parried an attack and kicked the man, sending him sprawling. She leapt into the air, sliding between the swing of a club and the stab of a pitchfork, and landed on all fours, blade in hand. Then she spun and kicked again, parried another blow from the club, and with a scream stabbed her sword up into the man's heart. She dropped to the grass, wet with blood, and rolled, only to leap up and stab another.

Her people followed her, taking down man after man, and finally they reached the remaining three guards. Astrid was relieved to see Eward among them.

"Have you seen Knot?" Astrid asked immediately.

The guards looked at each other.

Astrid reached up, grabbing Eward, and pulled him down to her eye-level. "Where is he?" she hissed.

"He… he ran away," Eward whispered, eyes wide.

"What the… what do you mean he ran away?"

"I think he had an episode."

Astrid released Eward, looking around frantically. *Shit*, she thought.

"He… he began acting like someone else, but for a moment I thought he might still fight with us. But he left us, ran into the woods."

"Who?" Astrid demanded. "Did he say who he was?" If he had reverted to Lathe once more, she might never find him. He might as well be dead.

"No," Eward said. "But… but he could fight. As well as Knot ever could."

That had to be Lathe. Astrid kicked a Kamite corpse, too angry for words. After taking a deep breath, she knew there was nothing to be done about Knot right now. "We'll find him later," she said, not believing her own words. "The Odenites need our help. There are still fifty or so Kamites left, killing your friends, your families. There are less than twenty of us. But we've got to help them anyway, do you understand?"

Each of them nodded.

"Good. I'm glad all of you are idiots. Now, here's what we're going to do…"

Lathe knew something was wrong by the time he made it to the trees. He was sweating, but it was not the sweat of battle. The perspiration was cold on his skin, he was shivering—and the memories wouldn't stop surfacing.

Just as before, he knew these memories were not his own. Or, at least, most of them were not. He remembered standing in a drawing room, looking out at dozens of people. He remembered facing nightmarish monsters underneath the Imperial Dome of Roden. He remembered the face of a tiellan woman framed in raven-black hair, eyes dark as midnight.

Lathe stumbled through the forest, catching himself on a tree branch to keep from collapsing.

What is happening to me?

Lathe had other memories, too: his own. He remembered the red and black and white marble of the Heart of the Void in the Nazaniin headquarters. He remembered missions he'd been assigned with the Nazaniin, in Triah and Mavenil and Turandel and Izet. He remembered waking up to see Sirana's face, smiling at him.

Lathe stumbled and fell to the earth, unable to catch himself this time. Were those his memories? Or were they simply the memories of someone else, and he… and he…

Who was he?

He looked up to see the sun streaming through the foliage above, and then collapsed.

Cinzia saw Arven running towards them as they emerged from the house. She looked on the verge of tears.

"You told me to lead the others here. So I did. I led them here, but not everyone. There were people who did not run fast enough. I tried to go back for more but they're dead… And the Beldam… the old woman… she left."

"Arven, if that woman chose to leave, it's not a bad thing."

"She left, but she took many followers with her."

"*What?*"

"She left, but she took—"

Jane put a hand on Arven's shoulder. "It's all right, Arven. You did all that you could do. We will deal with the Beldam another time. My disciples and I have business to attend to."

"The Kamites are still out there. You can't go."

"We are not going to the Kamites," Jane said.

Arven nodded, but it only confused Cinzia all the more. She had been hoping that Jane was somehow going to use Canta's power to defeat the horsemen. But if they were not going to confront their enemies, what *were* they doing?

Jane walked forward and the disciples followed. The four of them were the only people moving north instead of running south. Ahead of them, Cinzia saw guards fighting off a group of Kamites, trying to protect a group of fleeing Odenites. A small figure led the guards, and Cinzia knew immediately it was Astrid. She sent up a small prayer of thanks for the girl. But she did not see Knot. Anywhere. Where was he?

But, as Cinzia looked around, she realized that very few Kamites remained. There was a group engaged with Astrid and the guards, and another on horseback seemed to be moving towards Astrid as well, but without discipline. An even larger band of Kamites was already fleeing back up the hill.

Goddess, could the Odenites actually *win* this fight?

Cinzia berated herself immediately for thinking such a thought. Nothing she saw before her could be called a victory. Bodies lay everywhere.

"How could we have let this happen?" Cinzia asked, horrified.

Jane did not respond, but instead walked purposefully towards the nearest body on the ground. It was an old woman, a terrible wound gaping on her forehead. Blood soaked her face and once-gray hair.

Jane knelt down by the body, and put her ear next to the woman's mouth.

Listening for breath? Cinzia wondered. Is that why they were out here? To gather the wounded?

Jane stood and shook her head. "She is gone," she said, her

voice heavy. "We must find another."

"Another?" Cinzia asked, but Jane was already walking off, Elessa and Ocrestia following, leaving Cinzia with the body of the old woman. She looked down at the body, sadness gripping her heart. She knelt, and closed the woman's eyes.

"Canta take you home," Cinzia whispered. Then she followed quickly after Jane and the others, who had already stopped at someone else—a young man, barely fifteen summers, surrounded by a group of Odenites. The boy was clutching his abdomen, and from the amount of blood that ran between his fingers, Cinzia could tell the wound was deadly. The blood bubbling from his mouth was evidence enough that he would not last.

"Prophetess," a woman gasped, as Jane approached. "Why has this happened? Why has Canta taken my son? What did we do wrong?"

"Nothing," Jane whispered, and the Odenites kneeling around the boy made room for Jane as she knelt beside him. "Canta works in strange ways," she said, placing her hands on the boy's hands, covering the horrible wound. "Ways that are difficult to understand. But as she takes from us with one hand…"

A dull glow, almost invisible in the midday sun, began to form around Jane and the boy.

Cinzia gasped, taking a step back. She had seen this once before when Elessa had healed Jane after the first assassination attempt. Elessa had mumbled words in a language Cinzia had not been able to understand. This time, however, Jane said nothing as the soft glow enveloped her and the boy.

The boy coughed, blood still around his mouth and on his hands, but Cinzia knew, immediately, that he was better. The boy lifted his hands, revealing his bloodstained shirt and the scarred but healed skin beneath.

"Oh, Goddess," the mother exclaimed, hugging her son with a sob.

Cinzia stared, wide-eyed. Perhaps she should be used to such things by now; between Elessa's healing of Jane, and her own enhanced speed and strength when an assassin tried to kill her a second time—and, of course, the fact that they were friends with a vampire, a race of beings she had thought long gone, and of course there was Knot, and psimancy…

And yet here she was, still as shocked as ever. Would she ever get used to it?

"Thank you, thank you," the mother kept saying, over and over, and transferred her embrace from her son to Jane, nearly knocking Jane over.

Jane laughed. "It was not me," she said. "It was Canta. Canta healed your son, and She has many more yet to heal today."

"Of course," the mother sobbed. "Thank you," she kept repeating, turning back to her son.

"Is this why we're out here?" Cinzia asked Jane as they both stood up. Jane's forehead was beaded with sweat; the healing had taken a great deal of energy.

"Yes," Jane said. "We are here to heal. We are here to bind wounds with Canta's love."

Astrid stabbed her sword down, straight through the man's neck. She put one hand to her cheek, feeling the burned skin. Her hood had been partly knocked away from her face, and the sun had scorched her. It would heal within the hour, most likely, but it still hurt like a bitch.

Eward called out to her, and Astrid turned. He pointed toward the hill, where a large group of people—Odenites, not Kamites, Astrid realized—were fleeing. Astrid shook her head. Whatever was going on there was not their immediate concern. "As long as they're safe, we can't concern ourselves with them," Astrid said.

Then, to the left, Astrid heard a shout that she knew was not from one of their own.

"There they are! Get them!"

Astrid swore under her breath as she called a halt, and turned to face the oncoming threat. A dozen men on horseback bore down on Astrid and her guards, waving their weapons in the air.

"Form a line!" Astrid shouted.

The guards around her turned quickly, more disciplined than Astrid could have hoped. The men who bore down on them were screaming. That was good. That meant Astrid and her group had been noticed. Many of the attackers had fled, leaving their dead and wounded behind. Their biggest mistake had been splitting up, attacking the Odenites in small units. That had made it easy for Astrid and her guards to take them out one by one.

"Hold!" Astrid shouted. "Wait for my signal."

Then, Astrid moved forward, quickly. Horses, as a general rule, did not like her.

Sure enough, a couple of the horses spooked as Astrid approached, and when she ran up to them, ducking attacks from above her and stabbing a horse in the belly for good measure—if the creatures didn't care for her, why should she care for them?—the horses all but scattered.

"Charge!" Astrid shouted to the guards. Immediately they moved forward, shouting, weapons held high. As they crashed into the flank of the confused attackers, Astrid struck from the other side, stabbing and flailing about with her sword. Men and animals screamed around her, and in seconds the skirmish ended with a half-dozen of the enemy fleeing on horseback, while the other half lay dead and dying at Astrid's feet.

Astrid looked around, and she realized that the end of the skirmish might have marked the end of the battle, too. The only remaining Kamites she could see were fleeing. All around her were bodies, men and women groaning. And the smell of blood, everywhere.

Astrid scowled. In the distance she saw Jane and her disciples, wandering the grounds. It seemed the women had chosen to leave the house, despite what she'd told them.

"What are we going to do now?"

Astrid turned to see Eward approaching her. He was covered in blood and sweat, his voice hoarse. "We're going to regroup," she said, turning to address all of the remaining guards. "We're going to find Knot, tend to the wounded. And we're going to find out where that group of Odenites went."

Cinzia watched as Jane lifted her hands from the young girl. Almost immediately, the girl's eyes opened, and she looked around. When her eyes fell upon her parents, staring anxiously back down at her, they shone brightly in the light of dusk.

People gasped. "Praise Canta!" they whispered as the young girl stood, melting into her parents' embrace. "Bless the Prophetess!" As Jane and her disciples had walked through the grounds, a crowd had begun to gather around them to witness Jane's healing.

To witness the miracles.

Cinzia had lost count of how many people Jane had healed. Even those who seemed on the brink of death, who seemed impossible to bring back, Jane placed her hands on them, and soon afterwards they stood up, smiling, walking, as if they had just woken from a dream.

Jane reached for Cinzia's hand. Cinzia did not know how Jane was doing what she was doing, but it certainly took a physical toll on her sister. Jane was practically soaked through with perspiration; strands of her hair clung to her face. Her disciples had to help Jane up every time, one of them always by her side, holding her arm, as she walked from casualty to casualty.

"Where next?" Janc asked. Cinzia craned her neck, looking for the nearest person who might need healing. Elessa and Ocrestia had both begun healing as well, although it took them significantly longer than it took Jane. Cinzia noticed Elessa out of the corner of her eye—the woman looked exhausted.

Cinzia felt a sudden pull on her arm, and reached out as Jane's legs collapsed beneath her.

"Jane!" Cinzia knelt by her sister, prone in the grass. "You *must* rest, this is taking too much of a toll on you."

Jane shook her head. "I can't rest. Not yet."

"Jane, you can't possibly walk any further, you—"

"Then you will have to carry me, sister."

Cinzia stared at Jane. She did not know how much more her sister could take before the consequences became irreversible.

"If you don't, I will find someone else," Jane said quietly, her eyes pleading.

Someone rushed to Cinzia's side. It was Arven, breathing heavily.

"Disciple Cinzia, I found another group. There are so many of them, Goddess, it's like—" Arven stopped, looking down at Jane, eyes widening in surprise. "Oh! Is she all right? What happened?"

Before Cinzia could respond, Jane spoke. "There are people who need me, Cinzia. I can help them. *We* can help them. Please. Do as I ask."

Cinzia wrapped her arms around her sister almost before she knew what she was doing. Fear crawled across her heart, but she knew Jane was right. Her muscles strained as she lifted her sister. Jane held her tightly.

"Where are they?" Cinzia asked, turning to Arven.

"This way," Arven said, walking east towards the trees, towards the setting sun.

Cinzia followed, praying for the strength to carry her sister that far. She was not strong, and Jane was already heavy in her arms.

"How far?" Cinzia asked.

"Not very, just up ahead."

The crowd moved with them, having grown silent since Jane's collapse. Canta was silent today, too, at least for Cinzia. She felt no supernatural strength in her limbs, no imbued focus or speed. She could only trudge forward, one step at a time.

She had slapped Jane. She was not sure she deserved Canta's power. She was not sure she was ready to trust again.

Cinzia was suddenly ashamed for her thoughts. Jane had healed many people that day, dozens at least, and was about to heal more. She brought men and women and children back from the brink of death, with a power that Cinzia couldn't understand. And yet here Cinzia was, complaining that she couldn't carry her sister a dozen rods.

"Let me take her."

Cinzia turned in surprise, and saw Eward. Blood and sweat smeared together on his face and clothing, but he looked unharmed.

"Let me take her," he repeated.

No, Cinzia wanted to say. *I can carry her.*

Instead, she nodded, and handed Jane over to her brother.

Cinzia had not realized her cheeks were wet until after she gave Jane away. She sniffed, wiping her face with her sleeve.

Canta had not seen fit to give her strength today. Cinzia found it confusing that she felt both bitterness towards her Goddess for not deigning to give her that strength, and shame towards herself for not being worthy of it.

As they approached the crowd of wounded before them, Cinzia gasped. Arven was right; there were many of them. People groaned and sobbed on the bloodstained grass, clutching wounds. But the worst was how many people were silent, unmoving.

Ocrestia knelt down beside one of the wounded, and Cinzia witnessed the same soft glow she had seen around Jane envelop Ocrestia and the young man on which she laid her hands. Elessa, too, had reached down to an injured woman, soft light surrounding them both.

Eward helped Jane sit next to more of the wounded, and Jane began healing.

Eventually, Cinzia mustered the courage to kneel by a man, perhaps her father's age.

Trust comes first, she told herself. *I must trust.*

"You're going to be all right," Cinzia whispered. The man reached up to grab Cinzia's hand, his movement so sudden it startled her. His face was unnaturally pale, eyes wide in horror. Then he looked up at her and spoke, but his voice was different; hearing his voice, somehow, she *knew*.

It was not this man who spoke to her. The voice was dark, deep, wreathed in flame. The voice was the same voice that had spoken to her from Kovac, before she had killed him, in Izet.

"*You will all die,*" the man said, the words rumbling up from beneath him, his eyes wide and rolling up into his skull.

Cinzia tried to pull her arm away, but the man's grip was far too strong.

"*You will all die screaming,*" the man said, his hand squeezing

Cinzia's like a vice. Pain shot through her and she whimpered, looking around. Everyone was focused on Jane and the other two disciples, on the miraculous healing taking place. Cinzia wanted to cry out, but her voice made no sound, as if she were in a dream, in a nightmare.

"*You will all die screaming, and I will watch, and take pleasure in it.*"

Cinzia couldn't speak, but her thoughts were still her own. *I know who you are!* she cried, the words echoing in her mind. *I know who you are, and I am not afraid.*

"*You're right,*" the man rasped, and his lips parted, the corners shifting in an unnaturally wide, horrific grin. "*What you feel now, you think it is fear. But you know nothing. You will know true fear soon enough.*"

The man's grip tightened further on Cinzia's wrist; she felt the bones crunching in her hand, heard the snap of them grinding and breaking together. Cinzia let out a soft, silent sob.

"*We will consume you.*"

The man pulled, and Cinzia felt tears streaming down her face as she screamed silently at the pain. One of her knees pressed into the man's chest, and the man's horrifying grin faltered. In desperation, Cinzia moved her knee up to the man's throat, pressing with all her weight.

"*We will consume you, and all of your pride, and you will know it not.*"

Cinzia pressed harder, watched in horror as the man's face turned brighter and deeper red, almost purple. Then, she felt something give way beneath her knee, and the man's grip on her released. He lay there, his head lolled to one side, all the strength gone.

Cinzia cradled her arm, sobbing quietly to herself, the sound now suddenly audible. Behind her, she heard gasps of awe and reverence. Cinzia was grateful for that, as she stared down at the man she had just killed. Jane healed the people, while Cinzia killed them. Why such a dichotomy between the two of them? What was the purpose? She thought she had exercised faith during the inductions, when she saved Jane. Had she been wrong?

Cinzia sat back, holding her injured arm close to her chest. Behind her, Jane and the disciples continued to heal, and Cinzia stared at the dead man before her until the sun had set and all those who could be healed were healed and Jane had collapsed from exhaustion.

42

Forest surrounding the Harmoth estate

HE WOKE WITH DEW on his face and a strange, worming thought in his mind that something was wrong. He raised a hand to wipe the cold moisture away. The strange sensation that something was off, that either the world around him had changed, or that he had, was not so easily removed.

Who am I?

He tried to think, tried to search the deepest recesses of his mind, but it was like diving into a lake that had frozen solid. Where he had been the night before—or earlier that night, as the sun seemed to not have risen yet—was an impossible memory. Where he had been and what he had been doing a week prior even more so. He could think of no familiar face, no family member or friend or acquaintance or lover.

The man observed all of these things, or the lack of all of these things in his mind, with a strange indifference. It was as if he were watching someone else wake up in the middle of a forest with no memory of himself or his life before that moment.

Who am I?

As the man sat there, bent at the waist, his clothes damp with dew, there was only one thought that wormed its way through the rest, that gave way to real fear.

He did not know his own name.

It seemed a silly thing, a name. What did it matter what he

called himself, after all? What did a series of sounds matter in the face of a life, of an entire experience?

And yet, it did. As the man racked his brain to discern what others called him, the fear grew slowly into something greater, more tangible, a cold, bubbling terror in his gut. If he had no name, he had no identity. If he had no identity, he had nothing.

He might as well be in Oblivion itself.

A noise to his left. He turned his head sharply, and pain shot through his neck. A pulled muscle or kinked nerve. The man tried to stretch out the sharp, tweaking pain that ran from his shoulder to his skull, but it did not lessen.

The noise again. He twisted his torso to avoid moving his neck too much. He squinted into the foliage around him, dark and indiscernible. The terror bubbling within him had subsided with the sudden pain in his neck, but it now rushed back with a vengeance.

The forest was silent, now. It took the man a moment to realize that there was no noise at all, and the silence around him couldn't be natural.

Then, in the dark trees straight ahead of him, a shadow. A shadow within shadows, somehow darker than all of them. The shade was vaguely human-shaped, and was moving towards him.

His breathing quickened. He scrabbled backwards away from the shade. He felt a stabbing pain in his hand and stopped, holding his injured hand in front of his face. A large thorn protruded from his palm, a bead of blood just beginning to bloom at its base. He was in a briar patch, he realized. He had been lying in a briar. The man stared at the thorn in his hand in horror at the drop of blood, but his focus shifted from his hand to the shade that stalked him.

The shadow now stood directly in front of him, a shadow

cloaked in darkness, a black hood that overshadowed an even blacker pit where a face should be. The cloak hung loosely around the figure, and it was long, its folds reaching down into the foliage. The folds, the man realized, reached outward, blending with a dark fog that seemed to roil forth from the figure's feet. The fog moved forwards slowly, threatening to engulf him entirely.

He recoiled immediately, heedless of the pain in his hands, pushing himself backward, farther away from the terrible figure. More thorns pierced his hands, tore long scratches into his arms, but he did not care. The thorns did not matter, only getting away from this figure, only—

The briar beneath him began to move. The long, curving, entangled branches snaked around the man's arm. He tried to pull his arm free, but he couldn't. He looked up, saw the figure cloaked in darkness before him, at his feet once more. The figure's face was still nothing but a black pit, but as the man gazed into it he had the strangest sensation that this thing was smiling at him, smiling from beneath its shaded cowl, smiling as more branches wrapped around the man's other limbs, and then around his torso and neck, a dozen sharp thorns piercing his throat as a branch closed tightly around it.

He did not die.

The man knew, based on the length of the thorns—almost as long as his fingers—and how tightly the branch was constricted around his neck that he should be dead. He should be dead twice over.

"What… what do you want…" he rasped, barely forming the words.

The shadowy figure's hidden smile widened. "*This.*" It spread its arms wide. "*And her*."

And then, in a rush of air, the shadowy figure was gone, the thorns were gone, and the man was alone among dead leaves in the forest, and his name was Knot.

Knot gasped, gulping in air.

The figure was the same one he had seen in Izet, when Winter died. The figure was Azael, master of the Nine Daemons.

And as Knot remembered his name, and remembered Azael, he remembered what had happened before he found himself in this forest. The Kamites. The attack. The guards fighting, and Knot remembering, and then…

Knot swore. He had left them.

He leapt to his feet, and began sprinting west towards the sea, towards Harmoth.

43

Imperial palace, Izet

COVA RUSHED TO THE ballroom of the imperial palace, picking up the hem of her gown as best she could to move faster. She had lost track of time in the library, and now she would be late for her father's inaugural ball.

The ballroom, of course, was nothing compared to the throne hall, but while the great dome was being repaired, this was the best alternative.

She dropped the hem of her gown and stood outside the doors for a moment trying to regain control of her breathing. Running from the library to the ballroom in her childhood home would have been taxing enough, but the immensity of the imperial palace made Castle Amok seem a shack in comparison.

The buzz of hundreds of chattering voices drifted out of the ballroom. Cova could smell the food, too. Her stomach growled, and she realized she had not eaten since breakfast.

Goddess rising, there was just too much going on. Too much to do.

Cova smoothed her gown—a dark, deep purple dress, of the same new style she had worn to her engagement ball—and walked into the ballroom.

Her eyes immediately searched for Girgan, but they found her father first. He looked handsome in a newly tailored dark-blue suit, the emperor's gold circlet on his head. The imperial throne had been temporarily moved into the ballroom, and Daval stood at the bottom of the gilded steps that led up to it, a long line of people waiting to greet him. Urstadt and Winter both stood close by him, and Cova was surprised to see both were in gowns. Urstadt without her iconic rose-gold armor was a rare sight to behold, indeed. And yet she looked deceitfully comfortable in a fawn-colored gown, which contrasted well with her dark skin. The captain smiled politely and nodded at everyone who came to greet the emperor. Urstadt was bound to have a weapon somewhere in that dress, and her armor could not be far away.

Winter was almost unrecognizable in a dark crimson gown. Cova felt an immediate sense of pride as she saw that it was in the same style as her own; to have a tailor of Galce's skill imitate her own work was beyond flattering. Cova appreciated the dark color of Winter's gown, too; the two of them stood out among all of the pastels and muted colors of the other women's dresses. Winter's hair was down, too—the tiellan girl normally wore it braided tightly against her head, but now it cascaded over her shoulders and down her back, and Cova found herself envying its dark sheen.

She was jealous of more than that, too. Winter had been spending more time with Daval than Cova had lately, and while Cova did not particularly enjoy her father's company anymore—especially since their conversation a few days ago—she nevertheless found herself jealous.

And yet, who better to spend time with her father than this psychotic weapon of a girl? The image of Luce's body, bloody and upside down in the council chamber, still haunted Cova. She noticed the guests gave Winter a wide berth, too, even those who hadn't been present at the Council meeting where

Luce had met his death. It seemed to be on everyone's mind.

She pushed those thoughts away. This was her father's inaugural ball, and she had a duty to congratulate him. She was making her way to her father when the music began. Immediately, the attendees scattered to the edges of the ballroom, making space for the dancing.

"Welcome, lords and ladies, merchants and clergy!"

Daval had climbed the steps to the throne, and now stood by it, a wide smile on his face.

Cova snatched a glass from a servant's tray and took a sip.

"Allow me to express my gratitude for your support," Daval said. "The emperorship would mean nothing without that. And, by the grace of the gods, old and new, our empire will witness many incredible things in the coming years. We will accomplish much, for the good of Roden and her people!"

"*For the good of Roden and her people!*" the crowd shouted back. Cova shouted with them, raising her glass high into the air.

"It is my pleasure to announce the beginning of this evening's festivities," Daval continued. "Food, drink, dancing, and more. We are here to celebrate our great empire."

Daval saw Cova in the crowd, his smile growing wider. "And to begin the evening, I will invite my daughter and her husband onto the dance floor. Some of you saw their dazzling performance at their engagement ball; as a present for my inauguration, I'd like a reprise!"

Cheers went up throughout the crowd, and Cova blushed. She looked around for her husband, and found him walking towards her. Girgan held out his arm, Cova took it.

"We'd better give the people what they want, hadn't we?" Girgan asked.

Cova smiled. "Yes, we might as well."

Girgan swung Cova's arm above her head with a flourish, and Cova spun away from him, over and over again, as the crowd let out another great cheer.

Then, the musicians began the slow, wistful notes of a Rodenese waltz, and Girgan and Cova turned to face one another. Girgan raised his hand, and Cova moved towards him to take up position. They swayed once, twice, and then they moved with ease across the floor.

"You must admit, this isn't so bad," Cova whispered as they danced. They had grown comfortable enough with one another's dance styles that they could all but let their bodies take over as they moved.

"If you mean dancing with you, then you're right," Girgan said. "I've certainly done worse things."

Cova laughed. She would have elbowed him if they weren't otherwise occupied. "I mean this," she said, "the ball, the inauguration. My father."

"Forgive me," Girgan said, whispering now, "but I still have some reservations where your father is concerned. Have you forgotten Hirman Luce so quickly?"

"Hirman Luce was a traitor," Cova said, but even as she said it she knew the situation was far more complicated. And the manner of Luce's death... Cova shivered.

Which reminded her why she had been late.

"I went to the library, before the ball," Cova said. "To examine some of the older works regarding the Ceno order. I'd hoped they might help me understand the changes I've seen in my father lately."

They performed a series of spins, bodies locked together, and then came to a stop, stretching into a pose.

"Let me guess," Girgan said, as they resumed movement

once more, "they didn't help much?"

"They didn't help at all," Cova said, "because they weren't even there."

"Someone else had them?"

"No," Cova said quietly. "That was the strange thing—I asked the library keepers, and they said they had not seen anyone take those volumes in ages. But none of the volumes were there. Nothing about the Ceno order. Nothing about the Scorned Gods."

"That… that sounds more than strange."

"I know."

"That sounds like someone removed them on purpose."

They danced in silence. Cova lost herself in the music, in the movement. The song reached a crescendo, and then slowly started to fade. As it did, Girgan spun Cova away once more, and the crowd erupted in applause. They both bowed, and Cova took Girgan's arm as they left the dancefloor. Daval spoke again from the throne, but Cova was not paying attention. People had gathered around her and her husband, congratulating them.

Later, when the admirers had drifted away, Girgan took Cova aside. "I need to go," he said.

"What? The night has just begun, we haven't even—"

"I think this is important, Cova," Girgan said. "What you found in the library—or what you didn't find—I need to verify it. I'll be back shortly."

Cova took a deep breath. She had looked forward to spending the evening with Girgan by her side, showing him off to the other nobles. "Go," she said, with a sigh. "We've made an appearance together, at least, and I'll be able to cover for your absence."

"Thank you." Girgan bent to kiss her.

"Be safe," Cova said.

* * *

A few hours and a few more glasses of wine later, the inaugural ball finally began to wind down. Cova had been so wrapped up in chatting with the guests that she'd lost track of time. A part of her wondered why Girgan had not yet returned, but another part was not surprised. While Cova generally had a good time at balls and other social gatherings, they exhausted Girgan. He'd probably gone straight back to their room to rest.

Cova said her goodbyes. She had yet to pay her respects, so she made her way to her father. He had been a difficult man to corner tonight, though Cova was not sure she minded. She did not feel particularly inclined to have much of a conversation with him.

"Ah," Daval said as Cova approached. He smiled at the guests surrounding him. "Excuse me, please. Allow me to greet my daughter, I haven't spoken to her all night."The guests politely bowed away, and Daval wrapped his arms around Cova.

"Congratulations, Father," Cova said.

"Thank you, my dear." He released her, and put his hands on her shoulders. "One day," he said, his voice almost a whisper, "you will have a moment just like this. It will be a great time for Roden."

Cova smiled. This was the father she knew, the man she remembered. "You've thrown a grand party, I must say."

"Thank you again, but you know as well as I that I had nothing to do with this. I've got a host of people who plan these things." Daval looked over Cova's shoulder. "Where is your husband?"

"Girgan retired early," she said. "You know how he gets at parties."

Daval laughed. "I didn't know that, actually. But I suppose I've got all the time in the world to learn about him, don't I?"

"I suppose you do, Father."

"Well, I congratulate you both. You performed wonderfully this evening. You're radiant when you dance, my dear. I love to see it."

"Thank you."

"And give Girgan my compliments as well. He deserves them."

"Of course, Father." Cova yawned. "I'm afraid the hour grows late for me, and I'm going to find my way to bed."

"Good night," Daval said. "Sweet dreams."

"Good night, Father."

Making her way back to her bedroom was not as easy as she'd thought it would be. She was still new to the immensity of the imperial palace, its hallways were sometimes confusing, and it appeared she had had more to drink than she realized.

Eventually, she found the doorway to her bedroom. She pulled the large oak door open, slipped inside, and closed it behind her.

When Cova saw a single candle was lit on the desk in their bedroom, illuminating a small part of the large room, she smiled. Girgan had kept a light on for her; he knew how much she hated fumbling her way around.

Cova reached behind her, unlacing her dress, as she walked slowly towards the candlelight. A single square of paper rested on the desk next to the candle. At first Cova thought it was another draft of her proposal, but as she slipped out of her gown and into her shift, she realized it was not her handwriting.

My dearest Cova, the paper read at the top.

Curious, Cova picked it up in one hand, the candle in the other. Girgan had left her a note. Perhaps she would have to wake him up and… thank him. She was sure he wouldn't mind. He never did.

These past months have been the happiest of my life, the note continued.

Cova smiled, walking slowly towards the bed. The past few months had not been terrible for her, either. She couldn't have hoped for a better match in a husband.

But I am afraid that happiness can't last.

A seed of fear sprouted in Cova's heart, clawing its way out.

> I have not been honest with you, Cova, and for that I am sorry. The truth is, I have not been honest with anyone in Roden since I have returned from Khale. And I suppose there is no other way to tell you this other than in this letter. I am a spy.
>
> There is a long story behind why, and how, but it began at the Citadel. I was tasked with feeding Triah information from Roden. When I found myself married to you, living in the palace, it seemed too good to be true. Too easy. But the more I got to know you, the more I came to love you, and the more torn my heart became.
>
> I am a betrayer, Cova. I have betrayed your trust, and I have betrayed the trust of my empire. I have fabricated lies to implicate people of importance—you know of what I speak. Please disregard anything I said along those lines. They were lies, lies I now feel sick to my stomach that I ever whispered, especially to you.
>
> Please forgive me, my dear Cova. I now have realized that, at least in this life, I will never find happiness. I pray to all the gods that you still might.
>
> Yours always,
> Girgan

Cova, hands shaking, wiped at the tears streaming down her face.

"Girgan?" she asked. "What is this?"

She looked up, holding the candle up to the bed, and jumped out of her skin when she saw a pale white figure floating in midair before her.

Cova stepped back, muffling her scream, and her eyes refocused. The figure was not levitating. It was swinging, ever so slightly, back and forth. Hanging from the canopy framework of their four-poster bed.

"No," Cova whispered.

Then she leapt into action. She set the candle on the floor and rushed towards the desk, throwing open the drawer. There. The knife. She ran back and leapt onto the bed, holding the swinging body with one arm as she reached the knife upwards with the other.

No, no, no, no, no.

The candle on the floor only gave faint flickering light, and it took Cova a moment to find the rope, and another moment to saw through it. She was unprepared for the sheer weight of the body as it fell, taking her with it. Cova fell back onto the bed, and heard a sickening crunch as the body folded over the footboard.

That was when Cova finally screamed.

She screamed and screamed, and couldn't stop screaming.

Girgan's face was red and swollen, his lips purple. *This can't be him,* she thought, but she knew the folly of it. This was her husband, and her husband was dead.

The door crashed open, and bright light suddenly filled the room. Cova squinted at the torches. Voices asked her what happened.

"My husband," was all Cova could say, cradling the body in her arms.

My husband is a spy, Cova thought.

My husband was *a spy.*

Immediately she felt sick to her stomach. She dropped the body in disgust, standing and moving quickly away. People carrying torches approached her, but she shied away from them. She had to get out of the room. She brushed past as people called for the doctor, and ran through the wide corridors of the imperial palace.

She ran and ran until she got to the emperor's chambers. She needed her father. Her sprint slowed as she approached the ornate door, and just as Cova was about to start pounding on it, she stopped herself.

My husband is a spy, Cova thought.

A moment of doubt cracked through her horror.

Slowly, she backed away from her father's door. She realized she was shaking her head. It wasn't her father she needed to speak to.

She ran in the other direction, away from her father, towards a different bedroom in the palace living quarters. Towards the only person left who might be able to help her.

44

Harmoth estate

"You sure you want to do this, nomad?"

Knot couldn't blame Astrid for being suspicious. The *cotir* had helped them a great deal, but they still were Nazaniin. They could never be fully trusted. And the fact that they had been conspicuously absent during the massacre at the Harmoth estate did not help his view of them. But they were back now, at least, and Knot knew he couldn't risk losing himself. Waking up in the forest, not remembering who he was, seeing the shadowy figure...

He would die before he let that happen again.

The Tinskan *cotir* stood in the library with Knot, Astrid, and Cinzia. Wyle indicated that Knot should lie on the chaise longue. While Knot knew that the procedure Wyle proposed was necessary, he didn't like the idea of lying back and letting it happen.

"It shouldn't take too long," Wyle said. "I might be able to get it done in less than an hour. You said they implanted nine sifts in you?"

Knot nodded. "That's what they told me. You find any more in there, let me know."

Wyle smirked. "I certainly will. Are you ready?"

Cinzia squeezed his hand. "You don't have to do this." Her eyes met his, and he knew what they told him. *You don't have to put your life in their hands.* But Knot had made his decision.

"Jane said it herself," Knot said. "She won't always be able to heal me. Got to do something." He sat down on the chaise longue. "Let's get it over with. Ain't no sense in wasting more time."

"Then lie back," Wyle said.

Knot did as he was asked, looking up at the ceiling. A mural depicted a scene from Cantic history—Knot recognized Canta herself at the center, but her surroundings were unfamiliar. In the corner, a dark shape forming in shadow, seeming to writhe and twist even in the stasis of the mural.

Odd, Knot thought. He hadn't noticed that particular detail before.

"I wish I could say this wouldn't hurt," Wyle said, placing his hands on either side of Knot's head. "But I've never done it before, so I have no idea."

Knot was about to respond, when a sudden pressure began building in his head, soft at first but quickly becoming stronger, like he was being pushed deeper and deeper under water. As the pressure became an expansive pain, Knot screamed.

Cinzia rushed to Knot's side. "Stop!" she shouted over his screams, looking up at Wyle. "You're hurting him!"

But Wyle, eyes closed, hands on either side of Knot's head, ignored her. And then Knot's scream stopped, and he lay still. At first Cinzia feared Wyle had killed him, but a quick check told her Knot's heart still beat. The strain was gone from his face, and his breathing was shallow and easy. It was as if he were sleeping.

"Pain is often a necessary part of acumency," Cymbre said quietly. "He pushed through it quickly. That's a good sign."

"Tell me again about the procedure," Cinzia asked, glaring up at Wyle, surprised at the tears that burned in her eyes.

"He will not be able to answer you," Cymbre said. "Wyle has

delved into the Void to search for Knot's sifts. He can neither see nor hear us."

Cinzia clenched her jaw. She felt so *helpless*. She could not help but think of Kovac as she looked down at Knot. She had been powerless to stop what had happened to her Goddessguard. And, because of that powerlessness, she had been forced to kill him.

Cymbre recognized her pain. "I'm not an expert in acumency, but I can at least try to answer any questions you have."

Cinzia nodded, closing her eyes. She could feel more tears welling up, but she refused to let them fall. She did not want to appear weak. "Tell me what he is doing," she whispered. She nodded towards Wyle. "You said he is *delving* Knot. That is what he did to the Odenites?"

Cymbre sighed. "'Delve' may not be the most accurate term. When an acumen delves someone, it is an attempt to discern their thoughts. Wyle is going beyond that, although he is not deciphering Knot, either."

"Deciphering?"

"Deciphering is a complete exploration of another's sift. When an acumen performs a deciphering, he or she gains complete control over that person."

There was a rush of movement behind Cinzia—almost like a slight breeze, fluttering her hair and clothing. Cinzia looked over her shoulder to see Astrid, her dagger drawn and pressing into Cymbre's neck.

"You'd better tell me, right now, that that isn't what Wyle is doing to Knot."

"I already told you," Cymbre said, eyes wide. Her eyes flickered to Jendry. "It isn't."

Astrid glared at the voyant. "Try anything and she dies," she said.

"Don't move, Jendry," Cymbre said. "It's fine." Cymbre met Astrid's eyes. "Wyle is not deciphering Knot."

"How can we believe you?" Cinzia asked.

"Because when Knot wakes, he will still be himself. Deciphering is… an ugly process. The deciphered person is never the same. If Wyle is successful, Knot won't have changed at all. If anything, he will be *more* himself. Knot agreed to this. If you stop Wyle, you'd only be going against Knot's wishes."

Astrid relaxed, releasing Cymbre from her grip and sheathing her dagger, but Cinzia was not convinced. "What are Wyle's chances of success?"

Cymbre rubbed at her throat, glaring at Astrid. "We have no way of knowing. As I said, nothing like this has ever been attempted before. It is all theoretical."

"But you really think this will stop his episodes?" Cinzia asked.

"If Wyle can locate Knot's sifts in the Void and stabilize them, then yes."

Cinzia looked down at Knot. Everything seemed very far away. Knot, Wyle, Cymbre, Astrid. Cinzia felt as if she were in a vast expanse, and everything were moving quickly away from her at once. "The Void," Cinzia whispered. She shivered. It did not sound like a place she ever wanted to see.

Knot was alone but he was not, he was there but he was not, he could see the night sky and millions of tiny stars above him and below him and all around him but he couldn't feel their light, he was alone in an ocean of blackness but he was surrounded by infinite existence, he couldn't move or speak. The tiny lights offered no comfort, coiling instead around him in a quiet cacophony.

"Knot, can you hear me?"

Knot turned his head, but saw nothing but tiny mocking lights in the darkness.

"Knot. Focus."

The voice came from all around him. It was impossible to focus on something so all-encompassing.

Memories flooded through Knot's mind, more memories than there were stars in the sky. He was on Bahc's ship in the Gulf of Nahl, and Winter's eyes were on him. He held a child on his knee; he tilled the earth with a worn, rusted plow; he directed soldiers from a command tent on a battlefield; he fought for the people next to him on the front lines. He was murdering, he was loving, he was playing warsquares in a room of gold and marble. He lay with Winter's head on his chest, strands of her hair tangled in his beard. Winter arose, walking towards a crib illuminated in moonlight.

And then, in a vague memory, Knot recalled someone telling him that when the procedure began, he would need to find himself. He would need to sort the real from the unreal.

"Knot, focus on the sound of my voice."

Many of the memories were not his. Some of the memories seemed like they might've been, but Knot knew them to be false. He locked on to the one thing he knew was real.

He was on the deck of *The Swordsmith's Daughter*. Gray sky covered gray seas, and next to him stood Winter, her hair flowing around her face in the wind.

"Good," the voice said.

And Knot was back in the blackness, pinpoints of light twinkling around him.

Wyle stood in front of him.

Not Wyle, Knot realized. Not exactly. It was a translucent form of the man, faded and barely visible. If Knot squinted he could see points of light beyond Wyle's form, blinking in the dark distance.

Knot took a deep breath. He was in the Void. He'd always loved a clear night sky, and what he saw now was similar, but magnified. Tiny colored lights, looking very much like varyingly colored stars, surrounded him on all sides.

In the distance, there was something else. Far, far away, another source of light, but it seemed different than the other pinpoints everywhere else. It was somehow both light and dark at once, a glowing shadow, and the other lights congregated around it, moving towards it. Knot himself felt a faint tug, pulling him towards the thing.

"What is that?" Knot asked, staring at the strange phenomenon.

Wyle shook his head slowly. "An anomaly," he said. "Something we have never seen in the Void before. A few of us have traveled towards it, giving in to the pull. But those who have gone too close have not returned."

"Does that have anything to do with helping me stop the episodes?" Knot asked.

"I don't believe so," Wyle said.

"Then I don't care about it. Tell me what I need to do."

Wyle laughed, but the sound was halting. Unsure. "We need to try to understand what is going on inside you. Can you find Lathe?"

Knot looked around him. "How?" he asked.

"You're looking too far," Wyle said. "Lathe is a part of you. You need to look inward."

Knot frowned, looking down at himself. When he saw nothing—literally nothing, except for the strange lights blinking in the darkness—he felt panic surge in his… in his what? He was nothing. Where was his panic, then?

"Where *am* I?" Knot asked, fighting the tide of panic. *No,* he thought. He'd placed the emphasis on the wrong word. "Where am *I*?" he repeated.

"Don't be alarmed," Wyle said, stepping towards Knot. Wyle's steps made strange, tiny ripples in the blackness. "You can see me, but it's just an illusion. An ability of acumency. You are here, too, but just not in the form you know. You're still searching for yourself wrongly. Look within—beyond, and within."

Knot looked down again, but saw nothing but star-like lights deep in the blackness. *Beyond, and within*. He had no idea how he was supposed to do that.

"You still think you're trying to see yourself—your physical form. You aren't. You're looking beyond that. Not down, not backward. *Inward*. And… Goddess, when you see it, you'll understand. It's truly beautiful. I've never seen anything like it, in the Void or elsewhere."

"That doesn't make sense," Knot said. "Can't look inward if I have nothing to see into."

"You can," Wyle said. "It just takes time. Try it."

Knot closed his eyes, shaking his head. How was he supposed to—

There.

Knot had no eyes to close, he'd realized only after thinking about closing them, but after he'd thought about it—right after his body, if it were here, would have done it—something changed. Knot saw something… different.

A solid point of light, shining with a pinkish hue, like a miniature rose-colored sun. Surrounding the central light were a series of spherical glowing blurs. Each blur was translucent—almost like a perfect sphere of frayed, unraveling light-fabric—

shimmering and twisting around the central light, and each blur emitted a spectrum of color, all colors at once, and yet somehow no color at all, just light. More complex even than the night sky, than the countless tiny stars.

"You see it, don't you?"

And suddenly Knot was looking outward again, at Wyle's form in the Void.

"I… I did see it," Knot said. "But not anymore. You brought me out of it."

"That's all right," Wyle said. "Once you've seen it, it shouldn't be too difficult to see again. Do whatever you did last time."

Knot closed his eyes—his metaphorical eyes?—and, sure enough, the strange structure of light was before him once more.

"Do you see it?"

"Yes," Knot whispered. The fuzzes of light shimmered and shifted around the center. "This… this is me?"

Wyle laughed. "This is how you appear in the Void. Some say this is your true form. I can't help but say I'm a little jealous. Your form is much more complex than any I've seen."

"What do we do now?" Knot asked.

Wyle sighed. "I'm not entirely sure. But it seems to me that locating each of the sifts, defining where they are and their properties, might be a good next step."

"And the sifts are…?"

"The blurs of light surrounding the central source."

"And the central source is me?"

"I think so," Wyle said. "Your case is baffling, in more ways than one. If you truly only came into existence when each of the sifts within you combined two years ago, then you are, for all intents and purposes, a new sift. And the central source of light looks most similar to how other sifts appear in the Void, so yes, I think it's safe to guess that that is you."

Knot stared at the light that was, apparently, himself. Then his gaze shifted to one of the blurs. "How do I interact with this?" he asked. "If I have no form here—no form other than the one I'm looking at—how do I do what you need me to do?"

"You use *tendra*," Wyle said.

"I'm not a psimancer," Knot responded.

"A part of you is," Wyle said. "Lathe was a very talented telenic."

"I know, but… I burned myself out in Izet. I no longer have those powers." Knot had been a psimancer for a few moments, but in an effort—a failed effort—to save Winter, he had drawn in too much power, all but cutting himself off.

"I didn't know that. I'm sorry."

"Doesn't matter much to me."

"Even still, when a…" Wyle's voice trailed off. "Either way, that shouldn't matter. Even if you weren't a psimancer, you're in the Void. All people have *tendra* in the Void. The standard is two, although psimancers generally have more."

Knot concentrated. Using *tendra* in Izet had come easily to him, once they had killed the Ceno who had been blocking him. His *tendra* had just been there, as if he'd gained extra limbs.

Things were not so easy this time. He imagined waving his hands around but nothing happened. Then he focused on the light before him, imagining *tendra* moving forth from his mind. Still nothing happened.

Knot frowned, staring at the central light. *Why won't you just do what I ask?*

Knot paused. The light was himself. He was looking at himself, but the light *was* himself. He imagined *tendra* moving forth from the central light, reaching out into the hazes of color around him. Immediately he felt the difference. And, as Knot reached a *tendron* out into the haze of light surrounding him—surrounding the central light—he *saw* the difference, too. Tendrils of smoky light reached outward from the central glow.

"Well done," Wyle said.

As Knot drew one *tendron* up through the first sphere of fuzzy light, the light reacted strangely. Knot's *tendron* acted like a stone protruding from a river, and the fuzzy light diverted itself around the smoky essence.

"Can you sense anything about that sphere?" Wyle asked. "Anything that might be useful?"

"No," Knot said, moving his *tendron* about in the hazy sphere. "I feel nothing. In fact—"

Something passed through his *tendron*. Knot couldn't tell what it was, but it was *something*. Then it was gone. Knot grunted in frustration, waving his *tendron* about in the hazy sphere again. Almost immediately he felt the strange sensation, but just as quickly it slipped past.

After a few moments of dredging his *tendron* in the sphere of light, he felt it a third time, and wrapped his *tendron* around the sensation. Immediately, the sphere disappeared. Knot peered at his *tendron*, and nestled within the writhing smoke was a tiny particle of light.

Knot heard Wyle's laugh of delight behind him, but paid no attention to it. He knew the tiny spark he held before him.

It was Lathe.

He knew because of the memories. Many he'd seen already, in dreams and in visions; men and women dying by his hand. But there were other memories, too, memories he'd never seen before, but memories he immediately knew belonged to Lathe.

A woman with short red hair. A man—a Nazaniin—young, blond, with a smirk on his face. The particle felt like a cold lightning strike in his mind.

"That's one of the sifts," Wyle said. "Do you know whose it is?"

"Lathe's," Knot said, turning the particle of light over in his *tendron*. "How do I establish its properties?"

"I think you already have," Wyle said. "It's blue now, whereas it was no color before."

Sure enough, the particle was now emitting a bright blue light. "What do I do with it?" Knot asked.

"Let it go," Wyle said. "Let it go, and move on to the next."

Knot frowned.

"Don't worry, I think it will fall into place now that you've defined it."

Reluctantly, Knot released his *tendron*'s grip on the particle, and the thing disappeared. In its place, the hazy, spherical fuzz returned, but unlike the others it was now a steady pale blue.

"That's it?" Knot asked.

"We're treading new ground here, but yes. I think that might help."

Knot was about to ask how in Oblivion fiddling with a bunch of colored lights would help him, but in the context he wasn't sure he had any right to question. He was a man formed of other men's sifts. *A conglomeration of souls.*

Knot was himself. The rose-colored light at his center was proof of that. But, until this point, Knot had been so focused on preserving whatever made him *him* that he'd shunned the other sifts that comprised him. Now he realized something very simple he had not tried.

Acceptance.

Knot reached his *tendron* out further into the next haze. This had the same effect—a rock in a river, the haze splitting around his tendron. Knot grasped at the sift, and after a few attempts, secured it. He was once again flooded with memories, this time of life in a great marble palace, of a royal instructor who cared very much for him, and of a cruel father who beat him. Knot remembered running away from the palace, running away from his father because of the pain, and his instructor because of the fear.

These were not his memories. They belonged to someone else.

High Prince Dorian Gatama.

With the realization the sensation from the sift grew more concrete. The feeling that burst in one's chest right before leaping from a high point. The particle of light—Gatama's sift—began to glow a bright gold.

"Incredible," Wyle whispered.

Knot released the sift, and it disappeared just as Lathe's had, only to be replaced by a golden sphere of hazy light.

Knot smiled. This might not be as painful as he'd thought.

"Thank you," Knot said, inclining his head. "I'm truly grateful."

"Having seen what was going on in your head, I'm glad I could help. I don't know how you could bear it."

"Wait, so what about all the sifts? Who are they?" Astrid asked.

Knot chewed his cheek. Might as well get it out in the open.

"You already know about Lathe, the Nazaniin assassin, and Dorian Gatama, the Alizian high prince."

"And there are nine in total? Not including the you that is... just you?"

Knot nodded. "Nine. Darcen was a general, a master

strategist and military commander. I think I must have used his knowledge for the training of Jane's guard force. Another was Elenar. She was an investigator, a very intelligent woman who tracked down violent criminals."

"A woman?" Cinzia asked, the hint of a smile on her face.

Knot grunted. "Who would've thought, eh? And she wasn't the only one. Three of the sifts are less clear—I couldn't get names, just vague memories. One, the other woman, was a mariner. I imagine that's why fishing came so easily to me in Pranna. Another was a warsquares champion, a master at the game. The third was a philosopher of some kind, I think. Difficult to say for sure."

"So that makes seven," Astrid said. "Who are the last two?"

"Hoc," Knot said, "is a mystery. I stabilized his sift, but I have no clear memories of who he was or what he did. Not sure I ever will."

Knot paused, surprised at the emotion bubbling up within him. While he did not have clear memories of all the events in each of these people's lives, some were clearer than others. The memories of the last sift were the clearest. "Joze was a farmer," Knot said quietly. "A husband and a father." Knot refrained from mentioning Joze's painful memories; the deaths of small children were not something he felt keen to discuss.

"So that's it, then?" Astrid asked.

Knot shrugged. "I think that's it."

"Goddess, I hope so. I'm sick of meeting new people."

Knot couldn't help but laugh. He looked at Wyle. "I suppose you'll be wanting your information, now. I can tell you all I remember about Roden. About what they did to me. It's the least I can do."

"Actually," Wyle said, glancing at Cymbre, "I got everything I needed from you already. As we stabilized each of your sifts, I got a glimpse into Lathe's in particular. I saw what Roden did to him."

Knot frowned. "Can't say I'm happy about the way you came across it. But if it means we can part peacefully, then it's something I'm willing to accept."

Both Wyle and Jendry glanced at Cymbre again. After a moment, the woman nodded. "If you truly think you got what we came for, Wyle, then we can leave at first light."

"About damn time," Jendry said.

Knot gave a half-smile. He was grateful for what these people had done for him—he already felt more in control over the personalities vying for dominance in his head. But he was glad to see the *cotir* go. Last thing he wanted was three known assassins around Cinzia and Jane.

"We'll gather our things," Cymbre said.

The *cotir* left the room, leaving Knot, Cinzia, and Astrid alone. Astrid rushed to him, wrapping her arms around his waist, and Cinzia slowly followed with a timid embrace of her own. Knot held them both, feeling like himself for the first time in a long time. For the first time he could remember.

45

North wing of the imperial palace, Izet

THE DOOR OPENED ALMOST immediately after Cova knocked. Winter stood on the threshold, squinting in the torchlight from the corridor. Her long black hair fell in front of her face. She swept it aside and looked up at Cova.

"Yes?"

"Let me in," Cova said. "Please."

Winter opened the door, stepping back into the darkness, and Cova slipped inside.

"Light a candle," Cova said.

Cova heard a rustling, saw the spark of flint and steel, and a candle flame ignited in Winter's hands. "What do you want?" Winter asked.

Cova stood, still breathing heavily from her sprint from her father's door. Still shaking, from… Had she dreamed it? The candle, the letter, the hanging body. Had she dreamed cutting it down, and that awful sound?

"I want to sit," Cova finally said.

Winter sighed and indicated a chair in one corner of the room. "You're obviously upset, but I have no idea why you are here. What is it you think I can do for you?"

Cova collapsed onto the chair. She had to get herself together. Her husband was dead. There had been a note claiming he was a spy. Had the note been in Girgan's handwriting?

Cova couldn't remember. She had not noticed otherwise. But the note could explain how Girgan had been acting lately, his animosity towards her father, his cryptic references and all the times he went off on his own. The explanation made sense.

And yet.

Cova couldn't deny that there were no longer any books in the imperial library about the Ceno order or the Scorned Gods. She had heard the rumors about the succession vote, and the otherworldly bodies found in the rubble of the imperial dome. She knew her father had been acting strangely.

If her father had discovered that Girgan had even *entertained* the idea of a coup, this would be how he'd retaliate. Not an obvious murder, but enough of a suspicious circumstance to convince anyone else involved of its folly. Cova put her head in her hands. Could her father be responsible? Had he killed her husband?

"*Cova*."

Cova looked up, realizing that Winter had been saying her name.

"It's late. I'm tired. Either tell me what's going on or—"

"My husband is dead."

Silence.

"It looked like he'd killed himself."

"I… I'm sorry, Cova. I would never have thought he'd do something like that."

"Nor me," Cova said. She met Winter's eyes, flickering darkly in the candlelight. "It *looked* like he killed himself. I don't think he did."

"Cova…"

"That doesn't matter," Cova said sharply. "Not to you. But I'm here to make you an offer."

Cova felt Winter's hand touch hers. She recoiled,

remembering Luce's body hanging in the council chamber. But, when she saw Winter's face, she realized the gesture was timid, awkward, and Cova was suddenly overcome by the sincerity of the gesture. Her whole life, she had grown up thinking that tiellans were backward, uneducated, cruel beings, far below humans. But if Winter was any indicator, she would have to start changing her views. She still feared Winter. But she was beginning to fear her father more.

"My husband was killed," Winter said softly, her hand flittering away from Cova's. "Whatever happened to Girgan, I… I'm sorry."

Cova began to cry. She cried because of her father, she cried because the man she had just learned to love had been taken from her, and she would never be with him again, never feel his touch, hear his voice. He was gone, and she cried because she was now alone. Winter only stood there while Cova sobbed, but the woman's presence was strangely comforting. Cova had not known Winter had even been married, let alone that her husband had been killed.

Later, when Cova had cried all her tears, she realized she had two choices. She could believe the note she'd found with Girgan's body, that he was a spy, that he had lied to her.

Or she could believe her husband. Cova did not have to think long to decide.

"Do you want to kill my father?" Cova asked.

Winter's eyes widened, but she quickly hid her surprise, her face going blank. "I serve your father," she said. "Why would I want to kill him?"

"He killed my husband," Cova said, as if that was an answer.

"I thought you said he killed himself."

"It *looked* like he killed himself. I believe otherwise."

"And you think your father is behind it?"

"I see no other culprits. Girgan... Girgan had suspicions about my father. I can only imagine my father found out, and this is the consequence."

"You want your father dead?" Winter asked.

Cova thought long and hard before she answered. "No," she finally said. "I don't *want* him dead. He is my father, and I love him, but... but that does not change the fact that he must die."

Winter muttered something. Cova thought it sounded something like "loving to destroy" but she couldn't be sure.

Then Winter met Cova's eyes, her voice firm. "How do I know you aren't testing me?"

Cova blinked. "Testing you?"

"How do I know Daval did not send you to test my loyalty?"

"I..." Cova had not thought of that. "He didn't," she said. "My husband is *dead*, Winter."

Winter did not respond for a moment. She appeared to have her eyes closed. Had she fallen asleep?

"Again, I'm sorry about your husband," Winter said. "And... I believe you."

Cova nodded. That had been surprisingly easy. "Will you help me overthrow my father? Will you help me kill him?"

Winter stared at Cova for a moment, and then closed her eyes once more. Cova frowned. What was she doing?

Winter's eyes snapped open. She nodded. "I will help you."

"Very well," Cova said. *Now what?*

"We need a plan," Winter said. "Do you know when and where you want to do this?"

Cova stood. "I... I have no idea. I suppose it would be best to get him alone. Perhaps in the emperor's chambers. I think I could distract the Reapers that guard them, but if Urstadt is there we will not stand a chance."

"Urstadt might not be a problem," Winter said.

"What do you mean?"

"Currently, your father blocks my powers. But you saw what I did to Luce when I was given free rein. If he was not blocking me, I could handle Urstadt."

Cova said nothing to that. Given what she had seen in the council chamber, Winter was probably right.

"You think you can get around his blocks?" Cova asked.

"I may have a trick up my sleeve," Winter said.

"Anything else?"

Winter shrugged. "This was your idea. You tell me."

46

Harmoth estate

THE NEXT MORNING, CINZIA sat in her room alone, gazing out at the grounds. She was shocked at how empty they looked; a few hundred Odenites remained, but many more had left with the Beldam.

Between the Kamite attack, the Beldam's departure, the loss of the followers she had taken with her, and Wyle's work with Knot the previous night, too much had happened in the past few days. Cinzia was not sure she could keep up with it all. While she was relieved that Knot was himself again, she was uneasy. What Wyle had done to help Knot was beyond her understanding—as beyond her understanding as how Jane healed dozens of people.

The similarities between psimancy and Jane's abilities were not lost on Cinzia. Not to mention the way she herself had saved Jane, or even when she translated the Codex for that matter. Cinzia did not know enough about either form of power to make a judgment. But they were similar enough to make her uncomfortable.

And her unease did not end there. She may have succeeded in trusting Canta once, but the fact that Ocrestia and Elessa had healed others too, while Cinzia had been unable to, was evidence that she still had much to learn. She saw again the dark eyes of the man who had grasped her arm, his voice like burning darkness. She knew it had to be connected with whatever had possessed Kovac. The Nine Daemons. It seemed they were destined to face the otherworldly beings at some point. Cinzia did not know how to face such terror. She still had not told anyone of what she had experienced; she had murdered a helpless, wounded man. The man had been possessed by Azael, but Cinzia was not sure that excused her actions.

Cinzia jumped at a knock at the door. She rose from her seat at the desk and took a few deep breaths before opening it to find Wyle grinning at her. Cinzia blinked. Of all people, she had expected him the least.

"Hello, Wyle," she said, returning his smile with difficulty.

"We're leaving soon," Wyle said, glancing over Cinzia's shoulder. "As you know."

Cinzia nodded. "I do know," she said. "Do you require my assistance?" He was looking at her in an odd way. Almost nervously.

"No, no." Wyle cleared his throat. "I just..."

Then, before Cinzia knew what was happening, Wyle leaned forward. She felt herself lifting her face to his, and their lips met.

When they parted, Wyle's grin was wider than ever.

"I..." Cinzia wanted to say something, but she had no earthly idea what.

"Word has it you folks are headed to Triah," Wyle said.

"I... yes," Cinzia managed. "I think so."

"Look me up when you get there."

"I will."

Wyle nodded, and opened his mouth as if he were about to say something, but stopped.

Something in his eyes changed, in that moment. Cinzia couldn't pinpoint what it was exactly, but something changed. His smile faltered. Then, just like that, it was back.

"I look forward to it," Wyle said. "Until we meet again, Cinzia."

Before she could respond, he was gone.

Cinzia wandered down into the drawing room, still reeling from her encounter with Wyle.

She had just kissed a man for the first time.

She had kissed one or two boys, when she was young. She remembered Jonn Eyden, a few months before she left Navone for the seminary. Scrawny, with shaggy hair, but Cinzia remembered almost laughing at how much he had trembled when they kissed. That had been almost eight years ago.

Cinzia resisted the urge to place her fingers on her lips, remembering the unfamiliar excitement that had welled within her as Wyle had leaned down. Wyle was definitely not a boy, that much was sure.

And yet there was something about the encounter that made Cinzia uncomfortable. Not the kiss, but something Wyle had said…

Her parents were both in the drawing room, along with the triplets—Soffrena, Lana, and Wina—Knot, and Astrid. Cymbre and Jendry were there, too, and seeing them Cinzia felt her cheeks flush. She knew Wyle couldn't yet have told the rest of the *cotir* what had passed between them, but the thought of it still made her uncomfortable—although the feeling was not entirely negative, she was pleased to note.

She had to find Jane, Cinzia realized. To tell her about Wyle, of course, but for more important reasons as well. They had to decide what to do next—whether to pursue the Beldam and those who had followed her, or to leave them behind and continue on to Triah without them.

"Cinzia, you look flushed. Are you well?"

Cinzia smiled at Soffrena. She must have been blushing more than she thought. "I'm fine, sister, just looking for Jane."

At that moment Wyle walked into the room. He was no longer grinning, but had a purposeful expression on his face. Cinzia looked away, her mind still working over what he had said to her. He had told her to look him up when she arrived in Triah. Cinzia blinked. Knot had told her that Cymbre, Wyle, and Jendry were a Tinskan *cotir*. Why would they be going back to Triah, unless…

Unless they had been sent from the Circle City in the first place.

A crash echoed from the far end of the room. Cinzia turned to see that the sides of the huge inglenook fireplace had given way, smashing the massive marble mantelpiece into the ground. Splinters of wood and broken marble littered the floor.

"Goddess," Cinzia cried. She looked around. "Is everyone all right? Did…"

"Everyone, stay calm." Wyle walked to the center of the room, hands raised. "We don't want to hurt any of you. But we've just received new orders. And I'm afraid we have some unfinished business with Jane."

Cinzia's eyes narrowed. "Wyle," she said, striding towards him. "What are you talking about?"

"Cinzia," Knot shouted, "stay away from him!"

Cinzia turned to see Jendry holding a blade to Knot's throat while Cymbre bound his hands. Near them, the ruins of the fireplace shifted ever so slightly. Cinzia gaped in horror as she saw a small hand reach out from beneath the cracked marble of the mantel.

"Astrid?" Cinzia whispered.

"Watch him," Cymbre said, shoving Knot towards Jendry. "I need to focus on the vampire."

Cinzia's gaze returned to Wyle. Very different emotions began to well up within her than the ones she had felt when they had kissed minutes before.

"You're not from Tinska at all, are you?" Cinzia demanded. It all came together for her, now. The Nazaniin, first and foremost, were assassins. Jane was a marked woman. The *cotir* had not been sent from Tinska to help Knot. They had been sent from Triah to assassinate Jane. Helping Knot—and gleaning information from him—had only been a perk.

Wyle smiled, but the expression was empty. "I'm sorry, Cinzia," he said. "I didn't know we would be ordered to do this when I saw you last."

Cinzia shook her head. "But you knew it was a possibility."

Wyle shrugged. "Anything is a possibility."

"We will not give you Jane," Cinzia said. He could not kiss her, treat her like he did moments before, only to betray her. She would not let him.

Wyle took a step closer to Cinzia. He spoke more quietly this time. "I know this is difficult," he said. "But we're professionals, Cinzia. We're going to get the job done. Just… fetch your sister. Then we won't have to hurt anyone else."

Cinzia's rage bubbled up and she slapped him hard. Wyle rubbed his cheek but he did not seem angry. Instead his eyes were sad. Which made Cinzia furious.

"Lana," Wyle said, looking across the room at one of the triplets, "do you know where Jane is?"

Ehram and Pascia, who had already moved to stand between the triplets and Wyle, clasped their arms around them more firmly. Lana looked at each of her parents, then at Cinzia.

"Lana," Wyle said, "I need you to fetch Jane for me. I need you to do it now."

Ehram glared at Wyle. "We've taken you in. Given you food and shelter. This is how you repay us?"

"We've repaid you by fixing that facsimile of a man over there." Wyle nodded at Knot. His eyes remained on Lana. "Lana, if you don't do as I ask, there will be consequences."

"How *dare* you threaten my sister," Cinzia said. But she knew there was nothing she could do. Knot was incapacitated. So was Astrid. Unless… unless Canta granted her strength, the way She had given her strength and speed to save Jane. If Cinzia trusted, it could happen.

She began to pray.

Wyle sighed. He looked at Cinzia. "I'm sorry," he said.

Cinzia braced herself for whatever was about to happen, whatever pain he might cause her.

Then she heard the screaming.

Please, Goddess, Cinzia pleaded, *grant me strength.*

Soffrena had fallen to her knees, clutching her head between her hands.

"No!" Cinzia shouted, shoving Wyle in the chest with all her might, but he absorbed her attacks easily, his gaze focused on Soffrena. Slowly the girl's screams faded, and she collapsed to the floor, whimpering.

"Lana, do as I say, or your sister will suffer further."

Lana's terrified eyes moved back and forth between Ehram and Pascia.

"Go, Lana," Cinzia said. "Find Jane. It will be all right." Lana did not move. "*Go,*" Cinzia said.

Lana hesitated a moment more, and then rushed out of the room.

Please. Help me protect my family.

Cinzia rushed to Soffrena, her parents already kneeling at

their daughter's side. Wina was crying. Soffrena stared up at the ceiling, eyes blank.

"She'll be fine," Wyle said. "Give her a few hours. She'll have a splitting headache, but that's it. As long as Jane gets here."

Give me strength, Goddess, please...

Cinzia gritted her teeth. She did not feel any different. Time had not begun to slow. She felt no stronger. Would Canta really abandon her, now of all moments? She glanced over her shoulder at Knot, still bound and held at Jendry's swordpoint. He seemed to be concentrating on something, but on what Cinzia couldn't be sure. She looked over to where she could still see Astrid's hand protruding from the ruins of the fireplace. The girl groaned something incomprehensible, so at least she was alive. Cinzia was not sure how the vampire would be able to free herself before nightfall. It would take a dozen grown men to move it.

Cinzia shook her head. Then she stood, and walked towards Wyle, face hot with rage and helplessness.

Goddess, give me strength to help my family.

"What in Oblivion is wrong with you?"

"Look, Cinzia, I—"

"You expect me to let you kill my sister?"

"I expect you to know that you don't have a choice."

Cinzia glared at him. "You don't have to carry out your orders."

Wyle looked at her strangely.

"You can stay here with us," Cinzia continued.

Cinzia heard Jendry scoff. She ignored him, and took a step towards Wyle. They were close, now. Bodies almost touching. Cinzia raised her hand, as if to touch his face.

"We could spend more time together," she said quietly. "We could... see where this goes."

"What in Oblivion is she talking about, Wyle? Did you bang the bloody ex-priestess?" Jendry called out.

Cinzia continued to ignore him, hoping Wyle would do the same. He was looking into her eyes.

"You know I can't," he said quietly.

Cinzia stepped back. She had known he would respond that way, but had hoped otherwise. Not because she had any desire to spend time with the man, not after such a betrayal. Just to distract him, to stop him from doing the inevitable. Now, she was out of options. No help from Canta. No help from her friends. Nothing else left.

You can still trust.

Cinzia was not sure whether the voice was her own or someone else's. But as the words entered her mind, the strangest sensation trickled through her, beginning in her chest, spreading slowly throughout her whole body. She was suddenly as tranquil as a breezeless lake. Then, her prayer changed.

And in that moment, she understood. She had been praying for herself, praying that she might find strength. That was not trust at all—that was control, she realized. She had been praying for control. Faith implied giving up what little control she had. It didn't mean praying for her own power, to do what she thought was best. It meant trusting.

Goddess... give me strength to trust you.

The doors behind her creaked. Cinzia turned, and despite the peace she felt, still dreaded the sight of Jane. She had no idea what they could do to protect her. Jane was as good as dead.

Goddess, give me the strength to trust you.

As the doors opened, the brightest light Cinzia had ever seen sliced into the room. It was white and pure, brighter by far than the sun at noon. A figure stood at the light's center.

Cinzia squinted, shielding her eyes.

"Canta's breath," Wyle whispered.

Canta? Could it be?

The figure at the center of the light was certainly a woman. And while she couldn't recognize the woman's face—the light was far too bright—Cinzia felt acceptance. A sense of love. *Jane?*

Someone shouted to her left, and Cinzia turned. Knot had somehow freed his hands, and was struggling with Jendry. Cymbre moved towards them, but the light made it impossible to tell exactly what was happening, who had the upper hand.

But if Cymbre was distracted, Cinzia might be able to help Astrid. She rushed to the rubble, calling the girl's name. Astrid grunted something in response—it sounded more alert than the moan Cinzia had heard before, but she was still trapped under something Cinzia couldn't possibly lift.

Unless she had help.

Cinzia had experienced unnatural speed and strength once before. Perhaps, just for a moment, Canta was willing to grant her those things again.

"Hold on, Astrid," Cinzia whispered, getting as solid a grip as she could on the mantel. Then she planted her feet, and *lifted* with all she had.

The mantel did not move.

Cinzia released the huge object, breathing heavily. *Please*, she pleaded, *give me strength*... Cinzia paused. Had she forgotten what she had felt only moments ago so quickly? *Give me strength to trust you,* she said. She tried again, straining against the weight of the great marble mantelpiece with all of her might, but still it did not move.

Cinzia heard a muffled sound from beneath it, and she bent her head down. "Astrid, I can't understand you."

"I said, are you really trying to lift this entire thing by yourself, *you idiot?*"

Cinzia felt her cheeks flush, but before she could respond she noticed the light fading around her. She turned just in time to see Knot smash his fist into Cymbre's throat. The woman collapsed to the ground, where Jendry's body already lay.

Cinzia felt a tiny seed of pride well up within her. Knot would make a good Goddessguard. She must remember to talk to him about that—if a Goddessguard had a place in Jane's new Church.

"If they're dead, Kosarin won't be happy." Wyle was frowning. The light had completely faded now, and Jane stood in front of him. "All the more reason it's time I kill you, Jane."

Was my sister the source of the light? Cinzia wondered. The light had felt so… so strange, as if a very different presence had accompanied it.

Wyle drew a dagger from his belt. Knot rushed at him, but Wyle held up a hand, and Knot stopped immediately.

"Did you think I wouldn't set up any safety protocols while I fiddled around in that head of yours?"

Knot fell to his knees, immobilized.

Wyle frowned. "You're fighting it. You're stronger than I thought you'd be. It's a good thing I've been annexing dozens of sifts over the past few weeks, otherwise I don't think I'd be able to hold you back."

He turned back to Jane, raising his dagger.

Jane's eyes flashed from the dagger to Cinzia. In Jane's eyes, Cinzia saw the tiniest glimmer of white light. Jane nodded, slowly, and Cinzia found herself nodding in return.

Suddenly light burst forth once more from Jane's body, banishing every shadow from the room.

Wyle squinted, shielding his eyes with one arm, dagger

still held high in the other. "Your silly trick with the light won't worrrrrrrrrrrrr…"

Wyle's speech slowed, and the world around Cinzia stretched, everything elongating both away and towards herself. Her mind felt as if it were moving far ahead of her body, just as it had done when she had saved Jane from the second assassination attempt.

She stood and sprinted towards Wyle. He was frozen in place. Jane, too, was unmoving, although it was difficult for Cinzia to look at her sister, the focal point of the bright white light. The light, in fact, was the only thing other than Cinzia that moved. She could see it spreading slowly, reaching outward from her sister.

Cinzia slammed into Wyle, and they both crashed to the floor. Wyle did not react, his eyes staring blankly ahead.

Cinzia tore the dagger from his hand and flung it across the room. As soon as the dagger left her hand, it froze in midair. Cinzia ignored it, planting herself firmly atop Wyle. Just as she did, the world around her sped up once more, and the slow hum of the room turned to chaos.

As quickly as the light burst forth from Jane, it collapsed back into her. Wyle screamed, a ragged shriek. Cinzia blinked a few times as her eyes adjusted. She looked down at Wyle, whose scream had faded into low, ragged moans. She was shocked at what she saw.

The whites of his eyes were split and dotted with blood. More blood leaked from his nose, and he cradled both of his arms close to his body.

Slowly, Cinzia stood. Wyle wouldn't be getting up any time soon. Had she done this to him? She had only tackled him to the ground. She looked around. Knot was standing, shaking his head, but he seemed all right. Jane, too, was safe. Flustered, but safe.

That was when she noticed the frantic sobbing coming from the corner of the room where her parents and the triplets were cowered. Cinzia rushed over. Wyle must have hurt them somehow—

Cinzia's gut turned to lead when she saw the dagger protruding from her father's neck. The same dagger she had taken from Wyle, and tossed aside. It was buried up to its hilt.

The tears that blurred her vision were immediate and unstoppable. "Father," Cinzia whispered, kneeling next to him. Recovery from such a wound was impossible.

Unless...

"Jane," Cinzia said, her voice barely above a whisper. "*Jane*."

But Jane was already at her side, staring blankly down at their father.

"Heal him," Cinzia demanded.

Jane shook her head, tears streaming down her cheeks.

"*Heal him*."

"I can't, Cinzi," Jane whispered. "All of the healing I've done over the past few days, all of that power, the light... I have no more left in me. I... I can't..."

Cinzia shook her head. How could Jane be exhausted? Was not Canta Herself the source of Jane's power? How could that power fail?

"Lana, Wina, Soffrena." The triplets looked up at Cinzia. "Go find Elessa or Ocrestia, and send them here as quickly as you can. *Go*."

The three stood simultaneously, and ran quickly out the door. They, at least, did not hesitate to do what they could to help their father.

Cinzia looked back down at her father, fighting the panic clawing its way up her throat. She put her hand gently on his neck. "I can try to remove the dagger," she said, over her father's gurgling. "I can try to—"

She felt a hand on her own. It was Jane's.

You can still trust.

How can I trust that this is what you want to happen? Cinzia pleaded.

You can still trust.

Then, the same peaceful feeling that Cinzia had felt earlier returned, washing over her. *I can still trust. If this is what you want to happen, I will accept that it is for the greater good.*

I will accept it, because I trust you.

Then, slowly at first, then growing more and more intense, a warm glow wrapped itself around Cinzia and Ehram. She felt it envelop her, an embrace she never wanted to leave. Cinzia did not know how long the glow remained, but as it faded, she looked at her father. Tears fogged her vision, but even through them she saw his face, smiling up at her.

"Thank you," he said weakly.

The dagger no longer protruded from his neck. There was only a pink scar, just above his collarbone.

Thank you, Cinzia thought. Then she collapsed.

47

Imperial palace, Izet

WINTER HAD BEEN SUMMONED to the emperor's chambers. She knew the plans had been set in motion; she knew the decisions she had made, and how Chaos had helped her make those decisions. Winter knew the risks. She knew what was at stake. But she had made her choice.

She nodded to the Reapers guarding the door to the emperor's chambers. They would be taken care of, she had been assured.

Winter, the fire of frost burning in her veins, knocked on the emperor's door.

Cova wrung her hands, pacing back and forth in the corridor. She was in the royal wing, but not close enough to her father's chambers to appear suspicious—or so she hoped. Winter should be arriving there now, being admitted to the anteroom by Urstadt. Daval's retainer of Ceno monks had been called away, thanks to a diversion Cova had orchestrated with Hama Mandiat, Girgan's mother. While Winter claimed Cova's father was the source of her block, she did not want to risk having any monks around who might interfere.

The skin on the back of Cova's neck prickled. The fact that they were putting their hopes on Winter's powers did not seem wise. And yet it was their only option.

The image of Luce pinned against the wall of the council

chamber flashed into her mind. If Winter *could* access her magic, Cova did not think anything could stop her.

Cova took a deep breath. "Guards!" she screamed.

Kali waited impatiently in the Void. Winter had not been back since their altercation. But Kali had remained close to the dark immolating star that she had learned to recognize as Winter.

A battle was coming. Kali could sense it. If Winter was involved, she would use acumency. She wouldn't be able to resist. Or, at least, that's what Kali hoped. Kali had plans. Plans that just might get her out of the Void and into the real world once more.

The girl is here.

The Fear Lord's voice still gave Daval chills, the sound of a deep, dark, terrible fire, roaring as it consumed.

"Is that going to be a problem?" Daval asked. "She is coming around to our way of thinking."

Your daughter has drawn the Reapers away, as we suspected she would. And the girl… there is something different about her. They may be colluding.

"What do you mean?"

I am not certain. Be on guard around them both.

Daval was surprised; while the Fear Lord had told him to watch out for a power play from Cova, a part of him had still not expected it from his own daughter. The fact that she might be colluding with Winter… but what good would that do? Winter was powerless around him.

Daval tried to cover his emotions as best he could. "Of course, Lord. I accept your commands, as always."

The girl is important. Keep her alive if you can.

Daval nodded, although he felt a twinge of jealousy. Was he not enough for his lord?

No, Daval. You are not.

Winter entered the anteroom to the emperor's chambers and was not surprised to see Urstadt waiting for her.

"Dropping in unexpectedly once again, I see," Urstadt said.

Briefly, Winter passed through Urstadt's mind. Urstadt was worried about Daval—unsurprising, considering Cova's plot—but to Winter's surprise, Urstadt was also thinking about the Ziravi poem, what it means to love, and how destroying someone once you truly love them might be the hardest thing to do. Urstadt was thinking about the people she loved—her mother and brother back home, someone named Erial, and... and one more, one more person that Urstadt is not entirely sure whether she loves or not, but thinks she might. Someone she might love the way a daughter loves a father.

Daval.

"I need to see him," Winter said.

Urstadt stared at Winter. Then, knowing her orders, Urstadt led her into the emperor's chambers.

When the Reapers found Cova, they completely ignored her claims of an intruder.

"The emperor said you would do this, Your Highness," the Reaper captain said. Cova immediately regretted not spending more time getting to know the Reapers that served her father. If she had been friendly with them, this might have gone differently.

"Our orders are to take you to your father immediately," the captain said. She was an older woman, older than Cova would have expected, her hair gray and short. But she was broad, and looked strong. She turned to one of the other Reapers. "Call in another platoon, just in case. Meet us in the emperor's quarters."

The captain placed her hand on Cova's arm lightly. "Please, Your Highness, come with us. We would prefer you to come peacefully."

Cova went where the captain directed her. Inside, as the confused storm began to settle in her brain, she was left with fear. She hoped Winter hadn't acted yet. The best move would be to save their plan for another day.

If Cova saw another day.

Daval greeted Winter, but his face was oddly blank. He usually seemed happy to see her.

"Thank you for coming, Winter," Daval said. "I have a task for you."

Winter hesitated. This was not part of the plan. "You do?" she asked.

"Yes," Daval said. "A more delicate matter than anything you've done for me thus far."

Winter nodded, but her mind was already reaching towards Daval. She moved her acumenic *tendron* slowly, as if the slower her *tendron* moved, the less chance Daval would notice it.

"What is it you would like me to do?" she asked.

Then her *tendron* made contact. Daval was talking about her next target, but she was too distracted to listen. She just had to find a way to stop him blocking her telesis.

The moment her *tendron* attempted to enter Daval's mind, Winter's vision flashed, and she saw the terrible dark skull wreathed in darker flame. But her *tendron* didn't enter his mind. Winter's heart beat faster, and she attempted to delve Daval's mind again. But the moment her *tendron* touched him, there was the grinning skull.

The door behind her opened, and she immediately reached out to see who had entered. Reapers. Two in the chamber, and nearly a dozen more in the anteroom. And with the two…

Winter turned in surprise. Cova stood between the two Reapers. When her wide eyes met Winter's, Cova shook her head slowly.

Winter turned back to Daval. A quick delve into each of the Reapers' heads told her that they had been told to bring Cova in if she did anything suspicious. She concentrated on Cova. She wanted Winter to stop, so that they could attempt this another time.

Winter closed her eyes, and immediately Chaos was there. The sphere was black. She wouldn't stop now.

When Winter entered the Void, Kali was prepared. Winter ignored her, and Kali was all right with that. What she was about to attempt would probably be easier that way.

Winter looked around, her *tendra* immediately branching outward. Then, seeming to find what she was looking for, three *tendra* shot out, delving into three different stars in the Void. One of the stars, Kali suspected, was the one at the exact center of the black bubble around Izet.

Curious. What business Winter had with this force would have to be discovered later. For now, Kali waited. She couldn't make her move too soon, or Winter would sense what was happening. But if she moved too late…

Now was her chance. Winter was distracted, concentrating—surely attempting to rearrange these people for some reason. Kali moved to one of Winter's *tendra*, the one that was not connected to the star at the center of the veil—Kali did not want to join herself to that power until she knew what she was doing—joining it with her own just as she leapt directly into the stream with her ersatz body in the Void.

Her vision shifted, writhed, and Kali suddenly felt as if she were traveling down a very long, dark, twisting tunnel. Kali sent her *tendra* ahead of her, within Winter's. She could see what Winter was doing, but Kali did not have time to note the details.

Obliteration could be an easy process, especially with all of the practice Kali had. With her *tendra* she carefully carved out the mind she was entering, detaching it from its host. She wrapped her *tendra* around it, tying off the edges. She hoped, if she kept it intact, Winter wouldn't notice what was happening. Kali removed the sift, and rushed through the tunnel to her destination.

When she opened her eyes, she was in a room. A *real* room. A massive room, actually. Some noble's armory, by the looks of things. She was surrounded by racks of weapons and armor, some encrusted with precious stones.

"*Torun?*" a woman's voice said.

Kali turned to see a woman in a green robe frowning at her. Kali remembered these green robes, remembered the Ceno monks, from her last visit to Izet. She did not like these people. Kali's hand snapped out, grabbing a dagger hanging on the wall, and she rammed it into the woman's throat. She fell to the floor, choking, blood pooling around her.

Kali stepped over the dying Ceno woman and peeked out the door. Making it out of the Void was one thing; making it out of whatever situation she was in now was another task entirely. Winter was in the next room, as were two Reapers and two women Kali didn't recognize. The man who stood in the center of the group wore a golden circlet on his head.

Bloody Oblivion. Kali had made her way out of the Void, and into the emperor's chambers.

* * *

When the Reapers brought Daval's daughter into the room, he felt something he had not felt in a very long time. It was a hearkening back to something forgotten; to a time when he'd bounced her on his knee as she giggled uncontrollably. He realized that such times were gone, never to be experienced again.

"Father, why have you told them to bring me to you? I don't understand."

"We have had to keep a close eye on you, my dear. After the tragic death of your husband, we don't want anything to happen to you."

Take care of this quickly.

Daval took a deep breath. He loved his daughter. He loved her, and that meant he had to be willing to destroy her. Daval put on a smile, but before he could speak, Cova did.

"You had him killed, didn't you?"

The smile faded from Daval's lips. So it had come to this. She would give him no choice.

"He was plotting against me. Surely you can see I had no other option."

"I was keeping him in check, Father. I wouldn't have let him do anything that threatened the empire."

"He stood in your way."

"You mean he stood in *yours*."

Daval pressed his lips tightly together. How could it be that one of the things he loved most about Cova was her ability to try his patience? "Your way, my way, it doesn't matter. He was an obstacle."

"He was my husband."

Daval shook his head. His daughter's feelings for Girgan Mandiat had developed more quickly than he'd realized. The pair had matched a little too well. And now he had this mess to clean up. "I did what I did for the good of Roden," he said. If she would not see reason, he would have to do something about it.

"You may think that," Cova said. Her eyes bored into his, red-rimmed and dry. "But so did he. What gives you the right to think you matter more than he does?"

"I am the emperor. I matter more than everyone."

The girl, the Fear Lord's voice boomed in Daval's mind. *Stop her.*

Daval's gaze shifted to Winter, whose eyes were blank, staring off into space.

And then he felt it. His block was gone.

Raya? Torun? Daval asked, reaching out to the two Ceno monks in his armory, managing Winter's auxiliary blocks. *Are your telenic blocks in place, still?*

There was no response.

Daval looked back at Winter, a tremor echoing down his spine.

The tiellan smiled.

Winter smiled.

Her telenic *tendra* issued forth. The feeling liberated and invigorated her all at once. This time, someone else wasn't *allowing* her to use her power. This time, she was using it *herself.* This was what *faltira* was all about. The high was one thing, the burning blood and icy skin. But what did that matter in the face of real power?

"Urstadt," Daval said, his eyes widening, "stop her!"

Urstadt moved towards Winter, but she sent three *tendra* towards the woman, holding her by her armor, holding the short sword she attempted to draw from its sheath. Urstadt looked up at Winter with a frustrated scowl. And yet something was wrong. Urstadt was managing to push forward, straining against Winter's *tendra*. The woman's sword was halfway drawn.

Winter sensed movement behind her, and reached for Urstadt's glaive, left leaning against a wall. With one of her *tendra*, she rammed the glaive behind her, impaling one of the guards. The Reaper fell to the ground with a crash. Two more *tendra* picked up the woman's sword and shield.

Urstadt was much closer. In a panic, Winter pushed Urstadt back with more *tendra*, slamming the woman against the far wall and keeping her pinned there. The door to the emperor's chambers slammed open, and more Reapers poured in. Winter readied her weapons and prepared to meet them.

Cova had seen the tiellan woman kill Hirman Luce, watched the life drain from him. Cova never wanted to see such a thing again. What she hadn't realized at the time was that Luce's blood was as much on her father's hands as on Winter's, if not more so.

But that did not make what she saw now any easier. And there, standing calmly in the middle of it all, was Cova's father, staring intently at Winter as she defended herself from the Reapers flooding into the room.

Or the man who claimed to be her father. As far as Cova was concerned, her father had died long ago. This man was a murderer. He needed to be put down.

As quietly as she could, Cova moved to the edge of the room, trying to skirt around her father's vision. The guards had not bothered to search her for weapons. As always, she carried a small knife in a hidden pocket sewn into her dress. Cova reached for the blade and steeled herself for what she was about to do. This man had killed her husband, after all. This man might've killed the previous emperor, and the previous Tokal-Ceno, all "for the good of Roden." Cova did not care what he thought was for the good of Roden. If she knew anything, it was that her father was no longer fit to lead.

She crept along the wall until she stood behind him. Cova felt a brief stab of shame for such a cowardly attack, but it was quickly replaced with a wave of determination and a spreading wildfire of anger. This man deserved to die. With all of her strength, she rammed the dagger into his back.

He stumbled, but remained standing.

Cova blinked. Pain vibrated through her hands—it had been like stabbing a dagger into a steel plate. She saw the dagger had only sunk one or two fingers into her father's back. The blade had hardly penetrated. Slowly, Daval turned, his eyes locking on Cova.

"What *are* you?" Cova asked, taking a step back.

Daval's mouth moved in response, but the voice was not his. It was low, deep and rumbling, like the rush of an inferno.

I am fear.

Then Cova's father raised his hands, and all was blackness.

The moment Winter heard the crack of thunder, the moment the dark mist exploded into the room, she found herself back under the dome. A monster, larger than anything she could fathom, stood above her, its massive jaws rushing down to engulf her.

But in a flash the monsters were gone, and Winter was alone in darkness. But it was not the Void.

It was a place of terror.

Slowly, the blackness lifted and Winter found herself in the throne hall, intact once more. She saw the throne, the gilded steps upon which Lian was killed. She saw the great columns, unbroken by her psimancy. At the base of the throne, a form took shape. A tall, dark figure cloaked in black. The hood was drawn up, creating deep shadow where the man's face would be. The robe fell in folds that cascaded outward, blending with coiling, writhing black mist.

An image flashed in Winter's mind, the black skull engulfed in blacker flame.

"*You have surprised me. I should have told Daval not to kill his daughter's husband so quickly. It is my fault this has happened.*"

The Voice boomed, deep and rumbling, crackling like fire. Winter couldn't speak. Her whole body was frozen in fear.

"*In my pride, I thought our plans would come to fruition before the full effect of Girgan's death took place. I was wrong.*"

Slowly, Winter looked around. The tall figure was motionless. The black mist, other than the small wisps around the man's cloak, was nowhere to be seen.

"*You search for your mother*," the Voice said. "*You fear you will see her again.*"

"I always see her, when you bring me here," Winter whispered, finally finding her voice.

"*You will not see her this time, child. I have shown you many of your fears already. It is not necessary to show them to you again. Not yet.*"

Winter wanted to ask what the figure was, but she couldn't.

"*I am sorry about those close to you. Their deaths were necessary to bring you here. You are an essential component of the coming war. You will do great and terrible things, Winter. I have shown Daval a version of the future. Allow me to show it to you.*"

Winter's mind opened.

Knot and Astrid, Cinzia and Jane, facing a great mass of a beast—a Daemon—slithering towards them. Then Winter's vision shifted, and the Daemon changed into something elongated, feathered, taking flight. She saw Knot's mouth open wide. *He is dead*, Winter thought. *This vision is a trick.*

The colors of her friends swirled together, and then expanded again together in a different way, showing her a scene of war and destruction. Two armies clashed, an outcropping of great stones in their midst. Not any stones, Winter realized. *Rihnemin*, the ancient standing stones of her people. Just as one army seemed on the verge of victory, hundreds of tiny runes, previously invisible, began to appear on one of the *rihnemin*, each one glowing a bright blue.

The colors expanded and retracted once more, and Winter saw a great stone giant fall to his knees, crushing a bed of beautiful flowers beneath him. The giant crumbled and fell apart, and each stone fragment became a small feminine figurine, each one attending to a flower. Some were restored, others turned black and withered into nothing.

Then the first rays of dawn reached up over the horizon. Hundreds of daemons raced towards a great city, a city larger than any Winter could imagine. Between the daemons and the city, a pillar of light appeared. Each daemon the pillar touched burst into flame. As the sun rose the pillar of light became a pillar of fire, and then it exploded in a great ring of white flame.

Winter saw a ship just before dawn, searching for its final harbor. She saw her father touching her mother's swollen belly, and they smiled at one another. She saw Urstadt, without armor, holding hands with a young woman with a broken crown on her head. Urstadt leant down, but before they kissed, Winter was in her home in Pranna, moonlight streaming in through a window. A child slept soundly in a crib, moonlight streaking the baby's face.

Expand and retract, over, and over, and over, and over…

* * *

Daval shook his head, looking down at his daughter in pity. Everyone in the room—Winter, Urstadt, the Reapers, Cova—was silent, gaping, experiencing true terror in the face of the Fear Lord. Daval himself had experienced it many times—it hardly affected him anymore.

Cova's eyes were wide in frozen agony. *She used to come to me when she had nightmares,* Daval thought. *After her mother passed away.* Daval knelt down, cradling his daughter's head in his lap. He rolled his shoulders, and the knife Cova had embedded in his back clattered to the floor.

"It will be all right, my sweet girl. The nightmare will end soon." Daval reached for the knife.

"Sir."

Daval looked up in surprise. Who else could be conscious but him? Who else could withstand the Fear Lord?

Urstadt stood, looking down at him. She'd retrieved her glaive, holding it firmly in one hand.

"Urstadt," Daval said, his mind racing. He could not comprehend how his guard captain was able to speak to him. But never mind that. Now was his chance to take care of the final threats to his power.

"Urstadt, take care of Winter," he said. "I'm afraid she will have to return to her cell in the dungeon, under close watch."

"What about your daughter, sir?"

"I will do what I have to," Daval whispered, raising the knife.

"Sir?"

Daval grunted in frustration. He turned to look at Urstadt. "What part of my orders do you—"

The blow came fast and hard. Even with his enhanced strength, his hardened skin, it *hurt*. Urstadt hit him again and he fell to the ground, dropping the knife. He felt a sharp kick to his ribs. "Urstadt," he growled. He crawled onto his hands and knees in time to see another kick aimed at him. Daval caught it with his bare hands and *twisted,* throwing Urstadt to the floor.

"You think you love me enough to destroy me?" Daval had been imbued with strength by the Fear Lord. None would stand against him. "I'm flattered, Urstadt," Daval said, smiling. "And I love you, too."

Then he charged.

Cova climbed to her feet in time to see her father, screaming like an animal, barrel straight into Urstadt. He hit her with such force that the stone wall cracked behind them, and Urstadt cried out in pain.

"Goddess," Cova whispered. "What *are* you?"

Cova had seen Urstadt fight on the training ground, seen her take on the most skilled fighters in the empire and defeat them all. She had fought groups of men, sometimes a dozen at a time, hardly receiving a scratch. Daval, she assumed, had been a decent fighter in his prime, but he was old. And yet for every move Urstadt made, Daval moved quicker. He deflected every strike from Urstadt's glaive with his bare hands—and put her on the defensive.

Cova knew her father had changed. She had no idea *how much*.

In moments, Daval disarmed Urstadt, tossed the glaive aside, and lifted Urstadt, her rose-gold armor gleaming, above his head. With a roar he threw her into the mantel above the fireplace. Urstadt fell to the ground with a crash, and did not get up.

Daval turned to Cova, eyes blazing. "I have had enough betrayal for one day," he growled. He started moving towards her, picking up speed. Then something too fast to identify slammed into him, nearly lifting him off his feet. Daval looked around, bellowing, and was hit by something else—a large chunk of stone that had crumbled from the wall. Then Urstadt's sword flew at him, glancing across his skin with the sound of metal on stone.

Cova glanced around wildly, and saw Winter slowly rising to her feet, the woman's eyes trained on Daval.

"I won't be your prisoner anymore," Winter said evenly.

The emperor's desk, a huge antique thing of solid oak, flew across the room and smashed into Daval, splintering into a hundred pieces. Daval stumbled, falling to his knees. Two more blocks of stone flew through the air and smashed into one another, Daval's head between them. He wavered, then fell to the floor. The stones came down again and again on Daval's skull, until they crumbled to dust.

Daval lay still, not moving.

"One more thing," Winter said, Urstadt's glaive zipping across the room into her open palm. She walked over to the emperor. "I don't love you, you bastard," she said, raising the sword high, "and I never will."

She brought the glaive down with a scream and enough force to pierce straight through Daval's hardened skin.

When Urstadt stumbled to her feet, Winter was immediately on her guard. But the rose-gold-clad warrior raised her arms. "Our fight is not with each other," Urstadt rasped. Winter noticed the woman's eyes were wet. Around them, Reapers were slowly rising to their feet.

"We may have to fight our way out," Urstadt muttered. She wrenched her glaive from Daval's body. "Prepare yourself, girl."

Winter reached into the pouch at her side. The frost she'd taken before entering the emperor's chambers was beginning to wear off; she would need more if she wanted to be of any use against the Reapers.

The soldiers looked at Daval's body on the floor, and then at Winter and Urstadt. "The emperor is dead," one of them muttered.

"The emperor is dead!" another shouted.

"Vengeance!"

The Reapers rushed towards them.

"*Stop.*" Cova Amok stood by the corpse of her father. In her hands was the emperor's circlet. She raised it up, setting it on her own head. "Stop," she repeated. "Your empress commands it."

Winter looked back at the Reapers. A few of them looked confused, a few looked angry. But then one of them knelt. It did not take long for the others to follow.

Winter looked at Urstadt, a smile on her face. "Looks like we won't have to fight our way out after all."

48

Harmoth estate

THERE WERE TWENTY-SEVEN FRESH graves in the Harmoth cemetery. Each grave belonged to someone who had been killed in the Kamite attack.

The day was cloudy, with a light drizzle. Jane, Cinzia, Elessa, and Ocrestia stood at the south end of the cemetery after the funeral services, as the remaining followers paid their respects. Despite those lost in the attack and the group that had fled with the Beldam, the line of Odenites extended around the house and through the north side of the grounds. Hundreds of people had come to lay flowers and say prayers. Humans and tiellans alike mourned for friends and loved ones.

But Cinzia felt immense gratitude. The number of graves could have been triple this number if Jane, Elessa, and Ocrestia had not healed so many. There would be one more body in the family mausoleum, too, if Cinzia had not healed Ehram. While the twenty-seven lost lives were a tragedy, Cinzia thanked Canta that that number had not been higher.

Cinzia turned to Jane. Something had been on her mind since the Kamite attack. "We still have not found out whether a Daemon's influence was responsible for all of this."

"No," Jane said, "we have not."

Ocrestia sniffed. "I still ain't convinced there ever was one in the first place. People don't need the influence of a Daemon to commit evil acts."

"That may be true," Jane said, "but that does not change the fact that the Nine Daemons *are* rising. We will surely face one eventually. We need to be prepared."

"Has anyone considered that if a Daemon has inhabited anyone around here," Elessa said, "it might be the Beldam?"

Cinzia thought for a moment. "It is odd that an ex-high priestess knows so much about the Nine Daemons."

"And how many followers did she lead away?" Elessa asked, looking at Jane.

"More than two hundred people, if Arven's census is accurate," Jane said.

"And all of them human," Ocrestia added. "The Beldam preached hatred, and I say good riddance to those who left with her."

"We aren't going to try to get them back?" Elessa asked.

Jane breathed deeply. "I don't know. Our objective needs to be to travel to Triah. That is where more people will flock to our cause."

Cinzia hoped that, along the way, they would have the chance to confront the Beldam. What the Beldam taught had no place in the Sfaera, not when the world was already so full of fear and hatred.

"So what you're saying," Ocrestia said, "is that we just have to deal with Nine Daemons, a hate-filled woman who has manipulated our followers, and move hundreds of people across the nation to the capital city of Khale, to the doorstep of a rival religion—one that has tried to assassinate you three times?"

Jane nodded, her eyes focused in the distance. "And call six more disciples. And organize the rest of the Church of Canta's ministry." She met Cinzia's eyes. "And finish translating the Codex of Elwene. And…"

Cinzia burst out laughing. The other three woman stared at her until eventually they were all laughing, holding their sides, barely able to breathe.

"I admit, I ain't sure why we're laughing," Ocrestia said after a few moments, wiping away tears. "Don't see how we could accomplish all that in a lifetime, let alone the near future."

"We can't," Jane said, smiling. "Not alone, anyway. But with Canta's help…"

"If we learn to trust," Cinzia added.

"We might just have a chance," Jane finished.

"Well," Cinzia said, "before we go about saving the Sfaera, what about a cup of tea?"

"Sounds delightful."

"Wonderful."

"Guess I could have some tea, if that's what the rest of you want."

The four women smiled at one another, and walked back to the house.

EPILOGUE

Imperial palace, Izet

Cova watched as the Ceno order prepared her father's body, and felt nothing. She stood in the doorway to the imperial palace's Cantic chapel, watching the green-robed men and women move silently as they cleaned and dressed their former leader. The Ceno order had wanted to do the washing in the emperor's chambers, but Cova had refused. There was no way she was going to have her father's body taint that place more than he already had. The order had not been happy about being relocated to the sacred space of their rival religion. And the Denomination had not been happy about it, either. Cova did not have to care. She was the empress now, and both factions were obliged to obey her. She had burdens enough without worrying about two religious groups vying for power.

Fortunately, her father was no longer one of those burdens. As she stared at his pale corpse, she still felt nothing. It had been much more difficult to watch the Denomination prepare her husband's body. This did not seem to matter at all. What did matter was that her empire needed her. In her hand, she held a revised edition of the proposal Daval had tasked her with writing, outlining a war against Khale and the rebuilding of the palace. Seeing her father's body, knowing what his plans had been, Cova wanted to tear out the section that advocated war and burn it. But she knew she could not. There was too much at stake, now. What mattered was rebuilding Roden. Reforming her Ruling Council. Andia Luce was a good candidate. Cova had always been fond of her, and repairing the relationship between their two houses would go a long way towards peace in the empire.

What mattered was finding out the truth of the Ceno order and the Scorned Gods. Her father had been part of a cover-up, that much was clear. She would find out, and reveal, the truth.

All of these things mattered to Cova. And yet, as she stood there, looking at her father's corpse, only one memory occupied her mind. It was a memory of darkness, unfathomable fear, and a harbinger of things to come.

Imperial docks, Izet

Urstadt walked along the dock, looking around with curiosity. She had never been much for the water; she was better on dry land.

"Have you ever been to Khale?"

Urstadt shook her head. Winter walked beside her, eyeing the ships carefully.

"I wish I could say you'll enjoy it, but I can't. I'm not sure Khale is in any better shape than Roden."

They continued walking, the breeze from the Gulf of Nahl chilly on Urstadt's cheeks.

"And you're sure you want to come with me? Cova might need you here. Seems she has a lot on her hands."

"Cova can handle herself."

"Yes," Winter said, stepping toward one of the ships. "You're not wrong about that."

"Do you mind if I accompany you, my *garice*?"

They turned to see Galce the tailor standing on the docks, bundled in wools and fur, carrying a large knapsack.

Winter laughed. "Of course not, Galce. You're welcome in my company any time."

"Where in Khale will we go?" Urstadt asked.

"I wasn't sure at first," Winter said. "But I think I know now. I need to go back to where it all began. To the village of Pranna." Winter patted the wooden side of a ship. "This one will do."

Urstadt grunted. They were lucky Empress Cova had allowed them their pick of transportation. As much as Urstadt did not like the idea of being at sea, she liked even less the thought of walking straight up to the Blood Gate of Navone.

"Very good," Urstadt said, although she didn't care where they were going. She had her own reasons for accompanying Winter. Urstadt was learning to love the girl, in her own way. She *needed* to love her. Just as she had needed to learn to love Daval. The tiellan had power—too much power, as far as Urstadt was concerned. One day, Winter might overstep her bounds, just as Daval had done. And, on that day, Urstadt would be there, ready to destroy that which she loved. Ready for the wild calamity, and ready to stop it if need be.

Outskirts of Izet

Kali had made it halfway out of Izet when she stopped and vomited on the side of the road.

She wiped her brow with the sleeve of her dark-green robe. It was not very warm—spring was reluctant to show itself in Roden—and yet her face was drenched in cold sweat. Of course, that might be one of the side effects of being a man; Kali couldn't be sure. She'd caught a glimpse of herself, her new body, in a mirror as she left the palace, and had not been pleased. She was ugly. Portly. And a *man*, of all things.

That was something she could remedy soon, once she created a better lacuna to house her sift, but for now it would have to do.

Kali stumbled, her feet unsteady. This body was clumsy, too. Seemed to have no idea how to put one foot in front of the other. But despite the sweat, and the clumsiness, and the overwhelming nausea she couldn't shake, Kali was happy. She was finally free of the Void. She had not realized how much of a prison that place had become until she escaped it. She was not sure she ever wanted to willingly return, acumen or not.

She stumbled again, but this time fell to her knees. She grunted in frustration, and a few people walking by looked at her, but no one said anything or stopped to help. That was just as well. Kali hated being helped.

Her stomach twisted again, and Kali began to dry heave, her abdomen clenching and unclenching painfully. She tried to stand, but could not. Her strength ebbed at an alarming rate. She collapsed to the ground, her cheek against the dust of the road.

Then, Kali felt herself—her true self, her sift—being pulled backwards. Back and back and back, until she was falling through the twisting tunnel once more, into the Void, black sky full of stars.

No.

Absently, Kali reached for the note that would have been in her pocket, if she'd had a body, if she hadn't lost the note in Navone, if so many things hadn't happened. Not finding the note, despite being exactly what she expected, brought an unexpectedly powerful wave of sadness. Kali pushed it away. Sadness did not become her. This—her relationship with Winter, her attempt at inhabiting a body in the real world—had been far more of a success than a failure. She would try tagain. And again, after that. And again, and as many times as it took to get out of this place. Kali had tasted freedom.

She would taste it again.

Lathe awoke in the Void.

He had never seen the Void before, but then again… hadn't he? The black expanse, the countless lights of varying color looked familiar, and at the same time completely alien. He couldn't be sure. So much of him felt distant, as if he were trying to call out to himself across a wide canyon.

He tried to discern whether any of the lights in his vicinity looked familiar. Strangely, as he searched, he noticed an entire swathe of blackness completely devoid of any light whatsoever. Lathe moved hesitantly towards the empty space, then stopped. The space had shifted, just slightly.

Lathe was not alone. A slow, aching laugh echoed through the Void.

"Welcome back, Lathe Tallon." The voice was low, but smooth and melodious.

"Who's there?" Lathe called out. He tried to recall all he'd learned about the Void, at the Citadel and during his time with the Nazaniin, but… but none of what he'd learned referred to anything like this.

"I am she who woke you," the voice said. "I am Bazlamit."

Bazlamit. Lathe racked his brain. The name sounded familiar but everything was still so fuzzy he could hardly think straight.

"You woke me?" Lathe asked.

"I did," Bazlamit said. "I woke you because we can help one another. I woke you because you can help me access something we both want."

"What is that?" Lathe asked.

"*A body*."

Two months later

Astrid dreamt she was on a ship.

A ship, a boat, she wasn't exactly sure—she had never known much about seafaring vessels. But this one had sails, anyway, and cut through the water towards a clear, bright sunrise. Astrid knew, instinctively, that she was alone on the boat, but did not mind. It felt good to be on her own. It felt good because Astrid knew she was going to a good place.

The pink, orange, and purple sun rays streaking across the sky gave way to the sun itself, rising slowly above the water, transforming the ocean into a strange, beautiful sea of liquid gold.

The sun rose, and Astrid was not afraid. She did not burn. She remained whole with the light. The ship took a turn—Astrid wasn't sure how, or why, or where, but it turned, towards a massive fjord. Immense cliffs rose up on either side of the water. In that moment, Astrid knew where she was going, and the word rang in her mind like the tolling of a great bell.

She was going home.

Turandel

"Hey. You there?" Trave's gravelly voice brought Astrid back from her reverie.

She blinked. She felt as if she'd just woken up from a dream.

"Where'd you go?"

Astrid shook her head. Honestly, she didn't know. She couldn't remember experiencing anything quite like it.

"It was… a daydream, I think," she said. She hated ships. Why had she been on a ship in a daydream?

Astrid shook herself. She and Trave stood among the remains of Cabral's tower-house, now ash and rubble. They had sent the last of Cabral's former slaves far away, telling them never to return if they valued their freedom. They had killed Cabral's Fangs. Cabral himself was in the east, and wouldn't return for at least another week. Or so Trave said.

"It could take him a long time to rebuild," Trave said.

"But he will. And then he'll come after me." As Jane and her followers had moved south, it had been a simple matter for Astrid to slip away and contact Trave. He had told her that Cabral was gone; it was too good an opportunity to pass up.

"Aye. That he will."

"He'll have to find me first."

"He'll find you. He has cause, now. You were an amusement to him before. Now you're a threat."

Astrid didn't reply. She knew Trave was right. Cabral would come after her. He might not even take the time to rebuild first.

"But I'll be with him."

Astrid looked at Trave, one eyebrow raised. "What's that supposed to mean?"

"I mean I'll be with him. And I'll protect you."

"Why? Why did you help me do this?" Astrid spread her arms wide, indicating the carnage around them. Chaos, but so much better than what had been here before.

"Let's just say I'm looking for redemption as much as you, these days."

Astrid stirred some of the ash with her shoe. "Is this redemption, then?" she asked.

Trave shrugged. "Close enough."

"Feels more like revenge."

"I'm not sure there's a difference."

Astrid nodded. "I… I'm almost sure there is. I just don't know what it is yet."

"Let me know if you figure it out."

They stood in silence for a moment, and Astrid's thoughts returned to her strange daydream, whatever it was. She could almost feel the wind in her hair, the salt of the ocean on her lips.

Is this what redemption feels like? she wondered.

She did not have an answer.

ACKNOWLEDGEMENTS

IT IS A TRUTH universally acknowledged that *s*equels are really difficult to write, and this book was no exception. Fortunately, a host of top-notch people came to the rescue and offered their advice, support, and friendship. Let me tell you about just a few.

First and foremost: Rachel. I spend a lot of time at writing conferences, going to writing retreats, and, yeah, *writing*, and she supports me in every single one of those efforts. She's my best critic, and I simply couldn't do what I'm doing without her. My daughter, Buffy, has been a constant joy and inspiration since the day she was born. She even, on occasion, chills peacefully in her crib after waking up from a nap just to give me an extra few minutes of writing time. I'm grateful and humbled to be her father.

A HUGE thank you to Camille Johnson for being an incredible nanny and aunt to Buffy so I can write on a consistent basis. I couldn't imagine my daughter in the hands of a person better suited for the job. A shout out to Liz, Jaime, Chelsea, Buffy's grandparents, and my sister Deja for contributing on that front as well. I'm so grateful for all of you!

Speaking of my sister, she happened to marry a particularly awesome guy named Ben, and Ben built a particularly awesome website for me. Go to christopherhusberg.com to see what I'm talking about. (Also, Ben: thanks for always playing support in *Dota 2*. Seriously, you are the best.)

D.J. Butler is a great friend and an incredible writer, and I'm not sure *Dark Immolation* would have survived without the writing retreats he's so graciously hosted. Those retreats were instrumental in overcoming the many obstacles this novel threw at me. (Plus, we played lots of awesome board games.) Did I mention he's an incredible writer?

Writing can be a lonely gig, so a special thanks goes out to my writing group, affectionately and hilariously known as "Accidental Erotica": Megan Walker, Jenn Johansson, Tara Mayoros, Bree Despain, Heidi Summers, Michelle Argyle, Heather Clark, James Goldberg, Cavan Helps—and *especially* Janci Patterson, who went above and beyond and gave me an epic critique that was exactly what I needed. I'm grateful for everyone's friendship, feedback, and the opportunity to talk about writing with other fantastic writers. You guys rock. Additional thanks to Luke Tarzian for hosting an incredible book event at Flintridge Bookstore and Coffeehouse, and for giving me some great feedback on this novel.

Many thanks to the entire team at Titan Books, and particularly to my brilliant editor, Miranda Jewess. I'm always grateful for her notes and suggestions.

This book wouldn't exist without the support of the very fine people who work or have worked at JABberwocky. Joshua, Krystyna, Lisa, Brady, Eddie, Christa, Tae, Rebecca, Ben, and anyone else who may have slipped my mind. I'm grateful for the friendships I've developed with everyone at that agency, for all I've learned from them, and for the fantastic work they do.

Finally, my agent, Sam, is one of those agents that somehow knows exactly what to say to motivate and encourage me, no matter the situation. A few long conversations with him helped me hash out some of the major issues I had with this novel, and I'm very happy with the result. He's the best in the business.

ABOUT THE AUTHOR

CHRISTOPHER HUSBERG GREW UP in Eagle River, Alaska. He now lives in Utah, and spends his time writing, reading, hiking, and playing video games, but mostly hanging out with his wife, Rachel, and daughter, Buffy. He received an MFA in creative writing from Brigham Young University, and an honorary PhD in *Buffy the Vampire Slayer* from himself. The first novel in the Chaos Queen Quintet, *Duskfall,* was published in 2016. The third installment, *Blood Requiem*, will be published by Titan Books in June 2018.

www.christopherhusberg.com
@usbergo